Blood is Slicker than Water

Louise Furley

Blood is Slicker than Water

ISBN: 979-8-218-10138-1

Cover art by: *Pixel Mischief Design*
Photo: *Courtesy of Shutterstock*

Louise Furley

ALSO BY LOUISE FURLEY

Mafia Romance

Distilled Duplicity
His Winnings
Adara
Jozadak

Satan's Brood

Devil's Prince
Devil's Seed

Dutch Military Special Forces

Jungle Treasure
Jancarlo

Medieval

Cini and the Beast
Kultur's Keep
The Butcher Princess

Other titles

Jezábel and the Assassin
Bay's Bet
Solitar
Halo Valley

Jace's Elusive Woman

Isle of Orainn

iv

Blood is Slicker than Water

Neco's Rescue

Anastasia

The Kissing Number

Murder at Red Gem Farm

Blood is Slicker than Water

Capturing Dove

Auction Block

The Poser

Wrath of Wolf

Shawn's Prisoner

Rogan's Desire

Liquid Velvet

Vijay

The Sapphire Bell

Louise Furley

Blood is Slicker than Water

Prologue

Somehow she had gotten separated from her sisters and was now cold and alone in the blind darkness.

Struggling to stay on the sparse trail she fought off wicked branches that scraped her face and tugged at her clothes as if trying to keep her from leaving.

Not quite dawn, the silver moon's hazy sheen meagerly illuminated the path helping her avoid crashing into trees or tumbling down a deadly ravine.

"Where could they be?" she fretted out loud, picking her way through the forest. At first the little girl wasn't scared, but now her ears pricked at leaves rustling all around her from invisible nocturnal creatures.

Louder shifting bushes drew her nervous glance to the side. Peering through the web of vines she jumped with a squeal at the glow of yellow eyes watching her from within the dark shrubbery.

Scurrying faster, she stumbled along the obscure trail until she neared the lake. Stopping to catch her breath, she listened for any sound of her sisters, but there was nothing but empty silence.

Panic rising making her heart race, she called out, "Char! Hope! Where are you?" Having no idea how to find her way out of the forbidden woods, she had to find her sisters.

Her little feet hurt from stubbing against rocks and tripping over dead branches, she decided to just stand still for a second and rest. That's when she heard it.

A horrendous noise pierced the silent night, twisting terror in her belly. It came again, louder, goosebumps popped running up her arms. They were screams, inhuman agonizing screams that rent so violently through the tree-shrouded woods the branches shook.

More terrible screams followed, her hair stood on end. She recognized those screams, different from the first ones, they were her sisters' bloodcurdling shrieks. Heavy footsteps suddenly beat the earth rushing towards her.

Alarm striking like a baseball bat to the chest, her feet churned up and down without moving, then they caught traction. Her little legs powering like windmills she ran like the wind.

Praying the darkness hid her, heart slamming frantically against her ribs she dashed down the path and kept running. The footsteps pounding on the hard packed dirt after her struck such a brilliant fear in her she could hardly think.

She ran as far as she could until she had no breath left. A big tree loomed ahead, she darted around it. Pressing her back against the trunk, her quick shallow breaths were so loud she feared the stalking creature could hear her.

After an eternity, her breathing calmed, she stayed quiet to listen.

A few minutes passed and she heard absolutely nothing. The forest was as quiet and still as a cemetery. She peered around the tree. Her big frightened eyes saw that the path was empty, there was no noise, no screaming, no feet trampling the earth towards her.

Sighing deeply in relief, she emerged from behind the tree and cautiously made her way back to the trail.

"I'm so silly," she chastised herself. "I bet what I thought was a monster was just my sisters playing a trick on me."

Trotting steadily along the path she whispered to the trees, "I think I'll surprise them and scare them too!" Giggling with her revenge in mind, she moved more quickly down the trail.

Excited about her plan to ambush her sisters, she hesitated when she heard a sound just off the path.

"Oh!" she exclaimed. "I wonder if that's the bunny I was following earlier!"

She skipped to the bushes bordering the edge of the gorge.

"Here bunny, here bun-"

From behind, hard hands suddenly grabbed both her upper arms.

She was jerked her up, and before she could open her mouth to cry out- she was hurtling over the cliff.

Chapter One

14 Years Later

*T*he waves rolled the boat with the vigor of winter's end.

Kessa Kent didn't need to look for landmarks, even when it was pitch black and pea soup fog she knew the way.

But it wasn't dark and murky, it was mid-morning and the first days of spring were touching the pebbled lake shores of Maine.

She raised a hand to her brow to shade eyes that were as prismatic as the sea from the glare of the weak sun. Her rocking gaze trained on a tiny brown speck across the expanse of the choppy deep blue, a rustic beacon nestled amongst the pines. Heading home at a speeding clip, a flush wake trailed her.

The biting air crisp as a ripe Macintosh, Kessa tilted her head up enjoying the brusque wind slapping her hair back like a yellow flag, the chilly spray spitting at her red slicker.

Salty surf tingled the small straight nose and brightened the already the rosy cheeks. Beside her, a Belgian Tervuren braced himself with his paws on the dashboard.

Tongue hanging, like a dog with his head out the car window he also appeared to enjoy the wind sweeping through his fur and didn't seem to mind the cold water splashing his face.

Her pulse quickened. Kessa could see an unfamiliar car through the crowd of tall pines parked in her driveway on the side of the cabin. Slowing the engine, the roar lessened, the wake now barely cutting across the rough waters, the boat seemed as wary as she was.

Expertly docking the runabout and securing it, she killed the motor. Dropping the keys in a pocket, she gathered up her diving vest, fins and snorkel, she'd come back later for the other stuff; tanks, flag and the drysuit left on the deck where she'd peeled it off.

The dog leaped out of the boat and ran after a spindly-legged sandpiper dodging the rolling surf along the shore.

The busyness of collecting her things and climbing out of the boat gave Kessa something to do while she surreptitiously scanned her cabin for signs of human life. And there it was.

A man was sitting on her small deck making himself right at home. Seeing the boat come in, he rose lazily, stretched long arms then pulled on his jacket.

The cabin had blocked the wind and made it comfortably warm sitting in the direct sun, as feeble as it was for the time of year. He casually trod down the steps and made his way across the lawn towards Kessa.

Her heart fluttered back to normal. She called out as the man closed in, "What are you doing here?"

When he was an arm's length away, she smiled and turned her cheek up which he obligingly kissed. He took her gear from her and they headed back to the house.

Both in jeans and hiking boots, they walked under the blossoming linden trees draped in a feathery tunnel over the walk. They followed the crooked stone path that curved around the cabin to the front, behind them the dog ran to catch up.

The man held the porch screen door open while Kessa fished keys out of her pocket and unlocked the door.

Even with the curtains pulled back, the tiny cabin was still dim, the last of the frigid winter's sun struggled to pierce the small dusky windows.

Kessa flipped a light switch on and tossed her keys on a table by the front door. The rustic room, threadbare but cozy and clean, was now lit with a golden glow.

A stone fireplace anchored one end of the living room with a sofa and two old but comfy chairs in a semi-circle in front of it. A couple of worn and scarred tables bookended the chairs with a coffee table in the middle.

A work-table was beside the front window. A faint scent of smoky ash stirred from the hearth.

"Here, Matthew, I'll take 'em. You want some coffee?" Standing on one of the several warm knitted rugs covering the hardwood floor, she held out her arms.

He handed her back the dive gear. She plodded towards the kitchen not waiting for him to answer, he always wanted coffee.

Tossing his jacket on a chair, he dropped his long frame onto a recliner near the fireplace and relaxed back.

The dog started to follow Kessa then changed direction and settled down in a brown and gold mound beside Matthew's chair.

Matthew reached an arm down and scratched the dog's ears. In seconds the dog laid his head down on one paw and was sound asleep.

"Of course," he answered her coffee invitation, picking up a magazine off the side table. Boats, it figured. He tossed it back down.

"What are you doing diving in this freezing weather? And alone, you know that's wrong, girl," he scolded as she disappeared into the kitchen.

He heard water running and within seconds the coffee was percolating through the coffee maker. Cupboards opened, mugs tapped on the counter, the fridge door opened and closed.

A few minutes and she reappeared. "Here." She handed him a mug, the milk still in a swirl on the surface, steam undulated up and away. Pushing long, still half wet blonde hair off her shoulders, she moved to the thermostat on the wall and turned it up.

The sound of heat running through ducts was immediate, the dry burnt smell of the heat followed. Shrugging out of the damp slicker and boots, she padded across the hardwood floor in her socks to hang the slicker on a hook near the door and set the boots neatly to the side.

Tugging her sweater down over the jeans, she went back in the kitchen and came out with another mug and a plate of macadamia nut cookies, which she set on the table next to Matthew.

"It's freezing in here, I can start a fire," Matthew offered. Kicking off his own hiking boots, he noticed a hole in one of his socks. He pulled the toe a little to cover the hole. The dog snored at his feet.

"You're lucky Kato is very small for his breed or you'd have to step over him every time you moved through this miniature cabin."

"Uh huh. Don't bother starting a fire," she replied, sitting down on the old and lumpy but still comfortable sofa with stuffing tufting out the sides like an old man's hair. "The heater will take the edge off the chill tonight and it's supposed to warm up by morning."

Propping her feet on the coffee table, she cradled her mug in both hands in her lap. The steam rolled up misting her face, making the rosy cheeks from the brisk outdoors shiny.

"It's not freezing, Matthew, it's not really that cold diving with the drysuit on. You know there's no one here to dive with. And I like hurtling across the lake with the wind hitting my face, makes me feel fresh and free."

She watched him. He hadn't yet answered her question of why was he there; it was written all over his face something was up.

Matthew crossed one ankle over a knee, went to sip but pulled back quickly, it was still too hot. "Yeah, well. I think you like the cold, like an ice veil to shield you from the world…and your feelings." He blew on the coffee.

Kessa rolled her eyes. "Oh, really, so now you're a psychologist?" She leaned forward, set the mug on the table and her feet on the floor. Careful, cyan, more blue than green eyes studied his almost identical but slightly darker orbs.

"So, why are you here? Not that you're not always welcome my dear brother, but you always call first."

She nodded towards the side window. "I see a rental in the driveway. You flew in and it seems came right here. I could have picked you up at the airport. Something's going on?"

He uncrossed his legs and leaned forward to meet her frank gaze. "I tried to call when I landed, but," he wiggled his brows at the cellphone sitting on the table, message light blinking.

She smiled guiltily. "Oh. Yeah, I tend to forget it. No one but my publisher and agent calls me much anyway," a hesitation then, "thank God."

She set her elbows on her knees. "However, you didn't call before you left…" another hesitation, her mouth twisted like the word was distasteful on her pillow lips, "*home*."

Leaning back, she picked up her coffee and took a sip, pushed back a lock of hair and asked again, calmly "What's going on, Matthew?"

Matthew stood up, looked like he was about to pace then stopped and shoved his hands in his pockets. "Um, yeah." Tugging a hand out of his pocket, he ran it through his blond hair that was a few shades darker than hers which was so light it looked like corn silk.

"Well, Dad, uh…he's pretty sick." The words fell out. He peered through his lashes to gauge her reaction.

Her face retained a placid non-expression she had worked long and hard to develop. But she couldn't control the color draining, leaving her fair skin ashen, and pinching the light from her eyes.

Silently, she stared at the mug in her hand as if she could slip right inside it and melt away. The silence grew.

Not able to slide into the mug and disappear, Kessa drank some more coffee, but didn't look at her brother.

When the silence stretched, Matthew took a few steps closer to her. "Fai- I mean Kessa, geeze," impatiently, he palmed his hair again with his hand. "You'd think after all this time I could remember…" he waited for her to respond but she did not.

The air in the room stood still. Outside, a gust of wind rustled through the trees, around the cabin and then rippled out over the lake. Tied to the dock, the boat bobbed.

He pulled a chair around to face the sofa and plopped down on it. His eyes kind and sad, he leaned in and lightly touched her knee. "Kessa," she stared at his hand. "It's time. It's time to come home. To Resilir. You need to-"

"Really? Time to go home, really?" She set the mug none to gently on the table beside the sofa and abruptly stood up.

"Matthew, you know, I have no home." She corrected, "*This* is my home. I have nowhere I…I…really belong."

She held a hand out to stop him, her voice harsh, "No, you know it's true. They sent me away, discarded me like trash. They never came to see me, never called, it was like I no longer existed, like I… also disappeared."

She ignored the pain in his eyes. "No one, I heard from no one." Her voice gentled, loving, "Except you." She smiled fondly at him.

"And, my dear brother, I will never forget your persistence in sneaking into the folks' room and finding where they'd banished me and," she sighed, "and you wrote faithfully." Her lips puckered wryly when he shot her a look at her word, faithful.

"Until you were old enough to track me down and come visit me. I can't tell you how I cherished those contacts, you were the only one…" trailing off, she wandered over to the window.

Matthew sat back in his chair. "I know how lonely and unwanted you felt."

Kessa stood at the picture window looking out at the tulips she'd planted finally pushing their way further out of the cold, hard earth. Two weeks ago from a last freezing spurt they had worn little snow caps.

After a week of warmer weather and lots of sun, throughout the yard maple trees budded, every branch dripping a green teardrop.

Felipe, the next door neighbor's black cat chased a squirrel across the lawn. The squirrel ran up a tree. Felipe marched off like he had conquered an army.

To the right of the street, Mr. Cookman walked beside the road, his dog Horatio on a leash pulling him along, leftover shriveled leaves swirling around and behind them. She could tell Mr. Cookman was whistling, he always was.

On one side of the street the forest crept right up to the edge of the two lane road. The other side of the street, every house, bungalows mostly or cabins were in uneven clusters dotting all along the lake.

The woods, popular for hunting in season, teemed densely for acres upon acres. So tree shrouded it was a hard neighborhood to find unless you knew exactly where it was. It wasn't even recorded on most maps. Which suited Kessa perfectly.

Matthew stirred, slowly getting to his feet. Long and lean, his hands stuffed in his pockets. He looked at his slender sister over by the window, they were almost mirror images, except his coloring was slightly darker and he was a foot taller, and she was endowed with feminine curves.

"Kessa," he said to her back, "you know we can't change anything. What happened, happened. The folks did what they thought best at the time. But now-"

She swung around furiously, her fists clenched. "Really? What they thought best? Exiling an eight-year-old child to the other side of country, never seeing her, calling her, writing her? Acting as if she had never existed, that was best? For who?"

She spat the words out stalking a few steps towards him then she stopped, crossed her arms and went over to the fireplace and sat down on the hearth's stone ledge.

He waited a second then joined her, sitting on the cold bench. Twining his fingers, he hunched over slightly and rested his forearms on his knees. "Kess, we can't undo the past. You need to, uh…forgive" he stopped when she swung angry, hurt eyes at him.

"Okay, I…you know I understand. But," his voice mellowed. "Dad's getting old, Kess. He had Aria the oldest of us when he was in his forties. He's old and sick, and," he took a breath, "he's asking for you. He wants to see you before he-"

Kessa turned towards him, cocked her heart shaped face. "Are you saying he's dying, Matthew?"

Not looking her in the eye, he nodded slightly. "Yeah. Doc Aven said he needed to put his affairs in order. I think he wants to, I don't know, maybe apologize, set things right with you-"

"Ha-" Kessa snorted. "You can't throw a child away and then 14 years later ask to make amends." Her voice cracked, the sarcasm and pain rolled out filling the room.

Hearing the anguish in her voice, Kato's head popped up, he looked to see if she was okay. When she appeared to not be in any danger, he plopped his head back down and immediately commenced snoring.

Kessa stood up and went back to the window. Her mouth clamped shut hard, she stared blankly out the window. Even the fat red robins returning from the south bouncing in the grass after worms couldn't make her smile like they normally did.

Matthew sat for a moment. He stood up and retrieved his coffee. Tossing a cookie in his mouth, he washed it down, took another cookie and walked over to the desk by the window.

Holding the mug in one hand, he gestured at the desk with it.

"Is this your next book ready to come out?" He ate the cookie in two bites.

Her voice barely audible, not turning from the window, Kessa replied, "Yes. It'll be out by the end of May."

Matthew set the mug down on the desk and picked up the book. He read the back then flipped through a few pages.

Turning it back around, he read the title, "'The death of the Loose Goose.' Cute. This one is about Detective Fraser again. I'm glad you're sticking with him. When I read the novel I feel like I know the guy, like he's sitting in the den with me and other friends drinking beer and watching the game, but his mind is mulling whatever case he's working on."

He set the book down and moved to the work table next to the desk. His hands in his pockets, he studied the glass plates lined on a shelf. Below the shelf, paints, brushes, etching tools covered the table.

Looking from one plate to the next, he said, "These are magnificent as always. Are you still making money doing these glass paintings?"

Her arms crossed, Kessa shrugged. "Yeah." Still staring out the window, she said, "I only do ones I feel like. The boutique calls and tells me someone wants their wedding done, or their favorite scene like a sailboat on the water, or their spouse, pet, child, whatever. If I feel interested, and if it's a gift for someone I'm usually inclined to do it. But I only do one every 2-3 months."

"The way you are able to paint such a perfect picture on these glass plates is amazing. I guess you're the only one in the family that is creative-" he broke off awkwardly, red ran up his neck.

He swiveled around to face Kessa. "That was clumsy." He moved to stand near her. "You think about what I said about coming home and decide what you want to do. I'll be back Wednesday to help you pack. You can box up your work and I'll mail it, you can't fit much in that jeep of yours."

A grin tugged at the side of her mouth. "Sounds like you already decided for me."

Matthew gently grasped her arms. "You need to go, even if you don't want to. You need to. Not for them, or me, but for you. Come back and face the devil- devils. You can stay at my digs. I'll go with you to uh, there, um home, the house...when you go to see them."

He leaned in and kissed her on the top of her head. Then he plodded to the door, pulled his jacket off the chair and shrugged it on. He stepped across the smooth wood floor back to his chair, shoved his feet in his boots, and gave Kato a last scratch.

Kessa hadn't moved.

Matthew went to the door and opened it. The cool air rushed in, the dog whimpered. "I'll see you on Wednesday." He threw her a hopeful grin and slipped out the door closing it gently behind him.

Kessa stood at the window watching her brother climb in his rental car, back down the driveway. The robins flew and the squirrels scattered as he drove off down the street.

She looked around the compact furnished cabin that she leased.

There wouldn't be much to pack, she seldom bought anything. If you owned nothing then nothing could be taken from you, and vice versa.

There were no family pictures on the walls or desk to collect and wrap protectively, *really*, she thought, *why would there be*?

Chapter Two

Resilir

As much as she had prepared herself, as soon as Kessa saw the sign 'Welcome to Oregon' her skin tingled, her pulse pumped like a machinegun.

Many more miles and hours later when she saw the sign for Resilir, her heart palpitated so fast she had to pull over to catch her breath. Her stomach churned and heaved so horribly she thought she was going to throw up.

Parking the jeep on the shoulder, she got out. The fresh air blew her hair, she turned a bit so it wouldn't blow in her eyes. It had been well over a decade but the town looked almost the same as she remembered it.

The first years in exile she had lain in bed in the silent night picturing her town, Resilir, magical and shining with its arms held out, coming to gather her up and carry her back home.

In the beginning, she thought it was all a mistake, they'd come and get her and it would be over, just a bad dream. Except, every morning she would awaken and was still in the wretched little bed in the dismal room crammed with other little beds in the nasty orphanage.

As the time marched on and the years passed by with…nothing, the magical picture turned dark and menacing, hateful, and agonizingly lonely.

No one adopted her because she wasn't an orphan. She watched child after child leave with their new parents to their wonderful new homes. She was left behind with the misfits, the ones that were too weird, ugly, fat or dangerous to be adopted.

Their caretakers were cold, un-nurturing people working there because they were basically serving a sentence as well, albeit a religious sentence, they'd pretty much been banished for some sort of misdeeds too.

It had become an eternal hideous nightmare that finally sank into an empty aching hole she mentally sealed over with steel.

Watched 24 hours a day by nuns as well as other staff, the children were never allowed to leave the building, and they were switched with a stick or beaten over minor offenses.

Kessa had gotten her share of beatings because she got caught continuously trying to escape from the horrid place and run away. But she had survived the strict brutal orphanage and left as soon as she aged out.

Now, the flood of memories climbed in and shook her hardened heart, squeezing the air right out of her lungs-

"Bark! Bark!"

Kessa blinked, and abruptly returned to the present. Thank goodness. Memories of Convent Grisaille dissipated, dragging their hideous claws through her brain before disappearing, for now.

She turned and smiled at her dog. "Okay, you silly thing, out." She opened the jeep door and Kato sprang out like a cork and ran off into the woods.

"Hey!" she called. "Don't you go far!"

The jeep was parked just on the outskirts of Resilir, her hometown. A village cradled between forests on one side that eventually flowed like tree soldiers marching up the mountains, and flowering meadows on another side. The rest of the town was edged by a long crystalline lake.

She would never admit it, but where she'd settled in Maine closely resembled the area surrounding Resilir. Except where her home in Maine was totally rural, rustic and hidden, Resilir was a busy little town.

She stood on the dirt shoulder, breathing in the strong smell of pungent spruce. The dense forest to her right, Resilir was straight ahead. She had more miles of rolling hills to drive before farms would start to phase out and clutches of A-framed houses would begin to appear.

Like freckles on summer skin, there would first be the old Wallace Watham plantation, then the mills, then neighborhoods fanning throughout the valley.

She didn't have to call Kato, he came bounding out of the unfamiliar woods. A normally happy dog, he seemed uneasy now and hopped right into the jeep when she opened the door.

Stifling a shiver, "It's okay, buddy, I feel it too," she told him, rubbing his head, she kissed an ear.

When she put the jeep in gear, Kato inched over sitting almost on top of her, she drove back onto the two-lane paved highway.

Coming to the first stop light that basically announced she'd entered Resilir, not realizing she was holding her breath, she let out a long, deep sigh.

"Here we go, boy. I hope you're ready, 'cause I'm sure not." She pulled the map out from under the dog and folded it so it showed only Resilir. Never trusting GPS, Matthew had drawn with a highlighter the way to his house.

Looking left and right before going forward, there hadn't been much traffic the last several hours, she pulled out slowly but didn't realize the road to her left came curving sharply over a hill-

At the last second she saw a pick-up bearing down on her! She yanked the wheel as hard as she could to get out of the way, grabbed Kato with an arm holding him tight to her chest and ducked her head down.

The jeep lurched out of the way in the nick of time, but it jerked so hard it hit a gulley. Landing on its side, it bumped and jumped skidding across the grass where it came to a crunching stop against a picket fence.

All went black.

"My head..." Kessa put a hand to her spinning head and tried to sit up. *How long had she been lying there?*

"Wait, don't move-" a voice ordered her.

She struggled to sit up, but her head was whirling. Opening her eyes, she only saw stars, her stomach roiled, she shut her eyes.

"Here," the deep voice said, strong arms helped her sit up and leaned her against something hard and metallic. "Hold on, just breathe slow and steady. Keep your eyes closed for a sec until your brain stops reeling."

Kessa pushed her hair out of her face and slowly opened her eyes. She tried to focus on the blob wavering in front of her, it melded into a man. She cringed away from him.

"Kato?" She frantically looked for her dog. "Kato boy, where are you?"

The man tried to press her back against the metal which she now realized was her jeep lying on its side and she was sitting on the ground leaning back against it.

She slapped at the man and tried to climb to her feet. "Kato!" she yelled urgently, the abrupt move to get up sent her head spinning. Passing out again, she would have hit the ground but the man caught her and set her gently on the grass.

Lying unconscious, her mind spiraled backwards, going back, remembering that bewildering, fateful day that changed her world forever.

Chapter Three

It was Saturday morning, a still sleeping dawn on the verge of breaking into the promise of a beautiful summer day.

Eight-year-old Faith Mary Kenton bounced down the stairs and into the kitchen that was still dark. Singing off-key, she skipped gleefully into the kitchen.

"Hush!" At 11, Char was the middle child of the five siblings. She shushed Faith with a frown and a finger to her lips. "Do you want to get us caught you dope?" She turned to the picnic basket she was filling with goodies.

Faith held down her natural exuberance and tiptoed over to her sister, peaking in the basket.

"That looks so delish-"

"Shh!" Char admonished her again and slapped the basket lids closed.

"Are we ready?" A shrill voice popped from the doorway, the youngest at 5, Hope ran into the room.

"Shh!" Faith and Char whispered together.

Holding a paper, little Hope held her hands over her mouth, giggling behind them and tiptoed over to her sisters. She whispered loudly, "Are we going then? Now?"

Char smiled, setting a hand on her little sister's tiny shoulder. "Yes, as soon as we get dressed. But we must be as quiet as mice. You remember we talked about how we had to be quiet when we sneak out?"

Hope nodded emphatically, hand over her mouth, eyes twinkling laughter over the hand. "Lookit," she pushed the paper at Char.

But Char ignored her, turning to pick up the basket off the table and then went over to the door. She pulled the door open very slowly so it wouldn't creak, then opened up the screen door and slipped outside.

"Let me see, Hope." Faith took the picture from her sister. Admiring the work, she said, "You are really talented, Hope. I think you're going to be a famous artist when you grow up!"

"Wow," Hope gushed, her eyes big. "Really? My teacher Miss Penney said I'm the best drawer in the class!"

Within seconds, Char came back in and gingerly closed the door. "Okay," she leaned over, her hands on her knees to be eye-level with her younger sisters.

"This is the plan. We're gonna get dressed as quick as we can, put your bathing suits on under your clothes. Then we meet back here and then we sneak out the door real quiet."

The younger two sisters nodded enthusiastically.

"Mom thinks we're going skating with the Russells so she knows we're gonna be out, but she can't see our swim suits or the picnic basket 'cause we'll get a whipping if we get caught going in the woods. We'll stash our skates under the bush where I just hid the basket. Okay, got it?"

The girls again nodded emphatically.

"All right, then go- and be quick!"

The three girls stampeded to the stairs, but Char stopped abruptly and reproached them. "Quietly!" she whispered. The trio tiptoed quickly and quietly up the stairs.

Ten minutes later, Char and Hope were in the kitchen waiting for Faith. "Where is she?" Char asked petulantly.

Hope started for the stairs. "Ohh, I'll go get her, I'll be faster. You go wait outside."

Char stopped Hope. "But wait. Listen, since she made us wait let's play a trick on her."

"Yeah," Hope nodded happily agreeing. "What we do?"

Char thought for a moment. "Why don't we... when we get to the lake, when she's not looking we'll hide. When she gets upset we'll jump out and yell 'surprise!' That'll scare her and we get back at her, okay?"

"Yeah." Hope said, matter of fact without censor, "You always play mean tricks."

"I know. It's funny when people other than me get into trouble. Okay, so go outside and I'll get her and meet you outside." Char pointed to the door.

When she saw Hope sneaking out, Char ran to the stairs and up to Faith's room. When she got there she stepped inside,

"What're you doing?" she asked, then made a face. "Ugh. You look like a crippled flamingo. Come on, quit dancing, we gotta go."

She looked at the clock on the dresser. "You're gonna have to wear that stupid thing and grab your suit, you don't have time to change, the folks'll be up any second. Come on!"

Faith was humming to herself and watching her reflection in the mirror as she twirled and pirouetted in her pink tutu.

Often easily distracted, when she had come up stairs to change she saw her ballet outfit on a chair and was drawn to put it on. "All right." Reluctantly, she grabbed her bathing suit, pulled on her white sneakers and dashed out the door behind her sister.

By the time they got to the church where behind it there was an opening into the forest, it took them another twenty minutes to walk through the woods to the hidden lake.

Still very early, it was dark tromping through the thick woods. They kept to the well-worn path so they wouldn't get lost.

Being the biggest, Char carried the basket and led the way.

Faith trailed behind Char and Hope. Carrying her wadded up swimsuit in her hand, twigs kept catching at her gauzy tutu so she moved carefully to avoid them.

As they emerged from the dense forest they stood silently in awe. The dawn was now breaking, soft streams of sunlight shone down through the dissipating clouds on the lovely lake making it perfectly match the blue sky. Practically still, the water shimmered gently in the morning sun. It looked warm and inviting.

"It's so pretty," Faith said in wonderment, her eyes wide, lips parted slightly.

"Yeah, it is. I don't know why everyone freaks out about coming here. It's safe if you stay on the path. Come on, guys, I'll put the basket over on that tiny hill for when we get hungry. Hope, come and help me while Faith changes her clothes." Char gave the orders but they all dawdled a bit.

A pretty butterfly caught Char's eye, she followed it around the area.

Hope went and leaned over the water looking for fish.

Meanwhile, Faith was about to change, but then she saw a rabbit suddenly hop out from the underbrush and then hopped right back in.

"Oh!" she exclaimed. Dropping her suit, she ran after it. "Here bunny, here bunny," she called, disappearing into the thicket following the white cottontail.

The butterfly flew off so Char went to where she'd set the basket down, took out a plaid cloth and spread it out to be ready for when they ate. She looked up as Faith disappeared into the bush.

"Hey," she whispered loudly to Hope who had already stripped off her clothes. Hope turned to her.

Char motioned with her hand. "Now's our chance let's go hide!"

Hope's lips pulled in. she shook her head. Sandy blonde pigtails jiggled. "I wanna go swimming." She smoothed the blue swimsuit dusted with gold stars.

Char sighed and walked over to her little sister. She was almost identical to Hope with their sandy hair, green eyes and thin lips, they and teenaged sister Aria got their features and coloring from their mother.

Faith and her brother Matthew had very light blonde hair and turquoise eyes like their father.

"Come on," Char cajoled, "remember we said we were gonna play a trick on Faith for making us wait?"

Hope nodded.

"Okay then," Char smiled big, "let's go quickly before she comes back, it'll be really funny when she can't find us. Then we'll jump out and scare the poop out of her!" She raised her arms and curled her hands over like claws and made a snarly face.

Hope giggled. "Yeah, funny!" The sisters ran off hand in hand into the woods.

"Here bunny, bunny. Don't be afraid, come and play with me!" Faith veered off the main path to a lesser used one, bending under bushes and lifting branches to find the rabbit. The little girl wandered, stooping and kneeling, her legs and arms getting scratched, searching everywhere for the rabbit, but to no avail. Finally, she gave up.

Gasping, "Oh," she looked down, her pink tights were dirty from kneeling. "I'll wash them in the lake," she decided. Glancing around she realized she had gone quite a ways from the lake.

"Uh oh," she murmured. Her sisters might be worried about her she had been gone so long.

She turned and hurried back, but the trail was overgrown from lack of use and hard to follow. Several times she thought she was lost. She looked up and saw where the sun had risen.

At school last week Miss McMullen had taught them where the sun rises and sets and how to tell where you were by it. She thought for a second, trying to remember what direction the sun had shone on the lake. Remembering, she decided she was heading in the right direction.

Then, she heard screams, she frowned. It didn't sound like her sisters, but then she laughed. "Those sisters of mine, always trying to scare me. They've probably already eaten and are splashing in the lake." This spurred her to move faster.

There were more screams- She laughed. "Now those sound like my silly sisters!"

Finally, after some time, she burst out of the thicket with her arms raised high and shouting, "Here I am!"

There was nothing there but the lake and the basket and blanket on the hill. Her sisters were not there.

"*Hmmm*," she thought, "*they're playing a trick on me. I bet they're hiding and gonna jump out and try to scare me. But I'll fool them. I'll just ignore them when they come back. They're probably watching me right now and laughing at me.*"

Nonchalantly, she strolled over to the basket. She wasn't brave enough to go swimming by herself, she'd only had her first lesson this year and you never knew what might be lurking in the depths, so she went over and sat on the blanket.

Opening the basket, she took out a wrapped turkey and cheese sandwich, a container of potato salad and chips and popped open a soda. She ate slowly, keeping one eye peeled for the bushes to move and warn of her sisters' surprise whoops.

But after what seemed like ages and no one came, Faith grew worried. She put the stuff back in the basket and stood up.

"I guess I should go look for them, maybe they're lost." She cleaned her hands and wiped her knees with napkins and water from the lake. Leaving the basket, she went in search of her sisters.

Walking just a few minutes, she came upon a slight clearing off the path. The grass was pushed down all around.

Then…she saw something, like…a monster…? There was maybe two, a big and a little one, but it was so thick and still dim she couldn't quite make it out, then she heard one of the somethings yell.

Goosebumps shivered on her arms, the hair on her neck rose. Her feet pedaled up and down uselessly at first, then she ran away as fast as she could.

Her heart pounding, she ran blindly into the thick of the forest. Even over the pounding of her heart she could hear foot falls behind her, heavy steps crashing through the woods, right behind her! She tripped but was able to keep her balance. Panicked, she tore through the bramble not daring to look behind her.

Faith ran and ran and ran until she couldn't breathe any more. Staggering over behind a big tree, she leaned against it, panting like a dog. Trying to hear if the monster was there, all she could hear was her own frantic breathing and pulse racing in her ears.

After a moment, her breathing calmed, she stood still and listened.

The forest was silent. The leaves rustled, grasshoppers sprung out here and there, but nothing else made a sound.

She stood up straight staying behind the tree and peered very slowly around it. Not even knowing what she was looking for, she'd been so frightened when the something had yelled, her mind had blanked, colors flashed in her eyes and she had run without thinking.

Her eyes darted from tree to bush to tree, seeing nothing and hearing nothing. Maybe it was just her imagination. Her sisters had frightened her after all.

"Those goofs," she smiled. Shaking her head and talking to herself out loud, "I'm such a dope, running away like a scared baby. The thing I saw back there looked like two monsters, or people, maybe they were bears, but it was so hard to see in the dark and through the thick brush. It must have been my crazy sisters with towels over their heads or something. They're probably back at the lake laughing and laughing."

Taking one more scan of the area and listening carefully, she stepped out from behind the tree. Holding her breath, she tried to figure out where she was and how to get back to the main path.

The sun mottled through the tall trees casting wide shadows and skinny streaks of light. She found the scant trail and carefully picked her way over it moving slowly through the groves of trees and bushes.

A bee buzzed in her ear, she struggled not to run frantically back into the belly of the forest. She needed to stick to the path or she might get really lost, she shivered, and never be found.

Faith was following the little worn trail that ran close to the edge of a cliff when she came back to the weird area of mashed grass. Her head jerked up when she heard a thump then a rustling sound beyond the cliff.

"Oh," she said, "maybe the bunny is back!" Hurrying to the edge of the cliff, she carefully peeked over.

Then she heard movement behind her, and before she could turn around something grabbed her painfully hard around her upper arms and picked her up off the ground.

Screaming, she kicked and hit but she was thrown in the air- the last thing she saw was a chipmunk hunkered in the grass as she went flying over the cliff.

Chapter Four

When her daughters didn't come home by dusk, an annoyed Sophie Kenton called the Russells.

The panic started vaguely prickling at the back of her mind when Carrie Russell told her the girls had not been there at all today. That she didn't even know that they were going to come and skate.

In fact, her daughters, Bailey and Gwen, weren't even home, they were away this weekend with their father, and Carrie herself had been visiting her ill aunt in a hospital out of town and only just got home.

The panic started rising as Sophie called every person they knew and asked if they'd seen her girls. But no one had seen them today. She ran into the living room.

Geordie Kenton was relaxing in his recliner with the newspaper.

"Geordie!" Sophie exclaimed, bolting into the room, her anxious face white, green eyes alarmed.

"Good Lord, Soph, calm down, what's the matter, the meatloaf burned?" Geordie smiled good naturedly at his harried wife.

She halted in front of him wringing her hands. "The girls," her voice shaking, she said, "they- they were supposed to go to the Russells' today to skate but Carrie says they never came and weren't even expected."

She rushed through her words, "And I've called everybody and nobody has seen them. They haven't come home, it's dark, oh my god Geordie what if-"

Sighing, Geordie folded his paper setting it on the end table. There would be no peace and quiet now to read it. "Calm down, hon. I'm sure there's a mistake. They're probably at someone's house and the adults don't know it. They're fine, don't get yourself in an uproar for Pete's sake."

Sophie covered her face with her hands then rubbed her eyes. "Maybe, maybe you're right. But," the panic climbed again. "I called everyone, absolutely everyone, even Aria but she's with her boyfriend and Matthew is up in his room, I just don't see…"

Geordie groaned silently and grudgingly climbed out of his chair. He put an arm around his wife's shoulders. Gave them a slight squeeze.

"They're fine, you'll see." In his late fifties, Geordie's blond hair was thinning and his paunch was growing.

Sophie on the other hand was 15 years younger than him. Her shoulder length hair still glowed yellow with maybe some help from a bottle, however, she retained her lush figure.

Sophie Kenton was always dressed chic. Geordie made money in the stock market and they moved to a bigger, better house in Resilir. Some people still dissed them as new money, but they persisted, trying to gain a foothold in Resilir's upper crust.

Her country club was the most important thing in Sophie's life, other than of course her family. She made sure she always looked perfect, hair, nails, outfit, you never knew who was going to stop by.

They got Matthew to help and the family rechecked the house, garage, yard, neighborhood, and re-called everyone again just in case the girls where at someone's home and the other parents just didn't know it.

They patiently and politely asked folks to check all the rooms, closets, basements, attics, even under beds in their homes just in case the girls were hiding for some reason.

When the sun had completely set, the meatloaf sat burnt on top of the oven and they'd exhausted all avenues, the Kentons called the police.

An officer came fairly quickly, there wasn't a lot of rampant crime in the town. He took down the information, called a few of the friends and neighbors the Kentons had already called and then he called the sheriff's office.

Sheriff James, 'Jimmy' Lombardo was playing cards, drinking a very smooth scotch and smoking a probably illegal cigar. But his policy was usually, 'If I don't know about it I'm not guilty.'

The sheriff's plump wife, Isabelle, dressed in her normal attire of a below the knee, full skirted dress and low heeled pumps, stood in the doorway of the den. A couple of the men looked up and nodded polite greetings to her, the sheriff ignored her.

Saying, "Jimmy," Isabelle leaned an arm against the door frame and angled her upper half into the room keeping her feet in the doorway.

Her husband grunted and said, "I pass, it's to you, Bruce."

Isabelle crossed her arms and said louder, "Jimmy, it's the Kentons. Bobby called and said he went out there and their girls are missing."

Her brown hair slivered with grey was pulled back in a loose bun, glasses teetered on the top of her head, later she'd be looking all over the house for them.

Sheriff Lombardo grunted again, his jowls jiggled. Without taking his eyes off his cards, he said, "That hooligan girl of theirs, Aria, she's nuthin' but trouble. She's off with that punk boyfriend of hers, Dante Grange. They're shacked up somewhere doing drugs or robbing a bank. Tell Bobby to tell Geordie to keep his pants on, she'll be home when she's hungry."

He snapped at a man across the table, "You gonna marry those cards, Freddie, or play 'em? Come on, bid or throw, we ain't got all night." He swiveled towards his wife. "Bell, get me another scotch. Anybody else?" He glanced around the table.

"No, Jimmy." Isabelle took a step into the room, her hands twined tightly together in front of her. "It's not the oldest girl, it's the three little ones, you know, Char and Faith and baby Hope. They're missing. Bobby says Sophie said the girls said they were going skating with the Russells but the Russells weren't even in town today."

Her eyes flicked to the window. "And it's dark, Jim. The oldest is only 11. Something's not right."

"Uhhh," Jimmy sighed laboriously. He threw a card out then took one.

"Jimmy?" Isabelle repeated. "Something's not right."

The sheriff scratched his pillow of a belly and held up his empty glass. "Scotch, Bell, now."

Wayde, one of the sheriff's deputies tossed his cards in pile announcing, "I'm out." Tall and skinny, Wayde set pointy elbows on the table. "Jim, them girls are pretty young to be out this late. Maybe-"

The sheriff glared across at him.

Isabelle left to get the bottle of scotch.

"Let it be, Wayde. They are at someone's house playing hide-'n-seek, some parent will catch them and drag them home and Geordie'll beat hell out of them and that will be that. You out Bruce?" He gestured to the man next to him.

The men played on. Isabelle refilled glasses two more times before the doorbell rang.

Minutes later Isabelle ushered Geordie Kenton into the room.

Practically whispering, "Sheriff," sweating bullets, Geordie clutching his hat in both hands approached the sheriff.

Sheriff Lombardo, cigar hanging out one side of his fat mouth laid his hand of cards down and spread them out. "Read 'em and weep boys, I got me a full house. Cough up." He sucked on the cigar and reached both arms out to reel in his winnings.

The other men moaned and groaned around the table.

"Sheriff," Geordie said more urgently and moved to stand next to Lombardo. "Jimmy, my girls-"

Lombardo sat back, removed the cigar and placed it on a full ashtray. A haze of blue smoke clung in the masculine room. The walls were tan, the brown carpet was worn, bookcases of unread books lined the wall along with a variety of wild animals the sheriff had slaughtered on his hunts.

"Belle!" Lombardo barked. "Get in here and take care of these damned ashtrays, what're we living in a sewer for cryin' out loud?" He turned to Geordie whose panting breath was so loud it couldn't be ignored.

"Geordie my man, what can we do for you?" Sheriff Lombardo smiled an, 'I personally won't be doing anything for you but my minions will,' smile.

Before Geordie could speak, Lombardo put his beefy hands on the table and pushed his tonnage to stand up with a loud grunt.

"Listen, father to father," he leaned in, "you know how kids are, they will-"

Angrily, Geordie grabbed Lombardo's arm and spouted, "No, Sheriff, these are just little girls. They've never stayed out past six o'clock without an adult present. There's something wrong and I demand-" he trailed off at the look in the sheriff's eyes. Then the sheriff dropped his gaze to Geordie's hand on his arm.

Geordie immediately let go. "Uh, uh, I mean, Sophie and I are begging you, please, we need a search party for god's sake, now! The woods need checking! We need help to look for-"

"It's nigh on 11, past really, almost midnight, Sheriff," Freddie mentioned, keeping his eyes on his cards, not making eye contact with his boss.

"Okay, okay, Geord, settle down, get a grip." Lombardo set a hand on Geordie's shoulder and nodded to Deputy Wayde Smith.

Giving in, he sighed laboriously. "Wayde, you and Bruce go see Bobby and get a," he sighed heavily again, "a search party started. But the search will have to wait until tomorrow, it's too dark now. We'll set up the alarm and get volunteers-"

"What! Are you kidding? Tomorrow?" Geordie blasted out, his face reddening. "That's exactly the point, Jimmy, it's dark and they're little tiny girls." Tears filled his eyes, his throat clenched, beads of sweat popped out on his forehead which went back a ways.

"You have to start now! Check the forests, they could be hurt or in danger or- or- you can't let them stay out there-"

Isabelle collected the ashtrays and glasses on a tray. Tears filling her eyes, she sniffed, pulled an old tissue out of her pocket and wiped her eyes. She hurried to the kitchen to call her daughter to make sure her own infant grandson was tucked safe and sound in his bed.

Tall, narrow Wayde and rookie big-nosed Bruce stood up.

Lombardo patted Geordie's shoulder. "Now, now, Geord, calm down."

His voice softened, "You know we can't send people out in the woods for cryin' out loud. You know it's highly dangerous wandering around in the Blae even in sunlight. It's pitch black now, someone's bound to get hurt. I'd be sued up and down Elm Avenue if anyone got hurt, now you know that, right Geord?"

His campaign voice kicked in, friendly and empathetic, helpful but authoritative. "I tell you what, we'll send our men out to search the neighborhoods, stores that are still open and, uh, hospitals, but the woodlands will have to wait until morning."

"But-"

"That's all I can do for ya right now, Geord, okay? I mean I feel your pain," he kept an arm around Geordie and slowly ushered him out of the room and out of his house.

Chapter Five

Everyone, especially the sheriff, had expected that the Kenton girls would miraculously show up at home by morning, but they did not.

So, just about every able-bodied person in the town of Resilir either joined the search party or helped in some way like tacking up and handing out fliers, calling people etc.

The police department searched every building in the town, including garages, sheds, barns, fields, cars, and then finally they concentrated all of their efforts on the Blae Forest.

They had left the woods for last because other than during hunting season when people went out in groups, very few ventured into deeper forest. There were scant good trails because the ground was so rocky and peppered with hidden bogs.

The timberland went on densely for miles and miles, and further inside there were indiscernible underground lakes that spontaneously flooded into perilous rushing rapids.

Deep crevasses cut through the middle of the woods and jagged cliffs rutted along the perimeter that spooled like spokes on a wheel through the interior.

The rest of the harsh land was littered with shrubs chocked full of sharp leaves like serrated knives, and then there was that pesky legend about the chimera.

Due to the severe hazard of the forest, only lawmen and the most seasoned hunters and hikers were allowed to search deep in the woods. Since every building had been searched it was assumed that somehow the girls had wandered into the woods and had gotten lost, so the search was narrowed to there.

Everyone else who volunteered was to stay within eyesight of the tall Presbyterian Church's steeple. The people started fanning out beginning at the church because that was the closet entrance to the forest from the Kenton's home.

There weren't even church services on Sunday morning because the minister, choir, congregants, etc. everyone that could search was out looking.

Early on, the people were excited to be involved in such an important undertaking. Everyone thought they would be the ones to find and rescue the Kenton girls. Voices were boisterous and volunteers walked with energy and enthusiasm.

The enthusiasm increased when one of the deputies found the picnic basket and blanket.

Clutching each other, Geordie and Sophie identified the basket and blanket as theirs.

Tears erupting from Sophie, she cried, "That's our basket, but where are the girls?" Geordie hugged her, telling her everything would be all right, but his face was red and swollen with fear.

They were distracted by another officer that arrived, he had something in his hands. Everyone circled him to see what he carried.

He held out a tiny shirt and shorts.

Sophie whimpered and swooned. Geordie propped her up on one side an officer caught her on the other. A hand trembled at her throat, tears streamed down her face, her mouth opened and closed like she was a fish gasping for breath.

A CSI scurried over with a bag. He picked the clothes up with tongs and placed them in a bag. Another was right behind him with a paper and pen.

The CSI scowled at the officer who had handled the clothing. "Have you ever heard of evidence, you idiot? DNA? Chain of command? I'm reporting you to your superior. Please call us, don't touch anything else you find, don't move it, don't breathe on it. Do you think you can handle that?" The man browbeat the young officer who'd brought in the clothing. The officer backed up and wordlessly dropped his head.

The CSI said to the Kentons, "I apologize, Mr. and Mrs. Kenton. These local LEO's aren't used to handling this type of situation and forget all their training in the turmoil."

His voice softened. "Do you recognize, these," he reached in with a gloved hand and pulled the shirt a bit out of the bag so they could see it and identify it.

Sophie moaned again, her fingers scraped at her throat then covered her mouth. She nodded. "Yes, they're my- our- youngest, they're Hope's… why are her clothes," she turned frantic terror-stricken eyes to her husband.

"Geordie- what does this mean? Why are her clothes, was she- rap- attacked- what-" the words chugged, so afraid of what it could mean. What she was thinking, the horror, she couldn't get out any more words. She clung to Geordie's arm, her legs like water.

"Deputy?" Geordie's face a mask of fright breaking over denial, he begged, "Tell us,"

"It's okay," Deputy Wayde Smith said brightly. "This is a good sign. It means we know we're on the right track, looking in the right area. The things were found by Fey Lake."

"Are you kidding?" Geordie thundered. "A good sign? The basket is there in the damned woods, and their clothes, but the girls are gone! If they weren't there they must be-" Sophie gasped at his words.

Rubbing the side of his knife-blade nose with a long thin finger, Deputy Smith tried to calm them. "I know, I know, it sounds dire, um, but at least we've found a sign of them and we know where to focus the search.

"The girls could have gotten frightened of something and are hiding safely in a cave waiting for us to find them and bring them home." His words sounded ludicrous even to his own ears, but his job was to keep the family members calm.

Sophie managed to utter, "They always wore their suits under their clothes when we go to the lake…" she gulped at the air, grasping for calm. Her hand still at her throat, she stood a little straighter. "They, uh, basket, the bathing suits, I think, it sounds like they planned to sneak out to go swimming in the lake."

Geordie's head swung heavily back and forth in denial. "No, no, it's forbidden, they wouldn't-"

"Don't be ridiculous, Geordie," Sophie snapped at her husband's ignorance. "The kids do it all the time. The more you forbid something-"

"The more enticing it is," Deputy Smith added.

"Yes." Sophie smiled weakly at the young deputy through her tears.

Even the missing girls' hoodlum teenaged sister, Aria, looked scared clinging to her boyfriend, Dante Grange. In short-shorts, cropped shirt and straight blond hair, Aria's kohl lined eyes were glued to her scarecrow of a boyfriend with his long scraggily hair and filthy jeans that were a size too big.

Grange pulled his baseball hat down over his eyes. He had not wanted to be there, with all the cops running around. But Aria had begged, then threatened him if he didn't come and support her. She did not want to be alone with her freaky parents.

He tried to keep his bloodshot eyes averted and not betray the fact that he'd smoked a fat one before getting out of his truck.

Aria was high too but she didn't care who knew. If it pissed off her parents, all the much better. And the police weren't going to arrest the 15 year old sister of the missing children they were all there searching for, for smoking a little weed now would they? It might be legal but she was underage.

Deputy Smith tried again, "It cements the idea that at least we know where-"

Another deputy came running over waving something in his hand. Breathing hard from running a distance, he held it out for the Kenton's perusal. He gasped, "We found this near the Lake."

"Oh God, it's Faith's swim suit-" Sophie croaked. Geordie caught her just as she collapsed to the ground.

Almost 13, their son, Matthew stood next to his sister Aria. He whispered to her, "If the basket was found near the water, by Fey Lake, you know Hope can't really swim and Faith just started lessons. What if they find their bodies floating in the la-"

"Shut up, stupid," Aria snarled at him.

"I'm as worried as you are, Aria. At least I show it," Matthew said under his breath shooting her boyfriend Dante a sneering look that said 'you're a loser stoner.'

The entire grounds lit up with chattering volunteers wondering what it meant, finding the basket and then the clothes and then the swimsuit. Some argued about whether this was good news or bad news.

The police brought their findings to the sheriff inside the station. CSIs on hand waiting to see if they would be needed, followed the deputies inside.

The CSIs put the picnic basket in a big paper bag and labeled it and then put the swimsuit in a plastic bag and labeled it.

Wayde Smith said, "Sheriff, Mrs. Kenton identified the basket and the clothes. There was food packed it looked like for three people, but only one sandwich and soda looked like had been consumed. That's strange, why would only one of the three kids eat?"

He pulled out a notebook and flipped through it. "The shorts and shirt are the youngest one's, Hope. The suit is the middle girl, uh," he glanced down at his notes. "It's identified as Faith Kenton's suit. The basket was found beside Fey Lake. You know the little one in the woods, we skinny-dipped in it when we were kids playing hook-"

"Okay, I got ya." The hefty sheriff sent him a look.

Smith's neck reddened. "Um, anyway, the suit was found near the lake. It was on a path north of the water, and it was dry so that means the girls hadn't gone swimming."

"It's had a coupla days to dry, numbnuts," The sheriff said sarcastically to his deputy. The red crept up to Smith's face.

Another cop said, "It doesn't mean anything, Wayde, other than it places the girls in the woods. We don't even know if the kid was wearing it. No one saw the girls leave yesterday so they don't know if they were wearing or carrying their bathing suits. We don't even know if they are still in the woods."

"I got it, I know, Horace, you think you know every-"

"Shut up Wayde," Sheriff Lombardo growled at the cop. He turned to a CSI. "Margo, can you guys jump right on those? See if there's blood or prints, check out the inside of the basket, saliva, DNA, you know the drill." He smiled flirtatiously at the built brunette.

Under her white lab coat her skirt fell just at her thighs.

Lombardo's eyes travelled down then up Margo's long legs settling on her breasts. Without looking at her face, he said, "Why don't you bring your results personally, to me, to my office, hon."

Margo smirked. She had a string of boyfriends hot at her heels but she knew where her bread was buttered. Promotions, raises, even vacations with Jimmy Lombardo to Napa were on the plate when Jimmy favored you.

Of course, he favored a lot of the staff, as well as civilians. Bess Humpter was the last woman that tried to make a complaint against the sheriff. The word was she was transferred to another state, but then the word followed that she never got there, she disappeared.

Her disappearance was never investigated. The rumor was spread that she ran off with her neighbor's husband. This was never confirmed.

By the middle of the third day of the search of the woods, Sheriff Lombardo met with his deputies at the closest police station to the church. He didn't want civilian ears to hear what he had to say. He stood at the front of the room. Most of the deputies were wearing hiking clothes.

Lombardo addressed his staff. "Well, uh," he hemmed, smiling and nodding at everyone, his stomach strained to pop the buttons on his white shirt. He still wore his uniform of white, buttoned polyester shirt and green polyester slacks with a dark green line running down the side of the pant legs.

"I want to first start off with, well, I want to thank all of you for the hard work you're doing, each and every one of you." He grinned hugely and nodded some more.

A few people called out thanks to the sheriff, others waited to hear why he had gathered them there.

His hands in his pockets, he jingled some loose coins, he continued, "So, uh, I met with my captains and we decided, well, we decided that since it's been three days since anyone has seen hide or hair of these little girls, that, well, uh, it looks pretty much like the prognosis isn't," he took out a handkerchief and wiped his fleshy face.

"Well, at this point since we haven't found the children, it's pretty likely that they are…uh, deceased." He held up his hands for quiet as talking broke out in the room, objections bounced off the walls.

One deputy said loudly, "Sheriff, come on, we can't give up, they're little children, man, sir. I mean, they have to be somewhere."

Someone else said, "Yeah, they have to be somewhere, we have to-"

Jimmy Lombardo shook his head grimly. "No, no. At this point it would only be a recovery, not a rescue. We need to see how to play it so the police still look like heroes when the children are found dead. We need to find those bodies."

He heard some sniffling, his eyes narrowed at the group. "All right, buck up people. We need to show strength. Besides, they're not your kids." He tugged at his belt that hung well below his big belly.

"Sheriff!" one of the female deputies shouted.

He looked in her direction. "You got something to say, Tasha?"

The deputy shriveled. Crossing her arms over her chest she tried to sound firm. "Sheriff, they could be our kids. What if there's some maniac loose snatching the-"

The sheriff rolled his eyes then glared at her. She shrunk further. "Now don't get a bunch of stupid rumors started. We don't need no make-believe serial killer thing gettin' out there. We'd have panic, pandemonium, the town would get on us like ants on sugar. You just shut that pretty little mouth of yours, honey, and take notes. Now then," he smiled at the rest of the crowd. "Who has some ideas?"

Deputy Tasha Knowles dropped her head and shuffled discreetly to the back of the room.

Half an hour passed with deputies tossing out ideas on how to proceed when the door banged open.

All eyes turned to Wayde Smith lurching in the doorway.

Anxious brown eyes wide in his long face, he set a hand with long fingers against the frame to steady himself. He blurted, "They found one!" Then he turned and disappeared back out the door.

Seconds after Smith yelled, the room emptied. Everyone ran out following the deputy to the church lawn a few hundred yards away. They joined a crowd that was circled around something.

Sheriff Lombardo shoved people aside. "Lemme through, outta my way." He elbowed and pushed until he got to the center of the circle.

The circle hummed with voices, but everyone hushed when the sheriff got to the middle.

Jimmy wiped a fleshy hand across his eyes. He sighed. "Which one is it?" He leaned over, his hands on his squat knees and stared glumly down at the figure someone had set gently on the grass.

She looked like a broken doll. Blonde hair dirty and tangled, thin arms and legs curled towards her chest.

Deputy Wayde said quietly, "It's the eldest, Charity Rose Kenton. She was found at-"

She moaned.

The crowd gasped.

"What the-" Lombardo squawked.

Wayde yelled, "Get a bus, call the paramedics!" Wayde knelt beside the girl. He gingerly pushed her hair off her face. He said softly, "Charity, Charity Kenton, honey, can you hear me?"

Her eyelashes fluttered. He set a hand on her shoulder and shook her gently.

Sheriff Lombardo was still leaned over with his hands on his knees. No way he could squat down and then get back up again.

"Well, Wayde, what is it? Is she alive?"

Char slowly opened her eyes to a bare slit, she blinked unfocused once then they closed. "Mama," she cried weakly, "Mama."

Sophie and Geordie were told and they came running. They pushed through the crowd. "My baby!" Sophie cried and fell to the ground beside her prone daughter.

Geordie struggled to get down to his knees. Tears streamed down both parents' faces. "Is she- is she-" Geordie stammered.

Sophie set a tender hand on her daughter's cheek, her breath caught. She whispered, "She's warm, Geord, she's breathing! She's alive..."

She leaned over and said quietly, hopefully, "Char baby, it's mama. Mama's here, and papa, we're here baby." She stroked the fine blonde hair. "Talk to me baby, talk to mama." She patted the girl's face.

Char's eyes fluttered open again, she looked at her mother.

"Mama, I can't feel my legs."

Chapter Six

*C*har was rushed to the hospital where she fell back into unconsciousness for 16 hours.

Her parents never left her side. She had tubes and wires hooked to her small body to monitors and machines, and pouches dripping liquid. The machines monitoring her blood pressure and other vitals beeped and pulsed nonstop.

Her legs were in casts, her cuts had been cleaned, but she was covered in bruises and the side of one face was heavily bandaged.

Because she was a minor celebrity now due to the entire town's interest, Char was put in a private room with a private nurse and all of her hospital bills will be paid by the county.

Policemen hovered and paced outside her door. They weren't allowed to ask the child any questions yet, even if she could answer.

Sitting next to her bed, Sophie held Char's hand and turned desperate frightened eyes to her husband. He sat half asleep in a chair a few feet away. "Geordie-" he snored. "Geordie!" she snapped in a hushed voice.

He coughed and snorted, blinked rapidly in disorientation. Swallowing his drool, he struggled to sit up straight. "Wha… what Sophie, is she awake?"

His wife shook her head. Tears rolled off her cheeks and plopped on her hand in her lap. "No, she's still out. What if, what if," she gulped, tears streamed, "what if she's paralyzed-"

"Sophie! Hush! She'll hear you!" Geordie admonished her.

Sophie frowned at him. "I just told you she's still out. She can't-"

A policeman poked his head in the door. "Uh," he said politely, "is she awake? Can we ask her questions? We need to find the others-"

Sophie shook her head. "No, she's still out," she repeated. "Besides, you have to get the doctor's permission before you can talk to her, you know that, they told you."

The officer looked slightly sheepish. "Yes ma'am." He nodded. "I know, we're just, you know, we need to find your other children. She might know where they are. The sooner the-"

Sophie stood up angrily. "I do know, young man, I know very well what is at stake. My favorite, my youngest is out there, in the dark, in the cold, hungry," she cried.

Geordie hurried over and put his arms around his sobbing wife. He glared at the policeman. "Now see what you've done? Get out, get out before I call the-"

"Sorry sir. I apologize." The officer pulled his head back out and closed the door.

Shaking his head, still holding Sophie, Geordie sighed,

"Those bumbling police, they never know what the hell they're doing. If they'd gotten right out there the first night like I asked- uh I mean when I *told* Lombardo to go right that minute and look for our girls, well, you know..." he petered off.

"Mama?" a weak, pained voice murmured from the bed.

Both parents turned anxiously back to the bed.

Char was gazing up at them, green eyes anxious. "Where am I?" She glanced around fearfully. "Where's Faith and Hope?" She put a hand to her face. Feeling the bandage, confusion clouded her suffering eyes.

Sophie sat down quickly on the chair beside the bed and picked up the one hand her daughter didn't have something sticking out of.

"My little darling, it's okay, you're in the hospital. You're safe, and, well you had a little accident, but you'll be okay." She rushed her words, "Yes, you'll be just fine."

Geordie leaned over his daughter and smiled. "You'll be right as rain real soon, babygirl."

The little girl's eyes drifted back closed, the morphine was working.

Neither parent mentioned Char saying when she was found that she couldn't feel her legs. They were too scared to.

A couple of hours later, the doctor approved the police to question the child.

They were very patient and gentle while interrogating her.

Deputy Janey Leigh and Deputy Manuel Perez asked Char to tell them what happened.

She spoke with difficulty, the bandage covered part of her face.

They didn't tell her that in an hour the doctor was coming in to wire her jaw shut.

Unfortunately, Char was very vague. She was confused and scared, and in tremendous pain even with the meds. She told them about the lake and the picnic. She was about to tell them about the trick she and Hope played on Faith but didn't want to get in trouble so she kept it to herself. She just said they had all just wandered off to do different things.

Deputy Leigh was young and pretty, petite and friendly. She had strawberry colored hair and light blue eyes. She smiled kindly at the young girl. "What kinds of different things, honey?"

Char's shoulders squirmed, her eyes darted around the room. "Uh, you know, just stuff."

"Stuff?" Perez asked. He was medium height, stocky with dark skin, short buzz cut and a moustache.

The severely injured child nodded slightly. "Yeah, stuff. Like I saw the most beautiful butterfly ever and I followed it, but it got away." She sighed.

"Okay," Perez prompted, "what were the other girls doing?"

"Um, well, Faith went after a bunny. The bunny hopped off into the woods. I, I don't remember what Hope was doing." Her forehead wrinkled while she thought. The pain killers were befuddling her, and she kept squinting to keep the officers from wobbling.

Bigger than the pretty Deputy Leigh, Perez sat back to appear as nonthreatening as possible. He asked gently, "So honey, after you followed the butterfly and Faith looked for the bunny, what did you do?"

"Um," she tried to think back. "Faith disappeared, so Hope and I went for a walk. I think Faith was playing a trick on us." She peered at the officers from under her lashes to see if they could tell she was lying. They both smiled at her, waiting for her to continue.

Her words slurred from the medication and the bandages. "Uh huh, I think she was hiding, she wanted to scare us. I forget," her eyes flipped around the room as she pictured the scene in her mind.

"And then," Deputy Leigh prodded.

Char squinted, thinking hard. She shook her head and mumbled, "Don't remember."

Deputy Leigh suggested gently, "Did you eat your picnic? Maybe go for a swim? Try to think, honey."

The child reviewed their steps of that day, but she kept stopping at the butterfly. She shook her head. "Don't remember." She closed her lids, then opened them.

"I- I don't remember. But, we didn't eat. I don't think we went in the lake. I don't re-" her face paled. "I- I heard screams. They were horrible." Her face scrunched, tears welled.

"I couldn't really see anyone, maybe they were shadows, monsters, but, but then after the screams... I think then we, Hopey and me were screaming. I felt hands on my back- I think they were hands-" her eyes closed, she arched her neck as if physically remembering.

Suddenly her eyes flew wide open. She looked directly at the officers, her mouth trembled. "Where are Hope and Faith? Where are my sisters?"

The deputies just stared at her not knowing what to say. They hadn't known that she hadn't been made aware that her sisters are still missing.

Realizing something was dreadfully wrong, Char's face screwed up and turned red. "I want my mama," she said on a choke. The tears burst out of her eyes and down her cheeks.

"I want my mama," she cried louder. Then she wailed, "I want my-" the two officers got up quickly and left the room.

An hour later, the Kentons were in the hall speaking with the doctors and the police.

Deputy Wayde Smith stood with Deputy Leigh. Wayde watched the petite female deputy while she talked. The strawberry curls pulled back in a ponytail, the light eyes animating her face, he couldn't take his eyes off of her.

He slicked back his fine brown hair with one hand. She had a nice little figure, on the boyish side with small breasts and very little flare to her hips, made her look very young.

Leigh said, "She doesn't remember anything. She doesn't know where the other two girls are."

"Yes," Doctor Westfield affirmed. He studied a file he held. Flipping pages back and forth, he said, "It's hard to ascertain whether she has had um, a bit of brain injury, or it's traumatic amnesia, or something happened and she really didn't know what happened to them all. She might not have seen, uh, not seen it...coming, if it came from behind. She might not really be able tell us what happened to her much less the others."

Geordie's brows drew down. Confused, he said, "What do you mean something happened and she doesn't really know what, I mean, what does that mean?" He stuffed his hands in his pockets.

Sophie stood next to her husband with her arm through his.

He wore rumpled slacks and a plaid shirt. Sophie was dressed as carefully as always, in heels and a dress that was tight enough to showcase her curves, her hair and makeup were celebrity perfect.

Dragging his gaze from Janey Leigh, Wayde hesitated. He sucked his cheeks in making dimples in his gaunt face. "Well, uh, if, well if as she said someone, or something came at her from behind and she was suddenly attack- uh, knocked out, she could conceivably not have even seen who or what, uh, hurt her."

He had reviewed the doctor's appraisal of the child. Thank God she hadn't been raped. But what did happen? He and everyone else wondered. He turned to Dr. Westfield.

"What about her," he hesitated, he didn't want to sound insensitive or nosy, but, "her legs? Is she, can she, walk?" He tried to sound authoritative like he needed to know for police business not just wanted to know.

Everyone looked at Westfield. He stared at his file. He wasn't reading it, he knew what it contained.

"Well," he sighed heavily. "She has sustained severe trauma and injuries, damages that might have been caused by falling off a cliff. She was found at the bottom of one. Some of her ribs were broken, the rest were cracked, two fingers, both legs were broken, an arm was broken in three places." Everyone winced.

"I won't go into the complicated internal damage to her organs and such, but," he glanced at the file, "one of her facial cheeks was smashed, and, um, her vertebrae, as we discussed before," he nodded to the Kentons.

"There was damage to her vertebrae, but," he said swiftly as Geordie opened his mouth, "we have determined that it wasn't severed, it will heal. The problem is," his eyes flicked to the officers then to the Kentons. Geordie nodded.

"Well, she should walk again but the damage to her legs, we can put in rods and such, but she will never walk the same again," he finished with a long exhale.

Wayde tried to hide his horror. He was ambivalently astonished. On one hand the child will be able to walk, everyone had feared the worst. But on the other hand, a beautiful young girl with so much promise, crippled?

He asked, "Doc, what about her face? Will the damage be...permanent?" Hooking his thumb under his chin, he ran an unsteady finger down his sharp nose.

The doctor shot a veiled glance at the parents, but they were looking down the hall, the elevator had dinged. Dr. Westfield unperceptively nodded his head sadly at Wayde.

The officer put a hand over his mouth to hide his dismay.

Before the doctor could answer any more questions, Deputy Perez came out of the elevator and hurried to them. He was a little out of breath, his normally brown-toned face was white as a sheet.

"What is it?" Wayde asked urgently. It was apparent something had happened.

Sophie shoved her fist in her mouth. Geordie smoothed his thinning hair with his hands to still their shaking, petrified to ask, "Is it the girls? Are they, have they been found?"

Perez ran a finger under his nose then scratched his moustache. "Yes, it's one of them. I don't know which one. They've brought her to ICU."

Everyone skipped the elevators and rushed down the stairs.

Faith Mary Kenton's tiny body looked like a baby doll on the gurney. Only her wan, bruised face was visible, the rest covered by a sheet.

By the time her parents got to her they had already been advised that she did not seem to be in critical condition.

However, she had a broken arm, cuts, abrasions, bruises that were so big they covered both legs, and she also undoubtedly sustained a mild concussion. She also had a pair of cracked ribs.

And she was conscious.

Chapter Seven

Wayde Smith was summoned to Sheriff Lombardo's office. He wearily knocked then opened the door and went right in and flopped down in a chair in front of the sheriff's desk.

Jimmy had a bottle of scotch and a glass filled with some of the alcohol next to his left hand, a cigar in his mouth and he was reading a pornographic magazine.

Tearing his eyes away from the magazine, he raised his fuzzy grey brows at his officer. "Well? What's going on with the second kid?"

Wayde eyed him sharply but didn't comment. He trod to the sidebar and got himself a glass, came back, poured a full rock glass neat then flopped down with a grunt. He pushed back long fine hair. His legs straight out like skis, he crossed his ankles. His feet stuck up like black rabbit ears.

After taking a healthy swig, he replied, "They found the second youngest. Actually they didn't find her, they said she came stumbling out of the forest half dead I heard, in a tattered and dirty tutu, you know, one of those ballet things."

Jimmy arched an annoyed brow at him. "I'm not a moron, Wayde, I know what a damned tutu is." Then he huffed out a strange moan.

His brows flickered, Wayde nodded. "She was black and blue from head to toe. Has a couple of broken bones, she looks lucky to be alive. Luckier than the other one."

He gulped half the scotch down, opened his mouth wide, exhaled hard and shook his head. Limp light brown hair flipped back and forth over his forehead. "Boss, good stuff!" he hacked out.

The sheriff moaned again and took a sip of his own drink. "So, what'd the little git have to say? Who attacked them? Where's the third one? And what the hell was the kid doing wearing a ballerina outfit in the damned woods?" He groaned, rolling his head back.

"Geez Boss, you okay?" Wayde looked at Jimmy with concern.

Jimmy rolled his head again then leered at Wayde. "Oh, I'm good. So, what's going on?"

Wayde took another drink before he answered. He wiped his sleeve across his mouth. "Nothing. She could tell us nothing. Says she doesn't remember anything other than they got to the lake, got separated and she heard screams. Same tale the other one told, except they each claimed the other one was playing a hiding trick on them. We don't know if they're hiding something or what."

"Huh," Jimmy croaked. "Well, I'll finish up here and then I'll go question the little bitch."

Wayde tossed down the rest of the scotch and stood up. Stretching his long tapered body, he yawned then snapped his head as if to clear it. "Okay. I'm heading over to the Grub Grill. You comin' after?" He set the empty glass on the table.

Jimmy moaned then sipped. "Yeah. After I interrogate the kid."

"Okay. I'll see ya later. See ya, Trixie," Wayde said, heading for the door. He turned at the giggle.

A disheveled head peeped up from under Jimmy's desk, in front of his chair. Her lipstick was smeared, her mouth wet, she waved. "See ya Wayde!" And she slid back down under the desk.

Jimmy winked at Wayde as the officer turned and left the office.

Ten minutes later Sheriff Lombardo trudged over to the hospital. Everyone knew him, he was greeted as he crossed the street and as he made his way to pediatrics.

Faith Kenton had been stabilized, cleaned up, her injuries attended and her arm set. She also was hooked up to tubes and monitors. She was asleep when the sheriff came in.

Geordie was snoozing in a chair in the room.

The police had decided to keep the sisters separated until they had a handle on what had happened.

The sheriff kicked Geordie's chair.

Geordie jerked and snorted, arms and legs flailed, his eyes shot open. "Huh? What?" He sat up straight when he saw Jimmy Lombardo staring at him. He would have stood up but Jimmy was an imposing man and he was standing right in front of his chair.

Big, heavy, Jimmy was known for his lackadaisical attitude and mean streak. Geordie nervously pushed back a few thin strips of hair that had spilled over his eyes.

"Get the hell up, Geord." Jimmy stood with his hands on his hips, belly thrust out. "Where's Sophie?"

Geordie slid off the chair, squirmed around the sheriff and scurried to the door. "She uh, she's with our other one, Char. We felt it would be best to have one of us with one of them. You know, because-"

"You can shut up now. I need to speak to the girl. Get out. Go eat lunch, see your wife, just go away for 30 minutes or so."

"Uh, yeah, shouldn't I be here while you-" Geordie stuttered, wiping his hands together.

Lombardo opened the door. "Nah, it's okay. See ya later."

Not sure he should leave, Geordie hesitated a fraction then slid uneasily past the big man.

Jimmy closed the door behind him. He walked over to the child lying on the bed. He leaned over and studied her.

Her pale blonde hair was spread around her head like a halo, her skin was so white it was almost translucent. Long blonde eyelashes lay almost to her still baby round cheeks. The sheet was pulled almost up to her neck, but her broken arm in a cast was outside the sheet.

"I'm not wastin' time like those other shmucks, coddling the chit, I want quick, straight answers," Jimmy muttered. He pushed at the shoulder of the broken arm with a chubby finger. She didn't move.

He did it again harder, she made a tiny sound but slept on. Then he poked her quite hard.

Her eyes popped open, she looked confused and afraid. "Mr. Sheriff…"

Jimmy found the button that moved the head of the bed up, he pushed it. The bed moved up slowly until the child was sitting, the light hair fluffed around her shoulders.

He pulled a chair over next to the bed and lowered his heft onto it. He smiled at her. "How ya doin' there, honey?"

Huge turquoise eyes just stared at him.

His smile disappeared. Jimmy said, "I asked you how are you are doing, girl, are you deaf?" She still didn't answer, the eyes grew wider.

Jimmy reached over and pinched the skin above her cast, she cried out, tears sprung. He let go and said, "Now, girl, when I ask you a question you answer me unless you want another pinch. Is that understood?"

He leaned over putting his mealy face close to hers. She nodded frightened. Jimmy sat back and patted the girl's cast. "That's good, we have an understanding."

"So," Jimmy said, he set his beefy hands on his knees. "You need to tell me exactly what happened that day you and your sisters went into the woods. What happened that you came out all broken and bleeding?" He waited.

The child's lip trembled, the tears ran, she said nothing. He reached towards her arm with two fingers. "Do I need to prompt you again, girl?"

Faith shook her head vehemently and tried to pull her arm under the sheet but Jimmy grabbed a hold of it. "You talk now, girl, or," Jimmy growled at the child and went to touch her arm.

His liquor cigar breath blew in her face. A sweaty fat man smell lingered behind the boozy cigar odor.

"N- n- no, I'll, I'll tell you, please don't hurt me again, Mr. Sheriff, please!" Faith cried to him in a tiny wail. Her chin shook so hard her teeth chattered.

Jimmy set his hands back on his knees. "Well then, see, you can speak. So get talking. You and your sisters went into the woods to go to the lake, you had a picnic basket. What happened when you got to the lake?"

Faith pulled her other hand out from under the sheet and wiped at her eyes. She thought furiously trying to recall what they did, and why everyone wanted to know. "Uh, we, uh, my sisters and me got to the lake."

Then she told the same story she'd told before and that Char had told. They reached the lake, it was nice, she was chasing the bunny, then the shadows screamed and then her sisters screamed and then she felt herself lifted up in the air, she was flying- but it hurt- and the chipmunk watched her fall.

Jimmy yawned. "I know all that, girl. What happened after you fell? Where were you, how did you get out of the woods?"

Faith pulled her lips in to keep them from trembling. She was afraid to look away from the big man, she was sure he was about to pinch her again.

She closed her eyes trying to recall. "Um, I- I was asleep, down a hill. I woke up and didn't know where I was. The hill was there on one side and on the other side was a big hole. I was afraid I was gonna fall down the other side. It was dark." She shivered.

"And I was really cold, and," she looked at her cast, "and my arm hurt really bad, and I was scared. I cried for my daddy to come and get me, but he didn't." Her bottom lip stuck out, the tears came again.

"And? Get on with it girl. Was anyone with you? How did you get up the hill and out of the woods?" He jabbed her arm with a fleshy hard finger.

Faith used the sheet to wipe her eyes. Her tiny face hardened. She didn't look at Jimmy. "No one was there, I was all alone," her voice quavered, then she lifted her chin, bit her lip.

She turned to Jimmy. "No one came. I got up and walked until I found a shorter way up the hill. When I got up it, I found the little path I was on before and kept walking and walking until I was almost out of the woods and a policeman saw me."

Sounding relieved, she said wearily, "He picked me up and carried me to his car and I don't remember after that." Her lids drifted closed again.

"Girl!" Jimmy shouted roughly stabbing a finger into her tender skin. "Wake up!"

Her lids raised half-mast, the medication was pulling them down, her eyes swiveled towards him but she didn't move.

He jabbed her again hard with his finger. "You tell me right now young lady, you know what happened to your sisters. You saw what occurred."

She shook her head, he kept going. "Maybe *you* did it. Maybe you tried to drown them, or you pushed them down a hill and made up the story of falling over the cliff. Your sister is hurt a lot worse than you."

His finger dug into her arm to the bone. "We haven't found the other one yet. Did you hurt her? Did you hurt her real bad and then hide her body? Is that right? Am I right? You tell me everything right now or I'll-"

Faith pushed at his finger and sobbed, "No, I wouldn't! I mean I don't know, I don't know. I didn't do anything! I want my daddy-"

Blam! Jimmy slapped the injured child across the face.

Stunned, she stopped crying with her mouth open.

He bent over her and wagged a finger in her terrified face, his breath of booze and cigar covered her like a smelly mist. "You're gonna tell me, girl, you tell me what you did. You did it, didn't you? You hurt your sisters, didn't you? You tell me right now you little bitch or I'll tan your hide so hard you won't sit for a month!"

He raised his hand again and threatened, "You will never, ever go home until you confess, now, tell me everything."

A while later, Jimmy Lombardo had met with his officers and then the Kentons. He told the parents that Faith had confessed to hurting her sisters. He said she wouldn't be specific about what she did, and she refused to say where her baby sister, Hope, was.

A week later they called off the search.

Faith came home, Char would follow in another few weeks as her injuries were so extensive.

Faith was sitting on the sofa in the living room. She wore white frilly ankle socks and maryjanes, her legs stuck straight out as they couldn't reach the floor. Hair tied in neat braids laid like yellow silken ropes over her yellow dress. The arm in the cast rested on her other arm.

She sat silently listening to her parents talking in harsh whispers in the kitchen.

"She needs to go, Geordie. No, I can't hold my head up at the Club or the grocery store or even church. It's mortifying to have her in this house. Everyone is whispering and pointing, calling her a sociopath, they cross the street when they see her coming."

Geordie's grumble was inaudible.

"Beth Adderly actually pushed her out of the way when we were going in the grocery store. Faith fell to the ground and no one helped us. People have threatened to- to hurt her if she comes near them, called her the Devil's spawn."

A loud inhale was heard and more mumbles.

"And what about us? What about Char when she comes home? Are we safe? Will she try to hurt us too? Char will be mocked relentlessly when she goes to school having a murderer as a sister."

Geordie's voice had a low whine to it. "Sophie honey, you know Faith told us, that Jimmy made her say she did it. That he," he took a strained breath, "that he hit her and told her she could never go home until she admitted what she'd done. What he told her she'd done."

Their voices hushed a little as if they had moved away from the door. In a minute Faith could hear them again.

"Come on, Soph, you can't believe that, it isn't true. Everyone knows Jimmy lies, how brutal," his voice dropped off suddenly.

Sophie whispered harshly, "You better watch what you say, Geordie. Jimmy is the law in this town, and if he hears," her voice trailed away, then picked back up. "I don't believe Jimmy would hit a child, that's ridiculous. I don't know where that girl learned to lie so nastily."

Geordie tried to object but Sophie spoke over him, "No, Faith is the liar. Jimmy would never-"

Angrily sarcastic, Geordie said loudly, "What, your *boyfriend* wouldn't lie?"

Sophie gasped. "You don't know what you're talking about. I...Jimmy and I never-"

"Sure Soph, sure, you would never-"

"Oh yeah, Mister? What about you and your flooz-" her voice broke off, the pair moved away to their bedroom.

Faith sat still, and silently, tears falling on her braids.

At least she was not going to prison or reform school, or even to trial. The District Attorney decided not to prosecute Faith.

There was no evidence of any criminal behavior, and since she recanted her admission of guilt when she had confessed to the sheriff, and at only 8-years-old, the DA felt there just was not enough information to file charges against her.

The week before they brought Char home, Sophie drove Faith to a lawyer, Mr. Bennett.

Geordie couldn't make himself go. He let Sophie take his balls with her and he went to his own office, locked the door and got stinkin' drunk.

Mr. Bennett had advised the Kentons the best thing to do would be to send Faith away to stay at an orphanage for a while.

After paying a very large fee and then there will be yearly payments to Convent Grisaille, they would not tell the nuns what

Faith had done, just that she needed to be away from their home and they had no relatives for her to stay with.

They intimated that they were bringing Faith there for her own safety implying that someone in the family was abusing the child. They enrolled her as F. Mary Taylor. Taylor was Sophie's maiden name so no one would know who she really was and what she'd done.

Matthew screamed inconsolably for weeks when his mother told him what she'd done.

Sophie knelt down in front of Faith. Faith hadn't uttered a word since overhearing her parents' conversation weeks ago. Sophie smoothed the soft blonde hair and fixed Faith's collar that was astray.

She leaned in to give her daughter a kiss but Faith pulled back. Holding a teddy bear, she stared at the floor.

"Well, then, dear." Sophie stood up. "Just remember what Daddy and I told you. We love you very much, we know you didn't mean it. The nuns will take very good care of you. I'll write you every week. Most important to remember is you are not to ever, ever tell anyone at all about what happened, and you must always remember to use the name Mary Taylor. Okay baby?"

Faith stared blankly at the floor.

Sophie smiled brightly at Mr. Bennett. "So then, Sid, so you'll see her safely to the plane and then the nuns will pick her up in Maine as we talked about?"

"Yes, yes," the middle-aged lawyer dressed in a neat three-piece suit nodded emphatically. "The child will be just fine. I know this parting is very hard on you, it was wise of you and your husband to do it this way. I expect in a week or so, once the child is settled in you will go out and visit her, hmm?"

He smiled down at Faith who stared at the floor. "So, let's get on then…" he said.

Sophie handed a single suitcase to the attorney. "I guess this is it."

She said to Faith, "It'll be just for a little while honey, until all the hoopla dies down and then we'll bring you back. If you tell us where Hope is, maybe it could be sooner…"

Clutching her stuffed bear to her chest, Faith twisted away and marched out the door, to wait down the hall for Mr. Bennett.

Chapter Eight

Present Day

"Open your eyes, Miss, come on, open your eyes."

A deep male voice penetrated Kessa's dreams, dragging her back.

The little girl with the teddy bear went swirling down a tunnel out of sight, back into her memories. Kessa could feel a hand at her neck, pushing her hair back, she could feel his breath on her skin. She jerked away, slapping at his hand.

"Get your hands off of me!" she ordered. Her head was swimming, and it ached. She tried to open her eyes, but the light hurt.

The man had immediately removed his hand. It took a minute for her vision to clear. Painfully, she opened her eyes.

A man, late twenties maybe, with black hair and very dark blue eyes was kneeling in front of her. Dressed in black jeans and a black leather bomber jacket, with a rugged face and a scar over one eye he looked menacing. She thought, *like a- like a dangerous thug or motorcycle gangster or something.*

She shook her head to dispel the absurd thought and pressed back a smile at her nonsensical musing.

"You seem to be feeling better," the man said calmly. He knelt, sitting back on his heels in front of her on the grass.

Kessa looked around, *where am I?* She heard a bark.

"Where's my-"

"He's in the jeep. He's fine. He wouldn't let me near you so I had to lock him away."

Bewildered, Kessa pushed her hair back off her shoulders then brushed her palms over her face. "How did you get him into the," she looked at her hand, there was blood on it, she quailed. "What…"

"You were in an accident, you hit your head on the wheel. Those old jeeps don't have airbags. I was trying to see if you had any other injuries when you hit me."

Struggling to sit up straighter, she glowered at him. "I did not hit you. You were pawing me."

Black brows lowered. "I was not pawing you. I was trying to see if-"

"I remember now." Accusing, Kessa blurted angrily, "You came barreling out of nowhere straight at me, you hit me! I can't believe-"

Pushing his jacket sleeves up in frustration, his voice grew louder over hers, "I was not barreling, you were pulling out without looking. You-"

Kessa struggled to climb to her feet. "If I'm injured and you weren't manhandling me why haven't you called the paramedics?"

He smiled crookedly. "I have but," he took her arm to help her up, she tried to pull away but his grip tightened like a steel band.

"If you insist on standing, you will have to let me help you, otherwise you'll fall right back down and get hurt worse. And I don't want to get blamed for that too," he said lightly sarcastic then loosened his grip.

Kessa's rubbery legs gave out, she started to fall but the man grabbed her other arm and helped her lean against her jeep, actually more like pinned her against the vehicle.

Her hair covered her face, shooting bullets of pain struck her head. She shut her eyes against the agony, waiting for the pain to subside.

Still holding one of her arms, he stroked her hair back off her face. She opened her eyes slowly, the man's face was inches from hers, she cringed away. He leaned back, but still held her against the jeep.

"I am not attacking you, stop looking at me like I'm a big bad rapist, I usually prefer my women willing." He winced at her blatant fear of him.

"I can't help the way I look, still, I'm more used to women deliberately falling into my arms, not staring at me like I'm a monster. Here, drink some of this."

Bending his long frame, he picked a thermos up off the ground and held it to her lips. She eyed him warily with one eye, the other was still closed.

She knew she shouldn't drink anything from this stranger, but she was thirsty, and she was already in as vulnerable a position as she could be in. She shrugged and drank thirstily. It was cool water.

Still holding her, he took a step back. "Really," his voice softened. "I'm not going to hurt you. There was an accident. Your jeep took the brunt of it. Your dog is fine. You seem to maybe have a concussion, you have a lump on the side of your head and some cuts and bruises. That cut doesn't seem to be that bad," he pointed at the side of her head, she twisted away from his hand.

Exasperated, he said, "Anyway, don't worry, you won't end up looking like me." Wryly he pointed to his own scar.

Kessa bit back a smile. She leveled her gaze at him. "I am okay now, you can let go of me."

He looked her up and down. "Are you sure? I don't want-"

She smiled slightly. "Yes. Positive." He was so close to her she could feel the heat from his body. She looked at the muscular arm like an iron rod that was holding her against her vehicle, then up at him.

"Okay." He slowly released her. She swayed. He waited but she kept her balance, he took another step away from her.

"To answer your question, apparently you're not from a small, fairly rural town and aren't aware of our resources. We don't have a large retinue of ambulances to send out. I called it in, they had no one available. They said if you weren't in terribly serious condition, which to them meant if you were breathing, I can bring you to the hospital." He watched her to see her reaction to his words.

Her face a blank, she looked over at his cruiser. It was a three-quarter seated pick-up truck with Resilir County Sheriff printed on it.

"Your jeep will have to be towed but I checked it out, there doesn't seem to be any major damage. It should be good as new in a day or two. Now Mr. Franks' fence," he nodded at the white picket the jeep was nosed into.

"That may take a little more work. I'll call him later and explain things. We can get a work crew out here easy enough to fix it." When he moved, his jacket shifted exposing a gun and a sheriff's badge flashing against his belt.

Crossing her arms, Kessa considered her options. Stay here until a stranger came by and helped her, or get in the car now with a stranger. He had a gun, he was tall with wide strong shoulders and big hands, he could have hurt her already if he had wanted to.

She glanced down at her shirt and jeans. They weren't in any major disarray, it didn't look like he- she shook her head. It hurt. She squinted critically at him. "You don't look like a cop."

"Yeah, so I've been told. Come on," he said, gesturing to his vehicle for her to get in. "I won't bite. And speaking of biting, the dog can ride in the bed." He tromped to the back of the jeep and opened it.

Kato immediately barked and lunged. The man held up one hand and said, "Back. Stay. And be quiet."

Kessa was stunned when Kato obeyed. The dog didn't even seem angry, or scared, his tail wagged, tongue hung. He looked at the man, at Kessa then back at the man.

"Good boy," the man praised the dog. "We had a little chat, got to know each other while you were…out." He removed the jeep keys from the ignition and took out Kessa's single suitcase. He gave her a questioning look. "Not staying long?"

A corner of her mouth pulled back. "Actually, I'm staying for a while in Resilir. I don't need much."

"Uh huh, no woman travels light…" he muttered as he carried her bag over to his cruiser and put it in the back seat. "What's the dog's name? There's nothing indicating it on his tag."

Standing uncomfortably by her jeep, very unsure of her situation and what to do, "Uh, Kato," she said absently, vainly looking up and down the street hoping for someone to drive by. But there was not a car in sight on the rolling, curving rural road.

"Kato!" he called. The dog's ears pricked up. "Let's go."

Kato jumped out of the jeep and with no compunction hopped into the bed of the stranger's truck. The man turned to her. "Do you have family here?" He opened the passenger door for her and stood to the side for her to get in.

She hesitated, *well, she had to go with him now, the guy had her dog for Pete's sake*. She pushed off from her jeep and moved slowly, painfully to his cruiser.

It looked like the man struggled to not come and help her. He didn't need any more chastising or pawing accusations. But once she got to the cruiser she tried, but she couldn't lift her leg high enough to get in, her legs had taken a beating from the crash. *What was that saying- déjà vu all over again*. She sighed and looked at him.

He waited. She waited.

"You're going to have to ask, I'm not touching you again without you first giving me permission. I don't *manhandle* young women. Unless they ask," he added cheekily.

Kessa sighed again. "Fine. Would you help me?"

He crossed his arms and shook his head. "What's the magic word?"

Her eyes flared at him, mouth tightened. "Listen, you-"

He shook his head. "Nope. Magic word."

"Oh my God," Kessa groaned. "Fine. Fine, I can't stand out here all day. "Would you *please* help me into your truck?"

"I would love to help you, no problem." He suddenly swooped her up in his arms, turned sideways and gently set her down on the seat inside the cruiser. She was so surprised she was speechless.

He leaned across her, his chest slightly touching hers as he buckled her seatbelt before she could move. He took her hand, flipped it over palm up, dropped her keys in it, closed her door and locked it, then stuck his head back in the open window.

"You have anything else you need to get out of the car? You don't want to leave anything valuable."

Feeling like he'd waited deliberately until she was locked in his car before he gave her back her keys, Kessa ran a hand over her brow. "Yes, thanks. My purse is all, it's under the front seat. Please."

The man grinned at her. "And who said women aren't trainable!" He strode away before she could say anything.

He retrieved her purse, made sure the windows were up and secured then locked the jeep.

The pick-up rocked as he climbed in. Catching a glimpse of her white face, he tried to think of something to say to her to calm her fears, but drew a blank. He could see she tried to mask her fear with a false bravado, sitting up very straight, her chin raised, gaze direct.

He knew he could be rough looking, but a lot of women said his dangerous looks attracted them. Frowning, he ran a hand through his hair thinking that maybe that it was the type of women he dated, using the word date loosely, that found the danger exciting.

They rode in silence, bumping over rocky unevenly paved roads. They travelled away from the mountains, through meadows and farmland, corn was already knee-high.

He glanced at her. She looked anxious but like she was trying to hide it. He said, "So, you haven't told me your name."

When she didn't respond, he said, "I could just take your purse and look it up in your wallet, but I'd rather you tell me." He glanced over at her again, saw her eyes drop, like she was afraid, no, not afraid, but something. Maybe she was in trouble or trying to hide something.

He reached for her purse that was on the seat between them.

"No," she snatched up the bag and clutched it to her chest. "My name is... Kessa, Kessa Kent."

He nodded. "Okay, that's a nice name." He laid one arm on the hand rail and the other rested easily on the wheel.

Kessa peeked over at him without moving her head. His hair, black as night curled slightly over the back of his collar could use a clip. He had strong features to match his obviously strong body, he looked Italian or maybe Greek.

The dark blue eyes were a disconcerting contrast. "Listen, uh, whatever your name is, I don't need to go to the hospital. If you could just drop me off at a taxi place that would be just fine. Or somewhere I could call a taxi. My phone died hours ago."

"Uh huh. Well, since you asked so nicely," he said glibly, "my name is Grayson Whitewolf, that's Deputy Grayson Whitewolf. Pleasure to meet you, Kessa Kent." He nodded again but didn't look at her. "They do have cell chargers that work in cars you know."

"Yes, well, I forget to charge the thing. It sounds Indian, I mean Native American, your name I mean," Kessa said awkwardly but with interest. She turned her head slightly so she could see him.

"That explains your pitch black hair, but the deep blue eyes, uh," she closed her mouth, her expression clearly stating, *what is the matter with me, I don't want to get personal with him. I hope never to see him again once he drops me somewhere.*

64

Grayson shot her a grin. "Very observant. I am Atapante. I was born and raised a ways north of here. The blue eyes are from a Scottish ancestor."

He saw her mouth press together. He suppressed a sigh. She was closing off again, like she didn't want to get drawn into conversation with him. She was hiding something, or she was racist.

"Are you in some kind of trouble?" he probed gently, trying to watch her reaction, but her face stayed stony. It was intriguing, after all, a female traveling alone with only one suitcase that obviously cared less about her phone. Most people had it clutched in their hands even on their death beds. Plus, travelling to Resilir? It was so off the beaten track, what on earth was bringing her here?

She shook her head, said nonchalantly, "No, I am not in trouble. I am here to," she stopped, took a deep breath. "I am here to see family." Her exhale was long and heavy.

"There," she pointed out the window. They had entered the beginning of the town. A clutch of a few small stores, a diner and a bus station.

"You can let me off there. I can call a cab. Thank you so much for your," her mouth dropped as he passed by the street, kept going. "Um," she was afraid to look at him.

"Don't start that again. I am not kidnapping you, but I am not dropping you off in the middle of a town you are not familiar with. You have injuries, you need to go to the hospital."

She swung her head at him, her hands balled into fists. "I do not want to go to the hospital, I am fine. I insist you to stop this car."

He shook his head and kept driving. "Fine, if you don't want to go to the hospital then I will take you to your family." He frowned when he saw her face darken.

"Listen, babe, your options now are either I take you to your family, the hospital or to the police station. I am not leaving you stranded in the middle of the street. You decide." He clamped his mouth shut, a vein beat against his temple.

They drove through the small village area to a busier section. Kessa stared out the window. He kept his eyes on the road as the traffic had picked up.

She said to him, "You are very bossy and controlling." He didn't respond to that, just kept driving like he had all the time in the world and nowhere to go.

Kessa sighed. "Fine. You can take me to my brother's. And don't call me babe."

His shoulders relaxed. He hadn't wanted to haul her into the station like a criminal. Unless she was one. "All right then. What's his address?"

Kessa opened her purse and took out the directions Matthew had given her. "It's um, 135 Lake Avenue. He says it's over by the-"

Grayson swung the truck around quickly and turned down a street. "I know where it is."

They drove in silence until Grayson pulled up in front of a century old, two-story antique-white house that was surrounded by stately trees.

He pulled up and parked out front in the street. The driveway was an incline made of loose stones and there was another truck parked in it. He looked very puzzled.

"You're sure your brother lives here-" the front door opened and Matthew long-legged it down the slight green slope of the front yard to the cruiser, the screen door banged shut behind him.

He leaned in the window and gave Kessa a kiss on the nose.

"You made it!" He grinned at Grayson. "And in style! Hey Gray." He said to Kessa, "Where's your jeep? How'd you get hooked up with this tough cowboy?"

"Indian," Grayson corrected.

Matthew laughed. "Yeah." He asked his sister. "So what's going on?"

She unbuckled her seatbelt, unlocked and pushed the door open but couldn't get out. Her legs were screaming in agony.

"It's a long story. He hit me then he made me get in his car. My jeep is on the side of the road just outside Resilir," Kessa replied wearily. Her legs dangled out the door.

"He what?" Confusion written all over his face, Matthew said to Grayson, "You what? What the hell is go-"

Grayson hopped out, took out her suitcase from the back and came around the side. He handed the suitcase to Matthew. "I did not hit her."

One arm propped on the top of the passenger door, he leaned in and said to Kessa, "I did not hit you, you were in the way." He said to Matthew, "It's a long story. Can you open your front door for me?"

He reached in, scooped Kessa into his arms before her objections got out of her mouth and started tromping up the grass to the house. Matthew stood holding the suitcase, his mouth open.

"Mr. White- uh, Deputy, put me down right now, you're embarrassing me. People are watching, I can walk perfectly fine on my-"

"You can bluster all you want, Miss Kent. I much preferred it when you were out cold, you were a lot quieter and so much less annoying."

Kessa sputtered, then kicked her legs, which hurt her more than him, "What happened to your vow of asking my permission before touching me? I insist you put me down right now!"

"This is all still part of the initial permission. When I set you down safely inside, then you can do what you want." He shouted over his shoulder, "Kato! Come."

The dog leaped out of the truck and bounded after them.

Shaking his head, Matthew said, "What are we- in the Twilight Zone?" He hurried past them to open the screen door.

Inside, Gray set a fuming Kessa on Matthew's sofa. "You're welcome," he said then went over to where Matthew was setting the suitcase down. "Walk me to my truck," Gray said to him then strode out the door.

Matthew shot his sister a perplexed look. She shrugged. He followed the deputy out the door.

Kessa looked down at Kato who was standing in front of the couch, wagging his tail at her. "Traitor," Kessa muttered. He hopped up on the couch and sat down beside her and tucked his head in her lap.

The men walked down the yard to the street. At his truck, Gray said to Matthew, "Bro, you never mentioned you had a sister, I mean this one. And a seriously hot one at that. It's weird how much you two look alike with that pale blonde hair and blue-green eyes. So what's up with the secret sister?"

Matthew shrugged one shoulder. "Yeah, well, it's a long story. Now that she's here the news will be all over town shortly, you'll get an earful. Catch a beer with me tomorrow and I'll fill you in."

Grayson agreed and climbed in his truck and turned it on.

Matthew set a hand on the open window ledge of the truck.

"I like you and all Gray, you know I think of you as a brother."

Gray nodded at him.

Matthew went on, "But my sister has had it really rough. She's been away from home like… most of her life. She thinks she's strong as nails, but really she's quite fragile, and fairly inexperienced with the world, with…men. You know what I mean?" His brows arched at the deputy asking him to understand.

"No," Gray said, his eyes narrowed. "I don't. Explain it to me."

Matthew sighed. He glanced at the house to make sure Kessa was still inside, then looked down the tree-lined street, then back to Gray.

"What I mean is, I love ya man, but you're not right for my sister. You're, don't take this wrong bro, but you're kind of a tough, hard man. Because Lexi did you wrong, your female relationships consist of one-night stands, you use them with no emotional attachments.

"I'm not judging you, it's none of my business how you live your life," Matt smirked, "sometimes I really envy you. You have no strings, you're free of emotional ties and nagging women that keep you from hanging with your friends-"

"Yeah, yeah, where's this going, Matt?" Impatiently Gray cut him off.

Matthew set both hands on the window ledge. "I saw the way you looked at Fa- Kessa. She's more striking than technically beautiful, makes you keep looking at her though, and with that figure," he whistled, "guys are gonna be all over her here like bees on honey.

"But she's been living practically like a recluse for a few years, she's been hurt too, in a different way. I just don't want her hurt again, man. Mentally or physically," he wound down, sheepish, but gravely firm.

Gray sat quiet for a moment. Then he said to his friend, "Matt, you do not need to worry, seriously, she is not my type. Yeah, she's good lookin', but there's a lot of good looking women in the world. She's way too cold and secretive for me. You don't need to worry about me. I have zero interest in your sister. She's very touchy, and I'm not interested in inexperienced women. So, don't worry about me. Besides, if she's been in a nut house-"

Matthew shook his head vehemently. "No, no, that's not it. I'll explain tomorrow. She was… set up and treated wrong. This time she has me to protect her." His face darkened.

"Anyway, I don't want her screwed with. You're a decent guy, bro, I'd trust you with my life, you know that, and you might not mean to hurt her, but-"

Gray pulled back a slanted smile. "Don't worry, I don't go after naïve fragile women. Your sister is safe. I'll be like a big brother to her too, and watch out for her, okay?"

Matthew tapped a hand on the ledge. "Yeah, sure. You're not mad are you?"

Gray grinned. "We're good. You're her brother, I wouldn't expect any less from you, protecting her, watching out for her. You know I'd do the same with my sisters. So, I'm outta here. I have to do some paperwork at the station, then later I have an appointment with one of my, one-night stands." He laughed. "See ya tomorrow." He drove off

Matthew trudged back up to his house and went inside.

Sitting next to his sister on the couch, Matthew wrapped an arm around her shoulders and gave her a hug. "I'm glad you're here, sis. You take a few days to settle in and get healed up and then we'll make plans to, to go see the folks. Okay?"

"Sure, thanks." Kessa's face paled, but she smiled weakly.

Matthew squirmed back on the couch. He reached over her to scratch Kato's ear. "Listen, I'm gonna get us some take-out for dinner, but before I do, I want to talk to you about Grayson Whitewolf."

Kessa frowned irritably at him. "That obnoxious deputy? What about him?"

"Um," Matthew took a breath before answering. "I think it's best you don't get attached to him."

"What?" Kessa swung her head so hard her hair flew across her face. She pushed the strands out of her eyelashes, turquoise eyes flashing angrily. "What the heck do you mean? I have no interest in that bully, that- that- insufferable know-it-all. I have no interest in him, are you insane?"

Matthew patted her knee. "All right, calm down, I'm sorry. It's just, you know, the way you came in, in his arms and all, well, I just wanted to warn you about him."

Kessa pulled her knees up, wrapped her arms around them and set her cheek on a knee. "The beast grabbed me up in his arms, believe me, it was not romantic. I'm not into tall, dark and bossy. He looks like he eats nails for breakfast.

"He'd be good looking if he weren't so, I hate to use that overused cliché- rugged, and I find him menacing. There's an undercurrent of... I don't know, anger, violence? Whatever, not for me, thank you. He takes or does without asking, like he knows best. Anyway, what did he do?"

Her brother leaned back against the cushions. "It's a long story."

Kessa's lip curled. "I have time."

Matthew smiled. Pushing Kato aside a few inches, he crossed his long legs then dropped his hand on the dog's head to pet him.

"Yeah, ya do. All right, a few years ago he had this girlfriend, Lexi. He was away in the Army and she cheated on him with one of his best friends. He found out when he came back. He went after Joe, found him in a bar, with Lexi sitting on his lap." He slid a sideways glance at his sister.

She was watching him with mild interest while scratching Kato's ears.

"They got into it. Gray kicked Joe's ass, bad. Lexi left Joe bleeding on the ground and tried to go with Gray, but he shook her off and stalked away. She ran down the street after him. He turned on her, and apparently, according to her, in an ice cold empty voice told her to get lost."

"That's really sad, Matthew." Kessa moved so Kato could nestle onto her lap.

Matthew nodded, reaching over to keep petting the dog.

"Yeah, it was pretty bad. The beating he gave Joe put him in the hospital for weeks. But, the worst thing was, when Gray turned his back on Lexi, she had run back to Joe's car and took a pistol out of his glove box and ran back to Gray. She had called out to him, he turned, and… she shot at him."

Kessa's quick intake of breath was loud.

"Yeah," Matt said. "She shot him, but fortunately it only grazed him. The scar over his eye, that's where the bullet struck. Coulda killed or blinded him. As it turned out, he didn't press charges against her, and Joe didn't press charges against Gray.

"Gray said to me a couple years later that between being a military cop and the deputy job, it wasn't the first or the last time he'd been shot, he has at the least another bullet wound on his back that I've seen. He said though, as bad as he felt, he wasn't putting a woman in jail on his account."

"That is so awful," Kessa murmured sadly. She stroked the sleeping dog on her lap.

"Yeah. The worst was that it changed him. He became…well, he already was tough but now he has a hard edge, he grew quiet, reckless and quick to brawl. Not actually violent I wouldn't say, but, he has done damage with those fists. He's really a good guy, Kess, he's honest and has stiff integrity, the other thing is," he looked embarrassed.

"He uh, he doesn't go with like steady girlfriends now, he just sees a few, what do you call it, friends with benefits? Or he goes out of town to some of the other towns nearby and just picks up a girl for the night. Satisfies his needs but stays away from getting involved."

"Why are you telling me this, Matthew? I don't care about his past. I don't care about him at all. He called me babe for crying out loud. How sexist and demeaning is that? Especially coming from a law enforcement officer."

Her brother turned towards her and said gently, "He did that on purpose, to push your buttons, and it worked. He told me he thought you were cold and prim and he tried to get a rise out of you. I'm just saying, he's a great guy, brave as they come, he'll always have your back. If you're ever in trouble and I'm not around he's the guy I'd want you to go to. But I don't want you to get involved with him. He'll hurt you. He won't mean to, but he will. He's a player and would break your heart."

Kessa snorted. Raking her hands through her hair, she bent her head back, facing the ceiling. Then turned to him.

"Don't be ridiculous. First, I can take care of myself. Second, I repeat, I have absolutely no interest in that annoying man. My taste does not run to barbarians. Now, let's drop it, I'm hungry and I need some aspirin. What're you getting for take-out?"

Chapter Nine

On the late morning, Grayson Whitewolf stood in a dense thicket on the edge of the forest, near Lake Yana.

His horse, Sabbath, a Friesian, pure black, powerful, muscular, the feathers- the long silky hair on his lower legs was trimmed as they spent a lot of times in the forests and over scrubby land.

His short ears twitching, Sabbath grazed on grass a short ways back in a small opening concealed in a thatch of trees. Grayson didn't need to tether the horse, Sabbath would never leave him unless he told him to.

The deputy had been hiding for over two hours, waiting. He heard a motor. Finally. Dressed in army green cargoes and shirt, he stayed blended into the leaves watching the dory putter up to the hidden cove.

There was a single man at the wheel. He came in slowly from the sunlight to the shaded shore, looking all around the area making sure no one was watching him. A cap covered half his face.

Satisfied he was totally alone, the sailor pulled up a couple of feet from the shore and dropped the anchor. He slid over the side of the boat into two feet of water barely making a splash.

Throwing the boat's rope over his arm, he swished through knee-deep water slugging through cattails and tall grass to the shore. The water lapping over the rocky shore made a soft splashing sound.

The man was a big guy, like a wrestler. With dark hair and skin, tattoos inked on his neck and more showed on his arms when he pushed his sleeves up, a gun was holstered across his chest.

The deputy stood back in the brush still as a stone as the man pulled the boat onto the land and tied it off to a tree. He reached back into the boat. With a huge grunt, he lifted out a big box then heaved the box onto the higher dry ground.

He pulled the boat up further on the shore and pushed it closer under the cover of bushes. Then he picked up the box, and in soaking wet pants and boots, made his way along the hard sandy dirt following the curve of the woods.

Gray waited until he was out of sight. He had earlier found the man's car, a 10-year-old, blue Chevy Malibu hidden a hundred yards down near a dirt road, exactly where the thug was headed.

When the coast was clear, Gray jogged back to his horse and hopped on.

Whispering with a slight nudge of his heels, "Let's go, Sab," man and stallion sprinted through the woods.

Gray knew cutting straight through the forest he could get to the crest where the car would eventually leave the dirt road and enter a main road, and that road led to only one area where he was sure the smuggler was going.

Racing through, head ducked down, branches and bushes scraping and swatting him they reached the spot before the man did. Gray waited only a few minutes when he saw the Malibu fly by. They were on backside of the town, there was only one street that the car could be travelling to.

Emerging from the cover of the trees, he had Sabbath trod slowly down the street while he searched for the Malibu. Less than a quarter of a mile he saw it parked behind Taz Cache's place, Cache's Bar.

Gray slid off the horse and sidled up to the Malibu. Cautiously, he peered into the car, it was empty. He looked around, stumped.

The car would have just gotten there and was parked several yards behind the bar in the back parking lot. He scratched his head, mumbling, "How the hell did the guy get from the car to the bar without me seeing him?"

Down on the ground leading from the car were wet footprints. Gray followed them, they went behind a crowd of trees thick with wide, flat-leafed shrubbery and tall grass, then disappeared into the brush after only a few feet.

The ground was a mixture of loose and packed dirt, scattered small stones, exposed roots, and wispy layers of old cut and shredded grass.

Gray walked out to the front and studied the rest of the seedy street in both directions. Run-down, some decent but mostly derelict buildings rutted the street like bad teeth, separated by unevenly spaced, poorly maintained lots.

Cache's was the best of them. A grocery store, shops, drug store, a couple other bars, two banks, two gas stations, a gun shop, and a diner bunched both sides of the street.

The guy could have gone into any of them, but how? Gray would have seen him going inside. What, is he a ghost and walks through walls?

Gray jogged back to the horse and climbed on then pulled the reins to lead the horse down an alley heading back home, he didn't want to be seen nosing around and scare off the dealers.

He kept close to the side of the alley so Sabbath's rhythmic clip-clops would be more muffled. He needed to get back and call his CI, find out when the next delivery was planned for.

A week later, Kessa paced like a caged animal, Matthew almost bumped into her as he rounded the corner coming from the kitchen.

"Whoa, girl, watch out! What're you doing?" He carried a soda into the living room and sank down in an easy chair. He popped the tab and guzzled the cola, wiped his mouth with his sleeve.

"What's the matter?" he asked when she hadn't responded.

She wandered across the room. "I've got cabin fever, I'm going stir crazy. I need to go outside. I need to go on a run or rent a boat," she replied, pacing in front on him.

Matthew finished the rest of the soda and sat back. "I hear you. If I didn't have softball and the gym I'd go bananas too. You look a lot better, and you're walking with no problem."

She nodded absently.

"It's time I think, to go see the folks. I know you stayed inside while healing because you didn't want to take the chance of someone else seeing you and telling them you were here before you could."

Kessa pulled a kitchen chair over, turned it around and straddled it. She set her chin on the back of the chair. "I'm as ready as I'll ever be. When should we do it?" The edgy tightness in her throat made her sound like she was talking about a trip to the electric chair.

Matthew got up, went into the kitchen and tossed the can into the recycle trash then came back out with an apple in his hand. He polished it against his sweatshirt. "I know we talked about it, but I think I should go see them first, tell them, prepare them. I don't think they'd appreciate the surprise. We don't need any heart attacks."

Kessa nodded, let out her held breath. "Yeah, I don't think, really, that I could take their shock, their honest reactions. I'd rather they had some time to take it in, and then pretend they're happy to see me. If they have the grace to do that." She smiled wryly.

"Come on, Kess, they-"

Kessa stood up. "Don't placate me, Matthew. I'm not a child any more. I don't hold onto fairytale thinking anymore, not since I was 8. So, when?"

He was quiet, then, "A little belief in magic can be okay, you know." He sighed. "I'll go see them today and then, maybe we can plan dinner at their house tomorrow night, if of course they agree. What do you think?" He bit out a chunk of apple, it was juicy by the way it sounded.

Kessa wandered over to the mudroom. The house was pretty big for a single man, but it had been in foreclosure so Matthew had snapped it up at a very low price. The bad news was that it was a turn of the century house and needed continuous updates and upkeep.

The good news was it was uniquely designed with lots of cushy rooms and alcoves tucked here and there for a writing desk or sitting quietly to read a book.

Besides four bedrooms and three baths, it also had a den, even a small library, a huge eat-in kitchen plus a dining room. The living room faced the front of the leafy street of houses that were the same scale but each with different architecture, but all had a Victorian style.

All of the homes sat up on slight inclines with stone paths leading from the sidewalks up the lawns to the front doors. The back of the house was a glassed-in sunroom that looked out over a wide, long green lawn.

Coming back with a leash in her hands, she'd tucked her white-blonde hair up in a fedora type hat and put on sunglasses that covered half her face. "That's fine," she answered him looking around the room. "You'd better wear a bullet-proof vest. Come, Kato."

The dog didn't have to be asked twice. He popped up from under a chair next to the fireplace and pranced right over.

Matthew chomped the apple noisily, talking through bites, "Nice disguise. I think you will see they've mellowed somewhat."

"Huh." Her short laugh was joyless. She knelt to hook the leash on the dog. Standing up, Kessa said to her brother, "Really? Does Mother still go to the Wilton Club four times a week, shop daily, lunch daily, get her hair done weekly?"

"Kess-"

"Uh huh," she hummed drolly. "Is Dad still seeing Cassie Finestone on the sly, or has her husband moved the family away from the neighborhood? What about his other, *friends*?" She waited, but Matthew stood finishing the apple.

When he didn't respond, she said, "I see. He slops, she shops. Big changes." She headed for the door in a t-shirt and jeans.

When she opened the door, Matthew said, "Just give them a chance. They're your blood, you need-"

She pushed out the door with the dog. "I don't *need* anything." The door slammed behind her.

Matthew stood shaking his head. He went around to the back of the house. Opening a sliding glass door he tossed the apple core out for the deer then went to change out of his shorts and sweatshirt to go see his parents.

Chapter Ten

Dressed in jeans, a polo shirt and loafers, Matthew showed up an hour before lunch. He knew his mother had her book review group over for lunch, she wouldn't want him hanging around so he could pretty much hit and run.

Geordie stomped in from the garage. Sophie was giving her housekeeper, Alice, notes on when she wanted luncheon served and how the table was to be set. When she reached the dining room, Matthew, Geordie, sisters Aria and Char were already sitting at the long mahogany table.

Huffily, Sophie pulled out a chair opposite Geordie. Right behind her another one of her staff, Edna came in with a tray of glasses and a pitcher of iced tea. She set them on the table then poured each glass and passed it around until everyone had one.

"The fruit and cookies, Edna," Sophie reminded her.

Edna replied, "Yes, Ma'am." She scurried out of the room to return in seconds with a bowl of fruit and a plate of an assortment of cookies which she passed around then retreated to the kitchen, closing the door between the rooms.

"So…" Geordie smiled at his family. Matthew sat at the end of the table, his parents faced each other and his two sisters faced each other across the table.

"I have things to do, Matthew, why did you call us here today?" Sophie curbed her impatience, she didn't want to tick off her son. Some of her friends were bringing over some new ladies and a couple of them had daughters Matthew's age, and Sophie thought they might be perfect for her handsome, successful son.

The young ladies all had the blue-blooded ancestry Sophie would kill to get into her family.

Her eyes flit around the table settling first on Char. She rolled her eyes, *no chance there*, then to Aria, she shook her head in distaste. *Yes, Matthew will have to be the one to bring noble credibility and class to their family.*

"Yeah," Aria grumbled. "I got places to be, people to see." She scowled at her brother while reaching for a cookie.

"You mean crack houses to visit and crooks to go robbing with." Char's sardonic comment drew a glare from her mother.

"You're just jealous, heifer." Four years older than Char and two years older than Matthew, Aria fluffed her dark blonde hair. "Men are knocking down our door to date me, and you're stuck with that asshole husband of y-"

"More like the police are knocking down our door to arrest you and pimps to hire you." Char's green eyes burned across the table at her older sister. She sniffed and sipped her tea, tossed a long gnarl of hair identical to Aria's over one shoulder.

Aria slammed her glass on the table, tea spilled over sloshing on the table. "Oh yeah? Well your fat ass-"

"Girls!" Sophie slapped her hand on the table. "That's enough. Does it have to be this way every time we're all together?"

"As long as she's still a pig." Aria smiled, mocking her sister's look of disgust.

Sophie held a hand up at Char. "Not another word." She swung her other hand to Aria and ordered, "You too. That's enough and I mean it. I don't want another word out of either of you. Now, Matthew," she sighed wearily.

The sisters glowered at each other but kept quiet. Sophie had ways of punishing people who didn't obey her.

Matthew waited until the sniping simmered down, it usually took a couple of warnings before it completely stopped. He looked around, they were quiet for the moment.

"All right," he said, drawing the attention to him. These family get-togethers were always exhausting and he felt the need to go home and take a shower afterwards. All eyes turned to him.

Aria's were vacant, Char's disinterested, Geordie yawned and Sophie kept looking at the clock.

Matthew stayed seated to still his desire to run from his charming family. "So, I asked to speak with you today because I want to prepare you for something." Now the eyes turned with some interest to him.

Sophie's brows rose but she said nothing. Inside, she grew excited, maybe he was announcing a young lady, an engagement. The excitement dimmed, but he hadn't brought anyone around for quite a while. Her brows dropped, *she'd better be from good stock-*

"So, uh, you know I've tried to tell you, discuss with you a few times that, well, you know I've kept in contact over the years with Kess- uh, Faith."

He frowned at Sophie who was opening her mouth. "I am not calling her Mary." His tone of voice was enough to close his mother's mouth.

He pushed his chair back and stood up. "I have kept in touch and gone to see Faith regularly over the years."

Aria sat back, her interest gone, she shoved a cookie in her mouth. Geordie stared down guiltily at the table. Sophie's face reddened, she struggled to stifle her mounting fury. Char's expression was unreadable.

Matthew leaned over and braced his knuckles on the table. "There's no easy way to tell you, so," he took a deep breath. "Faith is here. In Resilir." He stood back crossed his arms. No one hid their shock.

"What?" Sophie exploded. "She's here? Now? Faith is…" she turned her head to see them all. Geordie's head lifted, he blinked blankly at his son, not sure if he was joking.

"Yes," Matthew said firmly, his face set and voice hard. "She's here. She's at my place right now. She's been here over a week, waiting," he coughed, "to see you." He looked around the table. "All of you."

Sophie shoved her chair back and stood up. Big beet-red blotches were spreading over her cheeks and down her neck. She stomped a few steps towards Matthew, blonde hair flouncing, then she stopped. Sputtering her anger and confusion, she said through clenched teeth, "What were you thinking bringing her here? What is the matter with you?"

His shoulders hiked up. Matthew responded, his voice low and even, "She's my sister and your daughter. You will see her and treat her kindly, respectfully and welcomingly, or you will never see me again."

Sophie's head reared back, her skin darkened like an eclipse in the desert. Her hands rolled up like hammers, elbows bent as if she was about to explode into a full blown tantrum. She shouted up at her son, "What? How dare you! What the-"

"Shut up, Sophie," Geordie said it so deathly hard, wearily dispirited that Sophie froze with her mouth hanging open.

Setting his palms flat on the table, Geordie pushed himself up on unsteady legs, his florid face wobbled. He said to Matthew, "Bring her." Then he asked him, "When?"

"Tomorrow," Matthew replied quietly, his bucked shoulders lowered somewhat at his father's acquiescent response.

Geordie turned to his wife and said coldly, "Tomorrow. Dinner."

Aghast, Sophie's mouth opened and closed like a bass catching flies. She said in a fluster, "But, but, I- I can't plan a dinner, I don't, there's no time, maybe next-"

"Tomorrow!" Geordie bellowed.

Sophie shrank back from her husband.

At the table, Aria looked with interest at her father who had apparently finally grown a backbone. Char still sat silently, her expression inscrutable.

Geordie took a couple of steps away, then turned back.

"She's our daughter. We can at least feed our child that we abandoned." Slumping shoulders, his head drooping, he plodded out of the room.

The aftermath was like a bomb had gone off in the middle of the table, and suddenly all the black air whooshed up dissipating into silence. No one moved.

Then Matthew said, "I mean it. Treat her right or I'm a ghost. Forever." He went over and gave his mother a light kiss on the cheek. "We'll be over, say at seven? Skip the early cocktails and hors d'oeuvres."

She didn't respond. He waved to the others and stalked out of dining room. Striding down the hall, his loafers clocking on the gleaming cherry wood floor, through the parlor, across the marble vestibule and out the front door.

Alice appeared out of nowhere and closed the door gently behind him. Matthew's engine could be heard all the way back to the kitchen as he roared down the street.

"Well, this outta be interesting, I'm inviting Peter." Aria jumped up and hurried out before Sophie could stop her.

Char said flatly, "Jaspar will be here too of course. He should have been here now as it was."

Sophie sighed. "He had to work, Char, and it was a family meeting-"

Char snapped, "He is family, Mother." She bent and picked up her cane that had fallen to the floor and used it to push to her feet then limped out of the room.

"Don't remind me," Sophie muttered after her. The doorbell rang, Sophie's head hurt, her reading group was already arriving.

Clenching her fists tight to her side, her neck straining, she ground out, "*Dammit all.*"

Chapter Eleven

$\mathcal{M}$atthew was already inside Cache's Bar nursing a beer when Gray arrived.

Smoking was allowed in the building as there was no food served. The room was hazy and moderately noisy. The oak floors and paneled walls didn't soak up much of the sound of the scraping of constantly moving chairs mixed with jukebox music and chatter.

The mahogany bar counter was a big circle and was almost full. In the low lights over in the corner was a pool table. Two men were playing, several others holding long necks stood around watching, others sat on stools waiting their turn.

The balls clacked periodically and there was an occasional cheer for a good shot.

On another side of the room a card game was in full swing. Several women hung over the men as they played. The rest of the room contained wooden tables and chairs, booths lined the walls.

Still in jeans and a polo shirt, Matthew took a pull on his beer, the meager light shined brightly on his blond head. "Whaddya havin'? Whiskey?" he asked Gray as the deputy sat down on the stool next to him.

Gray shook his head, waved two fingers at the bartender. "Nah, I'm working." He set a bill in front of him on the bar. "Hey, Rex," he said to the bartender who had come right over. "Just a draft, thanks, and bring Matt here another bottle."

"Hmm, must be nice," Matthew muttered into his beer, "wish I could drink while on the job."

"Uh huh. I have to blend into this place, you know," Gray said quietly to Matthew. He wore black jeans, black leather jacket and black boots. He took a few sips before discreetly perusing the room.

"They all know you're a cop, Gray. What're you working on in here?" Matthew asked curiously then snickered, "The female crowd?"

The bartender brought the beers.

Not responding to Matthew, Gray casually drank his draft. When the bartender took his money, brought back his change and then left, Gray leaned over to Matthew, whispered in his ear, "No women bro, you don't shit where you eat."

Matthew chuckled. "Yeah you've told me that before."

After he sucked down most of the beer, Gray said, "I need to find the connection between the drugs smuggled in at the cove and who they're going to. I know who's bringing them in, but I don't know exactly where or who he delivers them to."

Matthew turned to his friend. "I thought you said they were coming here."

Gray nodded. "I'm pretty sure they're coming here, but I haven't yet eyeballed the drop off. So," he set one foot on the bar rail and crossed an ankle over his knee, turned towards Matthew.

"You were gonna give me the heavy on your sister. What's the story?" He motioned to the bartender to bring him and Matthew another beer.

After twenty minutes or so, Matthew wound down his story about Kessa. "That leaves her here, why I made her return to Resilir. She's been on her own and alone for too long. She obliged me, but very resistant and reluctant needless to say." He sipped his beer.

"Not to say humiliated, afraid, ashamed, no idea what's going to happen to her, how she's going to be treated, welcomed, good or bad." His neck bent, his head drooped.

Matthew went on miserably, "She was a tiny child, Gray, she couldn't have done what they said she did. She told us Sheriff Lombardo made her confess or he wouldn't let her go home. I mean for God's sake, he told a child she would never go home again," he choked. "And basically, she didn't."

Gray silently sipped his beer, occasionally darting a commiserating eye to his friend.

"She even said he," Matthew broke off, his face angry and flushed. He sucked in a harsh breath before continuing. "She said the bastard pinched her real hard and then hit her. Across the face, more than once! Can you believe that?"

He curled his hands into tight fists and set them on the bar, his shoulders rigidly moved up by his ears. "My injured baby sister and that bastard animal struck her. I was too young myself. I wish I could have-"

Gray set a hand on his friend's shoulder. "You couldn't. Don't beat yourself up. It's too late to prove anything now, it's her word against his."

He shook his head cynically. "I believe you about Lombardo. I wouldn't put anything past him including beating a child." His face hardened, the vein pulsed at his temple.

The two men sat brooding, thinking about what Faith had endured and their feeling impotent to do anything about it then or now.

"Your parents, not believing her, sending her away, abandoning her, I have to say that's truly got to be one of the worse things I've ever heard. Totally heartless." Gray shook his head sadly. He said, "You keep calling her Faith, but her name is Kessa, what's up with that?"

"Yeah, that was all part of the tragedy. Her real name was Faith Mary Kenton. When the parents sent her away they changed her name so no one would know what she had allegedly done, or who she belonged to." His lips twisted.

"They entered her in the orphanage convent as F. Mary Taylor, Taylor was mother's maiden name. They called her Mary at the home."

"Uh huh." Gray listened while watching people come and go. The room was getting louder, more boisterous as people became drunker. The crowd thickened, people bumped and swayed off each other.

"Mary still isn't Kessa," Gray pointed out.

Michael nodded. "I know. When Faith aged-out she went to college for journalism and got a job while in school with one of those celebrity mags. While still at the orphanage she wrote a novel, and now she's had 3 out there and a 4th is coming out in May.

"Her stories are about mystery, murder, main character is Detective Fraser. They're actually quite good and she makes a decent living. Kessa Kent is her pen name. She didn't need her past weighing her down so she legally changed it. Kessa was a nickname our grandma called her, it's an old Indian word, means pudgy.

"Kinda funny now, she had the chubbiest cheeks as a toddler like peaches, hence the handle. Obviously she's quite slender now, but with killer curves that I'm sure you noticed."

Taking in this information, Gray's forehead furrowed. "I don't ogle teenagers, Matt. Sounds like she's stronger than she looks."

Matthew laughed. "Oh yeah, don't let that corn silk hair and turquoise eyes fool you. She's built quite an impenetrable little wall around her."

"Seems like she had to, to survive," Gray grunted.

"By the way, she's not a teenager, she's 22."

Gray sipped and replied, "That's baby in my book."

They sat in commiserate silence drinking.

After a moment, Matthew said, "There was a drifter in town that year, Woogie Montgomery. They questioned him once, but after they went after Faith they didn't bother with him again. Maybe someday we can look into it. You know, what really happened that day, my sister Hope's disappearance, and what happened to Char." He inclined his head to his friend.

His expression unreadable, Gray shrugged. "Maybe."

Matthew scooped up a handful of nuts in a dish on the bar in front of them, tossed a few in his mouth. "We all, we siblings, grew up under a terrible cloud of tragedy and mystery." He tossed in more nuts, crunched hard and fast. "That bastard, Lombardo, I wish I could-"

Both hands around his mug, Gray murmured, "It's okay, Matt. I'm on him. I'm taking him down. It'll take a while, but I'll get him." He turned briefly and looked at his angry friend. "When I do, I'll make sure he pays for what he did to her. I swear on my life, bro, he'll pay."

Matthew took in his friend's sincere, fixed gaze. He nodded.

Rex the bartender came over. "So guys, will it be another?"

Gray seemed to ponder whether or not he wanted another beer, then said, "Sure, I'll have another one. So Rex, are you full time here now?"

Late thirties with red hair, white skin and freckles, Rex Rodman the bartender, leaned a hip against the bar. He wore jeans and a buttoned down shirt with the sleeves rolled up and a black apron that covered his waist to mid-thigh.

He brushed at a thin streak of red fuzz over his lip. "Yeah. I work most days, my one day off changes." He sighed like it was hard work. He was long and lanky, narrow hips and shoulders.

"Uh huh." Gray nodded.

Matthew picked the label off his beer bottle with a fingernail, twisting the bits into little balls and dropping them in a pile in front of him.

Gray continued, "I heard there was a fight in here last Thursday. They said there was a lot of damage caused." He laid an elbow on the back of his stool and glanced around. "You guys cleaned up pretty well."

Rex laughed. "I don't know where you get your information, but there hasn't been a good fight in here in months. Last time was when Larry T knocked over Big Bill's motorcycle and was stupid enough to come in and ask whose it was!"

Recalling the sight of Big Bill picking up small, skinny Larry T by the neck and throwing him across the room into a table, he slapped a hand on the counter laughing. "You shoulda been here, Gray, helluva fight erupted after. Probably better you weren't, you woulda had to arrest Big Bill and half a dozen others that had joined in a free-for-all." He chuckled then grew thoughtful.

"But you asked about last Thursday? Nope, quiet as a mouse. I'll be right back." He tapped the bar with his knuckles and moved off to take care of a blowsy blonde a few stools down calling his name.

Matthew leaned close to Gray and asked, "What was that all about?"

Gray shrugged. "It was Thursday I followed the smuggler here, I wanted to know who else was around. Thursdays in the morning are pretty slow, couldn't have been a lot of people around. If I narrow down who was here, it could help. I'm sure he came in here, I just have to figure out how he actually entered the building and who he met."

"Sounds like a tall-" Matthew was cut off by a woman who pushed between him and Gray.

"Grayson," she purred. "You haven't been in lately, too busy chasing the bad guys?" The brunette barmaid fluttered false lashes at him while pressing her huge unauthentic breasts against his arm.

Matthew stared at her breasts, they were barely contained in the very low, very tight blouse. He decided he'd better go before the thin straps on the blouse broke and Gray would have to arrest her for indecent exposure, although that would be a sight to see. He tossed down a $20 and stood up. "Hey, Gray, catch ya on the flip side."

Gray grabbed the $20 and stuffed it in Matthew's hand. "On me, bro."

"Okay," Matthew said. "Next time it's on me." He smiled at the woman. "Bye Petra, you be good."

The woman batted her lashes at him, the shiny red lips curved up. Her mouth was so big the corners of her lips spread practically to her ears. "Matty honey, I don't want to be good. You don't need to rush off. Why don't you and me and Gray have a little fun out back?"

"I gotta go." Matthew bit back a chuckle thinking, *good luck Gray, you're gonna need it-*

Gray stoically watched him leave. He turned to the brunette. "So Petra, you always seem to be here when I come in, we've never gotten to get to know one another." That was because he avoided the lusty, busty woman every time she latched her eyes or boobs on him, and she had been dating Big Bill.

He didn't need that aggravation, even if he had the tiniest bit of interest in her, which he didn't. He doubted he could count the diseases she probably had on one hand. He asked, "Do you work here full time?"

She opened her mouth, before she could answer he asked her, "What're you drinking?"

She giggled coyly. "Oh, scotch and water neat, with a twist, but tell him to leave out the water, and the twist!" She wriggled against him.

Gray got their drinks and led her over to a fairly secluded table and helped her sit down. He reached for a chair for himself but she already grabbed a hold of it and pulled it close to her.

"Wow, honey, you are a gent. Don't see many of you around here." She laid her forearms on the table, crossed them, set her breasts on them then leaned as close to him as she could.

Gray sat back and crossed an ankle over a knee. "So, Petra, you look like you've already had a few scotch no water no twists." He nodded to her drink.

Her glassy eyes wavered at him, around the room, back at him. She kept losing her train of thought.

He watched the lashes starting to loosen at the edges, the lipstick smeared on her top lip, her head bobbed. She grinned, her mouth almost full of teeth, there were a couple of gaps here and there. She held up the drink in salute to him. "Oh, I can hold 'em with the best of 'em." She tossed the entire drink down.

Gray kept his face passive and waved at Rex to send over another.

Petra tilted towards him, set a hand on his arm, nudged her chair closer to his. "So, baby, whattya say we have some fun!"

90

Gray let her slouch into him. "Sure, sure, but you were telling me about your job here. Like last Thursday for instance. You were working, in the morning?"

She took the drink right off of the barmaid's tray before the girl could do it.

"Ain't you s'pposed to be working, Pet?" the barmaid asked, annoyed.

"Oh get on with you, bitch," Petra slurred, waving her hand up at the girl like she was pushing trash away. "I'm sittin' with a friend. You got a problem with that?" Her face hardened, painted on brows drew down over narrowed eyes. She outweighed the scrawny server by 30 pounds.

"Ugh," the girl threw over her shoulder, tossed her hair back and stalked away.

Petra turned back to Gray, set her hand, nails blue and long on his arm. She purred, "What were you saying before we were so rudely interrupted?" Her hand drifted to his thigh.

Gray waved over to Rex for another scotch then shifted like he was getting closer to her but wasn't really. "I was interested in your job. You look like you work hard. I heard there was a fight last Thursday morning and I wanted to make sure you weren't hurt. Tell me what happened." He dipped his face in towards hers and smiled.

The barmaid came right over with the drink, dropped it and kept moving. Petra scooched closer to Gray. "Aw, you are such a sweetheart, for a cop." She looked puzzled, shook her head.

"There wasn't a fight here Thursday, hasn't been one for months. It was real quiet Thursday. I didn't have to come in until 10 to help cut fruit and stuff." She downed the new scotch in one swallow, slammed the glass down.

Groaning, "Ahhh," her flaccid tongue flopped out, she dragged a hand crookedly across her face. She looked cross-eyed at Gray. "It's good, huh..." her head kept bobbing.

Pretending he was drinking his beer, Gray said, "Sounds like you work really hard, your feet must be killing you. Do you employees have to park in the back? I mean it's quite a walk to park back there then trudge in the dirt all the way around to the front..." His eyes shifted at her over his beer.

Her head drooped, dull hair fell over one side of her face. She shook her head, the hair flopped back and forth sweeping her face.

"Nah, Taz is really good about a couple of us, just like me and him, Rex and Suzette coming in the," she leered at Gray and steered off track. "Rex has it good for Suzette. He lets her do anything. I saw them one time getting out of his car and went straight to the tunnel in case her husband was watching."

Keeping his face an indifferent mask at the information she just gave him, Gray nodded. "Oh, wow. That's not good, huh? So, you were saying about not having to walk all the way around to the front, that Rex lets you come in, in where, Petra?"

He considered getting her another drink, but her eyes were wet and blurred and her face had turned into a pink bubble. Slowly, her head dropped, dangled down, she didn't answer him.

He gingerly shook her shoulder, which made her head loll, her hair swatted back and forth.

She tried to raise her head, blood red eyes blinked unfocused at him, her mouth hung open. "Huh? Wassat? C'n I hab anudder drinkie..."

Gray sat back in his chair. He wasn't going to get anything else out of her. The hitch of it was that it was now his responsibility to get her home.

He called over the testy barmaid. "Sara, where does Petra live, do you know?" She eyed him suspiciously. "Don't worry, I just need to get her home safely," he said at her reluctance.

She told him Petra lived just across the street in a run-down apartment complex. Petra's head banged on the table and stayed there.

"Good," Gray said, standing up. "Go tell Rex you're taking a break. You're coming with me."

Sara's mouth dropped open. "But I-"

"Off with you then, hurry and you won't miss anything."

Gray slipped an arm under Petra's arms and pulled her to her feet. He half carried the woman through the room to the front door where the other girl met him and they took her home.

Chapter Twelve

$\mathcal{T}$he siblings sat in the car in the wide driveway staring at the house.

"They got a bigger one," Kessa muttered redundantly.

"Uh huh, yeah. Dad made bigger bucks a couple years after you… after…"

"It's pretty ostentatious," Kessa said.

Matthew nodded. "Like Mom. Dad hates it. He says he hates having to go all over the house to find anyone, and there's help now, housekeepers. Dad says they're always underfoot, he has no privacy. They had to get older, homely looking maids so Jaspar, and probably Dad too, wouldn't bother them."

Matthew turned behind the wheel to face his sister. She had such a vulnerable appearance, but he knew she was made of sterner stuff.

"It'll be fine. No matter how bad it gets, I'll be there. They get nasty, we're gone. Okay?" He smiled at her and tried to push the corners of her mouth up with his fingers into a smile. That did make her smile.

"Come on, let's go. Face the dragons," Matthew said and opened his door. He came around to Kessa's side. Her turquoise eyes reflected back at her as she sat unmoving staring out the side window.

Matthew opened her door. "Come on." He held a hand out to her. Kessa took his hand and pushed out of the car to stand on uneasy legs. He closed the car door and wrapped an arm around her shoulders. The tow-headed siblings walked slowly up the drive together.

By the time they reached the front door there was already a slightly plump, middle-aged woman in a black and white uniform holding the door open.

The servant stood to the side and nodded at Matthew, grey curls bounced. Acknowledging Mathew, "Mr. Matthew," she said nothing to Kessa. Her eyes dropped to the floor, she knew she would betray her blazing curiosity if she looked at the girl.

Besides, she didn't know how to address the young woman. What could she say, "Hello murderer, what's new? Kill anyone lately?" She bit her tongue to still her giggle.

Then horrified at her sick humor, she closed the door and moved quickly in front of them. Keeping her eyes on the floor to hide her dismay at how identical they looked, except he was slightly darker all around and of course masculine.

The other sisters and Mrs. Kenton resembled each other, but life had etched them in drastically different ways. She chanced a peep at the pair.

They both retained a kind of sweet ingénue, still innocent of the deep disturbing cruelties of the adult world. Their faces and eyes were clear and open, both walked with good posture, confident but not arrogant.

The rest of the clan was sneaky and hunched, and half the time their ugly expressions matched their unhappy insides.

"I know the way, Alice," Matthew said.

"Yes, sir, it's better this way." Alice didn't want to say she had her instructions. "Please follow me to the salon."

The pair shrugged at each other and followed the maid through the large, round marble vestibule, so highly polished everything gleamed, reflecting them as they crossed the black and white patterned floor, around the huge vase overflowing with spring flowers, and down the hall.

The dark cherry wood floor glowed from hours of waxing and buffing. They passed several rooms, then the maid turned into the salon. She faltered at the door. Matthew moved in front of her and stepped into the room.

Their family was already ensconced inside, waiting.

The large drawing room was embraced by floor to ceiling windows. White with pale blue embroidered drapes were pulled back to let in the setting sunlight.

The room was filled with plush mostly white furniture centered on a Persian area rug. A white couch with pale blue pillows sat in front of the middle window with several cushioned chairs and glass tables. The chairs were white with thin red and blue stripes.

A white brick fireplace covered the left side wall with glass cabinets displaying china and crystal objects on both sides of it. Over the mantle hung an elaborately gold framed painting of Sophie when she had been around thirty.

In the painting, she was wearing a regal, very low cut formal gown. Her blonde hair in a chignon, she held a little white dog in her arms. Matthew had never seen the dog around. He asked about it but never got a straight answer. He assumed it had been a prop.

Sophie now stood like a queen awaiting her consorts in the center of the room.

Geordie was also standing, but he was looking out the back window. Char sat on a chair, her cane resting against the arm. Aria was off to the right side at a portable bar made of inlaid rosewood, pouring herself a drink.

"Well, everyone, we're here!" Matthew announced cheerfully.

Sophie stiffened. Geordie turned from the window, an uncertain frightened look on his face. Aria guzzled most of her drink before turning. Char sat as usual, expressionless.

Matthew pulled Kessa into the room and gently moved her to stand in front of him. He kept his hands on her shoulders.

No one said anything. A dropped feather could have been heard. Anxiety and awkwardness were like choking clouds filling the room.

Matthew cleared his throat. "Uh, Mother, have you nothing to say to *your daughter*?" He tried to keep his tone even, but he exaggerated the words 'your daughter' like Sophie didn't know she had another daughter.

All eyes turned to Sophie. Even at 50, she wore a powder blue dress that went to above the knee and very high beige heels. Her hair was swept up to one side, sapphire earrings twinkled in her ears, a matching necklace hugged her throat and a bracelet sparkled on her wrist.

Sophie's discomfited eyes directed warily at Kessa. She had waited for Kessa to come to her, but now she was forced to go to her.

Geordie stood frozen, a stricken look stamped on his face. He bent and gripped the back of the sofa.

Sophie had practiced all morning, "Darling…" She went to take Kessa's hand yet something in her daughter's eyes stopped her. She clasped her hands in front of her. "So, how lovely that you are here." Her smile was not wide enough to display her veneers.

Kessa stood mute.

Trying to suppress her consternation, Sophie said, "Well darling," she turned to address everyone in the room. "I thought we'd have a bit of time to get reacquainted before dinner, but," she sighed as if slightly distressed.

"Alice tells me dinner got done much more quickly than she'd planned and is ready to be served. Help these days…" she shook her head.

"Is so hard to find," Aria chirped in from the side of the room. She grinned with the rim of her glass in her mouth. "So, then," with her drink in one hand, she walked smiling over to Kessa and threw her arms around her, ignoring Kessa's stiffened reaction.

Aria stepped back and took in her younger sister. "Faith, it is so good to see you. Truly it is. You look," she took in the blonde hair much lighter than her own, and iridescent eyes that shone like the iridescent sea, then regarded her from head to toe.

"You look like dynamite. You turned out the best out of all of us." She rushed on when her mother made a sound, "You got the best part of Mom's figure, the full top part, but managed to make the rest of your shapely body all your own! You got a tiny waist and nice booty, small but shaped like the proverbial perfect onion."

She set her hands on her own square-ish hips. "Girl, you coulda made a killing as a dancer! Exotic I mean, you know what I mean-"

"Aria!" Sophie admonished, appalled.

"You mean a stripper," Char snarled. "Like you always wanted to be you tramp, but you're too skinny, all bones. So flat chested those implants Daddy bought you sit like two baseballs unevenly on your bony chest!"

Her voice a foul sneer, red veins stood out against her ashy skin, Char's dull green eyes scorned her sister. She gripped her cane, her knuckles white.

Aria turned a furious, jeering face to her sister. "Drop dead, you're jealous, you fat crippled pig-"

"Enough!" Shocked at her own shrill shriek, Sophie grabbed Aria's arm and shook it hard. "Stop it. Not tonight, no vulgarity tonight, please, it's bad enough-" her voice shook, she pushed a loose hair, tucking it back into the bun, trying to steady her hands and beating heart.

She smiled at her family. "Well then, now then, everyone, let's head into the dining room. Jaspar and," her lips pursed, "Peter should have arrived by time we get there." She held her arms in an arc, moving towards the door. "Shall we?"

"Faith." His eyes anguished, voice wreathed in misery, Geordie implored his daughter.

Kessa turned from Aria, who strolled back to the bar to get a refill, and faced her father.

"Daddy." Not knowing what to expect, she stood still. She tried to keep her reaction at seeing her aging father's decline. He'd been near 60 when she'd gone, he was mid-seventies now. He looked much older.

Most of his hair was gone except for some wisps he combed over the top. Most of his weight was in his stomach, his jowls hung, nose was longer. Tears fell from the turquoise eyes only Kessa and Matthew had inherited. He'd always been a weak man, never could stand up to his authoritative wife. Now he wished he'd had that devastating time 14-years-ago.

He held his arms out. He looked aggrieved when she hesitated, but then Kessa ran to her father. He folded her into his arms. His tears fell on her shoulders. He hugged her with regret and pain, loss and now regain. Father and daughter embraced like they would never let go again.

Sophie cleared her throat. "Uh, well then, Geordie, why don't you show Faith the way, we'll wait for you there. Come along everyone." The matriarch awkwardly ushered her family through the door.

By the time the Kentons neared the dining room, Char's husband Jaspar, and Aria's current boyfriend, Peter, were lounging in the living room, both had drinks.

Peter had a bottle of beer and Jaspar was cradling a large glass of cognac.

Jaspar's face was already shiny, cheeks cherry red from the alcohol, he held up his glass in greeting. "There you are, darling." He shoved off his chair and swaggered over to his wife. He bent and bussed her cheek. Char scowled but let him.

Leaning heavily on her cane, Char snarled under her breath, "You couldn't wait a few bloody minutes for us before," she glared at his drink.

Jaspar, medium height, stocky, a construction worker until he's married Char, now tried to dress and act like a genteel lord of the manor. Close-cropped brown hair and muddy brown eyes, he'd grown a mustache that lined down the sides of his mouth to his chin thinking it would make him appear more suave.

He wore a three-piece suit, a gold pocket-watch hanging from a chain was tucked in his vest pocket. Holding his drink in his hand, he slipped his arm around his wife's pudgy shoulders and snickered in her ear, "I felt libations were the proper course for the show that's about to play."

Char tried to tug from his arm, but he deliberately held her fast. He whispered, "I'll be expecting some of that angry fire later, my sweet, in our room."

Now it was Char who quivered in fear and arousal. Sex with Jaspar was painful torment. Yet, Char reveled in some of the pain, it enabled her to feel, for a change. Her body and heart had deadened to a hollow shell, she needed extreme physicality to feel anything.

But Jaspar would always go too far, for his own pleasure was in mastering and sadistically inflicting pain and suffering, like pulling the wings off a fly.

The family had to on occasion pay off several women that had threatened to go to the police after they left the hospital from an evening with Don Juan Jaspar.

Char, irate at the attention he drew, had once furiously told him that next time he should carry through and kill the girl, dead victims can't talk, or extort.

Everyone had been seated at the table by the time Geordie and Kessa came in. Loathe to let her go, Geordie brought his daughter to her chair and helped her to sit down.

His hands on her shoulders, he bent over and kissed the top of her head. After giving her shoulders a tender squeeze, he sluggishly made his way to his own seat at the head of the table.

Sophie was at the foot. Depending how you looked at the table, to make the seating even, Kessa sat between her brother and Peter on the right side. On the left, Jaspar was placed between Char and Aria.

Just as Geordie took his place, Alice and Edna entered with salads and toasted bread and butter. Alice left and came back with a pitcher of ice water and filled their glasses.

Jaspar held his cocktail glass up and said, "Alice, bring me another."

Alice nodded.

Kessa said, "Please."

Jaspar turned his attention to the blonde sitting across from him. He had taken a shifty gander at his sister-in-law when she came in and had become suddenly rigid at her startling appearance.

He had expected another version of Char or Aria, and worse even, after growing up in a nunnery. Now, he couldn't tear his eyes away from the unexpected intriguing beauty. Adding murderess to the mix, Jaspar could hardly contain his shiver of deviant anticipation.

His smile though to her was not pleasant. He said snidely, "Well, the beauty has manners."

Next to him, Char muttered, "Shut up, Jaspar."

Jaspar set his forearms on the table and started to talk but Char spoke over him. "Sister, dear," she said to Kessa, "since Mother ushered us in here so quickly, we haven't been able to greet each other. You certainly don't look the worst for wear." She speared some lettuce with her fork and stuffed it in her mouth.

"You are so snotty, Char-face, get it? Scar-face, Char-face." Aria the eldest of the siblings, chuckled, shoving her salad aside. She did not do rabbit food. "I should be a comedian I am so funny. We can't all have husbands who married us for our money. Anyway, you-"

"At least I'm not a bag whore," Char interjected sweetly.

"Actually," Aria said matter-of-fact. "Technically, Peter would be the bag whore because I'm the one with the money." She turned to Kessa. "So Faith, now that the pleasantries are over, do tell us how life at the orphanage was."

Slouching next to Kessa, Aria's boyfriend Peter, snickered. As addled with drugs as all of her boyfriends have been, Peter and Aria looked much alike. Emaciated bodies, clouded eyes and grimy, stringy blond hair. But where Aria had a cunning look, Peter always seemed in a fog.

"Aria," Matthew warned, glaring at her.

She stuck her tongue out at her younger brother.

Edna came in and cleared the barely touched salads and then she helped Alice serve a steaming platter of roast lamb and parsley buttered red potatoes, a bowl of buttered corn and more oven fresh bread.

After waiting to be served, Kessa put a pat of butter on a warm piece of bread and watched it melt. She took a bite, chewed and swallowed it, then said, "I go by Kessa now." She took another bite and said, "Convent Grisaille was profoundly horrible. How has life treated you, dear sister?"

Peter snickered again.

Jaspar's brows arched impressed, he said derisively, "Ooh, the kitten bites." Char jabbed him in the side with her elbow.

He leaned toward her slightly and said in her ear, but loud enough to be heard by everyone, "You do that again, my sweet, and you will pay for it later." He smiled, but it was an awful smile.

Char paled, realizing she'd gone too far. People started talking all at once to cover the uncomfortable moment.

"So," Sophie broke the tension in the room. "Um, Kes…sa, Matthew tells us you write brilliant books. I haven't read any of course, they're not my cup of tea, but-"

"Really mother?" Aria interjected sarcastically. "You don't even know what they're about because you've never bought any or looked at any or anything, because you have pretended all this time that she did not exist."

The noise in the room ground to a screeching halt. Everyone froze, except for Kessa who calmly ate her dinner.

Matthew cut a slice of lamb and pushed some mint jelly on it. "I think, for now, it would be best if we leave the elephant in the room alone for a while, until down the road when we have all become reacquainted we can discuss what has happened in the last 14 years." He slid the lamb into his mouth.

Geordie, white as a sheet, nodded, relieved. Jaspar drank, Peter sat in a stupor, stringy hair hanging over his wan face. Aria put butter and sour cream on her potatoes and gleefully mashed them. Sophie just stared at the table.

Char's face screwed up, the wine colored veins across her skin darkened. The side of her face that had been crushed was not symmetrical with the other side. It was like her head had been dropped and broke in half and they tried to glue it back together but they'd done a poor job of it.

Her hands clutched into taut fists on the table alongside her plate. "I don't *want* to ignore the situation." Her voice rose, higher, shriller. She slammed both fists on the table. "I don't want her here. Unless she wants to tell us what she did with Hope's body."

A few at the table gasped at her accusation said out loud.

She took a haggard breath and struggled to her feet. Pounded her fist on the table, her cane that was hooked to the edge of the table clattered to the floor. She screamed, "Look what she did to me!"

Everyone stared at the once pretty child that was now at 25 like a grotesquely broken mannequin.

"Char," Matthew started.

"Look what she did to me!" Char screamed louder, tears gushed out of her eyes, she pounded the table again with her fist. "Look what she did to me!"

Matthew motioned to Jaspar with his head.

Jaspar set his glass down, not bothering to cover his smirk and took Char by the shoulders. "Come on, Sweet, let's go, you're ruining the party." He pulled her from the table, but she kept screaming like a broken record, "Look what she did to me! *She ruined me!*"

"Yeah, we know, come on." Jaspar grasped her tightly and literally dragged her from the room.

Jaspar said at the door, "Sophie, be a dear and have Edna bring a bottle to our room. Thanks. The top-shelf of course. And don't forget our dessert." He laughed at Sophie's affronted expression.

Char's shrieks could be heard all the way down the hall until they finally disappeared when the pair went upstairs in the miniature elevator that was put in for Char's handicap.

The room grew uncomfortably quiet again.

Kessa wiped her mouth with a napkin and laid it neatly beside her plate. She pushed her chair back and glanced at Matthew.

"I think it would be best if I, we, leave. Thank you, Sophie," she turned an implacable face to Sophie who just sat dumbfounded, "for a lovely dinner."

She nodded at her sister, Aria, who still wore a slippery grin. Kessa didn't bother acknowledging the stupefied Peter.

She smiled sadly at her father who had expended all of his courage to hold her and bring her into dinner. Sophie will be speaking to him later about his behavior, he hadn't acted according to her wishes.

Getting up quickly, Matthew said cheerfully, "Sorry we can't stay for dessert, Alice makes a great apple pie." The siblings walked out of the room, down the hall, through the foyer and out the door.

Outside, Matthew started the car. Down the driveway and out to the street, he tried very hard not to speed away from the repulsive house.

He glanced at Kessa who sat still as sand, her face pale. "You did it, Kes, it's done. You don't have to see them again unless you want to. By the way, why did you call Mother by her given name? Was it a deliberate insult?"

Kessa murmured watching the houses go by in the twilight, "A mother would never do to her child what she did to me." She said quietly, "He's not really sick is he? You said it to trick me into coming here."

Matthew opened his mouth to say it wasn't true but then agreed with her, "Yeah. Sorry. I feel that you should to be here where I can watch over you, and you need to be with your family. Most importantly, you needed to come back and face this crap so you can get on with your life. Fix the hole." He patted her shoulder.

"It was hell, but you did it and I'm glad you came. The worst is over, right?"

Chapter Thirteen

At the station, while waiting for a return call from his confidential informant, and a sign-off on some incident reports, Gray opened his desk drawer and pulled out two thick files.

His space was in a room crowded with desks just like his, old and laminate, each containing a landline phone, computer, papers everywhere and sticky notes taped to the computers, desks and walls. Fortunately he didn't have to be sitting at it much.

He was usually out roaming around the town either in the cruiser, or on horseback when he searched the forests for illegal drugs grown and manufactured, fugitives, and fire-starters.

Since he had moved to Resilir a few years ago a lot of work had been done on the surrounding woodlands. Bogs were drained, crevasses filled in or warnings posted. The most dangerous cliffs were lined with protective rails.

The hunters and hikers had not been happy in the past because they had a beautiful wilderness to explore but it was too dangerous. So when Sledge Stirling ran for Mayor, part of his campaign block was that he promised to make the forests, at least for 10 miles in made safe.

He kept his promise. The bad part was that now smugglers and drug dealers and illegal growers of Papaver Somniferum, opium poppies, used the woods as cover.

He set the files on his desk and opened one, it was a couple of inches of clipped in papers pretty much in chronological order.

The other file had a hodgepodge of loose notes, summaries and maps crammed in it. He turned his attention to the clipped file.

On the first page there were pictures of three little girls. Charity, Faith and Hope Kenton. Hearing the story from Matthew had given Gray an itchy feeling in his stomach. When he got itchy, it was his internal intuition that something wasn't right.

Once he had that feeling he had to scratch until the itch went away, and that would only happen when he was satisfied with the truth. He had spent the last few days reviewing the file.

It pretty much stated what Matthew had told him. The file ended when Faith had been sent away. After threats were made against the eight-year-old child, the parents had sent her away, supposedly for her own good. His stomach itched.

The picture of a tiny Faith, well, Kessa, stared up at him. White blonde, thin like all energetic children yet with fat cheeks, and a big happy smile with a missing tooth and those unusual turquoise eyes aglow with mischief and intelligence, blissfully unaware her world was about to turn upside down and crash and burn.

He had already read through the file completely several times. There didn't appear to be anything done wrong, just not things done right. There had been that drifter Matt told him about, he flipped around until he found the information on the guy.

Reading, his lips pulled in, perturbed brows drew down. Officers passed by his desk, some said hey, he muttered a return greeting but kept reading.

Woogie Montgomery had hitchhiked in from California and did odd jobs. He had a minor arrest record of petit thefts, drug charges and drunk in public, there wasn't anything like assault in his history.

Once the police zeroed in on the child, Faith, as their prime suspect, they'd only given Montgomery a cursory interview. He'd had a thin alibi, said he had passed out at a flop house.

One man, a person who brought food to the shelter had said he remembered seeing Woogie there, but was vague about if he was there the entire time of when the children went missing.

Plus, there was an additional fact that Woogie had an ill-fitting prosthetic leg that would make it difficult, and unlikely for him to go in the woods at all much less chase after three little girls over rough terrain. But still, he could be a suspect.

Something else niggled at Gray too. He couldn't put his finger on it. There was a pack of maps rubber-banded together in the box he'd found the file in. The band had broken after all this time and the maps yellowed.

The maps had notes with them and there were places highlighted in different colors. They were the maps of the volunteers' as well as the sheriff's deputies' searches.

He took the maps and the notes out and looked at them like he had a few days ago. It was the last map that bothered him. He pushed the others aside and studied the one.

There was a house almost on the border between the town and the woods. The house belonged to Mrs. Arleen Goldbrooke. Gray tuned out the phones ringing as low beeping hums around the office area, and a deputy who was bringing in someone he had arrested.

The offender in handcuffs was filthy and sweaty, drunk and yelling obscenities. Used to this, the other occupants kept going about their business.

Gray reviewed the notes written about the property.

Mrs. Goldbrooke at 72 had been very ill at the time. She hadn't left the house for months. Her nurse practitioner, Brenda Bradshaw, was her caretaker and managed the house as well as filled in as the housekeeper.

There were notations made about different officers scheduled to interview Mrs. Goldbrooke, but she was on her deathbed practically, and the days around the girls' disappearance the nurse had been away to take care of her own sick mother.

Mrs. Goldbrooke was pretty much alone except for church members and the priest, Father Benedict, and Doc Aven and another nurse who stopped by periodically to check on her and provide food.

It was assumed that even if a deputy spoke with the sick patient, she was out of it those months according to Doc and Miss Bradshaw, so they figured she couldn't tell them anything anyway. Gray bent closer to the notes, then picked one up.

"What the," he set the note down shaking his head. Because the woman was so sickly, no one wanted to disturb her, therefore her house and the area around her property, right near the woods, had never been searched for the missing children.

"Hey Gray, what's doin'?" Deputy Wayde Smith swung his long narrow body onto a chair next to Gray's desk, the vinyl cushion whooshed air when he sat. Yawning, he pulled the file slightly so he could read the name on it.

"Uh, the Kenton girls. That was a tragic state of affairs, a long time ago though. I was a young rookie then." He yawned again pushing the file back with long fingers. "What's the interest after all this time?"

Gray leaned back in his chair and crossed his arms. As usual he wasn't wearing his uniform, he felt he was less conspicuous in civilian clothes when he was investigating or trying to set up CI's. The uniform made their tongues stop working.

He was wearing a black t-shirt, black jeans and boots. His arms bulged when he crossed them. Half of a tattoo of a military theme showed under his sleeve.

The beanpole deputy gestured at him. "What're you, in the gym every damned day, Gray?"

Gray shrugged still looking down at the file. "Sometimes." His dark blue eyes rolled up to the deputy. "There were some holes in the old investigation. Gaping holes, big enough to drive a train through."

Wayde wiped at his eyes and yawned again. "Oh yeah?" He sounded bored. "Everyone did the best they could at the time. Good enough for this poke of a town. What's bothering you in particular?" He leaned back with his hands behind his head, elbows out like bat wings.

"Mmm." Gray folded up some of the notes and the map and stuck them in his pocket. He stood up. "Nothing that probably can be fixed now. I gotta go. Catch ya later." He grabbed his black leather jacket off the back of his chair, his boots clumped across the linoleum.

"Sure, later," Wayde called out. He pulled the file over. "What interested him so much?" he mused, lazily flipping through. It all looked the same to him as it had almost 15 years ago, he pushed the file back.

He put his feet up on Gray's desk, crossed his ankles and his arms, dropped his head back, and even with the uneven commotion going on around him he fell asleep.

Once in his cruiser, Gray looked up Arleen Goldbrooke's address and phone number. Her number was listed as still active. He pulled out his cell and dialed it.

After a few rings an elderly voice said, "Hello?"

He introduced himself and said he was looking into the old missing Kenton girls' case.

There was a silence. Then a quavering voice, sounding surprised and cautious said, "Why are you asking about that? It was so long ago." She thought a moment then said, "It was about a decade or so past."

"Yes, Mrs. Goldbrooke. You're sounding quite well, they tell me you've been doing pretty good these past few years. Anyway, there's just a couple of loose ends that came into notice, um," he cleared his throat. "I'd like to come out there and talk with you, if I could. Today would be great."

Gray waited while the old lady pondered the call and the request. After a spell of silence, Gray said, "Mrs. Goldbrooke?"

She didn't respond.

"Mrs. Goldbrooke, I don't want to intrude or cause you any anxiety. I just have a couple of questions, and maybe I could look around your, uh, yard a little? I promise I won't get in your way or trample your flowers." He kept his voice upbeat and pleasant, like he was asking for a cup of tea.

Another moment, and the elderly voice replied weakly, "Um, well, sure, I guess that would be all right. I'd rather you came when my housekeeper is here. That won't be until tomorrow, after 10 in the morning. Would that be all right with you, Deputy, uh…"

"Whitewolf, Ma'am, that's Deputy Whitewolf. That'd be great. I'll stop by after 10 tomorrow. I appreciate it. Thank you." He rang off.

He sat for a second before turning on his cruiser.

She had sounded curious which was natural, but she also sounded…scared. *What was that all about*? He shrugged, he'd find out tomorrow.

Chapter Fourteen

Now that the worst part of meeting her parents was over, Kessa decided it was time she finally got out and about.

The mornings were still on the cool side so she threw a light jacket on over a lacey white blouse and pale pink jeans.

Hearing her keys jingle, Kato came tearing around the corner his nails clickety-clicking on the floor until he reached a rug, then went sliding across the floor almost crashing into the wall. He recovered quickly and hopped right over to her.

"Oh no, baby, not now. I have some errands to do, go to the bank and grocery store. You can't come." The dog recognized her negative tone and knew he wasn't going, his ears and tail drooped.

Kessa reached down and scratched his head. "When I come home we'll go for a run, how's that?" He recognized the change in her tone and the word run, the tail wagged. "Okay," she said, "you go-"

"Hey Kess," Matthew came down the stairs rubbing one eye. Plodding over to her in a long sleeved dress shirt and trousers, he asked, "Where you going?"

She picked her purse up off the table by the door. "I thought I'd go open an account at the bank to transfer my funds and pick up some," she smiled, "real food, like lettuce and fruit at the store."

"That sounds great." He rubbed his head, tousling his blond hair so it stuck out all over his head. His face grew serious.

"Listen, Kess," he stuck his hands in his pockets and stepped closer to her.

She smiled absently up at him while fumbling her grocery list out of her purse. "Sure, what do you need me to get?"

He looked sheepish, like he really didn't want to tell her what he was about to. "Yeah, uh, I mean no, I don't need anything, maybe some beer. But," he raked a hand through his hair. "What I'm trying to say is, Gorham called me, he wants me to go to-"

Her eyes flew to his. "No Matthew, you're not leaving?" Her head jerked to the hall in front of the kitchen. A set of suitcases were stacked against the wall.

He nodded dolefully. "I'm so sorry, you know it's the last thing I wanted to do." He leaned over and ran his hand down Kato's back so he didn't have to look at her.

Emotions scattered across her face; anxiety to panic to dread, then her expression turned resolute. "I'll be okay, really."

She turned a palm up in resignation. "You have to work, you have to work, you gotta do what you gotta do. Where is Omaplex sending you?" She looked cheerfully earnest, but her shoulders slumped slightly. Matthew's heart bled.

He set his hands on her shoulders. "I have to go to London. Donald Lamb totally messed up the installation out there for Wilson Prax Retailers. He missed an important part of their system when he was initiating the new computer program."

"Gorham, you know, my project manager, is sending me to clean up his mess. A taxi is already on the way to take me to the airport. I am so sorry, Sis, to drag you out here and drop you into the den of wolves. I never would have if I'd known. I think it would be best if you go back to Maine until I return."

Shaking her head, blonde waves furled over her shoulders.

"I'm a big girl, Matthew. I've lived on my own for almost four years. I'm not a coward or a quitter. I'll be fine here. Really."

Gripping her shoulders, his face a map of doubtfulness and agitation, he said, "I don't think it's a good idea for you to stay in Resilir alone. You have no one on your side, no one to turn to if you need help. For now, the family isn't on your side, yet. I'm going to be gone quite a while. No," he shook his head. "I think you need to-"

"Matthew, really," she stood on tiptoe and kissed his cheek. "Please don't worry, I lived in the woods pretty much isolated in Maine. I dove in the roughest waters and hiked the toughest hills. I can take care of myself."

Twisting from his grasp, she slung her purse over her shoulder and said to the dog, "Kato, stay."

Matthew stood with his mouth open, not knowing what to say. Eyes that matched his sister's twittered with fearful apprehension.

"It's not the wild animals I'm worried about, it's, I mean you've been tucked away, first in the convent and then in that cabin in the woods. Basically you don't have a lot of real world, real adult people dealings. Really, Kess," he stopped when he saw everything in her stern face and bearing showing she had no intentions of baling.

He sighed. "Okay. But listen. If you insist on staying, I'm calling Gray to keep an eye on you, check on you."

Her eyes shot a 'don't even think about it' warning at him.

"Don't give me that. I'm calling him. He's the only person I know I would trust with my life, and therefore yours too. The only way I'll agree to you staying is if he checks in on you." He held up a hand as her mouth opened. "No. That's final. No arguments. It's that way or no way."

"Geeze Matthew, I'm not a 5-year-old. You know I can't stand the guy, he's bossy and annoying." She wasn't five but she was starting to whine like one.

"Think of me, Kess. I'll just worry like crazy over you while I'm across the damned sea." He stood stolidly, arms crossed, hating to see her distressed, but hating worse to see her alone and vulnerable.

Seeing his set face, jaw hard, mouth in a firm line, she gave in. "Fine," she snapped in a huff. "I have to go. You have a safe trip, call me when you get to London. Leave any instructions I need on the table there. I love you." She kissed him again and then hurried out before he could see the tears welling in her eyes.

He did see the tears though, his stomach clenched. Standing in the doorway, Matthew palmed his phone out of his pocket.

Gray answered on the second ring.

"Hey bro," Matthew said. "I gotta ask you a big favor."

By the time she got to the bank, Kessa had regained her composure. In the parking lot, she sat at the wheel, her purse in her lap. For all her bravado to her brother, she hated to admit she was scared out of her mind.

She was back in Resilir, a place she had long ago closed off behind a steel door in her mind. Whenever the thought of it had popped in her head over time, she got the chills and closed her mind's door before the agony of her past could take a foothold.

And here she was, she looked out the window at the people coming and going into the bank, back into the lion's den. A shuddered sigh slid out. "Well, time to put my actions where my mouth is."

Pushing open the glass door, she walked inside as if she had been there a hundred times before. In fact, North Prime National Bank didn't exist when she'd lived there.

The town had tripled over the past 14 years. It had grown from a sleepy rural suburb to a bustling small town. On one side of North Prime was an upscale boutique and on the other a high-end salon.

Inside, the bank resembled an antique bank from a hundred years ago with vaulted ceilings and old fashioned teller's windows, but it was every bit a modern fiduciary. The lighting was pleasant, bright enough to see easily but low enough to cut the glare.

Wall-to-wall carpeting made all the sounds hushed like in a library. The men wore ties, the ladies suits, either pants or skirt. It was a relatively formal interior.

Kessa stood in line. When she got to the teller, the older woman told her she can't open an account at the window.

Sounding superior, she said snippy, "Don't you *know* that you have to go to a customer service representative?"

Kessa calmly asked how and where she was to do that.

The woman sighed and pointed to a counter where Kessa was to put her name on a list and wait to be called.

When Kessa, ignoring the woman's attitude, thanked her and headed to the sign-in counter, the woman rolled her eyes at her back.

The next person in line came up to her window. "Problem Bernice?" he asked friendly.

"Oh," Bernice rolled her eyes again. "These young people, they have no clue of the grown up world, do they?"

Kessa signed her name and sat down to wait.

A woman in a black pants suit with a cat pin on her lapel walked a customer out of her office and came over and crossed off the next name. She smiled at Kessa and inquired, "Miss Kent?"

Kessa nodded, smiling.

The lady said, "I'll be right with you, dear." She walked back towards her office but slowed suddenly, like she'd just thought of something and veered off to another office.

Almost immediately a man came out of the office. He looked over at Kessa. His face paled. He took a deep breath, smoothed his hair with his palms and then confidently strode over to her.

"Hey, is that you, Faith? Faith Kenton?" He greeted her in surprise.

Kessa suppressed a wince. She'd tried to prepare herself for this moment. The first time someone outside her family recognized her. She looked up at the trim man who was probably in his late twenties, but he looked older.

The sides of his hair were grey, he wore glasses and a suit and tie. He skin was sallow and pockmarked from young days of acne. She stared at him trying to figure out who he was.

She stood up. With a small smile, she said, "I'm sorry, I don't remem-"

He held out a hand. "Sure, sure, of course. I was in seventh grade, you were a little girl. You went to school with my brother Todd, Todd Gourdet. I'm Clayton Gourdet."

She nodded and smiled, shook his hand. "Of course. I remember your family. You lived on Granite Way in the big house at the end. How are you, Mr. Gourdet?"

"Oh, please, please call my Clay. It's been a long…" he trailed off not sure what to say. "You uh, your name, it's changed. Mrs. Kendall, the woman who spoke with you recognized your author's name. It got her attention."

He cleared his throat. "But she said there was also something else familiar about you, she says she looked more closely and realized you resembled Sophie Kenton, your mother. Well, sort of, she said you were obviously a lot younger and prettier. I don't follow books, Mrs. Kendall says you have a few out there and she loves them. I guess that's why the change of name…"

Kessa held her purse with both hands in front of her. "Yes. It's my pen name. Anyway," she rushed to avoid any more uncomfortable questions such as about where she's been the past 14 years.

"I'd like to open an account and transfer my money from Maine to here, under my name of Kessa Kent. It's all quite legal." She'd been F. Mary Taylor, Mary to the others, all the years at the covenant. As soon as she was 18 she legally changed her name to Kessa Kent. She couldn't burn or bury her past but she could cover it.

Clayton smoothed his tie with a nervous pale hand. He had almost feminine hands, white and slender and hairless. "Sure, sure. I guess you have all the proper ID and all, I don't see why we can't, uh-"

"Murderer!" A shriek let loose from a heavy woman filling out a deposit slip at the counter. Her face twisted and purple, she stood with her arm a rigid arrow pointing at Kessa.

Her face impassive, Kessa ignored the woman. Clayton looked about to have a heart attack.

The woman took a step away from the counter, towards them. "You deserve to fry, to burn in hell for what you did to your sisters!" Everyone in the bank was staring from the screaming woman to Kessa.

Kessa said politely to Clayton, "Why don't you have someone prepare the papers and I'll come back another time."

"Sure, sure," Clayton squawked. "Better if you come by before we open. Better yet," he tugged his tie, sweat pilled around his forehead. "I'll have the papers couriered to you and you can sign them and send them back."

The woman kept screaming. People were getting riled up, they moved closer towards them, like a mob crowd, curious, angry.

Kessa held out her hand to shake again. "Thank you."

He glanced anxiously at it, suddenly afraid to touch her.

Kessa kept her polite smile plastered on her face but dropped her hand.

"I'll wait for the papers." With calm dignity, she strolled to the door, the woman's screams ringing in her ears, the crowd like a tide followed her. She pushed out and forced herself to walk nonchalantly to her car.

She got in as slowly as her shaking legs would let her, closed the door and turned on the ignition. She backed out trying to pretend there weren't people standing on the street pointing at her as she drove away.

It wasn't until she was down the road that she let her held breath out. Her hands trembled on the wheel. But her heart hardened. She wasn't going to let them run her out of town like she was a thief in the night. She had every right to be there.

Despite wanting to go straight home, lock the door and get into bed, she drove to the grocery store.

Opening the glove box, it felt like giving in, but she didn't have the energy for another confrontation, Kessa took out a baseball hat and sunglasses and put them on before going onto the store.

Thirty minutes later, the disguise worked, no one recognized her, she went home and put the groceries away. All signs of her brother were gone. Missing him already, she pushed back the tears.

Mentally exhausted, Kessa dropped down on the couch, curled into a ball and fell into a restless sleep.

She was back at the lake with her sisters. Hope was standing by the lake's edge giggling at the fishes. Char was chasing a neon blue butterfly. A bunny hopping into the bushes caught Faith's eye.

The day was lovely, warm and peaceful. Then, as if a dark cloud lowered, Faith heard a terrifying scream, it turned her blood cold. She ran and ran, back to the lake. Hope was floating, face down, Char was screaming, "Help! Help!"

Faith froze, petrified. A shadow flew out of the bushes, Char screamed and ran away. Hope rolled over in the water, her lifeless eyes staring up. Faith let out a piercing cry and took off in Char's direction.

Hearing feet pounding behind her, Faith ran as fast as her little legs could go, she knew the shadow was snarling right behind her, it must be the chimera-

A discordant ringing woke her. Groggily, Kessa realized it was the phone. Pushing her hair out of her face, she wiped an eye, knelt on the cushions and grabbed up the phone that was on a table beside the sofa.

She took a couple of haggard breaths to chase away the horrendous nightmare that often knifed into her dreams. Clearing her throat, she said a husky, "Hello?" Her voice sounded unsteady in her own ears.

"That you, Faith?"

A corner of Kessa's lip pulled in. "This is Kessa Kent speaking."

"Oh yeah, I forgot. This is Aria. Your sister."

Kessa smiled wryly. "I know who you are. What's up?" She was surprised to hear her sister calling.

"Um, well, it's Char's husband's birthday and we're all going to the Wilton Club tonight for dinner. Mother said Matthew had to leave town and it wouldn't look right if we didn't, well Matthew made Mother promise to invite you. She doesn't ever go against Matthew, I'm sure you've noticed that," Aria said baldly.

When Kessa didn't answer her, Aria said, "Listen, I was given the job to call you. Please don't make me have to go back and tell her you won't go. She'll be happy you won't go, sorry, you know how tactless I am, but she'll be angry too, and she'll take it out on me. She always does. So, do big sis a favor here," Aria pleaded.

Kessa couldn't help but laugh at her sister's artless frankness. Aria really didn't care what people thought, she didn't care if she pissed them off, in fact, she was pleased when she did. Kessa figured she wasn't wanted, but she'd look like the bad guy if she said no, yet she also didn't want a repeat of the other night.

"How about," she said thoughtfully, "I come for dessert." She waited.

"You know, Fa- uh, Kessa, that sounds like a great idea. I'll tell her, Mother. I expect dinner is at 7 so if you come around 8, that should work. Boy, you sure grew up smart."

"Hmm." Kessa thought if she was really smart she never would have come to Resilir. But what's done is done, can't put the bullet back in the gun.

"So," Aria continued, "it's fairly dressy. Peter and I wear jeans, pretty much to annoy Mother, but the rest of them get dolled up. So, just so you know. So, uh, guess I'll see you there. You know where the Wilton Club is?"

"I can find it. I'll see you around 8. Bye." Kessa rang off. Too much of Aria was a drain. She went to iron a dress. She hadn't brought many so it wouldn't be hard to choose one.

Chapter Fifteen

At precisely 8 she drove up, ignored the valet parkers and drove to back of the lot and parked her jeep.

Her stomach in jitters, Kessa straightened her dress to give her hands something to do. The dress, white frilly bodice and a summer yellow printed skirt, fit sleekly on top and fell fluidly to above her knees.

It was an expensive dress and it showed. She looked elegant yet youthful. Her loose hair waved past her shoulders, she pulled her spine up and went up to the front glass doors. At least the 4-inch heels made her taller.

An attendant rushed over and opened the door for her eyeing her like she was frosting on a cake. She swished in, her head high. He stared at her legs as she walked with poise towards what she hoped was the dining room.

Once inside the Wilton Club, several hallways spread out from the lobby like fingers on a hand. Unsure of which way to go, Kessa chose the widest hall because it followed the huge windows that trimmed all around the brick building.

To the side and the back stretched the perfect green grass of a golf course. Tiny flags whipped in the evening breeze. On the other side were tennis courts and a pool.

Continuing her search for the dining room, Kessa finally spotted a sign directing the way to the restaurant, spas, rooms and more. She walked past a dark bar that was loud and busy, a barrage of voices and laughter tumbled out. Couples strolled around her, arm in arm enjoying their evening out.

Finally, she arrived at the main dining room. Holding her breath, she stepped in the doorway.

The walls were gold, the carpet, drapes, and tablecloths burgundy, male staff wore tuxes, the ladies wore black dresses with white Peter Pan collars.

All of the tables were round and filled with people. The dining room was packed. Like a beehive, patrons and staff buzzed sedately nonstop.

The immaculate maître d hurried right over to her.

"Madame," he greeted her austerely, looking around her for her date. Unescorted young women were not congenially welcomed in the dining room. Part of the town still clung to the social mores of the Dark Ages.

"I'm joining a party, the Kentons," Kessa said graciously.

"Oh!" His attitude became more punctilious. "Yes of course, please follow me." He clipped aloofly across the room.

Kessa was edgily aware many eyes followed her. Some curious, some looked in brazen interest at the beauty, and there was a fair share of jealous glares.

The maître d threaded imperiously through the tables until he stopped where the Kentons were seated at a round table. He pulled out the only empty chair between Geordie and Jaspar. "Madame."

Kessa sat primly and the maître d pushed in her chair.

Conversation halted as Kessa joined the table. Pleased to see her, Geordie leaned over and gave her a kiss on the cheek.

Sophie regally nodded at her daughter. "Darling, how lovely for you to join us. Lincoln, please have them bring our cake and coffee," she hesitated, "unless you'd like a drink?" She cocked her head at Kessa. "A cocktail perhaps," her lips pressed with uncertainty. "Um, you are of age, aren't..." her eyes narrowed awkwardly at Kessa.

Obviously Sophie had forgotten her daughter's age. One more stab to her heart. Swallowing the hurt, Kessa said diplomatically, "Coffee would be perfect, thank you." She nodded at Sophie and then smiled at her family without making eye contact with any of them.

"Certainly, Mrs. Kenton." Lincoln swiveled and cut arrogantly back the way he came. The lights dimmed and music started up. Off to the side of the room a band was playing, people strolled to the small dance floor in front of it.

"So," Sophie said glibly, "we heard you went to the bank today."

"Sophie," Geordie implored his wife. She looked down her nose at him until he wilted into silence.

"I did. Thank you," Kessa said to the server that set down a piece of cake and a cup of coffee in front of her. She ate the cake and sipped the coffee to uncomfortable silence.

Aria jumped up and grabbed Peter's arm pulling him to his unsteady feet. "Come on, I wanna dance." She linked arms with him dragging him to the dance floor. "I can't take anymore of Mother's contentious snits."

Char's husband Jaspar pushed his chair back and stood next to Kessa with his hand out. "Come on, come dance with me, let everyone settle down." He smiled over at his wife.

Char's face was like a cracked sheet of plastic with a plastered smile across it. She said, "Go on, Sister, he loves to dance and I," she glanced balefully at her cane, "it's not my best suit. Seriously, go on, have fun."

The last thing Kessa wanted to do was dance with her smarmy brother-in-law, however, it appeared that everyone at the table would be happier without her present, and it would have been way too discourteous for her to leave the Club already, and just as awkward to refuse him. She bit back a sigh and stood up.

He took her hand and drew her through the dining room and to the crowded dance floor where he immediately pulled her into a way too close embrace.

She tried to discreetly push out of his arms, but he only held her tighter. His hot hands on her back started moving down.

She placed her hands flat on his lapels and bent her elbows so her forearms were against his chest so he couldn't pull her closer.

When his hands kept moving lower, Kessa struggled to discreetly push him away, fearful of calling attention to them. That's all she needed, but he wouldn't let her go and his hands were about to take liberties.

She tried to grasp his wrists to stop him. "Jaspar, knock it off. Stop it, stop it right now," she whispered furiously.

"Oh honey, I know you want me, it was written all over your face at dinner the other night. As soon as we ditch the family, you and I can go to this little out-of-the-way place I know. Boy, you have a tiny waist, and a fine tight ass, I bet you exercise every day. Am I right? Huh?" His hands circled her waist then slid lower,

"C'mon, give me a kiss now, here turn away from the table, there's a crowd, they won't be able to see."

"Dammit, Jaspar, let go of me right now," Kessa hissed, twisting and jerking, but he held her tight, laughing in her ear.

Suddenly a hand came down on Jaspar's arm and squeezed it like a vise. "You heard her. Let go. Now."

The pair looked to see who owned the menacing voice.

Grayson Whitewolf's steel fingers dug into Jaspar's arm until it hurt so much Jaspar let go of Kessa.

Rage burning in his bloodshot eyes, Jaspar said, "You need to mind your own goddamned business, Whitewolf, you-"

Gray let go of Jaspar's arm but then clamped a hand on his collarbone, and squeezed with fingers like nails. His thumb dug into the hollow of his throat.

Gray said in a low voice, "If you leave quietly, I'll let you get out of here with your, dignity," he said dryly, "intact. Now, beat it." He let go of him.

The two men glared at each other.

Jaspar blinked first, giving in. "Fine. You've got a bad rep as a fierce scrapper, Whitewolf. I'm not going to let you make a scene with one of your brawls."

He narrowed a hard warning gaze at Kessa. "I'll be seeing you, Sister-in-law. Soon." He stalked off without waiting for her to say anything, which was good as she didn't know what to say.

"You all right?" Gray asked her. He was feeling guilty, her brother had asked him to keep an eye on her and here she was getting groped in public and no one lifted a hand to help. *People*, he spat. He set a few fingers gently on her arm.

Flustered, Kessa shook him off and pushed her hair back behind her ears. "Yes, um, I'm perfectly fine. I had everything under control, you needn't have gotten involved. Now everyone is staring."

Gray stood in front of her. "Babe, everyone was already staring, watching that gigolo feel you up. Your brother would have killed him. I was only going to break his arms."

Her eyes flashed at him. "He was not...not feeling me up, for crying out loud. You're a policeman, you shouldn't be out to break someone's arms."

Mortified at the whole scene, Kessa's eyes dropped to the floor. Her lips pressed tightly, she looked up at him. "Stop calling me babe. What are you doing here anyway?" She gestured to his uniform.

He crossed his arms. "So rurally far from other cities, this can be a lawless little town, like the old west sometimes. The sheriff's office has to show strength, not brutality, but we can't back down in the face of a threat either. I am here tonight because there was a reported theft in the lounge. I thought I'd take a glance into the dining room when I noticed that cretin pawing you."

The badge pinned to his shirt gleamed in the light. Tonight he wore the full regulation uniform of white polyester shirt and olive green slacks with the lighter green striped down the sides.

He went to take her arm. "Come on, I'll take you back to your table."

She snatched her arm out of his hand. "I can get there on my own. You're just causing a bigger scene. Please go away." Her face flushed, she tried to walk as gracefully as she could back to her family.

Gray stood for a second scratching his head. He shrugged, then, greeting people he knew here and there, he made his way out of the room.

Humiliated again, back at the table, Kessa picked up her purse and quickly said goodnight. "I uh, I have to get up early tomorrow, it, um, I should go," she stammered.

Aria smirked at her knowingly. As usual, Peter sat stupefied next to her. Geordie looked like he desperately wanted to do something to fix things but didn't know what to do.

Sophie for once was unreadable, sitting rigid as a light pole, fearful the club members were judging her.

On Char's face was an expression of unmitigated hatred, daggers in her eyes aimed at her sister. Kessa withered under the wrath and hate emanating like a scorching wind across the table at her.

Since no one objected, nodding briefly, Kessa swung around and as coolly as possible, forced herself to walk normally, without running out of the room.

It took all her will to walk unhurriedly to her car and drive home without going too far over the speed limit. She got inside, locked the door, went into the kitchen and poured herself a big glass of wine.

In her bedroom, she unzipped her dress letting it drop in a pile on the floor.

She moved into the bathroom, filled the tub with bubbles, turned on some soft music, and climbed in, letting the hot water, gentle music, and the wine soothe her body and soul.

Chapter Sixteen

At 10 the next morning, Gray pulled into Arleen Goldbrooke's driveway, the gravel crackling under his wheels, throwing up a trail of dust behind him.

The long winding drive led up to a house set on an acre of freshly mown grass. It used to be an old farmhouse generations back, and half a century ago it had been modernized.

A wide verandah flared around a one-story, weathered white building, topped with a sloping tin roof and numerous windows to let the light in even on gloomy winter days.

Gray was surprised to see a police car already there. Climbing out of his truck, he set his Stetson on his head. The gravel crunching under his boots he went directly to the deputy, who was often times his partner, and good friend, Rick Vanuu.

Rick was speaking with a chunky, dark-skinned woman.

"Hey, Rick," Gray said as he approached. "What's going on?" He tipped his hat to the woman. "Ma'am."

Deputy Vanuu greeted him. "It's poor old Mrs. Goldbrooke." He sounded appropriately sorrowful. The deputy was thick with muscles like a body builder, his head was shaved and he had a tiny brown soul patch under his bottom lip.

He looked more like a bouncer than a cop. But Gray had known him now for years and knew the deputy to be made of virtuous substance.

Taken aback, Gray felt chilling fingers run up his spine. He asked casually, "What happened? I didn't hear anything on the radio, dispatch."

Vanuu said to the lady, "Thank you Mrs.," no ring on her finger, "uh, Miss Bradshaw. If we need anything else we'll be in touch." He saw the beleaguered lady to her car and watched her drive away.

Rick tromped back to Gray and said, "I was standing by dispatch when the call came in so I took it. It appears that the old lady stumbled down the basement stairs and broke her neck." He reached over his shoulder to scratch his back then drew his finger and thumb under his eyes, rubbing gently.

"Miss Bradshaw came over to help her get started for the day and found her at the bottom of the stairs. It was quite a horrible shock for the poor nurse, she was beside herself when I arrived. They took Goldbrooke to the hospital but she was DOA. Looks like the poor thing just lost her footing."

He stuffed his notebook in his pocket. "So, Gray, what brings you way out here?"

His hands on his lean hips, Gray thoughtfully scanned the house and the surrounding grounds. "I had some questions I wanted to ask her. I guess it's out of bounds for me to take a look around."

Rick's lips pushed out, he brushed at his soul patch with a finger. "Well, I…"

"It's okay, Rick, I know until it's cleared no one can contaminate the premises. No worries. I'll wait for the CSI's before I check the place out in case it wasn't an accident." He glanced at his watch.

"On second thought, it's going to be quite a while before they get here and then longer for them to do their thing." He twisted to look down the long driveway. "I would have liked to talk to the housekeeper though." He turned back to Rick. "You got her address?"

"Sure." Rick opened his notebook and scanned it for a second. "Here it is, 1001 Southport St."

"Okay, thanks. I'll come back in a couple of hours. Later." Gray hopped in his cruiser, put the address in his GPS and took off. He went back to the station for a brief meeting with his commander, gulped down a quick sandwich then headed back out.

The GPS led him down a tree-shrouded street lined with large fancy homes. Finding the address, he parked in the driveway and took in the house.

Hmm, he ruminated, *nurses must get paid much more than they used to.*

The house, more like a mansion, had two levels and was made out of stone. Ivy crawled over the front, white-stenciled shutters flanked the windows, and in the dead center was a huge, dark red front door.

A detached three-car garage sat twenty feet to the side and slightly behind the building. Through the open garage door he could see a silver BMW parked inside.

He knocked.

The red door opened moments later. Brenda Bradshaw's surprised face appeared in the doorway. "Officer?"

His thumbs tucked over his belt, Gray said, "How d'ya do, Mrs. Bradshaw, I'm Deputy Grayson Whitewolf. I'd like to ask you a few questions. Do you mind if I come in?"

Brenda's middle-aged round, clove-colored face appeared confused, and there was something else. She seemed nervous about something, or fearful maybe? Gray waited patiently.

Brenda conspicuously glanced over his shoulder, dark almond eyes darted at the space behind him, back and forth.

"I just came from, um," there were still tear streaks on her cheeks. She dashed at them, smiled cautiously and stepped aside. "Sure, come on in."

Gray closed the door behind him, removed his hat and followed the plump woman through the entryway arched with a cathedral ceiling, down a hall and to a bright morning room.

"Please," she gestured, "have a seat. Would you care for something to drink? Coffee, water, tea?" She eyed his broad shoulders. "Something stronger perhaps?"

He shook his head, declining politely. "No thanks. I just have a few questions I'd like to ask you."

An angular blonde girl with a sharp face wearing a white maid's uniform stood in the doorway.

"Nothing right now, Evie," Brenda said in a voice used to giving commands. "See to the laundry."

Gray sat on a soft chair decorated with big, bold colored flowers. He set his hands on the arms of the chair but moved them to his lap. The flowery chair made him feel like he was at a ladies' party. He set his hat on his knee.

Brenda perched on a solid green divan kitty-corner to him. A pageboy wig framed her round face. She wore checkered slacks topped with a long sleeved white blouse. At first slightly nervous, she took a mental inventory of the man sitting there.

He would be handsome except for the hardness in his blue eyes, but that made him more interesting, and that strong body was alluring. She sat back, maybe it was the scar over his eye that made him appear excitingly dangerous. "What can I do for you…officer…?"

Gray leaned forward setting his forearms on his knees. "Whitewolf. Deputy Whitewolf. I have a few questions I'd like to ask you."

Brenda squirmed forward to the edge of the divan. "Your name sounds Native American?" It was a question not a statement. She studied his features. "The black hair I see, but the dark blue eyes and your features, you don't look quite the part."

Used to this, Gray said smoothly, "I have a few Scottish ancestors in the woodpile." He sat back and crossed his legs. "Anyway, can you tell me how long you've worked for Mrs. Goldbrooke?"

Brenda considered the question. "Well, it's been years. In the beginning, she was one of my first full time positions of an all-around, oh, what would you call it, I was her nurse, her caretaker, and her housekeeper.

"Another girl came in once a week to do the heavy cleaning and shopping, laundry and such, but I took care of Mrs.

Goldbrooke. It's been about," she thought back, "about twenty years now, I think. But now I just see to her every so often."

"Hmm. Do you mind if I ask if you're married, ever been married?" Gray asked politely.

Brenda shook her head, smiled. "No, I never met a man I could stand long enough to spend more than a few months with!" She laughed. "No, no husband, no children."

She appeared a little regretful at the lack of children in her life. "Fortunately I have nephews and a niece to fill that void."

"Uh huh, that's good." He glanced around the room.

A tall secretary desk was near the one long window, two flowery chairs and the divan dominated the small room. Several paintings of landscapes decorated the walls, the coffee table was littered with celebrity magazines and a cup with residue that looked like coffee. A table near the window was covered with frames of probably family.

"Were you born in Resilir?" he asked.

Brenda sat back against the cushions, crossed her legs and laid an arm on the arm of the divan. She inclined her head at him and answered, "Yes, born and raised. My mother was a stay at home mom, my father worked the mills. I had six brothers and sisters."

Her raised brows indicated she was obviously curious as to why he wanted to know about her background.

"Do you remember," he said slowly, "14 years ago when the little Kenton girls had their…their trouble?"

Brenda frowned, bent two fingers and tapped them on her chin. "Of course. It was big news then for this small country burg. Splashed the headlines for months." She shook her head.

"Devastating time for that family. One girl crippled, one missing, the other, the third was accused, they sent her away. Never heard a thing about her again." She dropped her hand and stared wistfully out the window.

Gray watched her for a moment then he asked casually, "Were you caring for Mrs. Goldbrooke during that time?" He watched her imperceptive flinch before her jaw set.

She turned slowly, carefully softening her expression when she faced him. "Yes, actually, I was. She was very sick then, on her deathbed we all thought. She was too sick to go to the doctor. Doc Aven used to come and see her. In those days in rural areas like this the local doctor did that. Fortunately," she smiled, "Mrs. Goldbrooke pulled through."

"Mrs. Goldbrooke lived on the edge of town. Kind of near where the children went missing. I understand the police at that time didn't question Mrs. Goldbrooke. Do you remember?" His voice mild and pleasant, he set his palms on his thighs.

"Sure, yes, she was practically in a coma for quite a while then. They asked me to come into the station for my statement. Of course I had nothing to offer them. I wasn't there those several days, I was away taking care of my own sick mother." Her lips quirked with guilt.

"I hated to leave Mrs. Goldbrooke then, but she pulled through and my own mother was quite ill. I had to go. You know, we were fairly isolated, nothing much came by the house, except deer and maybe the odd coyote."

"I could see that. You don't remember anything odd, anyone out of place that didn't fit in, didn't belong around the area?" Gray asked.

She bit her lip, eyes roamed to the left, remembering. She fiddled with an emerald ring on her finger. Gold and silver bangles jangled on both wrists with her movements. "No, really. But then I stayed inside with Mrs. Goldbrooke, there was no reason for me to be outside and she had very few visitors."

"Oh?" Interested, Gray asked, "Like who?"

Fidgeting, Brenda straightened the scalloped collar on her blouse, bent over and fingered the crease down her slacks as she tried to recall 14 years ago.

"I don't know, no one dangerous for sure. Mrs. Sanderson from church, my goodness, she was near 80 herself. A few other quite elderly, utterly harmless parishioners. The priest, Father Benedict came on Mondays to bring her the sacrament. No one else I can think-"

"A priest, really? Goldbrooke?" Gray interrupted.

Brenda smiled. "Her mother was Catholic, her father Jewish. She was brought up Catholic. But," she thought another minute.

"No, that was pretty much it. Church members and sometimes some other nurses came by to relieve me periodically. That was infrequent because the old lady slept most of the time so she needed very little actual hands on care.

"Of course the nurses and church members came by more often while I was away. We were so far off the beaten path that people didn't come often or stay long. With the gravel and stone driveway so lengthy you could hear someone coming long before they reached the house." She went to stand up. "I guess if that's all…"

"Uh huh," Gray's voice stopped her. He leaned back. "So, are your parents still around?"

Taken aback, Brenda stayed seated, said with some puzzlement, "Um, no, they've both passed." Unsure of his interest in her background, she said testily, "I don't see-"

He said like a smooth arrow, "Your folks left you some money to live comfortably," he deliberately looked around the wealthy home. "Quite comfortably?"

Her brows faltered, lips parted. A flustered flush rose up her neck. "Well, no, uh, yes, yes they saved every penny raising us and were able to- to invest, and then I, the stock market you know, well," she stood up. "Well, I have some errands to attend to, to do, and-"

Gray stood up too. "Sure. Thanks for your time." He slipped his hat on.

Their steps slapped the tiled floor as she quickly saw him to the front door. The door, like the rest of the house was large. Ornate molding framed it and the entire gold and sea-foam green foyer.

She opened the door. "Well, then…"

He took one last look around. "Yes," he said, "quite comfortably. Good for you." Tipping his hat to her, he strolled down the steps and to his vehicle.

In his truck, he watched Brenda Bradshaw stick her dark head out the door and again nervously look around before closing the enormous red door.

While Gray sat a moment making a few notes before leaving, he could see her peek out at him from a window, holding her cell phone next to her ear.

Chapter Seventeen

When she got up in the morning, Kessa had a bad feeling in the pit of her stomach.

On her way home last night she swore she was done with the family. Yesterday would be the last time she was going to see them unless she ran into them around town.

As soon as Matthew returned from England she was getting the heck out of Dodge. At least since she was a writer she could live anywhere and make her living.

Where to go would be the question, she found out the cabin she'd leased in Maine was already rented and occupied by new tenants.

In the mostly white kitchen with stainless steel appliances and beige curtains on the door and kitchen windows, she made herself some bacon and eggs, poured a glass of orange juice and a cup of coffee and sat at the kitchen table to eat her breakfast.

The top part of the Dutch kitchen door was glass. The morning sun streamed in through the glass bathing her in a yellow glow.

She spread open the morning Resilir Gazette and dug into a steaming heap of scrambled eggs. While reading, her mind became distracted, it kept pulling up Char's enraged face contorted in vile hatred, aimed at her. She set her fork down suddenly losing her appetite.

Pushing the plate away, she picked up her coffee cup. While sipping, her eyes kept drifting to the phone on the wall. She picked up her dishes, set them in the sink, refilled her coffee and sat on a stool by the phone. Her stomach tightened to the point she couldn't breathe.

Matthew had written the phone number on a pad on the counter. She picked up the phone and dialed the number. The phone rang. The butterflies in her stomach roiled up her chest and closed her throat. The phone rang. And rang. And rang. Mystified she hung it up.

She went upstairs, pulled on jeans, a gauzy blouse with four buttons down the front, and tugged on black booties, came back down and looked at the phone. She dialed the number again but it only rang.

"What the heck, they have no answering machine?" Thinking about it, it wasn't the weekend, so Jaspar and Geordie would likely be at work at Geordie's employment. Sophie probably had friends to visit and shopping to do.

Undoubtedly, Aria and Peter were off getting high somewhere, chances were Char was home alone as she seldom left the house. Matthew had told her that two days a week there were no servants in the house until dinnertime.

Kessa grabbed her purse and keys locking the door on the way out. It took her 15 minutes to get to her family's house. She parked the car on the pavers made up of interlinking multi-shades of rust and orange.

As she'd figured, the driveway was empty. She looked around the neighborhood with guarded quick glances in case one of them came in behind her. Walking up the drive she gawked at the house.

Grand, no, what she'd said before, ostentatious. It was a three-story Tudor with mullioned windows, herringbone brickwork with partial timbering and stucco. Several chimneys sprung up from the pitched roofs of the different wings.

It was a far cry from the cramped, four-bedroom family home she'd grown up- make that she was born in. She'd grown up in the orphanage.

Deciding to enter through the side porch, she knocked on the door, waited, knocked again, waited. "Where are all those servants they have for crying out loud?"

The door opened. Char stood in the threshold. Her face had cemented back into an unreadable statue. She said, not welcoming, "What do you want? No one is home right now."

Kessa pulled her lips in. This was, had been her dear sister, before. "I came to see you. Can I come in?"

Char stood and stared at her sister for what seemed like ages, then she turned to limp away. "Do what you want," she tossed over her shoulder.

Kessa walked up the steps and into the house. She closed the door behind her. She could hear Char's uneven clumping along with the cane every other step going down the hall from the porch. Kessa hurried after her.

She followed her sister into the white drawing room they'd been the other night.

Char clumped over to a red and blue striped white chair, flopped down and stared at the floor. Pudgy but not really fat, she wore a denim wrap-around dress which she pulled down over her knees. Her blonde hair fried from too many perms floated like fuzzy feathers to her shoulders.

Looking for an innocuous way to start a conversation, Kessa asked, "Where is all the help, Alice, Edna, how come there's no one here?"

"They get a day off, like you care. Dad wants at least one, actually two days when there's no strangers in the house." She smirked. "That's includes Aria's partner in crime, her junkie boyfriend, Peter."

Kessa lapsed into silence, trying to think of something to say that Char wouldn't take wrong. How to forge a relationship with her sister…

137

Before Kessa could come up with something, Char trained her empty eyes on her sister. "Well? You here to tell me you didn't hit on my husband at the Wilton?"

Kessa's eyes popped. She almost fell into the chair next to Char's. "What?" Her voice shrilled, "Me? Are you kidding? I-"

Char's face blackened to an unnatural gloaming of all that could not be good. The nonsymmetrical sides of her face shifted even more unevenly, the agonized green eyes spat accusation.

"You, yes you. It's always been about you!" She was so angry her entire body shook. She pointed at Kessa, shouting, "You got to leave, you got to get away!" She struggled to her feet, lines deepened in her face, the green eyes screamed in loathsome wretchedness.

"You weren't hurt. I was- damaged. I was crippled. Look at me, look at my face. You walked away from it all, scot free while I had to stay, here, with them! They cried for Hope for years!" She screeched like an insane witch, "You-"

Feeling like she'd been slapped, Kessa got up, clutching her purse. "Okay, I don't need this. I came here to make peace with you. I didn't get away, Char, I was sent away. I was thrown away like trash. I was nothing, I didn't even have an identity anymore, Char, they changed my name!

"I lived with strangers. I had no freedom, ever, not one second alone. They...they beat us almost daily. I didn't choose to leave home. I would have given a million bucks to have been allowed to stay here. No one even visited me until Matthew was old enough to find me."

Char lifted her cane and pounded it on the floor. "Don't you lie, Faith Mary Kenton! You hurt me and Hope ,and then you ran. You made a nice new life, a nice new name. You didn't stay and face your consequences!" She screamed so loud it was surprising her veins didn't pop.

Kessa's head dropped. Sadly, wearily, she said softly, "I had hoped we could-"

"Well we can't *do* anything. I don't want you here, no one wants you here! If only you'd been the one to die instead of baby

Hope! If only you were the one who had been brought out with a mangled face and broken back!" Char yelled at the top of her lungs, jabbing her cane at her sister in blind fury.

Feeling ill, Kessa said nothing, it was useless. She bolted out of the room and frantically ran down the hall praying she wouldn't get lost in the humongous hotel of a house.

She couldn't find the door she came in so when she stumbled onto a side door, she yanked it open and ran out and jumped in her car. Her trembling fingers pushed the key in, turned the car on and she peeled off down the street.

Driving in a directionless frenzy for miles, her hands hurt clenching the wheel so hard, tears streamed down her face.

After half an hour, she found herself at the Lake. Lake Yana. She pulled in and turned the car off. Her heart pounded, her breathing was so fast and hard she felt her throat scorching.

Her eyes trained on the lake, the crystalline blue water drained the awful emotions from her. She watched the gentle waves ebb and flow, gulls flew overhead, soft mounds of sand glinted in the sunlight.

After a while of meditating on the peaceful undulating water, anger started to stir in her. She looked in the rear view mirror at herself. Eyes red and puffy from crying, the painfully felt deep loss fading their vibrant color, mouth turned down.

She said to her reflection, "I can't believe I let her chase me out of that house without my saying my piece. I only wanted to mend things between us."

Kessa sat picturing the torment on her sister's crushed face. Fresh tears fell, this time for her sisters. She hadn't thought about how it had been for them.

She spoke to herself in the mirror. "She's right, she had to stay in that house, crippled, broken, disfigured. With the parents mourning their youngest child's disappearance."

Kessa had always felt sorry for herself being exiled. She'd never thought about how everyone else, especially Char felt. She lowered her head, the soft tresses fell over her face.

She wiped her eyes, blew her nose. "This is ridiculous, I need to clear the air with her. We need to be allies, be the friends, the sisters we used to be. I'm going to go make her understand, make her care about me again. Make her know, believe, that it wasn't me that hurt her and Hope. I just have to..." She turned the car on, backed out and drove back to the house.

Unsure, but hopeful, Kessa parked the jeep again and trod up the steps.

The side door was open. She must have left it open when she had stormed out. She knocked, rang the bell. No response.

Gingerly pushing the door open further, she peered inside. It was quiet as a morgue. "Char?" she called, trying to keep her voice strong and steady, unlike her jumping stomach. Still no answer.

Stepping inside, she made sure to close the door behind her.

"Char?" she called out louder, her voice echoing hollowly down the empty tiled hall. She moved slowly into the foyer, then beyond calling her sister's name.

Making her way all through the first floor maze in one direction without a sign of her sister, she tried to find her way back to the front.

Then, starting to search in the other direction, she tried the first room she came to. The door was closed. Cautiously, she turned the knob and opened the door. "Char?"

It was a large bathroom. Her sister lay sprawled in the middle of the cold, orange tile floor.

"Char!" Kessa hurried to her sister. Dropping to her knees, she pushed her sister over so she could see her face.

The fried yellow hair covered it, Kessa gently smoothed it back. Char's eyes were closed, her skin deathly pale, slack mouth open, white foaming drool trickled out of a corner and down her chin.

Kessa felt her cheek, it was cold. Panicking, Kessa felt her neck for a pulse. Her fear thumping in her ear, she wasn't sure she could feel a shallow, thready beating. She bent her head to put her ear near Char's mouth.

The air felt extremely slight, but it seemed she was breathing, barely. Kessa fumbled her phone out of her pocket. The numbers on the keypad were blurry and shaking, but she punched out 911.

"Hello?" a detached voice said flatly. "What is your emergency?"

"My- my sister, help me, she's passed out, maybe an OD. I can't tell if she's, I think she's breathing but it's shallow and she's very cold."

"Does she have a pulse?"

"I- I think, so, yes, very, very faint. Maybe."

The operator asked, "What's the address?"

Kessa's brain went blank. "Wait." She was able to look in her phone without losing the call. Running through her addresses, she found it. "Here...here...it's 333 Sanloquan Lane..."

"Got it. Do you know CPR?"

Kessa nodded, then realized she couldn't see her. "Yes, some."

"All right. Emergency is on the way. Keep checking to see if she has a pulse and she's breathing. If not, then begin CPR. Okay?" The voice sounded more kind.

"Yeah, yeah, I can, I mean, I have it. Thank you. Please tell them to hurry."

Chapter Eighteen

Deputy Wayde Smith pushed the heavy oak door of Cache's Bar open and was met with a thick smog of cigarette and cigar smoke. Letting his eyes adjust to the dimly lit bar, he looked around. Seeing the sheriff in the last booth along the wall, he went straight there.

Greeting, "Hey," he plopped down next to Deputy Bruce Sutton, and slicked back his fine hair that was always flopping in his eyes.

Sheriff Jimmy Lombardo had stuffed his girth in across the booth. A glass of amber liquid set on a wet cocktail napkin in front of Jimmy.

Bruce was sucking at a bottle of beer. The barmaid had apparently brought a frosty mug which Bruce had ignored and it now sat with a pool of water around it.

" 'Sup?" Bruce asked.

"Nuthin' bro." Wayde shot a quick look at the deputy. " 'Cept you still look like a baby giraffe. Maybe you should grow a 'stache or something, hit the gym and grow some shoulders. Try boxing maybe, man up a little."

Bruce paused mid-drink and almost choked, spitting out a mouthful of beer.

Wayde glanced at Lombardo then said woefully to Bruce who was wiping spit off his mouth, "But you can't do nuthin' 'bout that big long nose and that overbite," he shook his head.

"Too bad we don't make enough for you to get a nose job. Now the dentist could fix those-"

"Screw you, Wayde." Bruce put a hand over his mouth then plucked at his chin like he could pull whiskers out of it. Brushing the top of his short tussock-like hair with his palms, he glared at Smith.

At Wayde's smirk, Bruce retorted, "You're jealous that I'm younger than you and I don't have to live with a body shaped like a knife with narrow shoulders and hips and a gaunt old face like yours." He sniffed. "You might consider a trip to the gym yourself."

Barmaid Sara, despondent look on her dry flaky face, came right over with Wayde's drink. He always had the same bourbon and soda.

"Thanks, hon." Wrapping his long fingers of one hand like a hairless tarantula around the glass, Wayde asked, "What's the matter, Sara? A young girl like you shouldn't be looking so miserable."

Setting down a fresh bowl of peanuts, using her hand, the girl raked cracked shells and peanut dust into the almost empty bowl already on the table.

Tucking her hands in the apron tied over jeans and a shirt, she pushed her chin up and shrugged. "Nothin's wrong. Just, you know, my boyfriend, Eric, has to work next week on my birthday. It's not fair." She sighed like she'd lost a hundred dollars, picked up the dirty bowl then swept away, hair like wheat sheaves flouncing behind her.

The three men chuckled.

Jimmy Lombardo set his hands on his belly and twiddled his thumbs. "Ah, the troubles of youth. Anyway, I told you to meet me here, there's less ears than at the station." He glanced around.

There were only four other customers in the oak lined joint, like being inside an all wood casket.

Someone had played a series of ballads on the jukebox, the music flowed passively in the background. The last tune ended as

Wayde wrapped a few fingers around his drink. A low rumble of voices reverberated from the few occupied tables.

Wayde stretched his neck from side to side then downed his drink in two gulps. He looked over and caught Rex the bartender's eye and gestured for another drink. "So, we're here. What's up?"

Jimmy's piggy eyes darted around the room then back and forth at the two deputies across from him. He opened his mouth to speak but at that second a patron stuck a quarter in the juke box and a melancholy song flowed through the room.

"Great, Sam," Wayde called out sarcastically to the sorrowful looking guy swaying by the jukebox. "Thanks for the uplift." He saluted the man then said to the sheriff, "So?"

Jimmy pulled the wet napkin out from under his drink and wiped his forehead with it then dropped it on the table. "I want to know what's going on with Whitewolf. I hear he's rehashing the Kenton case. It's done, over, nothing else to dig up. No one asked me if that was okay, ya know? Ain't I the boss around these parts?" He grumbled his redundant question.

Wayde leaned back and crossed his long legs. One hand still wrapped around his empty glass, he brought it to his lips and shook some ice cubes into his mouth.

The long jaw bouncing up and down crunching on the ice, he said, "You know Gray was a captain at his last gig, the military police deal. He thinks he can still run his own show. I hear that the Kenton girl, the one they sent away has come back and is staying with her brother. They're probably stirring things up."

"I don't think Sophie or Geordie want any of this brought back again," Jimmy said, taking a few sips. Half a chewed cigar was perched unlit on the ashtray near him.

His eyelids levered open and closed like a reptile, he looked blandly at Wayde. "I want a lid shut on this thing. Now, before anything comes up that could appear-"

"I don't think so," Wayde interrupted, shaking his head at his boss. He accepted another drink from the mournful Sara.

Jimmy's brows popped up. "You-"

"I know Grayson Whitewolf. You make any kind of noise of any sort about the case and his radar will perk and he's like a dog with a bone. He'll figure because you're trying to shut it up there has to be something up with it. He will dig and dig until he gets something." He gulped the drink in two swallows again, the Adam's apple bobbing like a cork in water.

Jimmy glared at him but considered his words.

"Believe me," Wayde said, "you're better off leaving him alone. When he gets nothing, he'll get bored and move onto something else. Trust me."

"I hear that girl, the one that came back is a helluva looker," Bruce commented.

Jimmy partially turned to his left to look at him. "Oh yeah? She's just a kid."

Bruce twisted his beer between his palms. "Naw, she's like 21 or 22 now. Tyrone down at the bank says she's a sizzler, hot as hell, he says. Maybe that's Whitewolf's interest."

"Then she's gotta be a whore because that's all Gray goes for these days," Wayde said, and he and Bruce snickered.

Jimmy was silent, thinking.

"So, anyway, we on for some action tonight, Boss?" Wayde asked.

Jimmy took the unlit cigar and pensively stuck it in the corner of his mouth. "Yeah." He stared down at his glass. "Yeah. Okay. I agree with what you're saying, Wayde. We should let Whitewolf turn in circles until he gets tired of the case and the Kentons and moves on."

Cracking open a peanut, Wayde licked the nuts into his mouth and dropped the shell on the table. He said wryly, reaching for another one, "Well if his reputation is anything to go by, he only needs to bang the Kenton girl once and he'll move on."

Bruce giggled.

Jimmy barked in a loud voice, "Sara, get your ass over here, what, we gotta get our own drinks?" He pushed his empty glass to the end of the table and put his hands back on his belly. "Alright, next on the agenda, any information on the goods?"

Before anyone could answer, a man in a white button-down, long-sleeved shirt and crisp black slacks approached the table.

"Hey boys, how they hanging?" The thirtyish man with olive skin and short black hair greeted the trio. A tad shorter than medium height, filaments of black hair poked out of the top open button, gold chains linked down his chest, he set his hands on his hips. A gold Rolex glittered on his wrist.

"Taz, how's business?" Wayde greeted the bar owner.

Jimmy Lombardo grunted.

Bruce trilled, "How you doing, Mr. Cache?"

The bar owner barely glanced at the giraffe-nosed deputy, he said to Wayde, "Business is good," he nodded, "real good." To Lombardo, "I got some stuff to go over with you, Jimmy. When can we get together? Tonight?"

Lombardo studied his drink, picked it up with three bovine fingers around the rim and twirled the glass, watching the liquor swirl. "I can do that, Taz." His head bobbed, jowls shook. "You think you can come up with a big juicy T-bone for me?"

Taz smiled. "You bet. We'll go to Chanz's down the street. Let me know what time and I'll have the steak and mashed potatoes slathered in parmesan garlic butter waiting for you."

Jimmy sagged back in the booth like a relaxed hog. "That sounds good, Taz." He looked at his watch then labored to move into a more erect sitting pile of fat.

His thick lips blubbered when he let out a heavy sigh. "I gotta call Belle. In the meantime, Taz," he shifted his weight over on one arm propped on the vinyl seat, pig eyes slid up to the bar owner. "While I make my call, I need you to scare up Nefertiti. Have her waiting out back in your office."

Taz crossed his arms and laughed. "You got it, Chief. All right then," he acknowledge the three men. "I'll catch you guys later." He left and disappeared through a door to the side of the bar.

Wayde grinned lasciviously at his boss. "Oo, Nefertiti, huh. I thought you never paid for it, Boss."

Lombardo picked up the damp cocktail napkin and wiped his face again with it. He grinned at Wayde with half his mouth. "You know boy, I ain't paying for it. The Viagra neither."

Joining in, Bruce simpered, "That's that really young hooker, the one with the long red hair. She always wears those shorts that show her butt cheeks?" He smiled in admiration at his boss. "Good job, Boss. She don't even barely look legal."

Lombardo laid a hefty arm on the table. "All right, you guys get lost, I got business to do."

Chapter Nineteen

"What have you done?" Sophie screamed the second she saw Kessa.

She and Geordie were scurrying down the hospital hall towards Kessa who was sitting alone in a waiting room, perched on the tip of her seat, head down, hers hands clutched in prayer.

Her head shot up when she heard her mother. She stood up as her parents reached her.

"How is she? Where is she? What happened?" Sophie hollered all at once not letting Kessa get a word in.

"Come on, Soph, get a grip, we'll ask the doctor-"

Sophie cut off her husband, "I want to know now," her eyes narrowed at her daughter, "what did you do to her this time?"

Kessa folded her arms across her chest but kept her mouth closed.

Sophie grabbed her arms and shook her demanding, "Answer me! What did you do to her?"

Yelling for her to let go, Geordie grabbed Sophie's arms to pull her away from Kessa. Kessa stood mute with her neck snapping back and forth.

"People! Please!" A nurse hurried over to break up the melee. "Please, control yourselves, you're in a hospital-"

Sophie turned her face grotesquely warped in furor to the nurse. Pointing at Kessa, she snarled, "She- she did something to my child! You don't know what's she's capable of, what she's done! You need to call the police-"

"Please Madam, you really must compose yourself or I'll have to call security." The nurse stood with her hands on her hips trying to look compassionate and firm at the same time.

Geordie kept pulling on Sophie who would not let go of Kessa.

Kessa stayed mute, not fighting back at her mother. This only unhinged Sophie more, she started yelling at the top of her lungs for Kessa to answer her.

"What is going on here!" A bold authoritative male voice boomed into the scene. They all stopped and looked.

"Dr. DeBarra, thank goodness," the nurse said, with a huff of relief.

The doctor arrogantly strode to the group, his white lab coat flailing around his legs. A couple of years past thirty, with dark russet hair and cool, deep chocolate eyes, he was quite attractive, and he knew it.

Add good looks and being a doctor, Anthony DeBarra was quickly sleeping his way through the hospital staff. "What is going on, how can I help?" He studied the group, gauging what they could do for him.

Instantly, Sophie released Kessa who would have stumbled except Geordie let go of Sophie and caught his daughter. He wrapped an arm around her shoulders and held her.

Sophie pivoted like a dancer to face the doctor. "Oh, Doctor," Sophie cooed. She placed one hand over the other over her heart and gave him her most winning yet tinged with worry smile. "Yes, if you could *please* help us." She moved so she was between him and the others.

"Of course, Mrs., um," one russet brow arched in question.

"Oh, please call me Sophie." Sophie took a step closer to the gorgeous doctor.

"Of course, Sophie, how can I be of help?"

The nurse cut in. "Antho- uh, Doctor, these are the Kentons. They are here for the overdose-"

"Miss Domine," he frowned at the nurse. "Our patients are people, not just cases." He said to Sophie, but his eyes lingered on Kessa, "I know, your dear daughter was brought in a short time ago. Give me one second and I will check her status."

He patted Sophie's shoulder, his smile warm and commanding. His gaze flitted over Kessa as he turned and strode to the nurses' station.

Chastened, the nurse spun on her heel and stalked back where she had come from.

Completely shunning Kessa, Sophie grasped Geordie's wrist and pulled him away from his daughter. Holding his hand, she spouted angrily, "This is all her fault. When I find out what she-" Sophie smiled at the doctor who was moving briskly back to them.

Kessa spoke up, "Mother, I did nothing to Char. I came over and found her lying unconscious on the-"

Ignoring her, Sophie shifted her back to her daughter. "What can you tell us, Doctor?" she mewed at the doctor. Her head cocked coyly at him, she fluttered her lashes and smiled beguilingly.

Doctor DeBarra said, "Why don't we all have a seat. No," he held up his hands at their sudden concern, "nothing is wrong. Let's just talk, okay? Shall we?" He ushered them to a table with four chairs at it and they all took a seat.

"Now," DeBarra said, charisma oozing off him. "It does appear that, Charity, right?" Everyone nodded. "It appears that she is going to be all right. However," his expression grew serious, "it looks, um, I hate to say this, but it looks like she tried to commit suicide."

Sophie and Geordie gasped. "Surely not, Doctor, our little Char wouldn't ever dream of doing anything like that, never. Right Geordie?" Sophie appealed to her husband to confirm her statement. Her eyebrows were like inverted C's she was so distraught.

Geordie opened his mouth but no words came out.

Kessa also kept her peace. Matthew had told her that several times over the years Char had attempted suicide and had also accidentally overdosed on barbiturates before. Char had told him the barbiturates helped her look at her deformed image in the mirror without losing her mind.

"Don't you worry, Mrs. …Sophie, we'll help her get back on track. For now, she'll stay here for a few days until we get her stabilized and then we'll transfer her to the," he thought about the best way to say it. "Well, to the psychiatric ward. We have the best psychiatrists in the county here. Don't worry, we'll have her good as new in a…while…"

Sophie sat in horrified silence, her mouth gaping.

"So, uh, I need you to come and fill out the insurance and waivers and all that nuisance paperwork. Nurse Domine will be more than happy to assist you." He saw the groused glower the nurse shot him, and didn't care.

"Miss, I'm sorry, I don't know your name?" he said to Kessa. His dark eyes pulsated across the table at her, forcing her to acknowledge him.

"My daughter, Mary-" Sophie said before Kessa could open her mouth, but then Kessa very quietly said, "Please call me Kessa."

"Well then, Kessa," DeBarra replied, his smile wide and inviting. "While your parents are filling out the paperwork, perhaps we could have a private chat?"

Her face a blank, inside, Kessa moaned. It had been a horrible fright finding Char on the floor and fearing she was dead. The rush to the hospital, people running and yelling, wheeling her away, having to call her parents.

She just wanted to go home, get a glass of wine, sit with Kato and listen to some music. "Oh, well, since Char will be all right, I really need to get going, I have to-"

"Really, Kessa, you have nothing to do. It's not like you have a job for Pete's sake," Sophie snarked. She smiled at the handsome doctor. "She'll be thrilled to chat with you. When we get done with the paperwork I, we," she purred, "would love to chat with you as well. Would that be all right?"

"Huh?" DeBarra grunted, without sparing Sophie a glance. Then he said absently, "Yeah sure." He stood up as Nurse Domine came over to collect Sophie and Geordie.

At that moment, Doctor Aven wheeled around the corner. Recognizing the Kentons, he came right over. "Sophie, Geordie, I heard about Char. I want you to know I checked in on the lass. She'll be just fine." His Scottish burr like an old friend wrapped them in familiar comfort.

Gushing, Sophie plucked at his sleeve. "Oh, it is so good to see you, Dr. Aven. We've hardly seen you these past few years since the girls no longer see a pediatrician."

Geordie stood ill at ease off to the side. Whenever there was a man around, Sophie was on her airs.

Dr. Aven, in his early fifties, his hair greying, stomach pooching, pushed his glasses up his nose. He tucked the file he had in his hand under an arm and gave Sophie a quick hug.

In the meantime, Dr. DeBarra held a hand out to Kessa forcing her to take it or she'd look rude. "Excuse us for a moment," he said to the others, then grasping her hand tightly as she tried to slip it right out he led her down the hall.

Finding an empty room, he brought her inside and closed the door. He didn't turn on the light, she tugged her hand from his.

"You don't need to be nervous, honey. I'm not going to bite you. I just thought we could get to know each other a little since I'll be helping care for your sister." He took a small step in her direction.

Kessa crossed her arms. "Well, it sounded like Char isn't going to be in the ICU for very long, so I doubt our paths will cross again. So," she went to the door.

He leaned nonchalantly and dropped a hand on the doorknob so she couldn't. "Yes, yes, we hope she recovers quickly. But um, I was thinking, how about you and I going out to dinner one night? I know a fantastic seafood place."

Awkwardly humming, "Uh," Kessa pushed his hand off the knob and grasped it. As she pulled the door open, he had to step out of the way. "I don't think so. I don't date."

She tried to walk coolly past him into the hall. She was for once happy to see Sophie striding up the hall like a bull after a matador. "There you two are!" She hustled towards them.

"I thought you guys had to do paperwork?" Kessa asked.

"Oh, Geordie can handle it just fine. I wanted to thank you, Dr. DeBarra." Sophie leaned close to him.

Used to women behaving this way towards him, the doctor didn't react or move away. "Mrs...uh, Sophia-"

"Sophie," Sophie murmured. "But it does sound so much better as Sophia coming from your lips."

"Ah yes of course, Sophie. I was just trying to convince your daughter here to honor me with a dinner out, you know Banggero's over on First Street?"

Kessa sidled away from the pair, but Sophie said, "Oh yes, that's a very nice place. Something you're not used to, my dear."

"I was hoping you could talk her into going with me, Sophie," the charming doctor said silkily, his hands tucked in the lab coat's deep pockets.

Eyes rounded with warning, Sophie said to Kessa, "Of course she'll go out with you, won't you, dear?" Her voice was obviously threatening, but that didn't seem to bother the doctor. "When were you thinking of, this Saturday night?"

"Mother," Kessa pleaded.

"Yes, Saturday would be great. Give me your address, I'll pick you up at say, 8?" DeBarra was enthusiastic in his win.

"Oh, let me, dear." Sophie rummaged in her purse and pulled out a piece of paper and a pen and wrote down Kessa's address that Matthew had forced on her and quickly handed it to the doctor.

"There you go, it's a date! Now, Mary, uh, uh, Faith dear, we must be about seeing to your sister. After all, whatever you did, I don't know I'm sure, come along. So nice to meet you, Dr. DeBarra, hope to see you very soon," Sophie trilled, pulling Kessa with her down the hall.

When they were out of earshot, Kessa snapped, "Mother, what the hell were you-"

"Oh never mind you wretched girl. What are our friends going to think about Char and this mess? We managed to cover over the other…episodes, but this, this will be all over town by morning!" Sophie cried.

Seeing a man and a boy approaching, Kessa said under her breath, "Hush now."

"Don't you tell me what to-" Sophie exploded, but Kessa had moved ahead quickly to greet the man and boy.

"Clayton, hey, funny to see you again so soon. You remember my mother?" Kessa gestured a hand towards Sophie.

"Mother, this is Clayton Gourdet, you remember the Gourdets, they owned the liquor store at Ridgecourt Plaza?"

Sophie gave a curt nod and a short smile. "Of course, that's where we bought our dinner wine when we still lived on Bayshore, the lower side."

Kessa flicked an expression of apology to Clayton for her mother's obvious dig, that now they were wealthy they shopped on the other side of town.

An affable smile on Clayton's gaunt face, he said graciously, "Yes, it seems like eons ago. My parents have since sold the store and retired to Florida."

Before her mother could get another insulting word in, Kessa bent over slightly and smiled at the boy. "And, who is this?"

Clayton's paltry chest puffed slightly. He shoved his glasses on top of his head and smoothed back one side of his prematurely greying hair. He set a hand on the child's skeletal shoulder. "This is my son, Troy. Troy, say how-do-you-do to these ladies."

The boy looked around 7 or so. Blond shaggy hair and big blue eyes in a peaked face, ducking his head shyly, he mumbled, "How you do?"

"It's nice to meet you." Kessa smiled warmly at the boy again. Sophie didn't acknowledge his presence.

"We're here to…" Clayton considered how much personal business to tell them. Kessa was at this point still an unknown entity, but everyone knew what a gossipmonger Sophie Kenton was.

"Troy here is getting a check-up. Gotta keep on top of these things, right?" He held his wrist up to look at his watch. "Oh, and we have to be on the third floor in 5 minutes. Come on, Troy, we need to get a move on. So nice to see you again, Faith, Mrs. Kenton. I hope to see you around."

"Okay," Kessa said to their backs as the Gourdets moved weakly down the hall and out of sight.

"Harrumph." Sophie muttered, "Clayton looks just as sickly as the boy what with that sallow emaciated face and pock marks." She didn't bother lowering her voice.

"Did you get a load of that kid? Cute, but he looks very ill, his skin is paper thin. I wonder what kind of check-up he's getting? Isn't the third floor oncology?" She didn't come across sympathetic in the least. "Let's get up to Char and get out of here," she said. "I'm tired of this place."

Chapter Twenty

$\mathcal{G}$ray was writing up an event report for a drunk and disorderly arrest when Deputy Rick Vanuu came into the bull pen.

Rick started over to Gray. Just before he reached him, another deputy, a female with collar-length blonde hair stepped right in front of Rick and said to Gray, "Hey, I got that search warrant you asked for the Goldbrooke farm."

She stuck her tongue out at Rick as she cut him off and sat her butt on the corner of Gray's desk, moving as close to him as she could get. "I don't know how you got the judge to ok this after all these years, but," she waggled the warrant in Gray's face. When he went to take it she held it out of his reach.

"Oh no," the woman said. "I think I need some kind of reward for getting this for you, hotcheeks. What will you give me for it?" She dangled it up over her head, her leering smile saying what she really wanted for it.

In one move, Gray stood up, snatched the warrant out of her hand, shifted his chair a fraction and sat back down. "I'll tell you what I won't give you, Lindsey, I won't swat that big behind of yours. Now skedaddle." Gray shooed her with his hand.

Surprised, full figured Lindsey wasn't used to being shot down by men. She had thought she'd been wearing him down pursuing him blatantly for weeks, that now he must be ready to give in to her charms.

She leaned in at him. Coyly, she said, "Actually Gray, a spanking might just be the thing…" she ran a hand down his chest. "Maybe you can show me what those big muscles can do for me."

His attention on the warrant, Gray pushed her hand away like it was a pesky fly.

"Hey," affronted at the rejection, Lindsey started to talk but already slightly off balance sitting on the edge of the desk, when Gray gave her hand that little push, it caused her to slide to the side of his desk- if she didn't stand up she'd fall off and land on the floor.

She flailed for a second then scolded him, "Grayson Whitewolf! You're gonna be sorry you turned me dow-"

Gray looked around her to Rick. "Yeah, Rick, what is it?"

Muzzling his mirth at the hapless deputy, Rick stepped around her to talk to Gray. Shooting Rick a wrathful pout, Lindsey stormed off fuming.

"Laugh all you want, boyo, you'll be next on her menu," Gray warned.

This time Rick did laugh. "Oh I can hardly wait. You think she'll dig these tats and shaved head?"

"Sure, she'll think you're all the more badass for them. That's what turns her on. Bad boys and muscles. Those bench-pressing arms should do the trick. Maybe it's that Mr. 305 Pitbull thing you got going on, except you're like twice his size. Too bad you can't sing. You might need to shave that gnarly little soul patch though. So, what you got?" Gray settled back in his cushioned chair on wheels.

"You're a funny guy, hotcheeks," Rick said with a grin, sitting on the corner of Gray's desk. The mirth was eclipsed by a serious countenance. "You ain't gonna believe this, but the Assistant ME came back with the old lady's COD, Mrs. Goldbrooke. It was murder."

"Whoa, no kidding?" Gray wasn't shocked, but still, it was shocking. "I thought it could be. I mean, these past few years she's been fit as a fiddle, then I come around asking questions and she's dead before I can get to her. What'd Doc Klaus have to say?"

157

Rick crossed his arms, one foot on the floor, the other dangled. "Her neck was broken before she fell down the stairs. He said it looks weird, like she fell down the stairs, then her neck was broken, then she fell down the stairs again." A brow quirked in the oddness of it.

"There were bruises and cuts and stuff from the fall, but some wounds had bruised or bled and others hadn't so they occurred after she was dead. He said there were other signs, but it was definitely murder." He let the words soak in for a minute.

Gray crossed a leg over a knee, clasped his hands behind his head and leaned back. "What a bitch of a death. Poor old thing. I had this itch about the fact that she wasn't questioned, and the house and land not searched and it was so near where the Kenton girls had disappeared."

He thought some more. "But, how did anyone know that I was asking questions? I only briefly spoke with her on the phone."

Rick watched Gray's mind work until Gray squinted and sat forward so fast his chair jerked.

"What?" Rick asked.

Jumping to his feet, Gray yanked his phone out of his pocket and started dialing while walking. "I've got to get to the caretaker."

"I'm coming with you." Rick boogied quickly to his desk, opened a drawer, took out his gun and stuck it in the holster then jogged out after Gray who was already running down the stairs.

In the truck, Gray turned on the lights and siren and blazed like the speed of light down the highway.

"She's not answering her phone," Gray said to Rick then filled him in.

"There's something going on with the old lady and that nurse Bradshaw, they know something, I can just feel it. I believe that Mrs. Goldbrooke was killed for what she knew." He glanced at Rick then back to the road.

"The other thing is, I remember that Mrs. Goldbrooke said she didn't want to talk to me until the next day when her nurse would be there. So Bradshaw knew I was coming to ask questions about the Kentons. Plus, the day I spoke with the nurse, she was on pins and needles the whole time I was at her house."

"It doesn't make any sense, Gray, two defenseless females? I mean Goldbrooke was 72 at the time, and you said the nurse was much more overweight at the time of the girls' attack. They couldn't have had anything to do with the children going missing, could they? And why?"

Rick shook his head, muddling the thoughts around. A CZ 712 Utility semi-automatic shotgun braced on the rear window jiggled behind their heads.

Gray shrugged one shoulder. "Who knows. I don't think so. But they coulda seen something, heard something. Maybe someone was worried I would refresh their memories and something would pop."

He pulled hard on the wheel and skidded off the main highway to the bumpy two-lane road that led to the other side of town.

Rick threw out his arms to grab the dashboard. "Geeze, hotcheeks, take it easy, this ain't Daytona for God's sake."

Not taking his eyes off the road, Gray gripped the wheel with both hands, the speedometer was pushing 100. He said with a small tight smile, "I told you to put your seatbelt on."

A few miles later, he yanked the wheel again speeding off the jutting two-lane, forging back to a smoother paved four-lane road.

The siren wailed, the lights flashed blue and white like strobe lights, the truck raced down the road like it had wings.

"Should I call for back-up?" Already hitting his bald head on the ceiling from the rough road they had been on, Rick cinched his seatbelt on, held onto the hand grip over the side window and reached for the radio with his other.

"No. I don't want to pull deputies off the streets if it's just my overworked imagination. We're almost there."

The trees a green blur as they sped past, the men's heads jumped and rocked, the speedometer was passing 110. They left the main part of the city behind and were aiming for the suburbs.

"Bro, this thing hustles," Rick remarked in awe, his burly arm now braced against the side window. "I haven't been in this one yet. I guess you got this right after you totaled the F250 in that carjacking chase. This makes the F250 seem like a turtle. What's in it?"

Gray turned another corner and was hurtling down Brenda Bradshaw's wide street with the big rich houses and manicured green acres studded with enormous maple trees.

"I'll show you later." Unbuckling his seatbelt, he hardly slowed then jerked the wheel again into a skid up the nurse's long driveway to come to a squealing stop inches from the house.

Both men hopped out and ran to the house. Rick banged on the front door and rang the bell while Gray ran first to the garage and looked in the small rectangle windows. A silver BMW was inside.

Taking off around the house to the back, Gray yelled, "I think she's home, car in the garage!" Hitting on windows and a side door as he went along the back, he took out his phone and speed-dialed Rick.

Rick answered, breathing hard, "Nothing."

Gray could hear the deputy banging on the front door and yelling, "Police! Open up!" They were going to have a lot to apologize for if the lady was home and safe. But the itch intensified as they got no response. Gray made his way around the big house looking for a way in.

He reached the pool and patio that was fenced in. He hopped the fence and sprinted up to the door leading from the family room to the patio. He could still hear Rick yelling and pounding so he was spurred to move faster.

Gray ran up to the door, knocked, tried the knob it was locked. He jumped at the door, kicking it open. The door banged against the wall and rebounded right back- Gray blocked it with his forearm and kept going through.

He muttered into his phone, "I'm in."

As he shot through the house, Gray pulled out his firearm and called out Miss Bradshaw's name until he got to the front and let Rick in.

As he stepped inside, Rick noticed an open purse and keys on a table next to the door. Using one finger, he pulled the purse open further. "Wallet, I can see some loose bills, and a phone. Looks like she is home."

"You go south, I got north. If clear, the same upstairs," Gray said while moving. The men split off.

They each moved stealthily through the house checking each room, they no longer called out the nurse's name. If the noise they'd made gaining entrance hadn't woken her, nothing would.

The first floor was cleared and they moved quietly, nimbly up the carpeted stairs. On the second landing they split again.

As he slipped into one bedroom after another, Gray could hear Rick throwing open doors down the hall. Gray moved swiftly through each room, checked closets and under the beds then back out to the next, into bathrooms, checking showers, even linen closets.

Moments later they met back at the top of the stairs.

"She's not here," Rick said, huffing, his weapon in his hand. Sweat trickled down the side of his shaved head. He ran a knuckle across the damp soul patch.

His legs akimbo, Gray shoved his gun in the holster at his side and set his hands on his hips. He drew his fingers through his black hair. Turning his face up to the ceiling, he deliberated, replaying the file and the conversations he'd had this past week.

"Come on, bro, she's not here. Your radar is off. It's okay, it happens to all of us at one time or-" Rick broke off as Gray suddenly took off down the stairs. "Hey! Where you goin'?" Sighing, he ran after him.

At the first floor, Gray kept rushing through the foyer, down one hall then through the kitchen to the back.

Rick was at his heels. "What, Gray, man, what're you doing, we checked the kitchen."

On the table in the kitchen was a sandwich with one bite taken out and a tea cup filled with tea. A sweater was draped around a chair that was moved out from the table, the other three chairs were still tucked in around the table.

"She was alone," Rick mumbled, as he stuck a finger in the tea, it had cooled.

Gray stopped abruptly. "Over here, Rick. What're we, rookies?" He pointed at the cellar door.

The sliver of a door was in matching off-white paint of the kitchen and was just behind a protruding wall, almost invisible which is why they had missed it.

"Aw geeze." Rick shook his head. "Let's go."

Gray opened the door and patted around the inside walls for a light. He found a switch, flicked it a couple of times, nothing happened. He pulled a small penlight off his belt and turned it on.

He shined it down the stairs then swept it back and forth at the bottom, but there was little to see. The basement was a total black-out. Gray started down the stairs.

Behind him, Rick took out his own police-issued flashlight and followed, muttering under his breath, "Yeah, this is when in the movies the alien, or zombie, or gigantic spider is lurking in the dark and reaches out and-"

"Shut up, Rick," Gray growled, stepped cautiously, slowly.

"It's all right, I scared myself." Rick chuckled quietly behind him. Their boots a muffled tapping on the steps, the men moved like molasses until they reached the bottom. The basement split off at the end of the stairs.

"This time I think we should stay together, we can't see a damned thing and we could shoot each other in the dark," Gray said in a low voice. He shined the flashlight around, it was small though and only lit at a distance of a few feet.

"These tiny torches suck," he complained to Rick. He started walking to the left, he could hear Rick's breathing right behind him and he could see the beam from Rick's flashlight picking out cardboard boxes in a pile against a wall and a workbench beside them.

"You stay here, I'll take a look behind the boxes," Rick said and moved into the dark. While Rick checked out the boxes, Gray could see his flashlight bobbing and scrolling along the wall, up and down, sometimes disappearing entirely.

Meanwhile, Gray moved his meager light across the floor, over to the side where there was a washer and drier, laundry baskets, a double iron sink and a clothesline stretched from one wooden beam to another.

The setup looked new. He wondered why they hadn't made up this cellar as nice as the rest of the house, his light moved to a treadmill and a stationary bicycle.

A septic tank, water heater then he made out a workbench against the wall. There were tools laid out on the workbench but they were covered with dust, they hadn't been used in a good long while.

Gray figured Brenda Bradshaw probably bought the house from a family that had left some of their things, or she'd had a man at some point and had booted him.

Step-by-step, Gray moved slowly away from the group of boxes out to the center of the room, rolling his light up, down, back forth- up he swept the light across the rafters.

Then, "Aw hell." His discharge splintered into anger and resignation.

"What?" Rick called out.

Gray could hear him running to him. Stepping carefully, Rick stood beside Gray and followed the beam of his flashlight, it pointed up. To the ceiling, to the rafters.

"Oh my God, oh crap, damn," he sputtered, aiming his light up too.

Hanging from a cross-beam by a rope around her neck was Brenda Bradshaw. There was no air movement in the basement, her body hung still as a dead fly caught in a spider's web.

Rick yelled and started moving, "We need to get her down-"

"It's too late, she's gone, Rick. I'll call a bus. She's just evidence now. We need to locate her maid."

Gray could see the reflection of Brenda's blank opaque eyes in the flashlight's beam, they had already lost their color, their radiance. Her tongue hung out of her bloated face, and her head drooped oddly from her neck.

"Damn, Rick spat. He stood and stared uselessly up at the body.

Chapter Twenty-One

$\mathcal{L}$ater in the afternoon the next day, Kessa had just chatted with her brother on the phone.

Not wanting him to worry when he was too far away to do anything, she told him all was fine, and when is he coming home? He told her a few more weeks at least. They visited for half an hour, an expensive call and then hung up.

As soon as she hung the phone up it rang again. She answered right away, thinking it was Matthew again. "Hello? Matthew?"

"Hey, um, this is ah, Gray, Grayson Whitewolf." The now familiar, deeply masculine, but not loud voice came through the phone line.

Kessa slapped a hand over her mouth. *Oh no, not him.* She didn't say anything.

"Ah, you know," he said, "Deputy Whitewolf, your brother's friend."

Kessa said tightly into the phone, "I know who you are. How can I help you?" Her lips pursed, then she demanded, "Did Matthew tell you to call me, did he just speak with you?"

Gray could hear the tension in her voice. He cleared his throat. "No. It's been over a week since I've spoken with Matt. I'm calling you because, ah, well, maybe I came on a little too strong at the Wilton the other night. I can be a little hotheaded."

He paused as if to let her respond. When she didn't he went on.

"Maybe I should have just used the badge to make Jasper back off, but I've had run-ins with your brother-in-law before, he wouldn't have stopped hassling you if I'd only asked politely. It…it just twisted something in my gut seeing you so desperate to get out of his arms and he wouldn't let you go, treating you like a whore in public. I, ah, just wanted to, you know, apologize for acting like a- a barbarian, or-"

"I was thinking more like Genghis Kahn," she filled in.

He smiled, he could hear the humor in her voice. "Hey, that's okay, he was a good looking dude."

She choked. "Are you kidding? He was a bloodthirsty, vicious, lawless killer."

"Sure," he agreed, "but he was good looking. I've seen a few movies about him. Didn't John Wayne play him? And he got the skirt. He ended up with," he thought back. "I think it was Maureen O'Hara. Couldn't have been all that bad, huh?" He couldn't see her roll her eyes but he chuckled to himself knowing she was.

"You are incorrigible. Skirt? Seriously? I don't understand my genteel brother being friends with you," Kessa teased.

Now he choked. "Genteel? Matt? Girl, I could tell you some wild stories about your brother-" he broke off with a little laugh. "Uh, never mind. He'd kill me."

Kessa said with a fond smile, "I know my brother pretty well, nothing would surprise me. So, you called me because…"

"Uh, yeah. Actually," he paused. "I just wanted to make sure you were doing all right. I know it's tough being back here for you, and that crazy family of yours, except of course for Matt. Well, I guess I shouldn't disparage your family to you, that's ah, wrong. Anyway, I apologize again for being so heavy-handed. So, are we okay?"

Kessa nodded even though she knew he couldn't see her, just a habit. "Sure, yes, we're all right. You're Matthew's friend and I know you're looking out for me for him, and, I appreciate it. I do. Thank you."

"Okay, good, good," Gray said. "I guess that's all, just wanted to check on you." His voice turned slightly serious,

"Listen," he said mildly because she could be touchy. "I want you to contact me, any time, if you need help, day or night. I mean it. Please."

She didn't respond so he said, "Okay, well then, I'll see ya around, call me if you need me. Later babe."

Exasperated, Kessa said, "Don't call me-" he'd already hung up.

****

"Wake up Peter," Aria whined pushing him. She had been lying beside him until she couldn't stand his stupid snoring any longer. She pushed him harder.

"Huh, wha," Peter slobbered, eyelids flapping.

"Come on, get up," Aria huffed, rolling off her side of the bed to sit on the edge. Her bare legs dropped over the side. She sat in her underwear and one of Peter's undershirts.

She pitched back on her stomach and forearms and inched to her boyfriend. "I'm booored, Peter, bored to tears. We gotta go do something." She flipped over on her back and laid her head on Peter's stomach. Her head moved up and down with his breathing.

Peter shifted to sit up. He plumped a pillow behind him and leaned back.

Aria's head lurched with his movements. "Ow," she complained, "you have sharp hipbones." She wriggled to get back between his stomach and his ribs, not soft but there wasn't a bone jabbing her in the back of the head.

Peter reached over to a bedside table, picked up his pack of smokes and tapped one out. Sticking the cigarette between his lips, he flicked a light, pulled until it lit. He inhaled deeply then exhaled a plume of smoke.

Aria bent her head to look at him. "Cripes, Peter, you know mom will kill you for smoking in the house. She might even throw you out again."

He kept puffing. "Whatever. Who cares."

Aria watched him. His lean face, peanut colored sparse whiskers sprouted around his pointed jaw and sprinkled over his top lip. Hair like a camel's hung around his head in a messy nest.

Sighing, she settled back again. "I'm serious, Peter, I'm bored. We need to do something exciting. I wanna go do something now," she whined, bouncing her head up and down on his stomach.

Peter dropped a hand on her breast, his fingers splayed over it. "Sure doll." He squeezed her breast hard, smiled when she whimpered. "But we gotta do something else first."

He stubbed out his cigarette, blew out a lungful of smoke, pushed her off his stomach and rolled over on top of her.

Later, the pair was driving down the street in Aria's Lexus. In the passenger seat, Aria was looking out the window. Sighing she turned to her boyfriend. "Come on, Peter, let's do something."

His eyes on the road, Peter shrugged. "Whattaya wanna do?"

She'd been thinking about it. "Let's go rob some poor slobs. Let's do like we've been doing, when we hide in the park and then jump out at some lovers thinking they're alone and take 'em."

One of his shoulders jerked forward. "Whatever."

He slid a curious glance at her. "What is it with you, I mean robbing people. Your folks are loaded. They give you everything you want. Your allowance is automatically deposited into your account. You don't even have to have a job. Which is great, because it works for me, I don't have to work either."

He looked at the road then flicked back to her. "I mean, I don't care, I think it's funny, but what's your deal?"

Aria slumped in the seat then pulled her legs up so her feet were on the seat. "Like I said, I'm bored. I gotta do something to pass the time. I'm even bored with you, the drugs make you barely tolerable." He didn't care enough to be offended at her words.

Her feet dropped, she sat back up. "Okay, let's go to Lemintree Park."

Peter headed towards the park. Once inside, they parked right away.

As they got out of the car, Peter opened the glove box, took out a .38 and stuck it in the back of his pants, tucking it in the waistband.

Aria said, "Wait a sec," and she ran around to the trunk. Opening it, she took out a paper bag, closed the trunk then skipped back to Peter. Reaching into the bag, she twisted the top off and held the bottle in the bag to her lips and drank greedily.

Peter snatched the bag and top out of her hands. "Dammit, Ar, wait until we're in the damned bushes, you wanna get arrested?"

Screwing the lid back on the bottle, he stalked out of the parking lot and took off on a path for a few feet then disappeared into a thick hedge of bushes and trees. Aria ran after him giggling.

Walking through the undergrowth, they worked their way to a favorite area where they could hide without being in the thick of the bushes but had a good view of the path.

They could see when someone was coming and knew there was a clearing just on the other side of the path where a lot of young people came to make out.

Settling back against a tree, Peter twisted the top off the tequila and took a long swig. Wiping his mouth with his sleeve, he passed it to Aria, who duplicated his actions.

Fifteen or twenty minutes of drinking, they were heavy into their own make-out session, they almost didn't hear the couple coming up over the slight incline.

Aria was straddling Peter, sitting on his lap facing him when he suddenly shoved her off and rolled to his knees.

"Hey," Aria complained,

"Shh." Peter climbed to a crouch. He peered through the leaves. "We got us one."

Excited, Aria got on her knees and they both watched through the bushes as a couple, arm in arm, kissing while strolling came over the incline and swung off the path over towards the small clearing. The boy had a blanket under his arm, the girl carried a bottle of wine.

Peter whispered, "Oh goody, we got us a bottle of wine, too. I hope it's the good stuff, come on." He motioned to her. They climbed to their feet but walked bent over to stay hidden.

The couple, oblivious to anything but themselves, set the wine down and laid the blanket on the clearing then fell on it embracing, kissing and giggling.

Holding the gun out, Peter swaggered out from the bushes and over to the couple who were lying down now and peeling off each other's clothes.

"Hey there, you got a match?" Peter said.

Totally into themselves the couple didn't hear him, they just kept at it.

"Hey!" Peter shouted.

They froze, their heads popped up. "What the hell-" the surprised young man croaked, confused. Seeing the gun, his eyes bulged like satellite dishes and he sat up. The girl pulled her blouse closed.

"Okay, now you get the drift," Peter said, waggling the gun at the pair. "I want your money." The couple sat stunned, not moving.

"Now!" Peter barked low and loud and menacing. "Make it fast. I have no problem shooting one or both of you, so move it!"

Aria stood behind and to the side of him, a big excited grin on her face as she watched the incredulous couple.

Peter pointed the gun at the man. "Take out your wallet, toss it to the girl here," he nodded towards Aria.

"Why don't *you* drop *your* gun and put your hands over your head," a derisive voice said from behind them. "You're under arrest."

Before Peter and Aria swung around they saw smug looks on the couple's faces. They realized now weren't as young as they had first thought. Peter dropped the gun immediately.

"You're cops?" Aria blathered stupidly, staring at the couple, not believing they were caught in a sting.

The man stood up and helped the female to her feet. He said, "Yup. How moronic is it that you two keep returning to the same place to rob young, romantic couples?"

The girl laughed. "Yeah, like duh. You two have to be the dumbest thieves ever!"

The man went over to them and pushed Peter, turning him around and handcuffed him. Then he did the same to Aria who stood with her mouth open still not believing they were caught.

The man said, "It's the drugs you dopes. Dopes doing dope make you dopes and you make dumb mistakes." He gave Peter a little shove. "Let's go, I'm gonna read you your rights."

Peter and Aria now saw the two uniformed policemen that had been standing behind them when they turned around.

All four police officers marched Peter and Aria back up the path as the first officer read them their rights.

Chapter Twenty-Two

$\mathcal{K}$essa had just come in from a run and the phone was ringing. It was Matthew's landline. She wasn't sure she should or wanted to answer it.

She set her water bottle and keys on the table by the door and went into the kitchen and stared at the phone. It kept ringing, didn't go to voice mail. She realized she hadn't set the voice mail up after she went to the hospital the other night.

She had been so mad when she got home about her mother forcing her into a date with that doctor she'd unplugged the phone. She'd plugged it back in this morning as it's Matthew's phone and she felt she shouldn't be messing with it. In fact, maybe that was Matthew calling.

She snatched it up. "Hello?"

"Faith, it that you?"

"No," she said placidly, "this is Kessa."

"Whatever, listen Kessa, it's Aria," she said breathless, like she only had a short time to talk. "Listen, I'm, uh, I'm in jail and I need-"

"What? You're where?" Kessa said astounded, then waited thinking undoubtedly it's a joke.

"Yeah, yeah. Now listen, I only have a minute. I need you to come bail me out. As soon as you can."

Kessa thought for a second, trying to sort out what she meant. "You mean you were arrested? For what?"

"OMG, really, Kessa, it doesn't matter what we were arrested for, you need to come and bail me out." Aria sounded angry, like she was talking to a dull-witted child.

Kessa held the phone out in front of her, looked at it thinking, *I should just hang this up, she can't call back, she only gets one phone call, at least that's what they say on TV…*

"What do you mean *we*?" she asked. She could hear Aria take a deep breath then sigh loudly, annoyed.

"Gimme a break, who do ya think. Me and Peter. His bond is astronomical 'cause he has a big time record and he was holding the gun. You need to just-"

"Gun? What? Why don't you call the folks? Why are you calling me?" Kessa asked. She heard the big loud sigh again.

"Because the last time they bailed me out they said it was the last time." Her hard swallow was audible.

"Listen, you're my damned sister, you owe me. You left us all hanging, we had to suffer. You don't know what we had to go through, me and Char and Matt. You don't know, Faith, you weren't here."

Her voice softened. "Dad just fell apart after…afterwards. He felt so guilty because of his affairs. He felt if he had not been out running around he would have been home to have, you know, rescued us or whatever. Mother, well she," Aria laughed a harsh, short, ugly sound.

"She blamed Dad too, and she blamed Char 'cause Char was the one that took you all out there. And," she sighed, "she blamed me 'cause if I wasn't out sluttin' around and getting high, well, I'da been there. She even blamed Matt. I mean he was barely 13, what could he have done?"

Kessa sat silently listening. It continued to drive home that she wasn't the only one that had suffered through a tough time.

"Yeah," Aria laughed harshly again. "You know mainly she blamed you, and of course she didn't blame herself even a little. No, just because she was always at the Club or shopping and not with us, well, apparently that was our fault for being so annoying she had to get out of the house. Can you believe that? Can you believe she said that?" She sounded angry but also very sad, and lonely.

Kessa still just listened, made no comment.

"So, are you there Fa- Kessa?" Aria asked worried.

"Yes," Kessa answered.

A tiny sniff came through the wires. "Well, I'm sorry I said what I said about you. I know how bad it was for you. When we were older Matt would write with you and then tell us how bad you had it. We were all just," her voice trailed wistfully.

"Well, since you weren't around we could imagine you were like a princess off in a far-away land. We, Char and me, used to talk about how someday you'd come back wealthy and beautiful and whisk us up and take us...away...to...I don't know, paradise where there was just all love and happiness and nice crap like that."

Kessa wiped at her eyes.

Aria chuckled weakly. "Well, you did come back beautiful, there's no doubt about that. Matt told us about your books and says you're doing really good, you know, successful. Seriously, Fa- Kessa, sorry. We're kind of proud of you-" her words broke off uncomfortably.

"Aria..."

Aria laughed again. "Okay, don't get me wrong, we're jealous as hell and hate you for leaving, but..." she trailed, "we're proud of you too." Her sniffing was louder. "So, are you gonna-" the line suddenly went dead.

"Hello? Hello?" Kessa said into the phone. The dial tone came on, she hung up. "Well then, what do I do now?"

Dehydrated from her run, she walked to the sink poured a glass of water and drank it down then headed for the bathroom to take a shower. She could think about what to do while soaking.

An hour later, her hair still a little damp from the shower, Kessa dressed in slacks, heels and a short-sleeved light sweater. She looked up the jail on the internet. It was part of the main sheriff's station in the center of town. She slid into the car and put the address in the GPS and took off.

It was difficult to figure out how to park, everything was metered where you got a ticket and then had to find a station to pay when you were done.

She put the ticket in her purse and found her way to the jail. Inside, they told her she needed to go next door to the sheriff's office to fill out the paperwork. Finding out how to get there, Kessa made her way inside the station and to the proper bond counter.

She requested, received and filled out the paperwork using her credit card for the bail. They told her to have a seat and wait.

She sat in a waiting area and pulled out her phone. She had books saved on it. Pulling up one that she had been in the middle of reading last week, she settled back to read.

After a few minutes, a shadow fell over her. She looked up. It was Sheriff James Lombardo. She clicked off the phone and slipped it in her purse.

He had her at a disadvantage because he stood so very close right in front of her, she couldn't stand, she had to crane her neck back and look up at him like a child to an adult.

"Well, I'll be, it's little Faith Kenton come home to roost," Jimmy drawled. "Well, look at you, the rumors about your looks are dang true, girl." He studied her from head to foot then stepped back. "Git up on there, girl, come on into my office, let's get caught up."

Kessa didn't move. She remembered the last time she was alone with Jimmy Lombardo. He'd hit her. He'd forced her to confess to something she didn't do. She refused to cower, but it was all she could do to keep her back straight and look him in the eye.

"You still deaf, girl? I'm thinking you're here to bail out that scum of a sister of yours, arrested again, the little thug. Well, it's going to be a while before she's released, come in and visit."

When she didn't move, his eyes narrowed. Grey brows knit, he looked like a malevolent Santa Claus, except with thinning still brown hair.

He leaned over and said quietly, "You get up and you come with me or so help me God, it'll be years before you see that sister of yours again."

His big belly rolled over his belt. He stood back up, his fixed gaze tyrannical, coarse and devoid of compassion.

People moved all around the station, some hurried, some wandered, a man was being arrested, an officer hauled him across the room in handcuffs.

There was a constant clomp of boots, shoes and sandals, people chattering with others they knew, a lady was yelling at a woman sitting at a desk. For a small town it was rather chaotic in the station.

Hating to feel intimidated by the big man, Kessa could just walk out. But then could he cause Aria harm? Deny her bond? She took a deep, silent breath, clutched her purse and stood up.

He smiled at her. "There now, that's a good girl. You come with me and I'll see what I can do about getting' your sister released, later. It's all up to me, you know. Now, follow me."

He took a few steps then stopped and looked back at her. "I said now," he barked with a mean scowl.

Letting out the breath she was holding, Kessa walked with wooden legs beside the hefty sheriff. They went through a second metal detector and down a long hall. He turned into an office.

"In here," he said over his shoulder.

They walked past his secretary who eyed Kessa curiously but said nothing. Lombardo went to a door and opened it, stood aside and gestured for Kessa to go in.

Once she passed the threshold, Lombardo said to his secretary, "No calls, don't disturb me for nuthin'." He ignored her even more curious expression that was quickly followed by a knowing sly look. He followed Kessa into the office and closed the door behind him.

"Go on, have a seat." Jimmy pointed at a couch that was against one wall.

Two chairs were in front of his desk, and three others were at a round table in front of a corner window.

Kessa went and sat at one of the chairs near the window.

Jimmy shook his head, tossing his keys on his desk. "You still don't do what you're told, do you?"

He took a few heavy steps towards her, stopped right in front of her and ogled her breasts. "I always liked those thin sweaters you girls wear, they show your jugs loose and tight at the same time." His hand brushed the front of his trousers.

Kessa kept her face impassive, not letting him see she was scared to death. She stood up. "I haven't done anything wrong, Sheriff. You can't keep me here. I'm leav-"

"Sit down!" he bellowed and pushed her so she fell back on the chair.

Startled, Kessa jumped back up, but the sheriff towered over her, he was pulling his handcuffs out from the back of his belt.

"I'll show you, girl, how to learn to obey what I say, the first time I say it." He reached out to grab her, she ducked out of his reach and darted to the side.

"You're only going to make me mad, girl, and it'll just be harder for you, harder on you that is. Now come here." He started towards her, she ran for the door but he was fast for a heavy man, he got there first and slammed his hand against the door, holding it closed.

Hating herself for backing away from him, she wanted to be out of his reach. Then anger pushed aside the fear, Kessa demanded, "You let me out right now or I'll- I'll scream."

She knew there was no way she could win in a tussle with the big man. There were thick muscles under the fat, and he was a good foot taller than her.

She shook her head, she couldn't believe she might not be able to fight off this man, would he really...beat her? Frightful chills ran up her arms.

Jimmy laughed. "Honey, go ahead and holler," he told her while unbuckling his belt. "Macy out there has heard it all and she has orders to mind her own beeswax. And, you just try and complain, girl, I'm the law in this town."

"Ask around what happens to women who try to file a complaint, or refuse to…cooperate with me. Now, it'll be easier on you if you don't fight me. But then again, a little struggling excites me. Just don't blame me later for any bruises."

His intent finally dawned on Kessa, she was struck with a new terror.

He shrugged, his immoral mouth curled into a carnal leer.

"Usually a few whips from my belt calms you more reluctant girls down. C'mere," he took a sudden step at her. She wasn't expecting it- his hand snaked out and grasped her arm, he pulled her to him.

He had the handcuffs in the other hand, he snapped them open ready to slap on her wrist. "I'm gonna teach you a lesson girl." She twisted hard and with a curse he dropped the handcuffs trying to hold onto her.

"You little bitch-" He raised a beefy hand to slap her, but put it against her neck instead and shoved her back against the wall.

Her head hit the wall. He pressed his beefy palm hard against her neck cutting off her breath and holding her imprisoned. Quickly growing lightheaded, Kessa desperately clawed at his hands.

"This'll take the fight out of you. Don't get mad at me, you're making me do it this way. Another second and you'll be as malleable as a lamb, them legs'll open right up-"

The door flung open so suddenly Lombardo dropped his hands and stepped back from Kessa.

Her hands flew to her neck. Gasping and blinking, dizzy, Kessa floundered, trying to steady herself against the wall.

Grayson Whitewolf stood in the doorway. He moved quickly to Kessa and wrapped an arm around her shoulders to support her.

His face burning red with rage, he roared, "What the hell is going on here?" Not in his normal all black or uniform, he stood in khakis and a buttoned down, long-sleeved white shirt.

Lombardo nonchalantly kicked his handcuffs to the side and trod to his desk. Picking up a half-smoked cigar out of the ashtray he grabbed his lighter.

Stuffing the cigar in his mouth, he said, "Aren't you supposed to be in a meeting? The lady and I were just having chat. She came in here willingly. Wanted to talk about her…sister." The threat hung clearly, he lit the cigar, took a couple of puffs. "Didn't ya, honey?"

Kessa's eyes were so wide the whites shone clear around like whitewalls on tires. Her mouth dropped open then snapped closed.

"Yes," she took a jagged breath, "the- there's nothing going on." Her raspy voice was weak and shaky.

Grayson still held her trembling body, his arm tightened. Eyes narrowed to hard slits, his voice dangerously low, hard, husky, he said to Lombardo, "You know you're coming to the end, *Sheriff*." He said sheriff like it was a filthy word.

Lombardo puffed on his cigar, took it out, held it up, looked at it, then stuffed it back in. "Don't you threaten me, boy. Don't you forget I'm your boss. You'd 'a been out on your ass already if you weren't in the governor's pocket."

He pulled the cigar out. Brows slashed down, his hooded eyes contemptible, he sneered, "It's you, boy, that'll be out. Now get the hell out of my office. Both of you." He turned his back on them and made his way behind his desk.

Gray stalked over and snatched Kessa's purse off the table and handed it to her. He set a hand on her lower back and led her to the door. As Kessa went out the door, Gray turned back.

His face seething, he said in a stone-cold promise, "You ever touch her again, you're a dead man." He let the words hang in the air, then closed the door.

"Come on," he said to Kessa holding her arm just above the elbow. They walked past Macy who sat with her mouth hanging like a panting dog. She didn't say a word as they left. She jumped when she heard something hit the wall inside the sheriff's office. Her phone rang.

She looked at it, it was the sheriff. She knew there would be trouble the minute Grayson Whitewolf ignored her objections and stalked right past her into the sheriff's office. Last thing she wanted to do was answer it, but she knew better. "Hello?" she said anxiously.

"Call Nefertiti, tell her to come now!" Jimmy yelled into the phone.

Oh dear. "Uh, she's uh, I know she's out of town seeing her sick sister. Mina Mulligen down at the salon said-"

"Then get me Sally! Now!" he screamed and slammed the phone down.

Back out to the main lobby of the station, still gathering her composure, Kessa asked Gray, "How did you know I was, I mean, why did you come in there? He said his secretary wouldn't let anyone-"

Pushing his glowering brows back up, Gray said, "I heard you were here trying to bond your sister out. They told me you'd gone off with that damned snake. That could only mean one thing. Thank God he didn't lock the door, it would have looked really bad if I had to kick it in."

"I see. Watching out for your friend's little sister, that's nice. I...thank you. I know Matthew will be really grateful to you for doing this for him." She took a breath, "My sister-"

Gray ran a hand over his face. "Don't worry about Aria. The paperwork's done. She'll be released on bond but it'll take hours before she's out."

Kessa stood silently, her arms wrapped tightly around her body, obviously unnerved and desperately trying to pull herself together.

Gray gently grasped her arm. "Come on, I'll take you to your car. I can take care of the parking tab, give me your ticket."

Hands still shaking, Kessa pulled her ticket out of her purse and gratefully handed it to him. "Thank you, Deputy. I can't even fathom at the moment trying to figure out the payment system."

Smiling, he took the ticket and stuck it in his shirt pocket.

"I'll see that Aria gets a ride home after she bonds out. You need to get the hell out of here."

He walked her to her car and waited until she drove out of the lot before heading back inside.

Chapter Twenty~Three

Gray waited at the Mesa Diner for Rick. He had scarfed down a burger, tipped up his glass to drain the rest of the soda and was finishing his fries when Rick came in.

"Hey," Gray greeted him through a stack of fries he shoved in his mouth all at once.

Rick sat on the stool next to him. "Bro, that stuff's gonna kill ya." He patted his abs. "I just had a salad with baked chicken and a green tea. You have to take care of yourself."

Gray lifted up the bottom of his shirt to expose his own chiseled 6-pack, said while chewing, "You eat your bunny food and I'll take care of myself."

Rick cut a hand at the server as she approached. "We're leaving." He turned to Gray as the deputy was swiping the last two fries through a pile of catsup and stuck them in his mouth.

"What we both need is a steady girl. Women make sure we eat right, clean our clothes so they don't shrink or turn pink, besides the other, um, things they do for us. It's time to settle down, I think I'm ready. I want a girl that's nice deep inside but has a little edge. What about you?"

The server wrote on a pad, tore a check off and set it on the counter next to Gray's plate. "There ya go, hon, come back soon." She fluffed her curly brown hair and winked a brown eye at him. She sashayed away, swinging her hips.

"Not her," Rick advised. "Someone younger, better looking, and a really nice girl." Both men wore jeans and long sleeved thermals with the sleeves rolled up and braced their brawny forearms on the counter.

Gray licked his fingers then wiped them on his napkin and tossed the napkin on the counter. He picked up his check, put some money with it, set more dollars on the counter for a tip and slid off his stool.

"I'm fine the way I am. I don't need a woman to do those things I can do for myself. Besides, I've got Mrs. Butler comes in once a week to clean. What else do I need?"

"Sure." Rick looked at Gray's socks, they were both dark but slightly different shades. "You're doing just fine." Rick rolled his eyes.

"Seriously, Gray, don't you want to come home at night and someone who really cares about you and wants to be with you is there waiting for you, all soft and seductive?"

Gray scooped his keys up off the counter. "No. Last thing I want is some dame sitting on my couch drinking my bourbon, whining, and with her hand out for money, telling me what to do, where to go, who I can see. No thank you. It's easier my way."

Shaking his head, Rick said, "You're not seeing it the right way. You're thinking about the...kinds of women that you see. You need to find yourself a nice-"

"I don't want nice, Rick. Nice girls expect me to be nice too. And I'm not. Let's go." Gray turned and headed towards the door. Rick followed him.

Gray dropped the check and dollars on the cash counter and the two men left the diner and went to their vehicles. With Rick right behind him, Gray drove through town and to a seedier side of the city.

Down a street with uncut weedy lawns, old cars parked in torn up driveways of dilapidated apartments, Gray pulled over and parked in front of one of the apartments, Rick parked behind him.

The two men got out and went up to the building. Gray pushed a doorbell. They could hear it ring inside.

A young woman came to the door dressed in holey shorts and a sleeveless top. Disheveled red hair framed a pasty white face sprinkled with freckles and light brown eyes. Way too lean, the girl opened the door and the men went inside.

In the two room apartment, cigarette smoke hung heavy over a worn sofa and a worse carpet. The girl plodded over in bare feet and plopped down on the sofa that was covered in tiny flowers.

Gray sat next to her and Rick settled down on an old ratty easy chair. The curtains were drawn over the only window making the room dark and dingy.

A crucifix hung over the door to the small kitchen, otherwise the room was fairly empty except for some lamps, a handful of empty beer cans on the coffee table, candybar wrappers and magazines, cigarettes and ashtrays.

Gray said, "That's Rick," he jabbed a thumb in his direction. "So, Nefertiti, how're you doing?" He leaned back, one arm along the back of the couch and crossed his legs.

The girl pulled up skinny white legs and crossed them tailor-style on the couch. She picked up the pack of cigarettes, shook one out and went to light it. Gray pulled out a lighter and lit it for her. Then he took a cigarette from her pack, stuck it in his mouth and lit it.

"Damn, Gray, burgers *and* smoking?" Rick chided.

Gray peered at his friend through a veil of spiraling smoke. He sucked in then exhaled a grey cloud. "I quit, I just smoke once in a while."

"That's not called quitting, dude," Rick said sarcastically.

"Anyway," Gray held the cigarette between his second finger and thumb, curled it inside his palm. "What's going on, Nef-" he took a drag, squinted at the girl as he exhaled. "What is your real name? Is it Nefertiti?" He already knew of course but wanted to see what she would tell him.

One corner of the redhead's mouth turned up. "No, I think it makes me more, mysterious and exotic. It's really Donna. Donna Brown. How boring is that?" Her smile showed several crooked teeth. She leaned forward and tapped her ash into the ashtray on the table.

"Uh huh," Gray grunted noncommittally. "Whatcha got for me?"

"So, I heard they're opening the bar up extra early on Thursday. That's what they do when they're expecting a shipment." She sucked on her cigarette then blew out a stream of smoke, coughed. It sounded like her ribs were rattling.

Gray glanced at Rick. "Okay, that's great. This time I'll be prepared. Did you know there's a tunnel that goes into the basement in the back wooded area of the bar?" he asked the girl.

She looked surprised, shook her head. "No, really?" She thought about it. "So that's how they do it. That's why I've seen huge amounts of drugs get dispersed but I've never seen how they get there. Go figure."

Her arm in her lap, she set an elbow on the arm so she could hold the cigarette next to her lips. "Hey," she said, a slight animation to her wasted face. "I dodged a bullet the other night." She grinned, took a drag.

Gray swung his head at her. "What do you mean? A bullet? Are you-" he leaned towards her concerned.

"No, no, not a real bullet, silly. It's a figure of speech." She tapped his knee, laughing a little. Her teeth were still white but they were starting to have a yellowish glow to them. "No, it was," she glanced at Rick.

"He's okay," Gray said.

"Okay. It was Jimmy." She scowled, her expression darkened. "That pig. Takes it for free all the time like I'm his wife or something. And he's real rough, doesn't care if he hurts me..." she trailed off, looking down at a bruise on her arm then her eyes went vacant.

Gray put both feet on the floor and bent towards her, his hand on her leg. "What are you saying, Donna? I can go after him, what did he do to you?" He pushed back a lock of his black hair that had grown long enough to flop over one eye.

Donna blinked pale brown eyes then smiled half-heartedly at him. "It's okay, Gray. It's how I make my living. We've discussed this before. I don't want to quit, not yet anyway. He's not really much worse than some of the others. But what he did to Sally-"

"What?" Gray shot out. "What did the son of a bitch do to her?"

Donna pulled her lips in, crossed her arms. "I tell you, you have to promise to not do anything about it. It only makes it worse. I mean it. Promise." Faded eyes chastened him.

Gray's jaw clamped, the planes of his face sharpened, the dark blue eyes hardened. "Just tell me, Donna."

Sighing, Donna took a drag. "Well," she exhaled, watched the vapor float away and dissipate. "Apparently, he had this girl, not one of us, not a hooker, but a regular girl. I heard she was smokin', long super light blonde hair, unusual colored eyes but really pretty, long legs, and nice- you know what Jimmy likes," she held her hands under her breasts and pushed them up.

Gray leaned back against the arm of the sofa. "Go on," he told her.

"Anyway," she stubbed out the cigarette, "supposedly he was getting hot and heavy with her when something happened. I don't know what, but like someone interrupted them or something, but whatever it was, he didn't get her. And," her red brows rose sky high.

"Was he pissed. I mean, in a blind rage I heard. Anyways, he sent for me, but thank *God* I wasn't around, so he got Sally instead. And," she peeped sideways at Gray. The vein at his temple pulsed, his hands were clenched in fists on his knees. "Uh," she backed off.

"Just tell us, Donna. He's going to get his, soon, don't worry. We won't do anything now, right Gray?" Rick offered from the side of the room.

Gray stared at her, his jaw flexing.

Donna grew uncomfortable, squirmed. "Okay, I saw Sally yesterday, at the hospital. Jimmy was so steamed she said, he was out of control. Beat her with his belt, and fists," her eyes dropped from Gray's. "Afterwards, she was in pretty bad shape. At first she was mad at me that it wouldn't have happened to her if I'd been around." She held up a small hand and picked at her nails.

"Anyway," she set her hand on his leg again, pleaded with apathetic eyes. "Please don't do anything. You promised. Like I said, every time you go all vigilante we get hurt worse." She flapped her lids at him while he struggled with his rage.

"Just, stick with the drugs. I'll keep telling you when they're comin' in, eventually you take out whoever is dealing them and then maybe other things will lighten up, you know?" She picked up the pack of cigarettes and tapped out another one. Gray absently lit it for her.

He stood up. "I'm a cop, Donna, it's not vigilante when it's my job. Well," his voice craggy, Gray said through grinding teeth, "thanks for the info."

Rick stood up as well and stretched.

Gray pulled out some bills, peeled off a bunch and handed them to the girl.

She took them and rolled them up in her hand.

He said firmly but kind, "Try to stay out of that asshole's way, honey. Call me if you need to, you know that, right?"

She nodded.

Outside, Rick said, "Where are we going now?"

Hopping in his truck, Gray muttered through clenched teeth, "The hospital."

They saw Sally. She had told the doctors she'd fallen down the stairs. They didn't believe her but what could they do?

Covered in bruises, she had two black eyes, her arm was in a sling and she was lying half on her side because she said most of her backside was…damaged.

When Gray suggested filing charges or anything else, she got very upset. Begged the deputies to mind their own business. A doctor came in and asked them to leave.

Walking down the tiled floor of the hospital, his hands in his pockets, Rick said, "It's sad, Gray. Those girls are barely past 18 and they both look 10 years older. It's a hard life."

Gray's hands were tucked in his pockets too, his shoulders hunched. "I've talked to them until I'm blue in the face, but they won't leave the life. Arresting them only makes things harder on them. Their pimps are bad enough, but that bastard Lombardo," his hands balled into fists again, he spoke through grit teeth.

"The girls tie my hands, they plead with me to leave him alone, but-"

"You have to let it go for now, Gray. We'll get him. It'll just take time," Rick consoled him. "Look out!" He yelled as a young man came careening around the corner. All three men came to an abrupt stop.

"You need to slow down, fella." Rick admonished the man.

The young man was scowling but then he saw Gray's badge on his belt, his eyes raised to Gray's face, slight recognition appeared. "Hey, aren't you, Whitewolf, Deputy Whitewolf?"

Gray set his hands on his hips. "Yes, I am."

The man suddenly looked nervous, his eyes darted up and down the hall like he was afraid he was going to be caught at something. He pulled off his green, Oakland A's baseball cap and ran a hand over his crew cut while quickly glancing around the entire area.

He said, "You uh, you probably don't remember, but you arrested me back a few years ago, for DUI." He shoved the hat back on, pulling the bill down low over his face

Gray stood mute. Beside him, Rick set a hand surreptitiously on his holstered gun. The kid could be out for retaliation.

"It's not about that, dude. It's about my aunt, Brenda Bradshaw. I'm Brent Bradshaw, her nephew," the guy said, keeping his voice so low they could hardly hear him.

A sympathetic brow arched. "Oh?" was all Gray said.

Rick's hand on his gun relaxed slightly.

"Yeah." Brent twisted his head this way and that way, looking up and down the halls and behind them. He whispered, "I have to talk to you, about my aunt."

Interest spread across Gray's face. "Oh yeah, what about?"

Brent violently shook his head. "No, not here." He thought for a minute, then, "I don't want anyone to see us together. I have something, I know something about," he glanced around, gulped, "the old lady, Goldbrooke. And maybe about my aunt, too. I came across notes about money-"

A group of hospital staff came around the corner in a bunch.

Brent grew even jumpier, he tugged his green A's cap down lower over his face and slipped on a pair of sunglass.

"But not here. I have a jump on Tuesday. How 'bout you meet me at the café behind the jump school. You know, skydiving. The café is a dump, but no one goes there that I need to worry about. Okay?" he asked urgently moving away from them, his head down.

"Sure. No problem. What time?" Gray asked quickly.

"Uh, jump's at 11, I should be back by noon or 12:30 at the latest." Brent said.

Gray nodded. "Okay, I'll be there."

Brent dipped his head once sharply, then glanced around and took off down the hall with his head down.

"What the hell was that all about?" Rick wondered out loud.

Gray cracked a couple of knuckles, one shoulder rose up and down. "Dunno. But I can't wait to find out. Let's go, get out of here. I have to attend that formal award ceremony tonight. You're lucky you don't have to go," he groused.

When he caught Rick's grin, he swiped at his friend's shaved head. "You would have to cover up all those pretty tats, bro if you went." They laughed together going down the hall.

Chapter Twenty-Four

Saturday arrived, Kessa had been dreading it all week.

The last thing she needed right now was to go on a date. She forced herself to get dressed. She wished she had an old sack dress to wear, she didn't want to in any way tempt this guy, but she'd only brought a few dresses.

Standing in front of her closet, she decided it was time to go shopping. First thing Monday she was hitting the stores. She took a dress off the hanger and slid it over her head and went over to a mirror.

Bought off the rack for a premiere she hadn't attended, she hadn't worn it before. Unfortunately, the dress was fairly short, several inches above her knees. It was form fitting, black and lavender lace accented with sequins. The top had a lightly draped neckline.

Frowning at her reflection, she tugged up on the neckline, it showed more than she wanted it to but the dress fit snuggly to her body, the bodice just draped back down. She brushed her hair, put on some lipstick and glittery earrings and slipped into her high heels.

The evenings were warm now as they moved through spring towards summer, she didn't need a wrap. Stepping down the stairs, she went to find her purse and then wait for Dr. DeBarra.

She was so mad at her mother she could spit tacks. Sophie had served her daughter up on a silver platter. Against Kessa's objections, she insisted the doctor come to Matthew's house and pick her up there.

Kessa had argued that she would meet him at the restaurant but Sophie poo-pooed her in front of the good doctor claiming ladies are picked up at their home, not met at a tavern like some common streetwalker.

Sophie had made it practically clear that whatever the doctor wanted, he could have because Sophie wanted a doctor in the family to bring some noble class to the Kentons.

If Sophie wasn't married she'd go after him herself. He was so fine looking with that russet hair and deep chocolate eyes. She shivered just thinking about him. Of course Sophie didn't think about the age difference, she always pictured herself the way she had looked in her twenties.

The Doctor was at least 10 years older than Kessa and he was around 15 years younger than Sophie.

The phone rang, Kessa hurried over to answer it, maybe there was an emergency and she'd have to call off the date! She answered eagerly, "Hello?"

It was just Matthew checking in on her. She told him absolutely nothing about what had been going on, he'd find out about everything when he got home. They talked for a few minutes then hung up. The doorbell rang.

She opened the door. DeBarra was there wearing a very expensive, dark pin-striped suit and tie. The thick shiny hair was combed back, the chocolate eyes devoured her.

"Hey Sugar, you look great!" he said, making a move to come in. Quickly, she picked up her purse and turned off the lights and stepped out of the door before he could come in.

"Uh, hello, Doctor," she greeted him uncomfortably, even being a very handsome doctor, he kind of gave her the creeps.

He was surprised. "Aren't you going to invite me in? Maybe for a drink, or something? Let us get a little, acquainted?"

Kessa moved down the steps quickly and headed for his Mercedes parked out front. "Oh," she mumbled something entirely unintelligible over her shoulder so there was nothing for him to argue about.

She hurried to his car. Turning and waiting for him, she offered him a big beautiful smile to take the edge off her rudeness. The last thing she wanted was to be alone with this guy. Her heart was pounding already.

The smile softened him. He grinned, patting the top of his thickly moussed hair. He thought to himself, *there's always later, a few drinks, she'll loosen up.* He opened her door and stared blatantly at her legs as she slid inside.

On the way to the restaurant, he talked nonstop about his job, which made it easy on Kessa. He yakked about his schooling, the hours, how many lives he's saved, everybody loves him, patients and staff...on and on.

When they arrived, he had the car valeted and dropped his arm around her waist to walk her inside.

As soon as they crossed the threshold, Kessa maneuvered out of his grasp and tried to keep an arm's length away as they were led to their table. He had made reservations but the host advised there'd be a wait for a booth.

DeBarra didn't hide his displeasure. He'd wanted to get Kessa in a booth, against the wall where she couldn't get away from him. He wasn't used to having to woo his women, they usually chased after him, but this one was a little skittish.

Nevertheless, he'd lay on the charm and she'd drop in his lap like a duck shot out of the sky. He helped Kessa to her seat then instead of sitting opposite her, he took the chair next to her.

A young blonde woman in a barely thigh covering black and gold uniform cut in a low square in front came right over. "Can I get you a drink before dinner?" she asked.

DeBarra smiled his movie star smile, and took the wine list. Without asking Kessa what she would like, he ordered a dry white wine.

Handing the wine list to the woman, the dark rich eyes drifted down the front of her. He peered at her nametag pinned right at the edge of her décolletage. Showing every bright pearly, he said, "Thank you, Tiffany."

She smiled provocatively and thanked him, ignored Kessa and left.

"So," DeBarra nudged his chair closer to hers. "Tell me a little about you. I've heard some of course, the gossip mill, but no one seems to know where you've been for the past years."

He turned his chair slightly, laid a forearm on the table and leaned in towards her, cornering her off from the rest of the room.

Feeling an oppressive pressure on her chest, Kessa looked away from him and let her attention travel around the room.

Ruffled drapes in dark rose and gold were pulled back with gold tasseled ropes letting in the last vestiges of the setting sun.

Outside the floor to ceiling windows the sky blazed orange. The carpet and tablecloths were a deep rose color, candles in glass chalices flickered on every table. The cushions on the chairs were blush, all of the servers were male, dressed in black tuxes, the liquor and wine stewards were female.

"Sugar," DeBarra set a hand on Kessa's hand to draw her attention back to him.

Reluctantly, she looked back to him. He was gorgeous. He still gave her the creeps. "Um, I've been living in Maine."

Keeping his hand on hers, he settled back against his chair and crossed his legs. "Oh? And what did you do in Maine?"

The wine steward returned with a bucket of ice and a stand for it. She set it down between the pair and pulled out the bottle. Wrapping a napkin around the wet bottle, she turned it so he could see the label.

He said impatiently, "Yes, it's fine. Pour it. And move the stand over here." He pointed to the other side of him. The couple had to move apart when she set the stand down, irritating him because now Kessa put both of her hands in her lap.

The steward dried the bottle and pulled the cork. She poured a little in his glass, he swirled it, sniffed it, swallowed it and nodded curtly. "It's fine." This time he didn't look at her at all. He never took his eyes off of Kessa.

The steward filled their glasses, kept the napkin wrapped around the bottle, placed it in the bucket, moved it as he'd asked and flounced off.

Before DeBarra could speak again, the server was at their table.

The doctor ordered for both of them. He glanced sideways at Kessa to see her reaction. She just smiled politely at him. He ordered two filet mignons medium rare, duchess potatoes, asparagus. He did ask her, "Would you care for an appetizer?" She declined.

He handed their menus to the server and dismissed him. DeBarra talked about himself until dinner came then remembered Kessa hadn't told him anything about herself.

"So, how did you support yourself, while you were in Maine?" He cut a chunk of steak before saying, "Or were you, how do they say it, incapacitated?" He ate the chunk, cut another.

Kessa sprinkled salt and pepper over everything on her plate and added butter to her asparagus. "What do you mean by incapacitated?" She chewed wondering how long it would take to finish dinner and go home.

When she hadn't drank any wine, DeBarra lifted his glass holding it up to her, forcing her to do the same and touch glasses.

"Cheers, drink up, Sugar, don't you like the wine?" he asked with a chagrined pout.

"It's fine." Kessa took a little sip. She didn't want her faculties at all fuzzy when he took her home.

His chin up, he looked down at her, lids half lowered. "You know," he said with a reproving tone. "I would hate to have to run into Sophie and tell her that her darling daughter, was, oh, shall we say, uncooperative, maybe even rude?"

Kessa debated with herself whether to get up and walk out, or, she sighed. Sophie would make her life miserable until she left Resilir.

She lifted up the glass, smiled at him and said, "Cheers," then gulped half of it down. It took seconds before she felt her stomach warm, her cheeks grew rosy and her eyes shined.

DeBarra finished his wine then poured himself another and topped hers off. "That's better, my dear." He put the bottle back, and proceeded to cut another hunk of fairly rare steak.

"Maybe I meant incarcerated, not incapacitated, kind of the same thing. Were you, in prison I mean?" He said it with a touch of eagerness, like women in prison was a turn-on.

Kessa set her fork down and picked up her glass, took a few swallows. Murmuring, "No," she drank some more. "I was not in jail."

Skipping the convent part, she said, "I lived in a cabin on a lake, went scuba diving, fishing, hiking. I'm a writer, that's how I earn my living." Angrily, she finished off the wine. He quickly poured her more.

"I see, I've heard more that you-"

"Kessa."

The couple looked up.

Grayson Whitewolf was standing in front of their table. His eyes narrowed at the doctor, he shifted them to Kessa taking in the rosy cheeks and shining eyes. He looked pointedly at the glass of wine in her hand then back at her. "

Aren't you going to introduce me to your, friend?" he asked, a cold underline to his tone, he wasn't smiling.

Kessa's mouth parted slightly. "Um," she glanced at DeBarra her mind had gone blank.

DeBarra stood up and held out his right hand while buttoning his suit jacket with his left. "DeBarra, *Doctor* Anthony DeBarra, he arrogantly introduced himself.

Gray shook his hand briefly then said to Kessa, "Can I talk to you for a minute?"

Consternation made her cheeks redder. "Uh, I, I mean what for…"

"Listen here, I didn't catch your name," DeBarra huffed, taking a step closer to Gray.

Gray shot him down with a steely glance and said to Kessa, "Just for a minute."

DeBarra puffed his chest annoyed that Gray didn't tell him who he was. Although the doctor was tall and strongly built, Gray had a couple of inches on him, his shoulders were broader and his biceps strained against his suit with every movement.

"What are you doing here anyway," DeBarra sneered at Gray. "Where's *your* date?"

Gray was wearing a light grey suit and dress boots, and a tie.

Kessa couldn't believe it, he always seemed the jeans and leather jacket kind of guy. Surprisingly, the tough guy looked good in a suit.

Gray tossed off his words to DeBarra but without looking at him, "I'm at a police ceremony in the La Grande ballroom, not that it's any of your business. Come with me, Kessa."

"Listen, buddy," DeBarra huffed again.

Unsure of what Gray would do if she refused with that hot temper of his, Kessa folded her napkin and set it next to her plate and stood up. "I'll be right back," she said quickly then moved off with Gray before DeBarra could object.

The doctor stood there with his mouth open, then sat down with a grimace and poured himself more wine.

Gray grasped Kessa's arm above the elbow and ushered her out of the room and down a hall that led to party rooms and the restrooms.

"Deputy, let go of me!" Kessa tried to pull away from him, but he held onto her until they got way down the hall. Finally releasing her, he pushed the sides of his jacket back, set his hands on his hips, boots planted firmly apart and glowered at her.

"What the hell do you think you're doing with that- that pretty boy Casanova? He's years older than you, that makes him way more experienced. You can see what a smarmy guy he is, and you're drinking, are you even old enough? That makes you even more-" he broke off when he saw her riled expression.

Kessa stood as tall as she could. In 5-inch heels at least her head was almost to his shoulder. "Who do you think you are to tell me who I should or shouldn't see? I am an adult. And what do you think you know about my- my experience anyway? You don't know anything about me. You have some nerve!"

His angry expression matching hers, he pressed her against the wall, braced one hand next to her head and said, "I promised your brother I'd look after you. That gives me the right to protect you from some lecherous, what'd he say, *doctor*, even worse, they use and throw away women like they're post-it-notes for cripe's sake. Where's your sense, and what the hell is that you're wearing?"

His eyes raked her from collar to hem and back. "Are you trying to get yourself raped?" Slamming his hand at the wall, fury darkened his blue eyes to the color of the depths of the ocean, the scar whitened against his burning skin.

Kessa slid out from under his arm. Her face placid and voice calm, underneath she was shaking like a leaf, she said, "How dare you talk to me like that. You are not my keeper. You are way over-reacting to nothing. I will wear what I want and see whom I want. That comment is so misogynist. Stop ordering me around."

She stuck a finger in his face furthering her tirade, "You have some nerve calling Doctor DeBarra a Casanova, you need to look in your own mirror, Deputy. From what I hear, you're calling the kettle black."

She turned on her heel and strode gracefully back to her table. Gray watched her stride away in the very high heels, the angry hips snapping side to side swishing the short skirt against her slender thighs.

"So," DeBarra said when she returned, it was obvious she was mad, "who's that, some hotheaded ex?"

"No one important." She sat down and picked up her glass of wine. Taking a sip, she cocked and eyebrow at him indicating her interest. "You were telling me about the girl with the appendicitis you saved."

A big grin filled his handsome face. "Oh yes, she almost died, but let me tell you how I saved her life." He refilled her glass and relaxed back.

After what seemed a lifetime, they finally finished their dinner. Kessa couldn't remember a more boring evening, her head felt stuffed with cotton wool. DeBarra went on and on and on about himself. She refused coffee and dessert, and an after dinner drink.

"Boy," he said signing the credit card receipt. "You're a cheap date." He came around and pulled out her chair.

As they made their way through the dining room, Kessa couldn't help but look around for Gray. Every time she thought about his actions she fumed all over again.

How dare he tell her what to do! Warning her off Jaspar and now the doctor. Calling DeBarra a Casanova, with his own player reputation? Huh. And what's it to him if she wanted to sleep with the doctor.

Her shoulders quivered, *eew*, she had no desire to have any more contact, physical or otherwise with DeBarra.

Sensing her irritation, DeBarra dropped an arm over her shoulders and pulled her close. "What's wrong, sugar? That abrasive friend of yours get under your skin? I can make you forget him, hone. I can give those tense shoulders a rub that will get you all relaxed and…you know, feeling good."

When she remained mum, he said giving her a hug, "So who is that guy anyway, he has the manners of a goat."

"I told you, he's no one. A friend of my brother's. Not important. Can we go, I'm really tired." Kessa knew it was useless to try to shrug his arm off, the more she moved away from him the harder he hugged her.

He paid the valet, brushing both her butt and breasts helping her in the car.

Loosening his tie, he pulled it from around his neck, unbuttoned a couple of buttons on his shirt and removed his suit coat laying it and the tie in the back seat, then he climbed behind the wheel.

Turning on the ignition, he said, "How about we stop for an after dinner drink, maybe take in a dance, I know a great place." He could tell she still needed some loosening up. Most girls were all over him by now. Usually just mentioning he was a doctor got them spreading their legs.

Kessa covered a yawn. *Yeah, that's what she wants, him grinding all over her on a dance floor. First Jaspar now the doctor, what is in the water in this town that makes all the men grabby and randy?*

"No, thanks. Thanks for the offer, but, well, I'm just exhausted, I'd like to just go home, if you don't mind." She buckled her seatbelt and held her purse primly on her lap.

"Oh, that's fine with me. You are a little eager beaver after all." He grinned.

Pulling out of the parking lot, he paused before turning the wheel, his eyes black in the dark evening, fell to her bust then up to her lips. He smiled like a wolf sitting next to the rabbit. "Let's go."

She was too tired and perturbed to ask him what he meant by his comment. At least he was finally taking her home. Then he set a large, for a doctor not a very delicate hand on her thigh and squeezed, and left it there. Every time he went around a curve he slid his hand up further.

"Doctor DeBarra," she said, biting back her irritation, pushing his hand away. When she did that, he jerked the wheel and they swerved in the street.

"Hold on!" he yelled, gripping her leg tighter. Every time she tried to push his hand off of her thigh he did the same 'accidental' maneuver.

Patting her thigh, he said, "Listen, sugar, you can call me Anthony, or Tony would be fine. I think we're going to be good, uh, friends, you don't need to be so formal. Okay?" He gave her a hard squeeze.

Kessa figured he kept calling her sugar because he couldn't remember her name, he probably called all his girls sugar to avoid trouble. Her stomach quaked at the thought of being one of his girls. Ick.

He pulled up in front of Matthew's antique house. Kessa had unbuckled her belt as they came down the street and was opening the door before he put the car in park.

"Hey, honey, wait-" He turned the car off and hurried around the side. "Where you going so fast, can't wait, huh?" He reached out for her but she stepped back.

She held out a polite hand. "Listen, thank you for a lovely evening, dinner, and, and all. Um, I'll be seeing you."

His face fell. "What? You're not inviting me inside?" He couldn't believe it. He'd never been shot down before. "Come on, sugar, just for a second."

Kessa started to walk away, he jogged after her. "Please, just for a second. I need to- to use the restroom. Could I just use your bathroom? I live like thirty minutes away," his voice came out tinny and whiny. "Come on, honey, I'll leave right away, I promise."

Kessa blew out a deep breath. Against her better judgment she acquiesced. "All right. But just to use the bathroom. I really am tired, and I have, a, um, a big day ahead of me tomorrow."

"Okay, I'll be quick." He thought, *she's just playing hard to get.*

Chapter Twenty-Five

She unlocked the door and they went inside. Deliberately leaving the door open a fraction, she turned on a lamp and set her purse down. "It's the second door down there," she pointed, "on the right."

"Uh huh, thanks, sugar." DeBarra took off down the hall.

Her arms crossed tightly over her chest, Kessa kicked off her heels and paced, she didn't dare sit down, it would only be an invitation for him to stay.

She was standing in front of the picture window staring out, wondering what was taking him so long when he said in her ear, "Here I am, sugar, I'm all yours."

"Oh!" She turned around sharply, she hadn't heard him come up behind her. "You-"

Taking her by surprise, he suddenly grabbed her arms and latched his lips on hers. Kessa tried to pull her head away but he put one hand on her back and gripped the back of her neck with the other locking her. Mashing their mouths together, he tried to push his tongue in her mouth.

She struggled to turn her face away from his marauding tongue. "Let go of me," she demanded.

He let go of her neck to run both hands down her back and lower, cupping her derriere. He pulled her against his groin, grinding at her, then he pushed her skirt up.

Trying to stop his hands, she cried, "Stop it! Doctor! Stop!"

Grasping her jaw, he held her taut, said against her lips, "Oh yeah, baby, you want it. I love a little fire in my dates. I know you want me, your mother told me you couldn't wait to…be with me."

With all her might, Kessa wrenched out of his arms and ran towards the kitchen.

Right behind her, he grabbed her hair, jerked her back then spun her around. Wrapping his arm around her waist he dragged her back into the room. "You're going to make this tough on yourself, sugar. Just give it up and I'll be on my way. After thinking about you all week I'm not about to stop now and leave."

He could tell this was going to be his only chance, she wasn't going to let him near her again even with Sophie pressuring her. He wrestled her around to face him, holding her wrists. "What's it going to be, honey," he pulled her across the room.

"Let go of me, why are you doing this? What is wrong with this town!" she cried. "Does everyone just go around throwing women to the ground and assaulting them?"

Hating to be helpless, she hit him as hard as should could. He ducked from her blows, she hurt herself more than him when she punched his arms and chest. Kicking violently at him with her bare feet, she screamed, pushing and thrashing, twisting to get away.

Getting pissed, DeBarra gripped her arms and shook her like she was a rag doll until her eyes rattled in her head and she stopped struggling. "You got a nasty past, sweetheart. We males know we can take what we want from you, who're you going to complain to, huh? Murdering your own sister, who's going to believe a word you say? Your own mother tossed you to the wolves, girl."

Then he put his hand on her chin and dug his fingers in her skin, squeezing so hard she thought he'd break her jaw.

His face inches from hers with madness searing his eyes, he commanded, "Knock it off. I don't want to hurt you but I'm not leaving without getting what I came for. Submit to the inevitable."

Crushing her jaw, he snarled, "It's your fault everyone thinks you're easy game. You're a killer for God's sake. Not only does that make you more exciting, but knowing you're heartless and did time in the pen, no one is going to care, even if you go to the cops." His fingers dug painfully in her soft flesh.

"They sure aren't going to believe you, a criminal, against a well-known doctor. They'll only believe it was fully consensual. A killer wrapped up in an incredible package. I bet those girls in prison couldn't get enough of you, huh? Maybe you could tell me some stories while I-"

Kessa tried to scream but he held her jaw so tightly she could hardly breathe much less scream. She tried to twist her head out of his hand, but to no avail. His other arm was like a rope around her back holding her rigidly against him.

"Enough of this girl, now do what I tell you. When I get done ravishing you honey, you'll be begging me for more." He let go of her jaw but clamped his hand on the back of her neck dominating her. Forcing his mouth on hers, he held her so she couldn't move.

Bruising her lips, he leaned his head back and said, "Let's see that great rack of yours." He reached between them with both hands, grasped the top of her dress and tore it apart. Clinching a hand around her neck to hold her taut, he tried to yank the dress off with the other.

Kessa threw her head back and screamed at the top of her lungs.

DeBarra slapped her across the face then put his hand over her mouth so she couldn't scream again. "All right you bitch, I tried to be a nice guy." Holding her arms, he kicked her legs out from under her, lowered her down on the rug and climbed on top of her.

He yanked a computer cord out of the wall, then straddling her, he held her wrists over her head and tied them together. Holding her hands with one hand, he unbuckled his belt then unbuttoned and started to unzip his pants.

Kessa let out a piercing scream, thrashing back and forth under him.

"Damn it, don't make me gag you, girl, we don't need the neighbors getting involved in our fun." He clamped his hand back over her mouth. "I don't want to have to hit you again," he warned, "cooperate, woman."

Shifting his weight down past her thighs, he pushed her dress up. She bucked and screamed against his hand, tears of fury spilled from her eyes.

He tugged at her panties while sliding on top of her, thrusting his legs between hers, spreading them apart.

Chapter Twenty~Six

$\mathcal{G}$ray left at the conclusion of the ceremony. He shook out of the suit jacket and slung it over one shoulder, then untied the tie and yanked open the first few top buttons on his shirt.

When he reached his truck, he tossed the jacket on the passenger side of the bench seat and climbed in. As he stuck the key in the ignition he caught sight himself in the mirror.

Kessa's words came back to him. His crack about the doctor being a Casanova. Gray shook his head wryly muttering, "Yeah, she was right about me. Calling the kettle black." In discomfiture, he studied his reflection.

But the women he picked up knew the score with him. He was always clear up front, he didn't want any messy mixed feelings afterwards. Still...he hated to admit that her words rankled. He gave the mirror a little push and turned the key.

"What do I care what anyone thinks, I am who I am, that's the way it is. She can have her dumb, douchebag doctor." He left the restaurant and rolled onto the main road that led to his home.

Still, Kessa's words kept poking at him. He thought about her getting all bent out of shape about his comment about her being out with that slimeball. He smiled crookedly remembering what he said about her dress.

Then he winced recalling her hurt reaction. She was miffed, yeah, but she was hurt too. It's not his fault for crying out loud that she's so hot men are all up her skirt, and that dress just heated her up more. But she could have been wearing a paper bag and she still would- "Damn," he missed the turn-off to the road that led his street.

He rubbed his eyes to get the picture of Kessa in that dress out of his mind. "It's her fault," he mumbled, preparing to make a U-turn. "I'm only doing what Matt asked me to do, look out for her. If I was her brother I'd do the same thing."

He chuckled out loud. "Except I'd keep her locked in her room and not let her go out with assholes."

Instead of making the U-turn he kept going. Maybe he needed to apologize again. He didn't really think he owed her an apology, but he didn't want her telling Matt what a jerk he was.

He followed Swallowtail Road all the way to Lake Ave to Matt's house.

Seeing the Mercedes out in the street, he parked behind it. *Did she let that asshole inside?*

He sat for a second, debating what to do. It was her business if she invited the guy in. Yet, on the other hand, Matt said she was very green when it came to men, but it was still her business, but he didn't like the way the guy looked. Round and round he went in his mind.

DeBarra was good looking if you liked that metro-sexual thing, but to Gray he was slick, an operator. Kessa would be like a child in his hands. Besides, he'd felt a vibe when he had approached the table.

Kessa had not looked happy to be there, she had been leaning away from the creep while he had cornered her like a cat after a mouse. Gray dragged a hand through his hair and shut off the truck.

Shrugging into his suit jacket, he walked cautiously up the stone walk. What if they were just sitting there innocently sipping tea? He snorted, *sure, not with that smoking body sitting next to him*. That spurred him to move more quickly.

He took the steps two at a time, then hesitated, *that's weird*, the door was ajar about an inch.

Then he heard her scream!

Gray shoved the door open and saw the *doctor* assaulting Kessa on the floor. DeBarra was cursing at her, she screamed and he slapped her then shoved his hand between her legs-

"Motherfucker-" Gray roared. Tearing off his jacket, he threw it aside then ran and lunged at DeBarra knocking him off Kessa.

The two men flew then hit the floor. Gray jumped to his feet, DeBarra sat stunned for a second. Gray grabbed him by the shirt collar, jerked him up and bashed him in the jaw with his closed fist again and again.

Shocked, Kessa rolled to her knees, her hands still tied. She stood up, backing away from the fighting men that knocked over a table sending things flying.

DeBarra tried to block Gray's blows but to no avail. He got in a couple of punches, but Gray kept pummeling him, knocking him to the ground then picking him up and punching him to the ground again.

DeBarra tried to crawl away, blood streaming from his nose and mouth. "All right," he cried, "enough, enough…"

"Hit a woman you pitiful bastard! Assault her!" Gray shouted, kicking DeBarra.

The doctor put his hands up to deflect, but Gray shoved them aside and hit him in the stomach. As DeBarra doubled over, Gray shot an undercut to his jaw.

DeBarra slammed onto his back. He tried to roll over and cover his face but Gray grabbed his shirt, pulled him up and beat him, hitting and kicking him over and over and over.

"Deputy! Stop, my God you're going to kill him!" Kessa sobbed, pushing at Gray.

But the deputy, now in a blind rampage just hammered at the doctor who no longer tried to defend himself.

"Deputy Whitewolf! Stop! Stop!" Kessa kept screaming, pushing and pulling him.

Finally, her voice got through, Gray sat back on his heels, his fists on his on his knees, his chest heaving, panting. Hair damp with sweat hanging in his eyes, he stared at her like he was in a trance. His tie was still loose around his neck, blood spattered all over his white shirt and grey slacks.

Blinking, he wiped a bloody hand across his sweaty face and said to her, "Are you okay?" He stood up and took Kessa gently by the arms.

"Your face, you're bruised. That mother-" he turned to go back after the doctor who was choking and gagging and spitting out blood.

Kessa said quickly, "No, please, Deputy, stop, please!" Crying hysterically with tears streaming down her cheeks, her hands still tied together she grabbed his arm.

He turned back to her. Lifting a hand, he tenderly touched the tears with his fingers. "Okay, Okay," he said to calm her.

He brushed back a wisp of hair stuck to her cheek. "Did he, I mean, I need to take you to the hospital." He made to move with her, she stopped him.

"He didn't, he didn't do it. You have great timing." Her weakly sarcastic smile spurred tremulous.

DeBarra moaned. Gray looked over at him. "I'll haul his ass in and arrest him for-"

"No, please, please don't. It'll, you know, it'll be all over the news. I'll be a laughingstock, they'll blame it on me. They'll say it was consensual, that I wanted it, led him on or whatever."

"But I'm a witness, and I'm the law. I can't let him get away with this," he started.

"No, it doesn't matter. They'll blame it on me, they always have. You don't understand, it'll be all over the news. I'll come across as a despised Jezebel. Every female in the hospital, and probably a few men too are crazy about him. They'll say I tried to trap him. Please, please don't," she pleaded morosely, her head drooping, she broke into sobs. "Please."

"God," Gray groaned. He slipped his arms around her and pulled her head against his chest. "I'll do whatever you want. Please don't cry." He stroked her hair.

She wept against his chest. He took her hands and untied her wrists then irately threw the cord to the floor. Seeing an odd mark on the underside of her arm he touched it gently. "What's this?"

Reflexively, Kessa rubbed the mark. "It's a souvenir of my-uh... When my sisters and I were in the woods, something or someone had grabbed me so hard it made a permanent indentation. I've carried the mark ever since. It's like I'd been branded or something."

Still holding her, Gray delicately touched the unusual mark. "A horrible memory for you to have to carry," he murmured.

DeBarra moaned. Gray looked over. Gently setting Kessa aside, he trod over to the doctor.

"Deputy, don't-" Kessa called out in a panic.

"Don't worry, I'm just going to take out the garbage."

Shrinking away from Gray, the doctor zipped up his pants then held his hands up trying to ward off the expected blows.

Gray grasped his collar and jerked him to his feet.

He dragged him by the collar to the door, opened it and said, "You don't want me to ever hear again that you assaulted a woman, any woman, or struck one, or even slapped a girl. And don't ever talk to or even look in Miss Kent's direction again, ever," and he threw him out.

Closing the door to DeBarra's shrieks as the doctor tumbled down the stone steps, Gray locked the door.

Kessa's legs giving out, she plopped down numbly on the couch, her face stained with tears.

Gray went to the bathroom. She could hear the water running.

He came back out with his shirt sleeves rolled up and his hands and face washed. His collar and the hair around his face was wet. He jerked his head back to toss the damp black locks out of his eyes.

He had a handful of tissues. Sitting down next to her, he handed the tissues to her.

"Thanks," she mumbled, wiping her eyes.

Gray laid an arm along the back of the couch and turned towards her. "I warned you."

Kessa stopped mid-wipe. "What?"

Gray shrugged. "I told you he was an asshole and to watch out. I told you wearing that," he gestured at her, "dress, with your tits hanging out and cut up to here," he motioned to his thigh. "You were asking for trouble..."

Kessa stood up furious, her cheeks bloomed red. "Are you saying it's my fault that jerk attacked me?" She shook with anger. "What a chauvinistic, Neanderthal-"

He got to his feet. "Okay, calm down." He moved his palms down in a hushing motion, his knuckles cut and beginning to bruise. "I'm not saying any guy ever, ever has a right to take a woman against her will, force himself on her, it's just," he tucked his thumbs over his belt.

"Honey, when a girl looks the way you do, you're just throwing fuel on the fire dressing like that. Unless you're on a real man's arm, under his protection, well," he shook his head, "like I said, fuel on fire," he sucked in a breath.

"First of all," she sputtered, "the dress was not that sexy, my uh, I was not hanging out all over. I admit it was a bit, I don't know, I bought it for a premier. I've actually never worn it before. I bought it off the rack, anyway," she slammed her hands on her hips. "It doesn't matter what a person wears-"

He smiled. "Or has her tits hanging out, like I said," he motioned to her top with his head.

"What are you-" she glanced down. The bodice of the dress had been torn in two and was barely being held up by a thread. He was right, she was very exposed.

"It's not designed this way, you idiot, he tore it." She tugged the pieces of the dress together, glaring at him. Then she noticed he was looking down. She looked down and scowled. The rapacious doctor had torn the skirt of the dress as well.

"Here," Gray picked up his jacket and slung it over her shoulders. He pulled the lapels together to cover her exposed breasts.

Glowering at him, she slid her arms in the sleeves and held the jacket closed tightly, it was long enough to cover the torn skirt.

"You could have said something sooner, instead of- of letting me, instead of sitting there ogling me." Her lower lip pushed out, he was just as bad as the others.

He shifted a shoulder up lazily then dropped it. "Hey, I'm a red blooded male, you put it in front of us, we're gonna look." He straightened his rolled sleeves, dark hair was visible above the open top shirt buttons of his shirt.

"I admit it wasn't fair when you weren't aware. But, I swear to you, seriously, I didn't look, really. You're like my little sister for Pete's sake, and with your wrists tied together your arms covered you pretty well."

"You are a barbarian, you're no better than DeBarra. You even talk like a heathen. You use foul language, which I'm asking you not to use in front of me," she snipped primly, turning tartly away from him.

"Well, we did agree already that I am a barbarian. I'm sure Genghis Khan had better manners than me. But, like I said before, I usually like my women willing."

She half-turned back to face him. "This wasn't my fault, I didn't want to go out with him, Sophie forced me. I didn't want him to come in, he said he had to use the bathroom. I didn't dress provocatively on purpose, I," her voice cracking she turned away as the tears fell.

He gently pulled her into his arms again. When she stiffened, he said, "I'm not going to attack you. Just think of me as Matt's clone, like his older brother." With a sniff she lay against his chest waiting for the tears to subside.

"By the way," Gray said, his deep voice rumbled in her ear on his chest. "I'll do as you ask and not arrest that son-of-a-bitch, but I will be telling Matt. I owe him that much. Once he's home those freakin' wolves will back off. And it's not up for debate. Now," he put a finger under her chin and tilted it so he could see her.

"Go wash your face and grab a bag of clothes and whatever stuff you women need, you're coming to stay at my place tonight."

He let her go then flopped down on the sofa. "Go on."

She stood, astonishment ringing out of her. "Are you kidding? I'm not going with you to-"

"Yeah, ya are. We're not arguing about it. That doctor guy, when he can walk again, will be pretty mad. He may come back over here tonight, and I'm not leaving you here alone. I'd sleep here on the couch, it feels pretty comfy," he patted the cushion beside him.

"But I have to be somewhere very early tomorrow and it's way on the other side of town from here. So, you're just going to have to buck up and come with me." His tone brooked no argument. "Don't make me carry you out of here, because you know I will. So, get going. I'll wait here."

He looked around. "Where's the dog?"

Blowing her nose, Kessa replied, "He got in a scrap with another dog. Go figure." She sniffed, "Men. You're all alike, fighting all the time, I don't get it."

"Anyway," Gray said aggressively, "where the hell is he? He should have torn that guy apart."

Kessa smiled. "Yeah, he sure would have if he was here. The vet had to give him stiches and anesthesia. I could have brought him home to recover, but I couldn't carry him so he's staying at the Vet's for a few days."

"I see." Gray looked at her standing there, dress in shreds, his jacket covering her just past her thighs, not enough to cover those long bare legs. The light hair a soft halo in disarray around her shoulders, tear-streaked face. As vulnerable as a woman could be and she still put on airs that she was tough as nails.

He asked, "So, if Matt was here would he have gotten the dog home?"

She shrugged, not seeing where he was going. "Sure. Matthew wouldn't have had any trouble lifting Kato."

Gray leaned over with his forearms on his knees, hands clasped and looked up at her. Wet hair flopped over chastising dark blue eyes. He impatiently pushed the mop back.

"You still don't get it. I'm here for Matt. Whatever you need him to do, you call me." He leaned back against the couch. "I shouldn't have to tell you that again."

His long arm draped along the back of the couch, he dropped an ankle over his knee. "I'll get the dog and bring him back tomorrow."

Before she could sputter indignantly at him, he said, "I could really use a beer and it's a bit of a drive, so you need to get a move on." Dismissing her, he picked up some magazines that had been knocked off the table during the fight and settled back to read one.

Flabbergasted, Kessa could tell by his attitude he meant what he said. "Oh for the love of," she groaned and headed for the stairs. She didn't see his satisfied smile.

She closely followed him to his place in her jeep. He had told her if she didn't keep up with him, he'd come right back and get her and they were both too tired for that.

Chapter Twenty-Seven

$\mathcal{G}$ray parked in his driveway then walked back to where Kessa was pulling up behind him.

She put the jeep in park but didn't turn off the engine. He could see her pale face through the window. For all her bluster she was traumatized and frightened. She'd been through a harrowing night and was now sitting in the dark in a basically stranger's driveway.

He opened the car door, reached in and turned off the ignition. Pulling the keys out, he put them in her hand then took her by the arm and gently pulled her out.

She'd showered DeBarra's smell off her and changed into pale blue jeans and brought a small bag, it was on the passenger seat. He leaned in and got it, closed the door.

"Come on, it'll be fine, no worries. No one is going to hurt you here, including me," he added dryly. They were parked in front of a cabin somewhat like the one Kessa had been living in, in Maine.

In the twilight, tall oaks and conical firs loomed like gothic black spires. They should be frightening, but were oddly comforting like chess pieces clustered around the cabin. The cabin was bigger than hers in Maine, with a wide porch that appeared to wrap completely around the building.

A few chairs and wicker tables and even a rocking chair were on the porch. Fishing poles rested against the wood railing with a tackle-box nearby. Firewood was stacked neatly on the right side of the porch. A well-used ax leaned against the stack.

Gently taking her arm again, Gray helped her up the unfamiliar steps as it was very dark. The cabin was outside of town and there were few lights on the street as the other homes were on tree shrouded acres separated by groves of timberland.

As he unlocked the door, a whinny came from the near distance.

Kessa's head jerked up. "Is that a horse?"

Gray opened the front door, and with a hand on the small of her back, he ushered her inside. Switching on a lamp by the door, he set her bag down on a chair, closed the door and went to turn on another light.

"I have stables," he told her. "You can see them in the morning if you'd like."

"Really?" Kessa felt herself relax. A guy who had horses couldn't be all that bad. She took in her surroundings.

The inside was mostly made of teak and hemlock. A stone fireplace divided the room. There was a couch, a recliner and two other cushiony chairs.

On the other side of the fireplace was a sliding glass door with a table and chairs in front of it. He lived on a channel of the lake. The glass doors would lend a great view of the water during the day.

Gray moved around closing all of the curtains, then returned to her. Now he was the one who stood awkwardly.

Crouching, he unzipped the sides then kicked his boots off. "Go ahead and have a seat. I'm gonna get a beer, you want one? Or a soda or coffee, how about a sandwich?"

She shook her head.

Near the door, a saddle hung on a rack, cowboy boots under it, several different types of ropes looped around the rack. The floor was teak with rugs scattered all across it.

He left and came back in quietly in his socks, with a beer and a bottle of water. She was still standing. He twisted the lid off the water and handed it to her.

At her weak smile of thanks, he said diffidently, "You need something," then guzzled the beer.

His gaze settled lightly on her. He fumbled for something to say, to ease her uncomfortableness, but this was all foreign territory to him. He'd never had an innocent woman he'd just saved from being sexually assaulted in his house before. Most were racing to get their clothes off.

Vaguely cheerful, he said, "The um, there's two bathrooms, one at that end," he nodded down the hall to the right. "There's a room down there but I don't use it for much except sawing in the winter and stuff. Past the kitchen is a small den."

"On the other side," he gestured with the beer down the hall to the left, "there's my um, bedroom, and there's a bathroom in there too. I have a girl come in once a week to clean so you don't need to worry about…uh…whatever."

"A girl?" Kessa asked.

Holding the beer by the neck with two fingers, he took a swig, looked sheepish. "I mean, not a girl, it's Mrs. Butler. She's like 60. She'd kill me if she heard me refer to her as a girl."

His eyes darted around like she might be somewhere listening. "Anyway, my point is, the place is relatively clean. I know how you women are about-"

Crossing her arms, Kessa's brows arched comically, pretending she was insulted.

"So, uh, anyway, here, follow me." He picked up her bag and went down the hall. She followed him to a room where he reached in and flipped on a light.

The room was fairly sparse. A bed, nightstand, desk and chair in a corner, some clothes were lying over the chair. Plaid curtains, some books and papers piled on the desk, not much else. He walked over and set her bag on the bed.

"This is my room. You'll sleep here. There's a lock on the door. You don't need to worry about clean sheets, Mrs. Butler was here this morning. I'll be on the couch. You can use the bathroom in there," he pointed to another door to the side. "If you need anything, just ask. I'll be out there. So-"

"Oh no, Deputy, I can't take your room, that wouldn't be-"

Ignoring her protest, he moved to the doorway. "You don't have to argue about everything, Kessa. Good night, babe." He closed the door.

"Hey, don't call me-" she sighed. What was the use, the man was just impossible. The bed looked so inviting with a fluffy comforter and plump pillows.

It took her only a few minutes to brush her teeth, change into shorts and a t-shirt and was asleep before the man in the moon could yawn.

The morning sun streamed happily through the window pushing her sleepy eyes open.

Confused at first as to where she was, Kessa saw the dress hanging over the desk chair and the horrid memories of the last evening flooded her. Her cheeks flamed with humiliation and anger.

She climbed out of the bed and shuffled to the door. Turning the knob, she silently chastised herself, she hadn't even locked the door, would she never learn?

Padding down the hall, she made her way to the living room.

"Deputy?" she called out meekly. The place was silent except for birds chirping outside.

Pictures on the mantle of the fireplace drew her attention. She went over to inspect them. The big one in the middle was of two older people and four younger people. She recognized Gray as one of the younger people.

The three others were all female and looked a lot like Gray but with dark eyes. All the children looked like the older woman in the picture that Kessa assumed was Gray's mother. She moved closer to see the framed photo better. They were all smiling.

His mother was quite beautiful with high, sharp cheekbones and gleaming black eyes and hair. The girls were her spitting images.

The older man, again assuming it was his father, was handsome. He looked stern yet mischievous, just like Gray, but he had the dark eyes too. She remembered Gray saying he inherited his blue eyes from a Scottish ancestor.

The smaller pictures on the mantle were more of his sisters and apparently other family members as the resemblance ran through them. Not wanting to get caught snooping, Kessa left the pictures and went into the kitchen, there was a note on the table. She picked it up.

"Had to go early. There's juice, coffee and milk, bread, cereal and left over pizza. Make yourself at home. Gray"

That was it. Abrupt, just like him.

She made some toast with coffee then quickly got dressed. She pushed back the curtains in the bedroom.

A few hundred yards to the north of the cabin she could see stables. The sunlight sparkled on the yellow hay in bales outside the building and lit up the tin roof.

To the south was a leg of Lake Yana shimmering blue and white. A boat like the one she'd leased in Maine was moored to a small dock. She yearned to go out and explore the pastures, barns and the lake. But she didn't want to be there when he got back, so she packed up quickly and drove home.

When she walked in the house, Kato whimpered from near the couch. Kessa hurried over and knelt next to him, petting his head, she asked him, "How the heck did he get you here?"

His answer was a nose snuffling into her hand.

A few days later out at the Goldbrooke place, Gray pulled up at the same time as Rick.

"Hey," they greeted, bumping fists.

Rick said, "Quite a project you got cooking, bro."

Police vehicles and vans were strewn all around the property. City police officers and county deputies and forensic investigators mingled.

One sergeant separated from the group and approached the two deputies. He said to Gray, "You Whitewolf?"

"Yes. Sergeant Stiller?" Gray asked with a short nod. "This is Deputy Rick Vanuu."

"Pleasure," the sergeant said. Short neatly trimmed hair, brown eyes, thirtyish, strongly built like Gray and Rick, the sergeant asked, "So, what's the plan, what're we looking for? I mean I have an idea of course but my captain told me very little."

Gray crossed his arms, legs shoulder width apart, grounding him. "I believe there's something here, something to do with the trouble with the Kenton girls around 14-15 years ago."

Stiller pulled off his uniformed ball cap and scratched his head. "You're thinking the one that they never found might be here?" His expression was skeptical, yet he'd seen a lot in his years in law enforcement and nothing surprised him anymore.

Gray raised one shoulder. "I don't really know what could be here. This is the only place that was never searched at the time, there might be evidence inside or outside. The old lady, and now the housekeeper have been murdered.

"Although I spoke briefly with them before they died, they aren't my cases. However, I find it way too coincidental that they were both murdered almost immediately after I interviewed them. The middle Kenton girl returns after all this time and now bodies are piling up? My commander, Thomas Ross, gave me permission to search this place."

It was really the governor who he knew personally who gave him the permission, but he didn't want to sound like a name-dropper.

His hands in his pockets, Rick commented, "Ya ever think it's her?"

Gray turned a stony look at him. "What are you saying?"

"Come on, you're letting her pretty face dupe you. She shows up after what, 14 years and the killings start? Really? Have you considered revenge, or maybe she's eliminating witnesses?" Rick said with an eyebrow raised.

Bristling, Gray said, "Get off it, Rick, she's not running around town knocking people off. I think she did stir things up when she showed up after all these years. I think someone else is eliminating possible witnesses."

Shaking his head, Rick pulled a hand out of his pocket and pointed it loosely at Gray. "Oh, so you think the little old lady chased and caught the kids, killed then hid the body of the youngest, permanently damaged the older one, and now someone unknown took the old lady out? Dude, you need to be thinking with the big head that's up here not the one down-"

"Shut up, Rick. Don't be an ass. She's the little sister of a close friend for crying out loud. Drop it." A picture of Kessa after her assault wearing his jacket, half naked, tousled hair, tear streaked face with swollen trembling lips popped in his head.

He dragged a hand over his face dispelling the erotic picture. Geesh, it was practically incest for Pete's sake, Matt was one of his best friends.

Gruffly, he said to Sergeant Stiller, "I have a warrant for both the inside and the outside. We," he motioned his head over to another deputy, Janey Leigh who had a bag in her hand, "have some articles of clothing of the missing one, Hope Kenton."

"Shit, Deputy, it's been up on 14 years or more, you think the dogs can still pick up her scent?" Stiller asked.

"Who knows?" Gray shrugged. "But we won't know if we don't try."

"We got the K-9's here that detect remains," Rick said as he watched the deputy letting the canines out of his cruiser.

"Yeah," Gray added, "cadaver dogs. Let's get going. Sergeant, start with your squads near the house and then just have them work their way out, fanning at least to the woods. Then have two CSI teams, one begin in the basement, the other the first floor and go until they meet.

"Tell 'em anything at all, anything that could even resemble a blood drop, a child's toy, clothes, writing on the walls, they know the drill." He turned to Rick, "How about you go with the inside teams and I'll hit the outside."

Rick grinned, ribbing his friend. "Of course, you get the outdoors and I get stuck inside a musty, hot smelly old house."

"You got it, bro, have fun." Gray laughed at Rick as he left to go join the CSIs going in the house.

After hours with no results, Rick and Stiller found Gray and told him they were taking a food break and asked him to come with them.

Gray declined. "Thanks but I promised my mother I'd stop by." He wiped his hands on his jeans and dragged a sleeve across his dusty face.

"Geez, bro," Stiller grinned jabbing Rick in the side, "you didn't tell me your partner was a mama's boy." The sergeant and Rick guffawed and teased Gray all the way to his truck.

In his truck, Gray turned over the ignition and stuck his head out the window. "Sure guys, laugh. While you're choking down those greasy chili dogs and cold bland salads, you be sure Rick, to tell Stiller here about my mama's seafood chowder and blackened ribs." At the look on Rick's woebegone face he laughed and drove off.

His mother lived in a nice suburb outside of Resilir. His family had moved nearby after Gray had settled there but they didn't care for his rustic lifestyle, they preferred having shops and restaurants close by.

He drove down his parent's pleasant street of A-frames and split levels, neatly manicured lawns and shady maple trees that dropped colorful flowers in autumn by the buckets, children were playing hopscotch on the sidewalk.

As he pulled into the driveway the kitchen curtain fluttered letting him know his mother knew he was there.

He entered through the garage to the bright humming kitchen. His mother flurried right over giving him a hug and kiss. "About time, Grayson, you were supposed to come last week to Sunday dinner. We were very disappointed when you didn't-"

"Oh, but we've heard why you haven't been around, haven't we ma?" Identical to her mother only younger, Gray's sister Anaclara teased her brother. With the same black hair but hers went past her shoulders straight as an arrow, their mother's curled at her collar.

Glowing black eyes like her mother's twinkled impishly at him. He gave her a quick hug and went to the refrigerator taking out a soda. He popped the tab and took a hit.

"Really?" Gray washed his hands in the sink, dried them with a towel then he leaned a hip against the counter.

His mother, Shonna, bustled around putting a bowl of steaming gumbo loaded with plump shrimp and spicy sausage on the table and stuck a big serving spoon in it. "Anaclara," Shonna warned, now setting plates and cutlery on the table.

"Oh poo, mom, you know we're dying to know about her," she swiveled back to her brother. Her palms on the back of a chair she leaned in with taunting interest at him. "Tell us, Gray. The grapevine says you've been seen with this foxy, very young blonde with sick aquamarine eyes."

"Bewitching was what I heard," Shonna put her 2 cents in. She brought a bread basket, butter and a bowl of rice to the table. "Anaclara, please get the salad and dressings."

Anaclara's long hair swung around her shoulders as she leaned over the chair grinning at her brother. "So spill it, brother dear, we want to know all about it, her."

Gray finished his soda, tossed it in the trash and got himself another one. He pulled out a chair and sat at the table. "There's nothing to tell. Mmm, Ma, that smells spicy, I can't wait to dig in. You guys ready? Where's Dad and Haley?"

Pouting, Anaclara retrieved the salad and dressings put them on the table then she sat down and crossed her arms on the table.

"Dad's at work, sister's at school," she said pertly. "Come on, Gray, who is she? Give us the goods, don't be a spoilsport."

Shonna joined her children at the table. "Let's say Grace."

She led them in a short prayer then nodded to Gray to serve the gumbo. "If your brother wants to keep his personal life private from his loving family," Shonna said pleasantly holding her plate out for Gray to give her some of the seafood stew.

"Then that's fine. If he wants to keep secrets from his beloved, caring, interested mother, sisters, father," she sighed sadly, "well, then we shouldn't hassle him. Right dear?" She smiled innocently at her son as he rolled his eyes handing her the filled plate.

Gray stuck a spoon in his gumbo, blew on it before tasting it.

"Alright, I'll tell you, but," he wangled his spoon at his sister who was tearing off a chunk of bread, "let me explain the whole story with no interruptions, and there'll be no questions after, and" he eyeballed his mother, "get this straight. I am not involved with this girl, we are not an item, we are not going to be an item. I am simply assisting a friend. That's it."

Both women tentatively agreed with sly grins.

Shonna said, "You don't need to get cranky, dear. It's just that it's time for you to get a nice girl, settle down and give me some grandchildren."

Gray stirred his gumbo in agitation. "You have a grandchild already from Lily, remember? You all need to get off my back, I don't want to settle down. I don't need a nice girl, they're nothing but aggravation. Geesh, first Rick now you, let up already, will ya?" He shook his head as he took a mouthful.

Anaclara dipped her bread in her gumbo. "Uh huh, you need to move off those girls you date and step up, Gray."

The table grew quiet. Gray stared darkly at his stew, absently stirring it.

Anaclara shared a look with her mother. "Okay, we'll let it alone, for now. Anyway, tell us about this girl. I heard there's some major drama attached to her and that she went out with Dr. DeBarra, the hospital hunk. Word is, after their date he left town for a couple of weeks, he claimed for vacation. But, someone said he'd gotten beaten half to death on the date, but he wouldn't talk about it. I mean, who would beat up that gorgeous doctor, that fine, virile-"

"You interested in what I have to say or not?" Gray snapped surly. Ripping off a piece of bread then with ill temper he crammed the rest back in the basket.

Mother and daughter shared another 'we'll talk about this later look.' Shonna said soothing, "Of course, honey, we're dying to hear all about this young lady. Go on."

He'd heard all he ever wanted to hear about that asshole doctor, and relieved they were letting his love life go, for now anyway.

Chewing hungrily then swallowing, "Well," he added more rice to his plate and spooned gumbo loaded with shrimp, sausage, okra, peppers, tomatoes over it and said, "You know my friend, Matt Kenton…"

Chapter Twenty-Eight

Outside a fine drizzle had diminished and the sun was needling through the clouds.

Kessa pulled on jeans and an aqua colored chiffon blouse. Brushing her hair, she watched her reflection. "Hmm," she murmured looking at the blouse. It was almost sheer and draped lightly on her curves. "Maybe I should change."

Gray's depiction of her dressing pretty much as a slut came to mind. "It's warm out for heaven's sake, the blouse is appropriate. Screw Mr. Sexist Know-it-all," she said, dropping the brush on the dresser.

It had been over a week since the debacle with the doctor. Gray had left several messages but she had ignored them. She really didn't want to relive the incident sure that he was going to gloat or rub it in how green she was and had asked to be assaulted by the way she'd dressed. Archaic caveman.

She picked up her purse and keys, left water and a treat for Kato, locked the door and hopped in her jeep.

Driving to the hospital, she steadfastly pushed the other night out of her mind. She was worried though, what if DeBarra was there.

She smothered a smile picturing what the doctor must look like after the beating Gray gave him. It was doubtful he would be at the hospital. Well, she'd face that bridge if it came to it.

What was important was that she see Char and try to smooth things with her. There was no chance of doing that at the house so she hoped she could catch her alone at the hospital.

She found a spot in front of the building, the lot was only half full. She hopped out and walked to the entrance. A light breeze tickled her hair and ruffled the chiffon blouse.

The day had turned sunny and the air warm. When she entered the hospital she checked in at the visitor's booth and was given a sticker with VISITOR on it. She stuck it to one of the frills on the blouse and asked where she could find her sister.

The volunteer at the visitor booth directed her to Char's room. Kind of off-handedly, she asked if Dr. DeBarra was around.

The older woman behind the booth smiled. Kessa was in a line of many women that asked about the debonair doctor.

"I'm sorry, hon, the doctor is on a vacation. Called in the other day as a matter of fact."

Breathing a sigh of relief, Kessa thanked her and moved through the glass doors into the lobby and to the elevators. Getting off on the third floor, Kessa found Char's room right away.

Sucking in a calming breath, she gingerly pushed the door open.

Char was alone, sitting in bed, a book upside down on her leg. She turned towards the door as it opened expecting a nurse. Her eyes widened when she saw her sister, but she didn't look as angry as she usually did.

Kessa moved slowly to the bed, gauging Char's reaction. "Hi," she said softly.

"Hello," Char responded warily. She didn't appear to be about to spout curses at her.

Taking a deep breath, Kessa said, "Can we talk? If you say no, I'll leave quietly, no trouble." She waited, watching emotions flicker across her sister's damaged face.

Char pointed at a chair. "I'd like you to stay."

Relief washed over Kessa at the tiny smile her sister gave her. She pulled the chair over to the bed and sat down. "I," she started to talk but Char shook her head.

"No, please, let me first," she said quietly.

"Of course. I'm just glad you're not running me off," Kessa replied, hope hanging in the back of her mind that they could mend their relationship.

Char picked the book up that was on her leg and set it on the table next to her, then took a long breath before exhaling slowly.

"I'm sorry, Faith, I'm sorry the way I've treated you. No," she held a hand up as Kessa inched forward on her chair and opened her mouth. "Let me finish, please."

Kessa settled back in the chair and Char relaxed.

"Okay, what happened to us, all of us, well, I only ever thought about me. I'm crippled, my face is, well, it is what it is. I have been so bitter and there was no one to blame, so when Mother put you out there I centered all my anger, my resentment and bitterness on you, because there just was no one else."

She wriggled against the pillows to sit up straighter. "Actually, we have all felt some sort of guilt. Even me."

Helping her with her pillows Kessa frowned in disbelief. "There's nothing you could have done. You were a child yourself," Kessa told her, sitting back down.

"I know. But I always believed if I hadn't taken you guys there that day to the forbidden woods," she sighed in mental anguish. "Hope would be safe at home. You wouldn't have been sent away, and I," she smiled regretfully.

"When you came back and I saw your own pain," she sighed. "I finally had to admit to myself, as deep down I always knew, that you had nothing to do with what happened to us. Any of us. You were a scrawny, just turned eight-year-old kid, you couldn't have done it.

"Matthew kept telling us over the years the horrific life you lived at that detestable convent, but we all chose to use you as our scapegoat for our own shame and guilt, and hopelessness."

Kessa moved to the edge of her chair and took her sister's hand.

Staring unseeing at their hands, Char said, "They couldn't fix me, they couldn't find Hope, you weren't here so it was easy to blame you." Her eyes raised to Kessa's. "Instead of being grateful that I was at least alive and making something of myself, I grew bitter and depressed, turning self-hatred into an art. I always thought I was furious with you, but it was really me I hated."

"Oh, Char, that's-"

"Then there was Daddy. He was torn apart with guilt and grief. You know he was running around with Mrs. Finestone next door,"

Kessa nodded. "I didn't know then, Matthew told me. He said Mother looked the other way because it was the Finestones who were sponsoring them at the Club. Then Mr. Finestone found out and punched Dad in the nose and then they moved away. It would be comical if not so tragic."

Char grinned. When she smiled for real, her face somehow came back into symmetry and she was almost pretty again. "Yeah, I picture it whenever I'm mad at him, makes me feel better. Anyway, he always felt guilty that if he hadn't been over at her house doing her, he would have been home to protect us and this all never would have happened.

"It's even sadder because he only sought solace in another woman's arms because Mother was so ice cold and let the Club consume her. She loved the lifestyle, she believed the members' blueblood could rub off on her. Nonetheless, Daddy was eaten up with guilt."

Kessa's chewed her lip. "That's ridiculous, Mother and Dad were upstairs sleeping when we left that day, he couldn't have done anything."

"I know. Then he also felt guilty that he let Mother send you away. They fought about it all the time. He wanted to go get you and bring you home, or at least visit you. She put her foot down and said if he went she would divorce him and point the finger at him as being the perpetrator that day. That it was him that attacked us, his own daughters."

Kessa laughed derisively. "Dad? That's a joke. He went running screaming from that spider, remember?"

Char giggled, it was music to Kessa's ears.

"Yeah," Char agreed, recalling the incident. Her big dad running from a tiny bug. "That was hilarious, he couldn't hurt a fly, or spider. But other people, the police, well they might have believed her. I think Mother acts so horribly to you because she feels guilty too. Yes she does, Faith," she insisted at Kessa's scornful look.

"The Club had been her, has always been her God, still is actually. It was so important how the members all felt about her, the esteem they held her in. She was running around on Dad too, did Matthew tell you that?"

Nodding, Kessa said, "I couldn't believe it, it was ludicrous."

"Oh, but it was true. She was actually seeing a guy when what happened to us happened. He was the one that told her he wasn't going to see a woman who had a murderer in her house. He gave her an ultimatum. And she chose him over you." Char watched to see how her sister was taking this information.

Kessa just sat silently, waiting for Char to continue.

"Then he dumped her anyway. Plus, he wasn't the only one she had on a string. Anyway, so one can't help but think there had to be a smidgen of guilt in that botoxed body. Even Aria. You won't believe it, but Aria went into a tailspin after you were sent away and Hope was never found.

"She always had dabbled with weed and stuff, but she went hard core, like she had to shut it all out. She feels guilty too, that she should have been a better older sister, been around to take care of us. That's why she masks the pain and guilt with drugs and thugs, she doesn't feel she deserves any better. She said one time she'd wished she could have taken one of our places to save at least one of us."

Both sisters had tears in their eyes.

Char fell silent, each sat deep in her own regretful thoughts.

Sniffing, Char plucked a tissue out of a box on the table. She smiled sadly at Kessa. "And poor little you. I only felt my own pain, I never thought about how hard it had been for you. I mean your family disowned you, threw you away. What a dreadful, devastating time. You must have been so lonely..."

Kessa covered her face with her hands and bowed her head. She could hear Char crying.

Char sobbed, "I am so sorry, Faith, I am so very sorry. Can you ever forgive me?"

Kessa got up and sat down on the side of the bed and hugged her sister. "You didn't do anything wrong, Char. You have nothing to be sorry for. We were all dealt a wretched blow. The only thing you have to be sorry for is for still calling me Faith."

She could feel Char giggle against her arms, she laughed too, it broke the tension. They both took more tissues and wiped their eyes.

After a few moments, Kessa returned to the chair. Her expression serious, compassionate, nonjudgmental. "Char," she said cautiously. "It seems Aria wasn't the only one to drown her sorrows with drugs."

Char pulled at the wet tissues in her hands, wiped as a few more tears fell. She turned demoralized green eyes to her sister.

"It's true." She waved her arm. "I mean, how did I get here?" Her short laugh was grim. Her body shuddered, she closed her eyes and leaned back against the pillows.

Kessa sat and waited. She felt there was more Char wanted to say.

Char opened her eyes, her gaze settled lovingly on her younger sister like a tender shawl. "Yes, they had given me pain medication while I was in the hospital and then when I got out because I had broken bones, my face, my back, you know.

"I kept asking for them, and they kept giving them to me, out of guilt too I think because no one could fix me. I just, well, I spiraled, there was nothing to live for. Then," she rolled her eyes, "I met Jaspar. Actually, he met me, at a party. I didn't realize until a long time later that," she broke off, heartache striking her face.

"Char, you don't have to-"

Char held up her hand, shaking her head. "Yes I do. I have to get it all out. He, Jaspar had deliberately had someone introduce us. He was a hottie, I mean, he was a construction worker, and well, you know." She smiled sheepishly.

"Anyway, he knew Pops had money, and heaven knows we all know how I look, what would my prospects be, really. I married him. Deep down I knew, I knew he married me for my money. But it was better than living alone. How could I not know with Aria sniping about it all the time." Her face turned downcast.

Kessa scooted forward on her chair again and took Char's hand. "That's something else we're going to fix. We sisters all need to hang together, and Matthew too of course, to support each other. Maybe Dad too, I don't know."

Char's eyes shone. "Somehow I knew, dreamed, that your coming back would turn into a blessing. I had hoped," her eyes dropped, "that we could turn back the clock. Yet, when I first saw you, well, you were so beautiful and confident, a writer for Pete's sake! I mean, I was so envious, I...I behaved so horribly to you."

Kessa pressed Char's hand with affection. "We're starting fresh, Char. We'll pretend none of that ever happened. Be the sisters we were meant to be. Seriously. Okay?"

Char smiled radiantly at her. "You are such a saint, dear Faith, Kessa, I'll get used to it. Maybe a name tag would help."

They laughed in sisterly companionship. Char's smile drooped. "If only you could fix my marriage too."

"What do you mean?"

Char shrugged one shoulder. "Oh, I shouldn't say, but, I've put everything else out there." A deep breath fell into a suffering sigh. "Jaspar is a mean, cruel, brutal man who not only beats me but cheats on me all the time."

Wistfully, she lamented, "If only I'd waited. There's," she turned pink. "There's this man, actually he's a minister. I went to him for counseling and we," her cheeks blushed redder. "Well, we fell in love." Now a dreamy smile lit her disfigured face, softening and aligning the crookedness.

She blinked and said quickly, "But we never, I mean we never, ever, you know-"

"Consummated the friendship?" Kessa offered impishly

If possible, Char flushed even redder. "Yeah." She sobered. "No, we have not have sex. In fact," eyes and face drooped, "we haven't seen each other for months. I'm married. He's Episcopalian so he could get married, but, like I said, I'm married and we're not going to sin." She uttered adamantly with a scowl, "Even if Jaspar does."

Confused, Kessa asked, "I don't understand, why don't you divorce Jaspar?"

Suddenly Char looked ashamed. She held the tissues to her face, peered over them at her sister. She dropped her hands in her lap. "I wasn't exactly 100% truthful with you. The doctors eventually refused to fill my pain prescriptions. They said I had to get off them. They didn't understand," anguish wracked her body, she clenched the tissues in her fists.

"I couldn't, *can't*, stop. I can't stop." She wept bitterly, said on am anguished rasp, "I can't stop, and Jaspar is the one who gets me my- drugs."

She raised tear-sodden eyes to her sister. "He gets them, Kessa, you understand? If I divorce him he won't get them for me anymore, then what will I do?"

Chapter Twenty-Nine

After a few very early hours on the sixth day of searching, Gray walked up the driveway of the Goldbrooke home, his boots crunching over the mix of small stones and gravel.

Investigation of the house had been completed with zero results. The yard and house had been gone over twice. He made his way to where Rick and Sergeant Stiller and several other deputies were conversing.

The men greeted Gray.

"So, anything?" Gray asked, although he could already tell by their expressions nothing had turned up.

Stiller said, "I guess we're going to have to pull it in. There's nothing here, Whitewolf. Good try." The others nodded bleakly.

The group stood, feet shifting, hope gone. Already moving on to the next case in their minds.

Gray put a hand to his chin and tapped his fingers. "Hold on a sec, don't anybody move." He jogged away, around the house.

Everyone stared at each other puzzled.

Gray came back with something in his hand. He held his hand out. He was holding a stone.

"Yeah," Stiller said, "it's a stone. Why are you showing it to us?"

Gray grinned, motioned to an area behind and close to the house. There was a scattering of the same stones in a more or less four feet by two feet rectangle.

Gray said, "Look around. I got this stone from the driveway. The driveway is a mixture of these stones and gravel. There," he pointed at the rectangle, "and the driveway are the only places where these stones are in the entire property."

"So?" Stiller crossed his arms and stared in perplexity at Gray like he'd lost a brain cell or two.

Gesturing to the stone area, he went on, "There're no flowers or vegetables on or around the stones, there's nothing here at all, except a few blades of grass that's sprung up. Check out the rest of the yard," he spanned his hand out.

"There's none of these around any of the trees or bushes although there are wood chips around some. So, why would someone toss, I say toss because they're not placed in perfect rows, why would someone toss these rocks here?"

Stiller considered what he was saying. He raised a hand and called out, "Jeb, bring one of the dogs over."

When the officer jogged over with the K-9, Stiller told him to stop a few yards away. "Jeb, let the dog go around the house again, start him as close to the house as possible then let him go but don't lead him."

Jeb nodded and gave the dog a command. The dog took off right away, nose all over the ground. The group of five deputies watched with interest.

As soon as man and dog got close to the building the deputy let go of the leash. The dog kept going, sniffing back and forth and up and down along the base of the house.

When he got to the area with the stones, the dog hesitated, went around, over the rocks, sniffing like crazy. Then he came to a complete stop and alerted on the stones.

Jeb ran over and patted the dog, praising him. "Something's under these rocks. Blaster must have been too far away from the spot on the other search attempts and the rocks covered or muffled any scent."

Stiller pulled off his hat, rubbed his head and slapped the cap back on. "Well, I'll be. Whitewolf, I've heard things about you,

you have an uncanny 6th sense about things. This sure as hell proves it."

Gray said, "Just noticing things, that's all it is. We don't know if, or what's there yet. Could be a family pet. Let's go."

"Yeah." Stiller turned around, cupped his hands around his mouth and yelled, "Carol, call Craig Wagner, tell him to bring the hoes."

An officer out in the yard waved her hand and dipped her head to her radio on her shoulder to call dispatch.

"You're kidding, right?" Gray said, with a shake to his head. "You can't dig the ground up with a hoe. The forensic guys have to sift through, around, and even under if they find something."

The sergeant grinned. "Yeah, kidding. She's calling a specialty group trained specifically for this type of dissection, we nicknamed them the 'hoes.' Cute, huh?"

Rick and the others laughed. Gray rolled his eyes. His phone rang. He pulled it out and looked at it. The name Nefertiti displayed. He stepped aside to answer it. "Hello? Donna?"

"Yeah," she whispered, "it's me. Tuesday, it's gonna be Tuesday. Gotta go." She clicked off.

Gray went back over to the officers standing by the rectangle of stones.

He said, "We have to do this right, people. Everyone needs to step away. The CSI's will sift down and around until they get something. Any part of this area can be evidence. So, everyone, back away."

While waiting for news on the dig, Gray was kept busy the next couple days with a series of drug busts. They were bringing in a new strong breed of heroin now and kids were dying all over the place as a result.

Back at the Goldbrooke site watching the experts excavate the scene of the stones, Gray's direct supervisor called.

"Whitewolf," Gray answered.

"Hello Gray. Listen, your ex-partner, Ray Daniels, well, sorry to tell you, but he passed today. It was his heart. His wife is at the hospital, I thought you might want to see him and talk to her, while he's still, you know, there."

Gray's own heart hurt at the news. "Yeah, thanks." He slipped the phone back in his pocket and walked over to Rick.

"I've gotta go, this dig will take more hours, days probably. I'll get with you later." He hiked quickly to his truck and drove off to the hospital.

He said his goodbyes to his old partner. Ray always had heart trouble and he had been overweight and ate crap, it was only a matter of time. Didn't make it any easier though.

Gray spent some time with his widow, Gina. He had known her pretty well too. He was washed out, drained, by time he left the hospital. The funeral would be on Friday.

Hitting the walk to get to his truck, his stomach grumbled. Breakfast had been a long time ago. Wondering how the dig was going, thinking about what he wanted to eat, he ambled along with his head was down.

Just as he reached his truck he looked up. He saw a woman walking hastily out to the street, and she looked fit to be tied. He'd recognize that light blonde hair anywhere.

"Kessa!" he called out.

She looked up and stopped next to her jeep.

He jogged over to her. "Hey," he said when he reached her. "What are you doing here? You look nice." He admired the chiffon blouse. "Matches your eyes."

There were two vivid red circles on her cheeks and she was mad. "I came to see my sister, Char."

He grinned. "Good, that's good, how's she doing?"

"I am so upset, I can't think straight. I have to tell you something. You need to do something, tell me what to do," she rattled on disjointed then clutched his sleeve. "Deputy, please, can you help-"

Now he was concerned. "Of course I'll help you, whatever, whatever you need. Just chill down and tell me-"

"Oh my gosh!" Kessa shrieked. Her hands went over her mouth.

"What-" When Gray saw what had upset her so much he swore, "Oh shit."

Spray painted across the side of her jeep was the word MURDERER.

Gray set his hands on her shoulders and squeezed them gently to get her to look at him and away from the jeep. "It's okay, we can fix it. I got a guy that paints cars. It'll be all right."

But she just stood staring at the jeep in despair. "I don't get it, why, why do people insist on believing-"

Out of nowhere a rock came flying and cracked off Kessa's head, someone hollered, "Murderer!"

Gray caught her as she stumbled backwards. "What the hell was-" an arm around her back he levered Kessa back up. While steading her on her feet, Gray scanned the area to see who threw the rock, but whoever it was had already fled.

Kessa wobbled, putting a hand to her head, a red gash slashed across the side of her head.

"Let me see," Gray said. Tipping her chin, he lifted her head up so he could see her wound. "Son of a bitch," he spat.

"Deputy, I just, I'm okay," Kessa mumbled, wincing in pain.

"No, you're not. I'm taking you back inside. You're going to see a doctor." He looked down the street where the offender must have fled.

He debated trying to catch him but the person had a good head start and too many streets branched off the one they were on, there'd be no way to know which one he took. Besides, he didn't want to leave her alone, there could be accomplices.

Gray brought her inside and walked her back to the emergency room and demanded someone come and care for her.

Fortunately it was a slow day for emergencies and Kessa was seen to right away. Gray paced while an intern cleaned and dressed Kessa's wound.

The intern said he needed to get the clearance papers and he'd be right back.

Kessa sat on the edge of the gurney swinging her legs. There was a butterfly bandage on the upper corner of her temple. "I'm still trying to look like you." She giggled pointing at his scar.

He smiled, glad she was able to dredge up her sense of humor.

Then the corners of her mouth turned down, tears gleamed. Her voice breaking, she lamented, "When is it ever going to end?"

He stood beside the gurney and wrapped an arm around her.

"It will end when we catch the bastard who did this to you and your sisters." He pulled her head to his chest in solace like he had at her house after DeBarra had attacked her.

His chin set gently against her head, he said, "I swear to you, Kessa, I'll do everything I can to find out who was responsible for hurting you girls and taking Hope, and have them prosecuted."

Delicately stroking her hair with his stocky hand, he told her, "Matt has even brought it up to me, re-investigating it. He wants to clear your name." He didn't tell her about Mrs. Goldbrooke's house. The rectangle stone scene was too uncertain, no point in getting her hopes up.

"Here," he tugged his shirt from his belt and offered it to her. "Here, dry 'em up. It'll be okay, you'll be okay."

Kessa dabbed at her eyes then smiled up at him. "You go above and beyond for me, Deputy. I fear I've saturated half of your shirts with my tears. If Matthew were home it would be his shirts that would be sodden!"

A fleeting knot of chagrin nicked Gray's expression then it cleared. "Uh huh. I'll survive. So, what we're going to do now, is pick up some food and go to my house, and then go horseback riding for an hour or so, all right? We both need the ride and wind to clear our heads."

Grinning with delight, she said, "Have you always been this bossy?"

"Yes. There has to be someone in charge. Come on." Gray held her close while she slipped off the high gurney. Her body slid slowly down against his, so close they could feel every contour, supple softness skimming sinewy muscle.

The descent seemed to go on forever until she gently landed on her feet. Eyes connected, neither moved, each could feel the other's heart beating against their chest.

The intern dashed into the room with papers in his hand. The couple split apart and Gray moved to the door.

The intern said to Kessa, "Here you go. Just sign and you're free to go." Kessa signed and then the intern handed her some more papers.

"This is just information about taking aspirin for any pain and to call if you have questions, etc."

Kessa thanked him, took the papers, folded them up and put them in her purse. Gray was now standing by the door looking out into the hall. The intern left and Kessa joined Gray.

He smiled at her. "Ready?"

"Yup." She didn't know if it was a good idea to go to his house again, but it couldn't be any worse than what had already happened since she returned to this miserable town. Of course she also could not refuse the horseback-riding offer.

"When I get settled, someday," she sounded hopelessly plaintive, "I would love to get my own horse."

"That would be a great goal to shoot for." His palm on her back he propelled her out the door.

The corners of her lips turned up in a silly bow, she laughed, "Yeah, my new role will be a goal for a foal I can ride on a grassy knoll..."

His eyes rolled. "I didn't know you were a poet. A really bad poet." He grinned at her pretend insulted look.

"Come on. We'll go in my truck. You can't drive around in your jeep like it is. I'll send someone to come and take care of it."

They traveled down the hall and back out the door to the bright sunshine.

When they got to his truck, she said shyly, gratefully, "You always seem to be taking care of me and my car. Thank you."

"Well," he ducked his head, opened the passenger door for her. "I'm a cop, it's what we do. If your brother was here he'd be doing it. You know I told him I'd look out for you, be the big brother. Here, let me help you up."

Chapter Thirty

Gray stopped on the way and picked up BBQ with onion rings and slaw and cold sodas then drove back to his place.

He carried the food around to the back pasture while Kessa practically skipped over to the stables.

They went inside, she breathed deeply of the fresh cut hay and horses and mud. "Oh, it's been so long, so long since I've ridden. I've missed it so much. Who is this?" She went right over to Sabbath.

Petting his nose, she said, "He's beautiful. And big. Really big."

Gray put the food in a pack, set it on a barrel then went over and opened Sabbath's stall and walked the horse out. "This is Sabbath."

Sabbath rubbed his nose on Gray's sleeve then bumped his shoulder. "Yeah, I know, I've been neglecting you. It's all her fault," he whispered in the horse's ear. He got a bit and slipped it on the horse.

"Hey," Kessa complained with a pout.

"It's true." Gray left and went back inside his house and came out with a rifle and his saddle. A whiff of worn leather and gun oil came with him. He threw the saddle on the horse and buckled it, then stuck the gun in the side of the saddle.

He strode down the barn, straw and dust scattering under his boots and stopped at another stall. A palomino stuck her head out.

Gray opened the stall and led her out. She pranced with him to where Kessa and Sabbath waited. "This is Bamboo. She's for you."

Kessa rubbed Bamboo's ears and ran her hand down the golden horse's cream colored mane. "Hi Bamboo, you're very beautiful too." She glanced back at Sabbath. "Oh, I get it, Black Sabbath, right?"

"Yep. You're a smart one." Gray ambled over to a wall inside the barn, the hay strewn on the floor crackled under the crush of his boots. Several saddles hung on the wall, he took down the smallest one went back and tossed it on Bamboo's back.

Bamboo snorted and danced sideways. "All right, calm down, girl. Boy all you females are feisty lately." Gray got reins and put them on the horse.

"Do I get a gun too?" Kessa asked, letting the feisty comment go. She realized he said things to stir her up, get a reaction. Matthew had told her the deputy thought she was cold and rigid.

He studied her feminine slenderness. "Yeah, once I teach you how to use one. A woman with a weapon only gets it taken from her and then used on her. I can teach you.

"When I'm satisfied you know how to handle one and how to keep it hidden but quickly accessible, I'll get you your own. This town has grown way too dangerous." He turned back to finish getting the horses ready.

"Anyone ever tell you that you're a chauvinist?" Kessa asked him.

"You mean besides you? Yes." He retrieved the food pack and tied it to Sabbath's saddle.

Holding both reins, Gray led the horses outside. He dropped Sabbath's and went to the palomino. Next to the horse, he bent over with his fingers twined and said, "Hop on."

She looked uncertainly at his hands. He waited. She went over, put a foot on his hands and he hoisted her up and onto the horse.

Gray adjusted the stirrups. Then standing back, he held a hand over his eyes to shade them from the sun and looked up at her. "You sit a horse really well. Even Bamboo's a little big for you. Are you going to be able to handle her?"

For an answer, Kessa kicked the golden horse and they took off across the meadow.

"Hey!" Gray squawked then leaped on Sabbath and galloped after her.

He caught up and rode alongside her. He smiled because she had the biggest grin on her face. Her yellow hair bounced and flowed behind her, the chiffon blouse fluttered like a flower in the wind.

He said loudly over the galloping hooves, "It's good to see you finally really happy. You are, aren't you?" He asked, "I mean at this moment, not later or tomorrow maybe, but right at this moment?"

Decreasing briefly to a canter, she thought for a second, then smiled broadly. "Yes. I am blissfully happy at this moment."

After racing side-by-side for quite a distance, they eventually slowed the horses to a trot to enjoy the scenery.

Gray led them past the green pastures with tall tassels of waving grass to ride beside the vast lake. The day was warm and sunny, the breeze light, birds flew from tree to tree with singing chirps, the sky a clear blue dome.

The water sparkled, churning peacefully. They had the place to themselves, there wasn't a soul in sight. The horses' hooves clacked and clumped on the pebbles and wet dirt.

Gray headed closer the lake. There was a picnic table near the shore. He hopped off Sabbath, tossed the reins loosely over the saddle then went to help her. "Here," he held his arms up to her.

"It's okay, I can get down by my-"

He reached up and grabbed her around the waist pulling her to the side. She slipped off like she had off the gurney in the hospital, suspended for a heartbeat up in his hands, then, holding her securely, he pulled her down to him.

With the horse at her back she was pressed against Gray. He lowered her slowly, her hands on his shoulders, she slid down along his body. She felt the cordon of muscles under his shirt hard against her soft curves, then trailing down his stalwart legs in the frayed jeans, to her tiptoes finally to her feet. His hands stayed around her waist, their eyes held. He bent his head, she leaned back.

"Deputy, I-"

"Can you stop with the deputy stuff? I thought by now we're at least friends," Gray said, annoyed. His lopsided smile took the edge off. "My friends call me Gray."

Inside, he could kick himself for what he just did, again. She'd felt so exquisitely perfect against him when he held her in the hospital that he needed to feel it again. He was tempting fate and it was going to bite him.

He looked so boyish when he was irritated. Swallowing a grin, Kessa would never tell him that. "Okay, Gray. My fill-in foster-brother. I like your name. Your whole name. Are both your parents Native Americans?" she asked breaking the tension.

He stared at her for a second, emotions crossed his face, the pulse at his temple beat. He took the horses over to graze in some tall grass then retrieved the pack and brought it over and set it on the table.

"Yes," he answered her question. "My parents are both Atapante. Not full-blooded as I've told you, there's a Scottish relative from way back. Actually there's quite a few. The recessive blue gene beat out the dominant brown apparently. Unusual but it happens."

"Oh yes," she remembered, looking up at them, "the blue eyes."

The blue eyes searched her face for, for what? They dropped to her lips then back to her inquisitive gaze. Breaking the contact, he started taking the food out of the pack.

They sat down at the table and dug into barbeque sandwiches, coleslaw, crunching the crisp onion rings, washing it all down with soda.

After munching for a few minutes, Gray said, "Tell me about little Kessa. What were you like before, you know, before? I bet you were always bearing a Band-Aid somewhere." Motioning to her head at the butterfly bandage like a white slash of paint against her face.

Gray took a huge bite out of his sandwich. A dab of barbeque sauce left a spot next his mouth. Kessa reached up and wiped it with her finger. An uncomfortable silence fell between them.

Taking a drink of soda, Kessa set the can down and said, "You're right. On my knee, elbow, I was energetic and adventuresome, it didn't come without its dues. I was Faith then. I loved ballet, singing badly off key, gymnastics, Sunday school, my sisters and Matthew."

She nibbled at a ring, recalling her past. "It was, you know, innocent, carefree then. It was funny, even then, Matthew barely a teenager always tried to watch out for me and my sisters." She smiled at the memory. "In the summer we were always in our swim suits."

The picture of her in his jacket, dress in shreds blew into his mind. Through a mouthful of coleslaw, the thoughts came out loud, Gray said, "Bet he never got to see you almost naked like I did."

He swallowed awkwardly at her gasp, stuck his fork in the dish of slaw and wiped his mouth. Without looking at her, he mumbled, "I'm really sorry, Kess. That was so crass. I don't know where the hell that came from."

Scrunching his eyes at his awareness of his Freudian slip, he set his napkin down and turned to her. Her face was as pink as bubblegum. He went to touch her arm but stopped.

"Seriously, I'm really sorry. I was trying to make you laugh again, it was lame and boorish. I'm not used to being around ladies lately, nice ones anyway, except for my mother and sisters. My mother would even at my age wash my mouth out with soap if she'd heard me."

His face a broil of embarrassment, he said softly, "Can we forget I shot off my crude mouth?"

Kessa sipped her soda. The land all around them was breathtaking, full of lush meadows with spindly grass rippling in the breeze. They sat overlooking the crystal blue water, behind them lofty trees reached for the sun.

"Okay," she said, breathing in the fresh air and piney-grape smell of the wild Oregon grape. "It's so beautiful, isn't it?"

He looked at her then away. "Yeah, beautiful."

Holding her soda, Kessa indicated his horse with her hand. "He is unusually black. As jet black and shiny as your hair. It's rare for a horse to be that pure black."

Gulping his embarrassment at his stupid coarse comment, and grateful for the change in conversation, Gray said, "He's a Friesian. They're great horses. Energetic, muscular yet elegant." He leaned an elbow on the table and watched her watching his horse.

"He's fantastic, Gray." She turned towards him. She told him briefly about the orphanage, Convent Grisaille. The horror and pain effused so desperately from her entire being, Gray reached over and laid his hand over hers.

Kessa looked over at Sabbath, so strong, the way she wanted to be. After a shuddering deep breath, she turned back to Gray. His eyes reflected such sadness and compassion, and anger, it felt nice for a change to have someone care about her other than her brother.

She dismissed her egregious memories with a toss of her head and a warm smile. After all, she was outside riding horses on a gorgeous day in a beautiful place with a man, that although he could be crude and bossy, and unnerving with strength and vitality, and simmering aggression, he had a tender heart. "Tell me about you, you said you have sisters?"

He told her stories about his three sisters, two older, one younger about how they tormented and loved him.

They spent another half an hour sharing their lives. Looking at his watch, Gray reluctantly stood up and started packing up their remains.

"We gotta get going. I've got a crucial case to check into. I'm expecting a very important phone call. I've worked 14 hours straight, this was a great break."

Kessa helped him pack up. He hooked the pack on Bamboo's saddle.

"You ready?" he asked, cupping his hands for her to step into.

Kessa was a foot away when Gray suddenly put a hand on her chest and shoved her backwards- at the same time he pulled out a gun from seemingly nowhere and shot twice at the ground in rapid succession.

The horses whinnied and broke away galloping across the field into the woods.

Stunned, Kessa caught her balance. "What did you-" her face turned white when she saw why Gray was shooting. A dead snake lay in the tall grass.

Gray told her, "A western rattler, rattlesnake. Came out of that log there. Aw shi- crap," he muttered, watching the horses disappear. Kneeling, he shoved the small pistol back in an ankle holster.

Kessa was gawking wide-eyed at the dead snake with two bullet holes in its head. Then she saw his concern at the fleeing horses. "Are we stranded?" She knew they were quite a distance from his home.

Gray whistled.

In seconds, Sabbath appeared out of the woods cantering towards them.

"Bamboo will go straight back to the barn. She frightens easily and goes home."

When the horse reached them, Gray grabbed the reins to hold Sabbath steady, he was still skittish from the gunshots. Holding the reins, Gray watched Kessa petting the horse's powerful shoulders, his own shoulders arched up vicariously feeling the long warm strokes.

Tearing his envious gaze away, he scanned the countryside debating in his mind how to do this. They were too far out to walk back.

Whether he put Kessa in front of him, her butt bouncing pressed against his...legs, or, he took a deep breath, *he put her behind him where she'd have to lean against his back and hold onto him.* Neither bode well for him.

She looked at his long, lean strong legs in the jeans and said, "It looks like you're a runner. I love to run, I can easily do 8 or 10 miles, more. We can-"

He took in her pleasing full lips then looked down at the slender shapely legs encased in snug jeans. "We should go on a run together sometime." He held his watch up. "Unfortunately, I've got to be back in a few minutes and we're a good 15 miles out."

He bent and cupped his hands. "Come on," the words came out brusque.

She looked surprised. "How are we-"

"Go on, we'll ride double," he replied, keeping his expression blank.

"Are you sure? I can-"

"Kessa, just, get on."

"Okay." She put her foot on his hands and he pushed her up, she gracefully swung her leg around and landed lightly on the horse. She looked down at him. "Wow, this is a long way up!"

He didn't say anything, just wiped his hands on his jeans, stuck his boot in the stirrup and hauled himself up behind her. He made a tsk sound and the horse started a trot, the sudden motion knocked Kessa back, she fell against Gray, her hands landed on his thighs to catch her balance.

Gray rolled his eyes thinking *it's going to be a long ride.*

"Are you sure he's okay with us both on him?" Kessa asked, bending forward to pat the long mane.

An arm around her loosely holding the reins, Gray said quietly, "Yeah, he's fine."

His voice low in her ear, her hair tickling his face in the breeze, they spoke only the occasional word on the way back.

When they returned to the barn, Gray slid off and led Sabbath close to the stable. He could see Bamboo off to the side innocently chomping on grass like she'd done nothing wrong, but he could see her peek at him, so he knew she knew she had been bad.

247

Near the stable, Gray reached up for Kessa, but this time he slid one arm around her waist and the other under her legs and lifted her off the horse and set her down on her feet.

"Go on inside," Gray said to Sabbath, giving him a pat.

The horse obliged and trotted into the stable. Gray took Kessa's hand, boots sloughing through the tall grass, and led her over to the wooden fence that cordoned off a part of the pasture for training the horses.

He leaned back against the fence, pulled Kessa to stand in front of him then let go of her hand. Wide open meadows dotted with wildflowers flowed soft to the forest. Except for the occasional velvety breeze, they were enveloped in stillness.

"Uh," he cleared his throat. "Listen, Kess. I have to be straight up with you. This brother thing is not going to work." He looked at her then lowered his head.

"Um, I want you to absolutely turn to me when you have problems or need any kind of help, but, uh, I'm going to have to have someone else, uh, actually assist you." He glanced up, but she looked so hurt he dropped his eyes again, staring at his boots.

"I, I don't understand. What did I do? Was it the murderer thing on my jeep? The rock? I didn't mean to be so much trouble," her voice was tight.

He raised his head. "It's not you, Kess, it's me." He hesitated, then said, "It's this," he grasped her shoulders and pulled her to him, expecting a slap and retort, his lips crushed hers.

When he didn't feel a slap, his control vanished and the kiss turned insanely wild.

At first taken by surprise, Kessa froze. Unable to stop his onslaught even if she wanted to, and she didn't want to- her hands pressing against his chest slid up to his shoulders and wrapped around his neck, pulling him tighter to her, responding with ignited passion to his unrelenting needful kiss.

"Kessa," he moaned against her mouth, then, pulled back slightly. "Matt is gonna kill me." Unable to resist, he cradled her head with one hand, the other spanned her back, he could feel her heat through the sheer blouse.

Even as he was telling himself to back off, get away, he lowered his head and took her into bruising, euphoric torment. Lost in the fire blazing between them, his brain burning, Gray fervently tasted the lips he hadn't been able to take his eyes off since the day they met.

His hands moved, tethering her to him, cinching her waist, stroked up her back, crushing her against his body.

Kessa's palms cupped his face. Feeling the planes and afternoon bristles on his jaw, her fingers roamed up to twine in his hair, tugging the locks in desire.

Her response knocked away any reserve Gray had left. He swept her up in his arms, lips still bound, he started towards his house. He was so gone he didn't hear his phone ringing.

Kessa struggled to pull away, to speak. "Gray, Gray, your phone."

He looked at her dazed, the pulse over his temple pounding.

The ringing finally broke through his muddled brain. He set her on her feet. Keeping an iron arm around her, he pulled the phone out of his pocket, pushed the button trying to steady his shaking hand.

Never taking his eyes off her, he said into the phone, "Whitewolf."

A voice came through, Kessa could just barely hear it.

"Yeah, Rick. Tell me," Gray said hoarsely.

Tingling with sensation, her heart beating like a drum, Kessa felt dizzy, drunk with ardor. She watched Gray deliberately keep his face impassive as he listened, but she'd seen a flicker of, something, she couldn't tell, he'd masked it quickly.

He listened for a moment then said, "I'll be right there, I'm at my house." He clicked the phone off and slipped it in his pocket.

Still locking eyes, it was like he was drinking her in. Her lips swollen and red, eyes glowing and sultry. "God, you're so beautiful." Blinking hard with a sigh, he said reluctantly, "I have to go."

He still held her tightly, tensely with one arm, slowly he forced himself to loosen his grip. "I'm so sorry, Kessa. Thank God

Rick called and broke, the- the spell. I didn't mean for that to happen. I was taking you to my bed, I wasn't thinking clearly. I've never lost my mind like this before. It's like I'm a match and you're a matchbook. It was instant flames for me when we connected."

He looked off to the horizon then dragged his eyes back to hers. His tone turned hard. "That's why I- I can't be like a brother to you, because I don't have brotherly feelings towards you. I'm as bad as that bastard DeBarra.

"I was so crazed with jealousy when I saw you with him that night at the restaurant, but I denied it to myself. Told myself I was just looking out for you. But now, I…I took advantage of you, and I broke my promise to Matt that I wouldn't."

Kessa moved to say something but he kept on, "From the moment we collided that day, I've fought to keep my hands off you, to not dream about you at night, to," he wiped an arm across his face. "I'm sorry, I shouldn't have done it. I wish to God I was, but I'm not the man you deserve." He dropped his arm and started to walk to the stables.

"What?" Kessa shook her head, then jogged after him.

"What?" she repeated catching up. "I don't have a say in the matter?"

He kept walking, she had to hurry to keep up with his long, quick strides. He didn't answer her, kept his eyes on the stable.

Kessa grabbed his sleeve and yanked. He finally stopped, turned still smoldering, pained eyes on her.

She cried, "Gray, I'm a big girl, an adult. I make my own decisions. You can't just-"

He went to touch her, but stuffed his hands in his pockets instead. "That's the thing. You're barely an adult. I'm the one that knows better and I acted before I could stop myself. I'm afraid if I don't get away from you right now I won't ever let you go. I'm as unscrupulous as a damned dog. It was wrong and it's not going to happen again. You don't know me, really, Kessa, I'm not a good man. I have to go now. They found bones at the old Goldbrooke place. Small, child sized bones."

Her head spinning, Kessa's mouth dropped, speechless.

"I wasn't going to tell you, Kessa, but it'll hit the news and I don't want you to hear it that way."

"Is it, is it…" she couldn't say the words.

"We don't know. I didn't want to get your hopes, emotions up, but," he turned away from her. "I have to see to the horses. I have a guy bringing your jeep around."

"Wait, Gray. I can take care of the horses. I've done it a hundred times. You just go, all right?"

He paused, regarding her earnestness. Struggling to keep the passion and the ache out of his face and voice, he nodded and said. "Okay. Call me if you need me."

He gave her a last look then took off for his truck.

Chapter Thirty-One

*G*ray went straight to the Goldbrooke house.

The jangle of police vehicles and vans still covered the area.

"So much for keeping the scene clean," he muttered, exiting his truck. He spotted Rick's shaved head and strode across the lawn to where he was standing near a van and other people all dressed in white from jackets to booties to hairnets.

Rick saw him and separated from the group to meet up.

"Hey," Rick started cheerfully, but then took in Gray's grim demeanor. "What's up?" he asked as they bumped fists once.

Gray stuffed his hands in his black jean pockets and hunched his shoulders. "Nothing. What's going on here? What'd they find?"

Rick considered Gray's stiff dismal bearing with an odd look. Even the normal vibrancy of his tanned face was subdued. Something had obviously happened to greatly disturb the deputy.

But Rick knew his friend, he was very close-mouthed about things. They'd need a few beers together before he could pry anything out of him.

He said, "Okay. Yeah, about six feet down they got to the bones. They're mostly out, including all the soil over, around and under them. There's rock further down so the person could have only dug so deep."

Gray observed the activity going on between the place behind the house and the forensic vans. "Well, there's something, it's not in vain, even if it's not the Kenton girl."

"Yup," Rick concurred. "Except they found faded fragments of what looks like a child's bathing suit. Blue with little stars on it." He'd read the notes on the missing child too.

A bit of awe and levity in his revelry, he said, "You got some kind of intuition bro. Never ceases to amaze me. It's gonna be days at least before they can identify the body. I just wanted you to see it before it goes. You're owed that. Come on."

The grass had grown and was now unkempt since Mrs. Goldbrooke's death. It partially covered their boots as they crossed to a van. Tubs and a mass amount of containers and tools littered tarps laid out on the lawn.

After viewing the bits of bones the CSI's had unearthed and meeting with Sergeant Stiller, Rick said, "So, let's go have that beer." Gray agreed. The tiny bones, few locks of blonde hair and child's swim suit was heartbreaking.

They went to Cache's Bar. Skipping the beer, Gray went for the hard stuff, throwing back shot after shot of bourbon and within an hour was trashed. He blabbed the whole scene with Kessa.

Rick shook his head from side-to-side and whistled. "I warned you about that piece, didn't I? I told you she's going to cause you trouble. You thought you hid it, but it was all over your face every time you looked at her, talked about her." He was drinking bourbon neat glass for glass with Gray.

"Yeah, she aggravated the hell out of you, that's the first sign you're toast." Rick chuckled with his lips on the rim of his glass.

Gray scowled at his friend. "She's not a *piece*, man. That's why I have to step away. She is a good kid, woman. I feel like shit. I let down my friend, and I took advantage of a situation like a mangy dog. I am such a jerk."

Rick threw back his drink, slammed the glass on the table and wiped his mouth with the back of his hand. He said, "Having feelings for a woman who reciprocates your advances is not the same thing as just taking advantage of her. It's obvious you feel more than just lust for her. You're just not used to that…um…in-strong-like-feeling anymore. I say go for it, bro, hit it."

Gray stared despondently down at his glass then sent his friend a short grin. "She'd have a field day on you if she heard you keep talking about her like she's an object instead of a person. Your ears would burn all day." He shook his head.

"I can't 'hit it' as you so eloquently put it. She deserves a hell of a lot better than me. Even Matt knows what a dog I am, he warned me off her."

He took a hard swallow, feeling the slow burn down his throat from the liquor. "Unfortunately, I can't trust myself around her anymore, and right now, until Matt gets back, she needs someone looking out for her." He chuckled mirthlessly.

"She thinks she's tough, can take care of herself, huh. The thing is, she trusts everybody. Including me. That's what happens when they're young and not familiar with this cold, hard world." He waved at the bartender, ordering them another shot.

Rick swiveled to smile at Gray and offered, "Hey, I'll watch over the little-"

Gray grabbed the front of his friend's shirt, his brows down low in a scowl. "Oh no you won't. You stay the hell away from her. I'll get, uh," he let go of Rick's shirt.

Rick smoothed his shirt and ordered yet another drink grinning at his friend.

Gray said, slurring his words, "I'll find the oldest deputy eunuch in the department. No wait, better, I'll get one of those really tough older female cops to keep an eye on her. Yeah, that's what I'll do."

Rick swung his bobbing head at Gray, grinning foolishly. "You got it bad, bro. You're gone on that girl, she's more than just a situation to you."

"Shut up, Rick," Gray slurred to his glass.

They drank and talked and drank some more then called a cab.

The sun burned through the window, he hadn't closed the curtains when he passed out in bed last night.

Struggling to get up, Gray had the hangover from hell. Groggy and head pounding, he climbed into the shower, dried off and pulled on a light blue t-shirt, black jeans and boots. Combing his hair, he ambled into the kitchen.

Tossing down several aspirin along with the strongest cup of coffee he could make, he pushed down a dry piece of toast. Leaning against the counter eating the toast, he saw the note on the table he'd left Kessa. A knife twisted in his heart. He set the coffee mug and plate in the sink, grabbed his keys and left.

He was driving towards the station when his phone rang. He looked at it, Nefertiti. "Hello, Donna, how's it going?"

She whispered, "Now, it's now. The guy has already come in from the lake and is heading to the bar." Click.

He stuffed the phone in his pocket and stepped on the gas hurtling across town to the bar, praying he'd get there, stash his truck and be hiding in the bushes by time the smuggler arrived.

He drove past Cache's, searching both sides of the street for the Malibu the guy he'd trailed before drove. Nothing.

At the end of the street, he swung back around and parked a few buildings down from the bar. The backs of the buildings on the street ran right up to the bordering forest.

Opening the glove box, he took out a .357 Magnum and stuck in the back of his belt then slipped into the woods and jogged through the cover of the trees until he neared the bar.

There wasn't another car in the lot and not a sign of the smuggler. He hunkered down but didn't have to wait long before he heard a car pulling into the lot. Peering through the leaves, he saw the Malibu go to the next building and park in their back lot.

The guy got out of the car, went to the trunk and pulled out a big box, just like before.

Tattoos crawling around the guy's neck and sleeved down his arms, he carried what looked like a heavy box staying close to the back trees as he made his way over to Cache's lot.

Just as he crossed the property line, he ducked into the woods.

Gray crept silently to where he saw him disappear. He thought he'd lost him when he saw movement only ten feet away. Leaves suddenly flew up.

"Oh yeah," he muttered, hurrying over to the disturbed land.

Crouching down, one hand braced on the ground, he brushed at the dirt with the other. He felt it. There was a door. It was covered with a sheet of fake grass and leaves. There was a tarnished brass circle as a lever.

He waited a few minutes to make sure the guy didn't see him following him, then he carefully opened the trap door and climbed in.

It was dark, but not pitch black inside. A ladder was attached to the inside wall.

Gray closed the door and climbed down the ladder until his feet hit solid ground. Staying close to the wall, he let his eyes adjust to the dark and then surveyed the area. It was definitely a tunnel, smelled of dank damp earth. It went in only one direction.

He could see electric lanterns spaced every 30-40 feet along the wall. Not enough to read by but enough to find his way. He looked down at his shirt. He wished he'd had time to change from the pale blue t-shirt to a black one.

And, he must have shrunk it last washing because it wasn't skintight but it was snug enough that if he was going to go pump iron the short sleeves could tear. The light color would show like a spotlight in the dark, but there was nothing he could do about it now.

He trod slowly and quietly down the tunnel staying in the shadows close to the wall opposite of the lanterns. He walked a good hundred yards before it looked like he was approaching the end.

A few more steps and he could see the tunnel opened into a big room, a basement, made out of rock, cement and dirt like the tunnel.

He took out his cell to call Rick for back-up but there was no reception, he slid it back in his pocket. He pulled the magnum out from his waistband, then with his back against the wall, he craned his neck around the opening to peer inside the room.

It was a little but not a lot brighter than the tunnel. Not much inside, some crates, boxes, a wooden table off to the side with some sturdy wood chairs with slates for backs. It looked like there wasn't anyone inside. The smuggler must have gone up into the bar. Gray tucked the gun back in his jeans.

Creeping inside, he debated whether to hide in the room, against a dark wall, to catch someone when they came in or out of the tunnel, or go up the stairs and see whom the smuggler went to meet. He waited, listening, nothing.

He decided to move. Slipping a few feet in- BLAM!

He was hit in the head with a board, he dropped to his knees.

"Grab him you idiots."

Even with his head spinning and eyesight blurred, Gray recognized Sheriff Lombardo's voice. Gray's arms were seized on both sides and he was jerked to his feet.

Two brawny men held him, twisting his arms behind his back. Lombardo, yanking his pants up but not completely over the big belly sauntered over to Gray.

"Well, well, well, Whitewolf. Gotcha."

Gray tried to hold his vision steady on the sheriff when Lombardo hauled his fist back and drove it into Gray's stomach. Grunting, Gray folded and would have fallen if the men weren't holding him.

"I told you I saw his truck over on 2nd Ave. We got him 'cause of me!" a voice bragged nearby.

Gray's head hung over, he squinted up through the hair flopped over his eyes. Deputy Bruce Sutton, skinny with the nose like a giraffe and overbite, was hopping up and down.

"Get a grip, Bruce, before you pee your pants," Deputy Wayde Smith said, coming out of the shadows. The room was an illusion, there were walls that couldn't be seen in the dusky light.

"You boys better hold him good, he's a helluva bruiser. He gets loose he'll break all your necks in a New York minute," Jimmy Lombardo warned.

Two powerful men held Gray. The boxer-like smuggler was on one side, and another muscle-bound male he didn't know held him on the other.

"Go tie him up. Tight. Bruce, get one of those chairs, bring it over."

Gray's head swaying, his vision grew steadier, he could make out the sheriff, Wayde, Bruce, the smuggler and the other man holding him. Besides them, there were three other burly men entering the room. His vision clearing, he suddenly jerked both arms to break free.

"Little help!" the smuggler yelled as both men struggled to hold him.

The other three thugs ran over, one punched Gray in the stomach, he doubled over again, another delivered a hard upper cut snapping Gray's head back, but he kept fighting. All five men struggled with him, dragging him to the chair, they shoved him down.

"Tie him up you fools, quick!" Lombardo ordered.

Gray thrashed to get his arms free. The men still held him while Wayde and Bruce tied his wrists behind the back of the chair so tightly he was pulled back and couldn't even kick out with his legs.

Straining against the ropes, Gray fought to get loose, but he was tied tight and secure. He could tell they had taken his .357 when they'd nailed him with the board, he couldn't feel the gun pressing into his back.

Wayde knelt and frisked him, taking out his cell. Then he checked his legs. Smiling at the gun he pulled out of Gray's ankle holster.

Lombardo stomped over to stand in front of him. He leaned over with a fat hand on a fat knee and grabbed Gray's hair, holding his head up so he couldn't move it. Then he smashed his hefty fist in Gray's face, the blow bashing his head to the left. Lombardo punched him again then let go of his hair.

"That's for taking that tasty piece away from me. Which now, without you butting in, I can take care of unfinished business." Shaking the pain out of his fist, Lombardo grinned hugely, the piggy eyes disappeared in his fleshy face.

Gray's blood ran cold, but his impassive expression didn't betray his fear for Kessa.

The sheriff gloated, "I'd like to bring her here and make you watch, but, you're a wily one. I can't take any chances keeping you alive for long. The guys are gonna have to take care of you right away."

His face bloody, Gray bucked, twisting with all his might to break the bonds. "You hit like a girl Jimmy," he snarled, "and you're a shit coward." He spat blood, trying to goad the sheriff into freeing him. "Untie me and I'll-"

Lombardo punched him again, Gray's head wrenched to the side. "You ain't doing nothin' anymore, boy," the fat man said. "That chair is like steel, it ain't gonna break, and these fools aren't stupid enough to let you loose."

"Yeah," Bruce giggled. "Look at those muscular guns and chest, he'd give that Thor guy a run for his money, huh? He gets you against the ropes you're done for."

Gray's biceps were pumped from straining against his bindings, the light blue shirt spattered with blood stretched tight across his arms and chest.

Wayde sniped at Bruce, jeering, "What, are you in love with him? Should we leave you two alone?" The other men laughed.

Bruce scowled then went over and punched Gray to show them he was a tough guy. Puffing up his chest, he said with a huff to Wayde, "I'll show you what I can do. Boss says when he gets done with the girl we get her, I'll show you-"

"How tiny you are?" Wayde laughed, holding his thumb and finger apart an inch.

Lombardo gave Bruce a shove out of the way then he slapped Gray. "Threaten me, son, you threatened me in my own office," he hit the deputy again. "Then you come here to take down my drug empire?" He back-handed him.

Gray shook his head to clear it, blood and sweat flew. Lombardo stepped back.

His face swelling, Gray looked up at Lombardo through a mess of sweaty hair. "You force yourself on defenseless women and beat them. You're nothing but scum, filth, Jimmy, a disgrace to the uniform. A cockroach has more honor than you." He looked at him in disgust.

"You'd better kill me, you loathsome piece of shit," Gray's voice like ice, he vowed, "because if you don't, you're dead." He spat out more blood.

Lombardo pulled his belt up again under his belly and looped his thumbs over the belt. "There ya go again, Whitewolf, threatening me." He clubbed Gray as hard as he could with his fist. Gray's head snapped then dropped forward on his chest.

The sheriff turned to his men. "All right boys. I got business to do. Do enough damage to him so he can't put up a fight, but not enough to kill him. Don't break anything yet, you're gonna have to walk him out of here, I can't have any suspicious bundles coming outta the bar.

"Escorting a passed out drunk won't raise any attention. As soon as the sun sets, slap a hat low on his head to hide his face and take him out through the tunnel. I don't want his body showing up, so do a good disposal job."

Lombardo said to Wayde and Bruce, "I need these other guys for an hour, you two stay here and watch him."

They all looked at Gray, slumped over, his face bruised and split open, covered with blood, his head hung down, hair covering his eyes. He didn't look like he was going anywhere on his own steam.

Lombardo tromped across the room and up the stairs and out the door. The rest of the men went over and took turns hammering and battering Gray until he blacked out and couldn't feel anything anymore. Then they left Wayde and Bruce alone with him.

His arms crossed over his chest, Wayde watched Gray. He wasn't moving. Wayde grabbed a handful of hair like Lombardo had done and lifted Gray's head up. His bruised eyes were closed,

Wayde let go of his hair and his head dropped. "He's out. I don't need to be here, I've got things to do. I'll be back at sunset." He turned and strode towards the tunnel.

"Hey!" Bruce bleated. "You can't leave me here alone with this brute. The boss said-" he was talking to an empty room, Wayde was gone.

Bruce ambled cautiously over to the unconscious deputy and poked him gingerly in the arm. Gray didn't move or make a sound. Bruce pushed his shoulder, nothing. "Aw, he's not going anywhere, he looks dead already. I got things to do too."

He skittered over to the entrance to the tunnel. At the threshold, he took a look back, Gray hadn't stirred.

Bruce scampered into the tunnel and was gone.

Chapter Thirty-Two

Sitting in the back of a cab, Kessa pressed her face against the side window.

"Lady," the driver said, "what are you waiting for? Sitting here is going to cost you a fortune."

"You'll get paid, just wait until I tell you."

They had been parked down the street from her parents' house for the better part of an hour.

Another half hour passed, the driver grumbling the whole time, when finally the garage door opened and a red corvette pulled out. The door closed automatically as the vette wound down the drive and out to the street.

"Now," Kessa said, tension in her voice. "Follow that corvette, discreetly, I don't want him to notice us."

The driver pulled out from the curb following the corvette at a distance. It was easy to see the bright red car.

"Why didn't you tell me you were spying on your boyfriend? Trying to catch him with another woman?"

Her eyes peeled out the window, Kessa said, "Just don't lose him."

The cab followed the corvette through the wealthier side of town, into the city where they almost lost him twice, then to the farther, seedier side of the city.

"Slow down," Kessa ordered, the vette looked like it was about to pull in somewhere. He turned into Cache's Bar and drove around back.

"Let me out here, now." Kessa said urgently, "Stop the car."

"Geez lady what the-" he pulled over and stopped.

Kessa tossed a couple of hundred dollar bills over the front seat and got out of the car.

She ran to the side of the building so as not to be seen. Just as she got to the back of the building, she saw Jaspar had already parked and was disappearing into a crowd of trees behind the parking lot.

Taking the chance of being seen, Kessa dashed across the lot into the woods and ducked behind the first big tree she got to. Just in time, she saw Jaspar kneeling and brush some leaves off the ground.

What on earth?

Then he pulled and opened a door, a trap door going into the ground. He disappeared into the door and closed it behind him.

Kessa stood there in disbelief. She couldn't believe her eyes. She waited for what seemed like hours but was more like ten minutes, for him to come back out but he didn't. She didn't know what to do.

Well, she thought, *I've come this far...*she trod as quietly as possible over the grass and crackly leaves. This time she had dressed like Gray usually did in black jeans and t-shirt and boots she used for hiking.

When she reached where Jaspar had vanished, she knelt down, she could see the ground had been disturbed. A piece of metal glinted in the sun's closing light.

"Here goes," she muttered and slid her hand around the metal handle and pulled the lid up. Bending over the hole, she tried to see inside. She spotted the ladder attached to the wall.

Sitting on the ground, she swung her legs around and into the hole onto the first rung and pulled the lid closed. It was dark, but she could see well enough.

At the bottom of the hole, she could see there was a tunnel made partially of bricks and dirt. Praying she didn't encounter a rat, rodent or human kind, she forged ahead slowly down the tunnel. It was cool and damp, musty smelling.

Not thinking about covering her bright hair with a hat, the lit lanterns glowed on the flaxen locks as she passed under them. Every few feet she stopped and listened for someone ahead or behind her.

Eventually she reached the end of the tunnel. It led to an opening to the mostly cement and dirt cellar below the bar.

Holding her breath, Kessa inched to the doorway. Standing to the side of the doorway behind the wall, she stretched her neck to see inside.

Inside was darkly amber from just a few lanterns. There was someone in there! She snatched her head back. She had a weird impression of someone sitting in a chair near the middle of the room.

Her curiosity got the best of her, she carefully peeped around the corner again. "Oh!" There was a man in the chair, and he was tied to the chair. His head was down. She blinked trying to see better.

Her eyes widened. "Oh my gosh, it looks like-"

Forgetting her own peril, she ran through the door and across the room.

"Gray!" she cried when she got to him.

He was tied up, his head hanging, she could see blood all over his shirt and jeans. Putting her hands gently under his chin, she raised his head.

"Oh God," she choked.

He'd been horribly beaten. His face black and blue, deep cuts were bleeding profusely, and his eyes were swollen and closed. She couldn't tell if he was dead or alive.

She whispered his name, "Gray, Gray, oh please, are you all right?" Holding his head, she pushed his hair out of his face. His eyes fluttered.

"Gray, can you hear me?"

He struggled to open his beaten eyes. Her face wavered in front him. "Kessa?" Through swollen lips, he mumbled, "Either I'm dead and you're an angel, nice one at that, or," then he remembered where he was. His breath expelled harshly, "What the hell are you doing here?"

"Oh! Thank goodness you're alive!" She pulled his head to her heaving bosom, stroked his hair and wept.

His voice muffled against her chest, he said wryly, "Remember the part where I said I was a red-blooded male? If you don't stop what you're doing I'm going to be in worse straights than I am already. Apparently most of my body parts are still working."

She pushed his head back, gently. "Gray, what-"

"You need to get out of here, now," he told her.

"But I need to-"

"No!" he barked. "Get out now. Right now, run, run as fast as you can, get the hell out, now. Leave me-" he twisted his head. "What the hell are you doing? I told you to go."

Kessa knelt behind the chair. "You're so bossy. I'm trying to untie you."

He groaned. "No, Kessa, leave me, there's no time. You've got to go. You don't know what they'll do to you if they catch you, that DeBarra freak will seem like an infant in comparison." His voice weakened to a hoarse whisper, he begged, "Please baby, go."

Kessa struggled with his binds. The rope itself was large twine and tied so tightly she tugged and tugged at the knots barely moving them.

Gray's head fell back. He croaked at the ceiling, "God you're so obstinate."

"You're obstinate," Kessa groused under her breath, pulling at the ties.

He gasped in pain, trying to stay conscious. He warned her, "They're only gonna kill me, they'll do a lot worse to you. They'll have to untie me to get me out of here, I'll have another chance to get away. But you, you won't have a...Kessa," his throat raw, he trailed off in a pained rasp.

Her voice muffled behind him, "Really Gray, the condition you're in, there's no way-"

Wheezing, Gray struggled to breathe. He hoped the pain in his chest was only cracked, not broken ribs. "Just get out, you have to get out of here before someone-" the door to the basement opened. "*Run Kessa,*" Gray demanded, barely audible.

Kessa ran and hid behind a wall. A second later the smuggler came into view.

"You're still here," he commented redundantly with a grin. Gray's head lolled. "And still alive I see." The man scanned the room. "Where are your babysitters? Those two morons bail? Boss is gonna fry them alive."

He walked closer to Gray, stopping a few feet in front of him.

"Sorry, dude, I'm gonna have to pop you some more. Boss was very specific about making sure you were out. I guess you got quite a rep as a hell of a combatant, like a warrior or something and he don't want to take any chances on you getting free. Anyway, no offense bro," he rolled his hand into a fist and slammed it into Gray's face, then raised it again-

WHACK!

Kessa swung the board Gray had been hit with earlier and the guy went down. She closed her eyes as she hit him again then dropped the wood, it clattered on the cement floor.

"Now go Kessa, get out," Gray sputtered, hardly understandable. He was fading so fast she could hardly hear him.

Kessa ran over to work on the ropes when out of the shadows like a vampire stepped her brother-in-law, Jaspar. He looked shocked.

"How the hell did you get here?" he asked Kessa with bugged eyes.

She stood warily, she had dropped the board and now had no weapon. With more bravado and gusto than she felt, she said, "You've been keeping my sister doped up to keep her with you so you could have money. That's over with now. There'll be no more giving her drugs. She has a chance to get clean in the hospital. You need to pack your things and get out of my parent's house. Immediately."

He just stared at her for a minute, stunned at her audacity. Then he laughed. "Uh huh, sure. You won't be giving me or anyone else any orders, honey. Sheriff Lombardo has plans for you."

He glanced at Gray, taunting him, "I heard he already told you, deputy, that when he's done with her we all get a shot, so all your blustering at the Club was for nothing."

Switching his attention back to Kessa, he said, "Lombardo's gonna be ecstatic that you came here on your own steam, dropped yourself right in his lap so to speak."

He chuckled at Kessa's aghast expression. "Oh yeah, honey, he wasn't even gonna nab you until this guy," he shot a thumb at Gray, "was already taken out."

"So," Jaspar said, reaching out a hand out to her. "Come quietly, there's no need to make a big fuss. Lombardo's not going to want you all bruised and battered, he likes to do that himself."

He frowned when she backed away from him. "So that's how you want it? Okay, makes no difference to me." He started for her.

Kessa searched for a place to run or a weapon she could get to before Jaspar could get to her.

She had loosened Gray's restraints enough that he kept straining and working his wrists trying to tug free.

As Jaspar moved past him to go after Kessa, Gray vaulted from the chair like lightning, tackling the former construction worker. They hit the ground and punches started flying.

Fighting like wild gladiators, Jaspar got the upper hand because Gray was weakened. He got Gray on his back then straddled his hips and pummeled him.

Kessa ran to get the board. Gray bucked and at the same time cracked Jaspar with a crosscut knocking him off, and in a flash rolled and jumped on Jaspar, jabbing and jabbing with his fist like a boxer so rapidly his fist was a blur, until Jaspar fell back gasping.

Gray grabbed the guy by his hair. Lifting his head up, he slammed it on the concrete floor. Jaspar was screaming, blood was flying.

Gray bashed Jaspar's head until he ceased to move, then he rolled off him onto his hands and knees, his head hanging.

Kessa could hear his heaving breaths from where she was. She ran to him, knelt down and put an arm around him. Trying not to look at the pulverized bloody mess next to him, she asked, "Is he dead?"

Panting, Gray shook his head, blood and sweat sprayed. "Don't know, don't care."

"Come on." Kessa pulled at his arm, trying to get him to stand up. He had given Jaspar all that he'd had left, he was spent. He didn't move, he was about to fall flat down when Kessa yanked his arm up as hard as she could.

"Come on, I'm not leaving without you."

He struggled to his feet, Kessa put his arm over her shoulder to help him walk, and they moved like going through quicksand to the door.

It took a lifetime for them to get through the tunnel.

Kessa prayed they wouldn't come across anyone else. When they reached the ladder, Kessa climbed up and opened the trap door. She crawled out then stuck her head back down.

"Gray, you have to do this, I can't get you up here."

He was leaning back against the rocky wall to keep from collapsing. He bent over with his hands on his knees, garnering all the strength he had left.

Grasping a rung, like a 90-year-old man, huffing and grunting, he climbed up the ladder. As soon as he got out he dropped on the grass rolling over on his back, his chest heaving.

"Gray, I think we need to keep going, someone's bound to come."

"Kess," he wheezed, "you got your phone?"

Puzzled, she said, "Yes."

He took a pained breath. "You need to call my partner, Rick." He told her the number. She dialed, Rick answered right away. Kessa handed the phone to Gray.

He spoke hoarsely, laboring for air, he was sure his ribs were screwed, maybe had a collapsed lung. He choked out briefly what happened and where and gave the phone back to Kessa.

She was kneeling beside him. She wanted to touch him but there wasn't a place that wasn't bloody or bruised or cut so she pushed back a lock of hair.

Smiling weakly up at her, "You are so goddamned stubborn," he grumbled.

She gave an affronted huff. "Again with the calling the kettle black!"

He tried to maneuver over onto his stomach, she helped him. He struggled to his hands and knees and staggered to his feet. Leaning on her, he hacked out, "Where's your car?"

"I don't have it. I took a cab. I followed Jaspar and didn't want him to recognize my jeep."

Suddenly a loud bang rang out.

Gray pushed Kessa to the ground and dropped on top of her, covering her with his body and ducked his head. A second passed before he realized it had been a car backfiring.

He lifted his head, grinned weakly at her. "Sorry, just a car." He pushed up on his forearms, stared down at her, faces an inch apart.

"Gray, we need to go."

He nodded faintly. "Yeah. Feel in my pocket, I don't think they took my keys."

Kessa stuck her hand in his left side pocket.

His voice tight, he mumbled, "The other side. You need to find them quickly, believe it or not there are parts of my body that are still working." He smiled sheepishly at her.

"Men," she exclaimed, feeling herself blush. She pulled out the keys, crawled out from under him and started walking.

"Hey," he called out. "I thought you were helping me."

She went back and let him drape a heavy arm over her shoulders.

It took some time but they got to his truck. Kessa helped him into the passenger side then ran around and climbed up the driver's side. She stuck the key in and turned the engine on.

His head rolled back on the seat. He sighed with relief, and pain. "Now," he said, "you're driving my baby, so be nice to him. Be gentle." His grin crooked, he laughed. "You're the babe and he's the baby."

Kessa hit the seat lever and slammed the seat forward so fast his legs got jammed up. "Hey!" he protested.

"You are such an ass," she told him, biting back a grin. She pulled out of the lot.

His tired eyes flickered over her. He let his injured head settle against back the head rest. "I know."

Chapter Thirty-Three

$\mathcal{K}$essa didn't tell him she was taking him to the hospital, he would only have argued about it.

She pulled up in the back at the emergency room entrance, shut off the truck and ran inside to get help. Gray had passed out. It didn't take long for the staff to get him inside and into ICU.

While she waited, Kessa called the guy Rick back to see what was going on and tell him where Gray was.

"We got most of them," Rick said, out of breath. "We got the sheriff, we'll get the one or two that got away. We even picked up Taz Cache running out the front of the bar. You wouldn't believe it, there were drugs every-freakin-where. We even got the smuggler's boat using Gray's directions." He chuckled gleefully.

"That Lombardo, what a trip. Ordering us to let him go, threatening to fire us, then threatening to kill us. I had to, I couldn't help it, I had to punch him right in his fat face. He dropped like a shot hog and cried on the ground like a baby. It was hilarious. I kicked him in the nads as hard as I could, then leaned over and told him, 'that was for Gray.'" He took a deep breath. "So, how is my man? What're they doing to him?"

Kessa relaxed back in the chair in the room they were preparing to put Gray in. "He'll be all right. They told me he's actually in much better shape than he deserves to be after the beating he took."

She hesitated as tears threatened. The image of Gray unconscious on the gurney painfully gripped her heart. She gulped and said, "His ribs are slightly cracked, not broken, he's mostly bruised really bad, but nothing life threatening. Thank the Lord."

Rick could hear the strain in her voice. "You are just as he said," he said with mirth.

"Huh? What did he say?"

He chuckled again. "He said you were stubborn as all get out, and as brave as they come. How did he put it," Rick thought for a minute. "Yeah, he said 'she's a courageous, willful, annoying, beautiful little girlie package.' "

She gagged. "Are you serious? He's such a jerk."

"Yeah, he knows," Rick said, the smile evident in his voice. "I'll call his family." He paused then said, "So, I took your sister home the other day, when she bonded out. Aria."

"Oh? That was nice of you, I mean, was it an order?"

"Nah. I saw her standing outside just watching the cars go by. Gray had made arrangements for her ride home but the guy bailed. No one was coming to pick her up, she looked so…forlorn. She told me you were her sister, I had to help her out after that. Gray would have wanted me to."

Pausing before she spoke, Kessa said, "Oh, um. That was kind of you, Rick."

Now he hesitated. "Well, uh, she's really a good kid, woman I mean. I think you all got a raw deal and it affected you all in different ways. Beside, she's pretty in a winsome waifish kind of way."

She laughed. "Nice way of saying scrawny."

He laughed too. "Yeah. Anyway, I actually ended up taking her to lunch, learned a lot about her. I don't think anyone has ever much asked her about herself. She suffered her share of guilt and blame for what happened to you girls."

"We all forget none of us had it good."

"Yeah. So I think she acts all bawdy for attention. All the focus was on you little ones for a long time. She acts out and dates scumbags to get your parents to notice her. I think she does drugs because she's bored. She needs a job. We'll deal with her sentencing, then I told her I would help her. So, anyway…"

"You're a nice man, Rick. I appreciate your kindness." Kessa thanked him warmly.

"Yeah. Anyway, tell my man when he's alert, tomorrow, that I'll be by with the whole story, okay?"

"I will. Take care, Rick."

"You done good girl, you done real good," Rick praised her then clicked off.

Kessa put her phone in her pocket as a nurse came into the room. "They're bringing him in now," the nurse said, "he'll be fine, dear."

"Okay, thanks." Kessa stood up and moved over by the window to be out of the way. They brought him in on a gurney.

When they got inside the room, he told them he didn't need their help and rolled off the gurney and fell onto the bed.

The staff fiddled with instruments and trying to get him settled until he barked at them to get out and leave him alone. They fussed some more then left.

Kessa slipped over to the bed and looked down at Gray. He was cleaned up but his face was a mass of cuts and bruises. He'd been washed and someone had combed his hair. The dark blue eyes opened, he looked right at her.

"Hey," he said.

"Hey yourself." She smiled then sat on the edge of the bed. "So, you remember what happened?"

His eyes fluttered, he winced. "Yeah. I remember. You saved my damned life. Did you talk to Rick?"

She nodded. "I just spoke with him and told him how you're doing. He said he'd be by probably tomorrow and tell you the whole story. They got most of them but a couple got away. He punched Lombardo then kicked him in the crotch for you. Said he dropped like a shot hog."

A corner of his mouth turned up. "Good." His half-closed eyes slid over at her again then he frowned. "I do remember the part where you were being stubborn as hell." He smiled crookedly. "You're icorrgible, uh, incorrimable, ahh…"

Kessa gently set her hand on his arm. "The pain meds are taking you out."

"Ya know," his words slurred. "I had a talk with that dog of yours, Kappy,"

"Kato."

"Whatever. An' I told him 'no more fights.' That he needed to stay out of scraps and do his job watching over his mistress." Gray yawned.

"Someone else should heed this fine advice," Kessa murmured, stroking his arm in between cuts. "Gray, the bones, is it, her? My sister?"

He touched her upper arm, rubbed the mark from her past with his thumb. He peered at it through slit eyelids. He slurred, "They don't know yet…pretty sure it's her…" Then he rambled nonsense unintelligibly for a bit and yawned.

"What happened to tall, dark and silent?" Kessa remarked with a grin and slid off the bed, it was time to go. She leaned over and kissed him light as a feather on his forehead then turned to leave.

"Love you, Kessa." The words poured out in a low, anguished sigh.

She swung back around, her mouth agape.

He was asleep.

Chapter Thirty-Four

$\mathcal{T}$he next day Kessa waited until later in the morning to check on him.

When she peeked in, his room was full of deputies. They were laughing and joking, they were quite jolly and loud for being in a hospital.

She decided to leave him to his friends and walked away.

Gray looked up just as she turned. He waved and called out, but then one of the guys said something that made everyone roar with laughter.

When she returned later in the afternoon his room was empty. A twinge of fear struck her, she sought out his nurse, Ms. Collyfield and asked where he was.

Seeing Kessa was upset, the nurse laid a hand on her shoulder. "He's just fine, honey. He refused to stay longer. He left without the doctor's consent. Apparently that could get him in trouble with his superiors, but he said he wasn't too worried about them. He's very stubborn, you know?"

Her lip curled, Kessa said with a wry nod, "Yes, I know. Thank you." She left and went home.

She was far behind in her work. Her agent had been calling and leaving messages which she had not returned. She called him when she got home. Then she called Matthew.

He was flabbergasted at the whole affair. She was careful to leave out the part about the danger she had put herself in.

"So," Matthew drawled. "Last week you intimated that you were outta here as soon as I return. Still feel that way? I'd really like you to take some time, give it a chance. I know it's been hard on you."

You have no idea, Kessa mused. Then she told him about her talks with both Char and Aria and the hopes she had for them all reuniting and working on repairing their relationships.

"That's what I'd hoped for Kess, I'm so glad. Maybe we can be a family again," Matthew said hopefully.

They chatted for another few minutes then hung up. Kessa went into the small study. Sitting at the desk she plugged in her laptop, muttering, "Time to get to work."

A couple of days later, still no word on whether the bones were Hope's or not, Kessa wanted to see how Gray was doing, she called him but he didn't answer. He didn't call her back after she left a message either.

She called Rick who said Gray was supposed to go into work today for the first day since he left the hospital. Now starting to worry, Kessa drove across town to Gray's place.

There was another car in his driveway. She parked behind it and walked up the porch steps, the door was open, she could hear voices. She called, "Gray?"

He must not be able to hear her. She pushed the door open and went inside.

"Gray, are you-" she broke off when she saw him standing in the middle of the room with his arms around a woman.

The color drained from Kessa's face, she spun and ran out the door.

Gray called her name, she flew down the steps and to her jeep. Jumping in, she drove away as he came out the door, his injuries slowing him down. He stood in the driveway watching her disappear down the street.

Her phone on the seat next to her rang almost immediately. She could see his name light up. It kept going to voice mail and then ringing again. She picked it up, shut it off and flung it to the floor.

When she reached her home she dashed inside and packed a quick suitcase. She left Kato with her neighbor and then went to a hotel several miles away. Knowing Gray, he would come to her house.

Talking out loud to herself, Kessa said petulantly, "After of course, he was done with his floozy. Must have been one of the one-night stand hussies. Well, I am not going to be one of his slam bam thank you ma'am women."

Matthew was right to warn her about him. Gray had even warned her himself that he was a player. She had no one to blame for the pain in her heart but herself.

Gray picked up Rick and they drove to the sky-jumping school to speak with Brent Bradshaw, the murdered caretaker's nephew. His eyes fixed on the road, Gray hadn't said two words.

"Well," Rick chatted, seeing the planes of Gray's face sharp, the vein beating at his temple, his jaw clamped, eyes so dark the blue looked charcoal. "You sure are in a foul mood, what happened between you two now?"

Gray ground through gritted teeth, "Nothing. Stop assuming everything I do is wrapped around...Kessa." His voice dropped from churlish to dismal. "You want to gab and gossip like a couple of hens?"

Before Rick could respond, Gray said, "My phone had gotten smashed when I was at Cache's. I was out of it on pain meds for a few days so I couldn't make any calls and I couldn't receive any. I'd just gotten the dammed phone back. She thinks she saw something, but she didn't, I mean she did, but it wasn't, then-"

"What? You're not making any sense, bro. Start over."

"Never mind, we're here." Gray pulled into the lot, he slowed immediately. In wonderment, he asked, "What's going on?"

The two deputies looked around the parking area. There were ambulances, fire trucks and police cars, red, blue and white lights twirling everywhere like a wild disco party.

They got out of the truck and checked the area for the highest ranking officer. Rick nudged Gray and pointed to Sergeant Stiller, they made straight for him.

They all fist bumped. "What's going on?" Gray asked.

Stiller glanced over one shoulder. "You won't believe this, but one of the newbies jumping today, took a total flyer. Chute didn't open. Big damned splat. It's marked down to amateur error."

"No shit?" Rick exclaimed.

Gray gaped dubiously at the sergeant then scoped out a fast visual of the scene.

More cars drove up, people hurried out and ran to join the melee. His head moved in a sharp shake. "No way, Stiller," Gray stated, "that can't be, there's something going on. No way it was an acc-"

"Not an accident. My conclusion exactly," Stiller agreed. "When I heard over the radio the name of the deceased," he shook his head, his lips pulled in. "It was way, way too coincidental that two Bradshaws die in freak ways in such a short period of time. I was actually just about to call you." One brow drew down over an eye in suspicion. "So, what are you guys doing here?"

"It was Brent Bradshaw," Gray said more as a statement than a question.

Rick's head jerked at Gray. "No way." He looked at Stiller. His mouth dropped in disbelief. "It can't be."

Stiller pierced Gray with wary discernment. "What's going on, Gray?"

The body was already stuffed in a cadaver bag. A green baseball cap with a big white A on it lay on the ground several feet away.

Gray let a long breath drain from his taut lungs, shaking his head. "The boy stopped us in the hospital the other day. He said he had something to tell us about the death of his aunt. He said he thought he knew who did it, or why or something." Gray's eyes closed, he rubbed his head.

"He refused to tell us there, he was scared out of his mind. He asked us to meet him here today after his jump, after noon."

His eyes narrowed at Stiller, Gray gestured at him. "Get a roster of everyone here, coming, going, went, everyone who works here, on the planes, pilots, jumpers, instructors, guests. Even everyone at the diner behind the school, staff, customers, deliverers, all of it. We'll break it up, there has to be someone in common, some connection."

Nodding affirmatively, Stiller pulled out his phone.

"This is just damned," Gray's face scrunched, brows grooved in aggravation. "The second I talk to someone they're killed. We're in different places each time," he shook his head. "I don't freaking get it."

"So you're the common factor," Stiller advised Gray.

Gray's eyes slashed sideways at him, he nodded. "Yeah, I am. But there's someone else too. Someone who didn't want these people, Goldbrooke, Brenda Bradshaw and Brent talking to me."

A corner of his mouth pulled in, Stiller said with a wink, "Hey, do me a favor, don't talk to me."

Gray scowled at him. "You're a funny guy, Stiller." He gestured to Rick. "Let's go check it out, ask some questions."

"You think we're really going to get anything? So far the perp has been pretty careful, leaving no trail."

Gray's face darkened in chagrin. "No, I think the guy, or girl is too careful. But you're wrong about there being no trail, there's always a trail. There's always evidence no matter how careful the perp, no matter how miniscule the trace. We'll find it. Let's go."

The three men strode quickly to the hub of the scene.

For a week Kessa stayed away from her house.

Gray called every day, all day, but she didn't even listen to his messages. It was good anyway, there'd been so much drama she hadn't been writing and she has a deadline.

She set her work up on the motel desk. But when she looked at the computer screen, Gray's face, all battered and hurt floated in front of her eyes. Then the picture of him with another woman in his arms-

"*Damn him*," she slammed the cover closed. She went out, bought a bottle of wine and got herself good and stinkin' drunk.

When she woke, dawn was breaking. She swore that was the last time she would drink away her sorrow, her head was throbbing.

Her phone buzzed on the nightstand. It wasn't Gray. It was an unknown number. "It better not be him," she said dourly and answered.

"Hi sweetie, it's Mora Aven, you remember, Dr. Aven's wife? It's been such a long time."

Kessa was taken by surprise. "Uh, uh, yes, Mrs. Aven, of course I remember you. You were our Choir leader for years when I was a child…"

"Yes, dear. So sorry for what happened to you, to all of you. Such a tragedy." She paused to let the sympathy soak in.

"So, Skip, um, I mean my husband, Dr. Aven, of course his real name in Clarence but he's always been Skip as long as I've known him. Sorry dear, I tend to digress. Bad habit Skip always says. Anyway, Skip occasionally runs into your darling brother Matthew and he says that Matthew always goes on and on about how successful you are. He's very proud of you, my dear." She waited for Kessa to respond.

"Oh, uh, yes, Matthew is a great brother. I'm lucky to have him." She wanted to say 'get to the point,' but of course she was way too polite to do that.

"Um," Mora paused again. "Matthew had told Skip what a great little artist you were. That you painted these incredible pictures on glass plates." She waited again.

Kessa sighed. "Yes, when someone asks me to do a painting for something special I sometimes do."

"Yes, yes," excitement entered Mora's voice. "That's what he said. I'm calling you because, well I'm sure you've guessed by now that I would so love it if you could do one for me."

"Oh, I'm uh, sorry, Mrs. Aven, but I don't do self-portraits, I only-"

"No darling, not of me, heavens no." She laughed with self-deprecation. "No, what I'm asking for is, well Skip has this dog that he just loves to pieces. You know, men and their dogs, hmm? The thing is, Benson, that's the dog of course, well, Benson is on his last, well you know, he's coming to the end. Skip is so depressed about it."

"I don't see how-"

"Yes dear, what I'm asking is if you could do a picture of well, of Benson." Moving on quickly, she gushed, "Oh you don't understand, Skip would be over the moon, something to keep of his buddy. A photo isn't the same you know, dear, no not the same. I hear that your pictures, well, that they actually seem to *breathe!* It would be so, so wonderful if you could, I mean can you, please…?" she tapered off with a mournful sigh.

Kessa sat feeling sulky. Why couldn't people leave her alone to feel sorry for herself for crying out loud. "Oh, fine, Mrs. Aven, I think I can manage it. When do you want-"

"Isn't that fabulous!" Mora Aven squealed. "I can't wait to see it!" Her voice dropped, she now sounded a bit nervous. "The thing is honey, that we're leaving town for a few weeks tomorrow, and I don't have a driver's license. I was wondering if I begged you, could you please come here and get a couple of pictures of Benson, then-"

"Mrs. Aven, maybe you could email some pictures to me?"

Mora chuckled. "Dear, that's not something I've ever cottoned to. I can hardly work this fangled phone. Skip insisted I have one, took forever to get the hang of it. So, if you could *please* come here, today, *please* dear? It's important that you see little Benson's personality, that doesn't show in a photograph."

At Kessa's silence, she pleaded, "It won't take but a moment and it would mean so much…"

Kessa saw no way out without being mean or rude. Holding a hand over the phone, she exhaled her irritation. Forcing herself to speak kindly, she acquiesced, "Sure, sure, I can do that. When would-"

"Oh thank you, so much, thank you. Can you be here in about say an hour? We can have a little tea and biscuits and discuss your price. Now it is a secret, so please don't tell anyone, I want to surprise him!"

The sooner she got this over the sooner she could come back to the motel and wallow in her depression. "All right. No problem. Um, just out of curiosity, how did you get my number?" Kessa asked.

She had an unlisted number. As a writer she didn't want some nut-job showing up on her front porch asking for an autographed book.

"Oh," Mrs. Aven chuckled. "Of course your mother gave it to me. She is just the nicest person, isn't she? We see her all the time at the Club."

Of course. "Sure, she's so nice." Kessa scraped the sarcasm off her tone. "Okay, I know where your residence is. I'll see you in," she looked at the clock and winced, "an hour."

After polite goodbyes, they rang off.

Chapter Thirty-Five

Deputy Lindsey Covin strutted over to Gray as he was getting a cup of coffee. She stood as close to him as she could without touching him. Then her arm grazed his.

"Hey hotcheeks, where've you been?" She wriggled nearer to him, trying to brush the side of her breast against his arm that was holding the mug.

"Lindsey," Gray growled, taking a very obvious step away from her. "Stop calling me that stupid name. It's not professional."

She wormed closer. "I can't help it, honey, you have a fine-"

Barking, "Deputy, knock it off," he twitched away from her and poured coffee into the mug then replaced the decanter on the coffee machine.

Even though he knew it would be boiling hot, Gray put the cup to his lips anyway to keep the blowsy deputy an arm's length away. He took a painful sip, winced. "Don't you have a boyfriend, didn't I see you smooching with some guy at the party last month?"

Fluttering her eyelashes at him like she was a movie star bombshell, patting her blonde collar length bob, she said, "You drink your coffee black, Gray? Just like you, hot and strong." She strung an arm through his that wasn't holding the coffee and slithered her body against his side.

Lowering her head to his shoulder, she looked up at him through a fringe of dark brown eyelashes. "Yes, Benjie Storm down in the crime lab and I have a thing going on, but that doesn't mean I can't taste some other sugar. You know what I mean?"

Chafing her body against his, she traced a heart with her finger on his chest then kneaded his bicep with her hand. "Grayson Whitewolf, you are so unbelievably buff,"

Gray pulled his arm out of her clutches and took a step back. With his luck Kessa would be coming right around the corner and he'd look even more the boor.

"Lindsey, keep your hands, and your," he raked her bosom with a glare, "body off of me." His severe tone barely made an impression on the sensual gaze she directed at him.

Voice gravelly and forbidding, he said with a scowl, "I don't have the time or desire to play touchy-feely with you. So knock it off."

He started to leave but she said to him, "Hey, don't leave without the reports I have for you." One hand behind her back so her chest thrust out, she handed a file crammed with sheaves of papers out to him.

Unrepentant, she tilted her head flirtatiously. She waved the file at him. "It's everyone's reports on the triple-murders, interviews and bank accounts, all the information. It's all in the computer too, but I know you like to lay…all the papers out and look at them at the same time."

He went to take the file but she moved it behind her back. Tilting her head up, she stuck her lips out at him. "You have to pay for them," she said kittenish with her eyes closed.

Gray stepped around her, snagged the file out of her hands and strode off quickly, her curses at his back falling on deaf ears.

When he got back to his desk, he set his mug and the file down. Sitting down, he opened the file.

Since the murders weren't his cases, a dozen people had already reviewed and studied the paperwork. Comments, notes and summaries were included. Still, he reviewed every word, every number, every comparison.

After a couple of hours, he came to the same conclusion as those before him. Nothing showed a connection, nothing came up wrong or even circumspect. None of the three people had ever been arrested or even made a complaint with the police. His elbows on the desk, he lowered his head into his hands.

His phone rang bringing his head up with a grimace. He answered it stiffly, "Whitewolf."

It was his Commander, Thomas Ross. He told Gray that H.R. was on his back for Gray's clearance to work. He told him to get his ass back to the hospital for his follow up or he'd take his gun and badge until he did.

Before Gray could say he didn't need a follow up, that he was fine, Ross hung up. It was an order.

"Like I got time for this," Gray bitched. He needed to find Kessa and square things with her. He scratched his shoulder to keep from clenching his fists.

Indignantly, he told himself he didn't need to apologize to her for anything, he had been up front about the kind of man he was. Yet, the thing was, he hadn't been doing anything.

And it was tearing him up inside thinking about what she assumed about him. Even though they couldn't have a relationship, he still hated her thinking he nobly pushed her away for her own good then went right to another woman.

He sped to the hospital, the sooner he got the ridiculous follow up done the better.

It took a lot longer than he thought it would. He had to wait at the discharge nurse's station to complete his paperwork.

Several doctors were gathered at the counter having a discussion about a new cholesterol medication.

Filling out the paperwork, Gray glanced over at the doctors periodically. Apparently they didn't have a lot to do today. Something caught his eye.

A dark purple and silver ring flashed in the overhead fluorescent lights making him think of something he had seen before. He completed the forms and went out to his truck.

It nagged at him, he sat for a second trying to recall what he had seen before that was familiar, that pulled at his memory. Why did that purple ring make him think he'd seen it before?

Suddenly, pinpricks of panic and fear pricked along the backs of his shoulders then ran down his arms. He pulled out his cell and called Matthew.

Matthew answered tersely. Gray could hear the censor in his greeting. "Hey Gray."

"Matt, listen, yeah we have a lot to talk about. I- I- but listen, right now, I need to know where Kessa is staying."

Matthew blurted a few choice words, Gray cut him off, "You can beat the shit out of me when you get home, Matt, but right now, she might be in danger, and I need to get to her- *now*."

That shut Matthew up. For a moment.

Then Matthew said half worried, half angry with his friend, "What the hell are you talking about, Gray, what is she-"

"Dammit Matt, I need to know right now."

Knowing his friend, and ultimately trusting him, even though he wasn't really sure what was up with the deputy and his sister, Matthew told him where she was staying. He'd deal with her wrath later.

Gray told him he'd keep him apprised and hung up. He switched on the ignition and peeled down the road.

Chapter Thirty-Six

Kessa pulled into the Avens' driveway within the hour.

After going for a short but fast run then popping aspirin, drinking a pot of coffee followed by a cold shower, she was feeling a little better. However, the last thing she felt like doing right now was paint a plate for someone.

Her heart was aching and she just wanted to crawl in a corner and die. Gray had broken her heart and yet she still missed the big jerk. Gulping down the sigh and the verging tears, she turned off the car and climbed out.

Of course the doctor's house was immense. Taking up a huge hunk of the acre it sat on with three stories of brick and windows, white columns and even lion statues at the entrance like Solomon's temple.

"Talk about ego," Kessa muttered under her breath and tromped up the steps to the broad porch. Wearing dark blue jeans and a burgundy short sleeved sweater, she felt her heart twinge. The color of her jeans reminded her of Gray's eyes.

Her chin up and spine straight, she ordered herself to get a grip and move on.

As she lifted her hand to ring the doorbell, she saw a note taped to one of the large, tempered glass double doors. Seeing her name on it, she peeled it off the door.

Unfolding it, she read:

'Dear Faith, we are enjoying our mid-morning repast
around back on our lovely patio.
Please come around the house and join us.
Yours, Doctor and Mrs. Aven.'

"Huh. So much for the surprise." She laid the note on the stone parapet and went back to the driveway to get to the walkway that appeared to go around the side of the house.

Traipsing beside the brick walk, she muttered, "Not much security for such a wealthy establishment." She glanced around and listened for barking. "Not even a guard dog."

She had noticed security cameras on her way up the drive and on the house so maybe there was inside computer surveillance.

Behind the house was a raised terrace, the floor made of glossy pavers. Trees in full spring blossom, crabapple and dogwood blooming with colorful flowers made a beautiful frame for the patio, sweet fragrance permeated the air.

When she got all the way around and up to the patio, she saw the Avens sitting at a white wrought iron table on matching chairs. Bowls of fruit and plates of toast were on the table with butter and jam, along with a teapot, cream and sugar.

Both of them held a tea cup and both were reading the newspaper. There were several brick steps leading up to the terraced landing.

Her shoes scuffing across the yard, the scent of freshly mown grass tingled Kessa's nose. "Um, hello there," she announced her presence. She couldn't believe no one was patrolling this extravagant house, and the pair hadn't even looked up at her approach.

Mrs. Aven set down her paper first. "Well, good morning dear, you are true to your word, aren't you? Right on time. Isn't that such good manners, Skippy, darling?"

The doctor's face was hidden by the newspaper he was still holding up.

"Come along, dear, come and join us." Mrs. Aven motioned for Kessa to come up on the patio.

Kessa wasn't the least bit hungry, she just wanted to get some pictures of the dog and move on. She expected to see the beloved animal lying at the doctor's feet but he was not. She assumed he must be inside as Mrs. Aven had indicated that the dog was not well.

She trod up the three steps leading to the patio.

Mrs. Aven stood up and pulled out a chair between her and her husband, her smile wide and welcoming. "How nice that you are here, my dear, please, have a seat."

"Um, sure, okay." Kessa sat down. She smiled politely at Mrs. Aven then turned her face to Doctor Aven.

He crunched the paper and crumpled it on the table. "Well, hello little Faith." His Scottish burr was a blast from the past.

Kessa's brow furrowed. It was more than him being her pediatrician, there was something else, something that gave her a slight chill. She frowned, straining to think what it was.

He chuckled. "I can see the thoughts spinning in there." He tapped a finger against her forehead.

She leaned back, perturbed that he would touch her.

He continued to smile, but it wasn't a nice, friendly smile, it was…sinister?

"It'll come back to you, girl, in time. I couldn't take that chance you know." He watched the memories play across her face.

The turquoise eyes darkened, there was something tucked way back in her subconscious, but she couldn't grasp it.

"I don't understand," Kessa said, puzzled and disconcerted. The husband and wife staring at her made her feel like Little Red Riding Hood and she was sitting at the witch's table with the cauldron brewing in the corner.

The doctor sighed, reached over and clasped her wrist to the chair arm with a surprisingly strong hand.

"Um, Doctor Aven, I don't, ah, I need to go-"

He gripped her wrist to the chair harder, like a steel clamp. Shaking his head with a faux sad smile, he said, "I'm sorry, little Faith, but you're not going to get to go home this time."

The way he said it, the burr, the underlying tone of malevolence, something niggled at her brain. The voice peculiarly familiar from back... back in the woods, but softer now, yet with the burr and the evil still present.

Tinglings of memory lifted the hairs on the back of her neck, apprehension turned to alarm. She could feel the color drain from her face right down to her suddenly churning stomach.

Her eyes widened like plates, her mouth dropped. She cried horrorstruck, "It was you!" She yanked at her wrist like it was about to be guillotined.

But the doctor held her locked to the chair with an iron hand. He leaned back a bit more relaxed and nodded. "I thought for sure you would have said something the day they found you, but when you didn't, I realized you hadn't clearly seen me."

He leaned in, his eyes narrowed in inquisition. "But you did see something, didn't you, my dear?"

Kessa's eyes darted to Mrs. Aven, but the older woman sat in her expensive mid-length satiny green dress with puffy short sleeves, her salt and pepper hair in a bun, still smiling benevolently behind round glasses like she was a fairy godmother and all was well with the world.

Kessa turned her attention back to the doctor. He looked anything but benevolent. In his mid-fifties, wearing trousers and a shirt, his still thick, wavy hair was also flecked with grey like his wife's, and he also wore glasses, however his eyes glinted unpleasantly behind the lenses.

Kessa stuttered, "I- I don't- don't understand. I didn't see anything, really. I need to leave." She tugged at her hand but he held her fast to the arm of the chair.

She swung her head to his matronly wife imploring, "Mrs. Aven, please, help me!"

The doctor's wife just stared vacuously, smiling a Mona Lisa smile at Kessa and said nothing.

Kessa yanked at her arm. "I must insist," she demanded with bluster, "you let me go this instant or else I will call the- the police." She was pulling her arm so hard her wrist was red.

She tried to pry his hand off with the fingers of her other hand but his long fingers were wrapped around the chair arm and she couldn't get to them.

"With what?" Dr. Aven pointed out she had no purse or phone, she must have left them in the car. The doctor's smile turned into a malignant downward gash.

Kessa looked into virtually empty eyes, strange brown holes of fearsome abomination. She struggled to stand up, her wrist scraped, the skin tore from his harsh grip and slashed from the sharp angle of the metal chair arm.

Then he grabbed her wrist and pulled it up between them. Holding it immobile at a painfully awkward angle, "Sit down," he ordered, his voice flat, all sense of humanity nonexistent. He pushed her with the hand holding her wrist until she fell back against the chair.

Tears blurred her vision, she blinked them away refusing to give in to the terror. Kessa worked to keep her voice calm, she said coolly, "What do you want with me, Doctor Aven?"

He relaxed back again, holding her wrist. It was raw and bleeding from where she'd tried to pull away. "What I want, dear little Faith, is to dispose of the last person who can take me down."

He leaned in, his face close to hers, she could smell the fusty chamomile tea on his breath. With a fake benign smile, he said, "Please satisfy my curiosity, tell me what you remember." He shook her wrist causing shooting pain to lance up her arm.

Biting back a cry, Kessa closed her eyes. Gray's face danced behind her lids, worried, looking for her in her mind like the witch looked in the glass globe in the Wizard of Oz.

She shook her head, opened her eyes and gazed withering at the doctor. "I'll tell you. I remember the dreams I had for a long time when I was sent away. I remember," she closed her eyes again going back in time.

That day the breaking sun was warm on her face, she could smell the pine trees and earthy dirt. She saw herself looking for her sisters, thinking they were playing a prank on her.

She said quietly, slowly, "I remember in the woods, hearing screams, different screams. At first, I thought it was my sisters trying to scare me, but then, they sounded like screams of," she shivered, "pain, agony. Cries of horrendous torment."

She opened her eyes and looked at him. "I always thought I'd fancied that, I mean really, cries of torment?"

Her eyes shifted blankly about as she remembered more. "Then there were the other screams, of," Kessa's breathing grew shallow, rapid and uneven, she felt queasy. The corners of her eyes tightened as the event unraveled in her mind.

"The screams were bone chilling, blood curdling terror. They were my sisters' screams. They were real, very real, they weren't pretending. I can still hear them…" Her hand pressed to her ear, shaking her head, she still felt the incredulity, and the flood of dread that had followed.

"It all seemed illusory, a movie reel, yet," in agonizing, shocking recall she pictured Char being carried back, irreparably broken. Hope never found. Kessa's eyes flashed hatred at the doctor.

"But it was real, wasn't it? All of it? What did I see?" she asked with demanding, tortured, frightened eyes, wanting to know what had hunted her like prey in her nightmares.

He smiled again, the lips turning up obscenely, like a vile satyr. An immoral and lethal fiend, half man half beast. "Oh, it's a long story, one I don't think you have time for, my dear."

"Please, it has haunted my life, my family's lives. You at least owe me the knowledge of what destroyed my home, my childhood."

She stopped twisting her arm trying to get free, it was only tearing the skin on her wrist. If he held her any tighter the delicate bones would break.

"Hmmm," he brightened. The doctor loved to talk about himself.

Mrs. Aven calmly poured her and her husband some more tea.

"All right. I don't owe you a damned thing, however, I will tell you. As it turns out," he took a sip of tea, set the cup down, added sugar, stirred it, tasted it again, all the while gripping Kessa's wrist so hard it was turning numb.

"Hmm, better." He set the cup down. "As I was saying, although I have been happily married for," he looked at his wife cheerfully, "how long has it been, my darling?"

Mrs. Aven added sugar to her own tea, smiled a mild chastisement at him like he was a forgetful child. "Thirty-one years, dear." She sipped demurely with her pinky out.

"Ah yes, 31 wonderful years." His head drooped, his lips curved down. "Sadly we never had any children." His callous eyes swerved from his wife to Kessa.

"The thing is, I would have loved to have had some kids, boys. Little boys. You see," his degenerate gaze flowed out to the woods way in the back of the yard.

"It was the young boys that I liked. It took Mora a year or two before accepting that part of me. She decided she could let go of the sex and romance for all of this." His spanning hand designated the area, indicating the majestic house and elaborate gardens and lush acres.

Trying to keep from vomiting her fear, Kessa pressed a hand to her stomach while nodding, thinking she was hiding her revulsion.

The doctor drank some more tea. There was a buttered piece of toast on a plate in front of him but he didn't touch it. "Anyway, that's why I became a pediatrician. What better way to be touching those lovely young bodies."

He shivered with delight, Kessa shuddered with disgust.

"The thing of it was, the problem was, I could touch, fondle without them being any the wiser, but alas," he sighed. "I needed more of course. I couldn't do what I wanted to do with them so I had to venture outside the job and search for…game if you will." He smirked sadistically at his terminology.

It was all Kessa could do to keep her mouth shut and remain very still, almost relaxed. She let her wrist rest on the chair arm, no longer fighting to get away.

"So, I had to recruit, my, um, dates. So I sought out kids that their parents were either divorced or just never around, kids that were looking for a father figure of sorts. Actually, my first one, you're not going to believe this," he leaned in conspiratorially. "Was Sledge Stirling." He giggled at Kessa's astonished expression.

"The mayor?" she asked with skepticism.

"Well, dear, he wasn't the mayor then, now was he?" Aven laughed at her struggle to take in what he was saying. "He's the youngest mayor we've had, but I think he does a great job. Don't you, dear?" he said pleasantly to his wife. She nodded with a cultured smile.

"Anyway," Aven continued, "the one that caused all this trouble was, I think you went to school with his brother, you were younger, Clayton Gourdet." His brows rose in question.

Shock and horror struck Kessa's face like a slap.

Aven nodded happily. "Yes, he was a cutie. All blond hair and blue eyes, adorably chubby. What did they used to call him?"

"Gordy," Kessa said, swallowing the sudden anguish that ate at her soul.

"Yes, yes, that was it, Gordy. My, my, what a spirited child he was then. Mellowed quite soon after he hit his teens. Of course that's when I let them go and move on to a younger treat."

Kessa bit back her retort, said instead, "I'm sure it had nothing to do with you, um," she didn't know what to say.

"Rutting with him?" Aven fit in, laughing at her look of contemptuous revulsion. "Yes, it was little Gordy you girls saw that day. I thought we were totally alone out there in that spot in the forest. I thought no one would come across us.

"Not only was most of the forest dangerous to travel through, but I'd spent years cultivating that chimera legend to keep people out. I did things to scare people to keep them out of the woods, like putting on a horror Halloween mask of a grotesque mutant and playing a recording of inhuman sounds I'd recorded from movies of abominable monsters screeching and yowling, and of the ground being pounded by heavy feet like an enormous creature was coming."

Aven was amused at his own antics, he enjoyed being able to tell someone else how clever he'd been.

He said with pomposity swelling his head and chest, "When I got the very young patients alone in my examination rooms without their parents present, I'd tell them grisly stories about a grotesque miscreation that lived in the woods.

"It would snatch a person, rip them in half and then sit on a boulder eating their innards. I'd tell them that once in a while, one would survive. Someone would venture too far in the woods but manage to get away, they come running out screaming totally out of their minds. They would be taken to the insane asylum where they would stay for the rest of their lives in a catatonic state."

"They believed that ridiculous tale?" Kessa found her voice.

He shrugged, draining his teacup. "They were impressionable children. I'd start when they were tiny tots, they'd grow up with the idea tucked in the back of their unconscious. They were too little to tell anyone or remember where they first heard it.

"Some of them even told me about the chimera in the woods. Hilarious, huh?" He was enjoying himself.

Kessa bit her tongue to keep her comments to herself. She needed to stall, keep him yakking while she figured out how to get away from the macabre insane couple.

Aven cheerfully continued his tale to his captive audience.

"So, what happened that day, the first screams, the ones you describe of as of torment happened to be Gordy. It was his first time. I guess it hurt a little." He paused, lips pursed into a avaricious smile of remembrance of the event

"Anyway, I thought we were safe where we were. I usually had a blanket laid out for our comfort when I brought others there, but that day I was in too much of a hurry, just too excited to," he stopped at her loathing revulsion.

"Keep looking at me like that, little Faith, and I may give you a taste of my," his tongue rolled around his lips, "skills."

Mrs. Aven narrowed her eyes at her husband, but he was in charge. He disregarded the venomous look she conveyed across the table.

Doctor Aven, impervious to her attitude at his high-handedness said, "Mora, be a dear and get a fresh pot."

Balking at first, she resentfully pushed up from the table and stomped off to do his bidding.

Still holding Kessa's wrist, Aven suddenly yanked it up, pulling her close to him, his nose almost touching hers. The depravity trawled from his eyes, winding around her like a spider trussing a net, snaring and pulling her like a bug into his abysmal pit of a black soul.

To Kessa it was like looking into the true depths of hell.

"Listen girl, I like the little boys, but over the years I've had my taste of the females too."

He glanced towards the house. "I never let on to Mora, because," his mouth curdled in distaste, "well let's leave it at I was never stimulated to arousal by my loving wife and she would expect it if she knew I was actually bisexual."

He pulled Kessa closer, his eyes dropped to her mouth then back up to the turquoise orbs. She couldn't hide the fear, it radiated from them.

Drawling, "I may show you what I'm talking about," he glanced at the house again, "later." Then he licked the side of her face and pushed her back.

Kessa wiped her face with her short sweater sleeve. Expressing her repugnance would only give him more enjoyment so she pressed her lips into firm line.

Aven crossed his legs, never letting go over her wrist. "So, as I was saying, the first screams were Gordy's and you were always correct when you asserted that the other screams were your sisters'.

"Alas, your sisters came upon us quite by surprise, for all of us. The youngest one, Hope, she saw what we were doing. Charity was behind her and some trees. She saw something but not enough to make sense of it, and she didn't see me. Even as young as she was, Hope realized something was not, well, right. You know, with Gordy crying and the blood and all. So, she screamed and ran. I had to abort my tryst and leave Gordy to go after them."

Kessa strained to keep her face impassive. She was picturing the scene, as it was when she was there. Goose-bumps ran up her arms making her feel clammy, her heart was racing.

"When Hope screamed and ran, it incited Charity to do the same. They ran but of course I was faster. I caught Hope, grabbed her up around the neck, her little legs swung in the air."

Kessa would not give him the thrill of seeing her react, she kept her arms stiff resisting covering her roiling stomach.

"She was so small, I snapped her neck like a twig and dropped her." He watched Kessa through hooded lids like a snake waiting patiently for the quarry to get closer.

"I then easily caught Charity, she never knew what hit her. I pushed her over a cliff from behind, more blood curdling screams for you to hear. Then, you," he sniffed, his eyes gleamed.

Kessa's body trembled with the effort not to vomit or scream, or thrash away from the sick fiend as he told her the truth of what happened to her beloved sisters that day.

"I tossed a rock over the cliff to draw your attention, then when you went to look, I picked you up from behind because you weren't close enough to push over. What a fighter you were, a little tiger. Regardless, I threw you over what I thought was a steep cliff. You can't imagine my astonishment when you made it back home."

He reached over and picked up a lock of Kessa's hair letting it curl gently around his finger. Then he twisted the curl tightly on his finger, pulling her head closer to his. She turned her head so she didn't have to see the horrid gleeful eyes trying to bore into her soul.

"Lovely, light blonde. I bet many a boy, man, has pictured those tresses spread across a pillow, looking down at eyes the color of the sea. Or, maybe they would be looking up at you, yellow silk falling over your face, tickling theirs," his breath hot on her skin.

"Here we go," Mora Aven announced as she bustled out of the door carrying a tray with a fresh pot of tea and two clean cups. Apparently Kessa wasn't staying for tea.

Aven dropped Kessa's hair. "Oh, there you are, darling. I'm so parched." He waited for his wife to set the tray down and pour him a cup.

Chapter Thirty-Seven

*G*ray hustled to the hotel.

He parked right out front and hurried inside. Matt had told him her room number so he hit the stairs two at a time to the third floor. He found her room and knocked, and knocked.

He was pretty sure she wasn't in it anyway because her jeep wasn't anywhere in the vicinity. He swiftly jogged back down the stairs, to the front desk and asked for the manager right away.

A fortyish man in a suit and tie, hair combed over his receding hairline, slim, average height approached Gray.

"How can I help you sir?" He inquired with a professional smile.

Because he was wearing a dark sapphire thermal and black jeans, Gray flashed his badge and told the manager he needed to access Kessa's room.

As the man shook his head and started to speak, Gray leaned in and said very quietly. "This is matter of life and death. I hate to be melodramatic but it's the truth. Let me in now. I won't tell anyone you did, or I'll come back with a warrant and shut this place down for as long as I can get away with."

The manager took one look in Gray's inarguable eyes then straightened his tie, cleared his throat, slicked back an errant two hairs. "Of course, sir. Come with me." He went to the desk clerk and asked for the main card key that opened all the rooms and headed for the elevator.

At Kessa's room, he slid the card in the lock and opened the door. "Shall I-"

"No. Thanks. You can go about your business." Gray shut the door in the manager's face. Turning around, he studied the room. It was as he expected, relatively empty.

On the desk there was a laptop and notebooks and other miscellaneous items she would need to write. A jacket draped over a chair, a small suitcase was stashed in a corner, and on the bed was her cell phone.

"Of course," he muttered. "Why that woman never carries that damned thing I can't freakin' figure out." He stalked around the room, opening drawers, looking in the closet, under the bed, in the bathroom.

It was obvious she hadn't planned on staying long, even so, Matt had told him she didn't have many belongings anyway. That she didn't want to be attached to things that can be taken from her. Or vice versa.

Gray needed to know where she had gone. He could feel the itch at the back of his neck. He just felt something was wrong.

He stood in the middle of the room, looking, thinking. He went over and picked up her phone. Naturally it was password protected.

He pushed in 'Kato.' It unlocked. "Oh Kessa, that's why you need someone looking out for you." Scrolling to the recent calls, he started at the first one and dialed it.

It rang five times before the voice mail came on with, "Hello, you have reached the residence of Doctor and Mrs. Aven. We can't-" he clicked it off and dropped the cell in his pocket and strode to the door.

Running down the back stairs and out the door, before a match could spark he was in his truck barreling down the street.

Trying to gain as much time as she could, the doctor had to get tired of holding her so tightly and eventually loosen his grip. He'd already let go of her wrist and was holding her upper arm. Kessa said, "I don't understand, Dr. Aven, why didn't they tell on you? The boys you...hurt. I can see as children, you threaten to harm them or their families or the shame, or guilt," her lip curled in revulsion. "But as adults, why wouldn't they tell?"

The cocky smirk spread across his thickening face. Age was softening the once patrician features. He had developed a nose twitch over the years to push his glasses up without having to touch them. The twitch caused deep grooves etching along and across his nose and between his eyes.

He twitched now, rapidly three times like a compulsive mannerism. He took off the glasses and set them on the table. Still maintaining a snobbish air, he fussed with his slacks picking off a miniscule leaf that had attached to them.

A glow lit the heartless eyes. The smirk flattened into a satisfied smile. Reliving all of this was like doing the actual acts again, it thrilled and titillated him, he just loved it!

"Well, my dear, there's always something you can have over someone. Say for instance Mayor Stirling, Sledge Stirling. Harrumph," he grunted. "What parent names their child Sledge for Pete's sake?"

He sipped his tea, the toast sat untouched on his plate. He was filling up with a gluttonous sordid mental feast.

"Stirling, as a mayor, as he was fairly young while campaigning he had to at least have a façade of strength and maturity. He wasn't about to tell the world he was sodomized at the tender age of," he thought about it then shrugged.

He said glibly, "Who remembers how old he was. The point is, he had kept quiet over the years. Sure, I may have threatened him here and there when he was a terrified young child, however, as an adult, he couldn't look like a scaredy-cat with a terrible secret, could he?

"John Q. Public would wonder what other secrets did he have? He certainly couldn't be trusted if he had one secret. And they would think he was weak, let himself be cowed by a lecherous doctor." He said it like it excused his abominable acts.

"They also would have been angry with him for not speaking up and saving however many other victims he let suffer because he was too afraid to tell what I'd done to him." He snickered. "Not that I see them as victims but they've referred to themselves as such, so, semantics, whatever."

"Uh huh," Kessa uttered mechanically. "I can see that." She slid a glimpse at Mrs. Aven.

The doctor's wife hadn't spoken or moved for quite a while. She could see why.

The matronly lady's lids were shut behind the round glasses. She was taking a little snooze sitting up. How the despicable horrors her husband committed could have zero effect on her was beyond Kessa's comprehension.

Kessa said to the egregious doctor, "What about Clayton Gourdet, he had nothing to lose, why hasn't he told? Why didn't he tell about what happened to me and my sisters?"

The doctor grinned like the cat that ate the rat. "Him. Gordy. Have you seen that boy of his?"

Puzzled, Kessa nodded. "Yes, Troy."

"Did you notice how sickly child he is?"

Of course she'd noticed, the boy was very skinny, very pale, lacked any vitality at all. "Yes, but I don't see how that-"

"I'm a doctor. The boy is seriously ill, always has been. Clayton never had great insurance. Besides, the child was born with a pre-existing disease. Since I am a doctor, I can get medicine that may be unobtainable for others but not for me." He sat back exultant.

The information flowed over Kessa as she grasped what he was saying. "You're saying you supplied Troy's medication, I'm sure at a cost but much less than what the pharmacy charged. Basically, you black mailed him to keep quiet about how you had abused him as a child?"

An offended brow arched. "Or, you could say he was blackmailing or extorting from me. It's all on how you look at it." He squeezed her arm. "All right, enough discourse, we-"

"Doctor Aven, please," Kessa said anxiously, stalling for more time. "I heard the elderly lady, Mrs. Goldbrooke, and her housekeeper were- were murdered. Could you now satisfy *my* curiosity on, I mean if you had anything to do with those…uh…deaths."

Aven couldn't help but break into a self-satisfied grin. "Well, I di-"

"Don't you even start, Clarence Aven." Mora Aven had woken. She moved to sit up straighter, corrected her crooked glasses and snapped at her husband.

"Don't you play the almighty mercenary. You see, my dear, it was I," she shifted to face Kessa looking every bit the sweet grandmother.

"*I* was the one who always told him what to do. *I* was the one who told him he'd need to tell Sledge Stirling not to talk or he'd lose the campaign. And when Clayton Gourdet grew up and started making noise like he was going to tell, I told Skip to bribe him to save his son."

Kessa could not hide how appalled and surprised she was.

Mrs. Aven grinned proudly. "It was me. I went to see Arleen Goldbrooke. Deputy Whitewolf had called her, wanted to ask her questions about that day in the woods. Arleen had always been suspicious of Skip.

"The town kept talking about who was in the area that day, who had access to that section of the forest, who wouldn't have stood out like a sore thumb. She'd practically been on her deathbed at the time it happened, and Skippy was seeing to her almost daily. But over the years the questions kept coming back to her. Until, when the deputy called, she got confused. She called my Skippy to ask him what she should do."

Eyes wide in incredulous horror, Kessa said to Dr. Aven, "And you went and killed some poor innocent elderly woman because she might have mentioned that you were frequently in the area at that time?"

"No," Mora shook her head. "It was me. I went to see her. I was always cleaning up his messes," she shot a thumb disgustedly at her husband. "He couldn't think past the nubile young children."

Contemptuous scorn ground her words, letting her feelings be clear how she felt about his repulsive actions. She sighed grievously, shooting an irate glare at her husband.

"Of course after all this time I didn't want to lose what I had. So I went to see her." Her smile mirrored the evil sickness of her equally depraved husband,

"Naturally she wasn't wary or afraid of me, I know how demure I appear. The docile doctor's wife. She offered me tea and scones and I offered her a shove down the stairs." The unrepentant Mora looked about to laugh out loud over her cold, cruel, sociopathic actions.

"Unfortunately, she was stunned, gravely injured, but not dead. I called Skip to come and break her neck. Didn't I?" she asked her husband for confirmation of her dastardly acts.

He just nodded sullenly, rankled she was taking his thunder.

Mora moved her head up and down emphatically, her double chin wobbling. "Yes, and the stupid housekeeper, what's her name?"

"Brenda Bradshaw," Aven filled in quietly.

"Yes. What an idiot. She freaked out after Whitewolf came over to question her. He made comments about her fancy house and expensive car. Asked where she got the money. Scared, she also called Skip to ask him what to do. You see, she was *really* blackmailing Skip. Wasn't she, dear?"

He barely moved his head. He said in hushed lackluster, "Yes dear."

Mora scooted to the edge of her seat, she was getting excited over her cunning actions. "So, I went to see her as well. I told her I was there to work things out. Of course she felt non-threatened by me and just let me in. The fool." Snorting in derision she slapped the table with her hand.

"So, soon after we got inside I pushed her down the stairs too. Damned if she wouldn't die either. Tough old birds these ladies." She hooted.

"Well, I clobbered her good too with a frying pan then called ol' Skippy here. He hightailed it right over, snapped that neck and strung her up. We thought they might just take the old lady's death as an accident and the housekeeper's as a suicide. But alas, they went ahead and did autopsies. It's that deputy's fault, *Whitewolf*," she snarled his name.

That brought the doctor back to life. His face dark, Aven said crossly, "Yes, all of this is his fault. He came in and started digging through things, stirring people up."

Aven said to his wife, his tone affectionate, "What do you say darling, after we take care of this one," he nodded to Kessa, "we put him next on our list."

This made Mora very happy. She clapped her plump hands. "Oh yes. He'll be a tough one. We'll have to plan carefully, I hear he's quite intuitive and aggressive. Oh what fun, Skippy!" She freshened her husband's tea.

"Just for you, my-" he was patting her hand across the table when Kessa suddenly grabbed his teacup and tossed the hot liquid in his eyes, wrenched her arm loose and ran.

Startled, Dr. Aven shrieked and covered his eyes. Mrs. Aven sat frozen, surprised at Kessa's abrupt escape.

Breaking her stunned reverie, Mora reproached, "I told you, Skip, to take her out right away. Break her neck, throw the body in a crevasse. But no, you wanted to play with her." She tossed a napkin at him to wipe his eyes and hobbled to her feet.

"Now go get her and no more toying with her. Do it quickly, don't let your hideous lust mess you about again. She looks like a bit of a fast runner the way she sleekly took off over the grass as if in flight." She pointed a finger in the direction Kessa had run.

"However, she doesn't know there's only one way into the woods, the way she just went, and where it leads to, but you do and you'll get there first. Now go!"

Fortunately for Aven, the tea wasn't boiling hot. He wiped his eyes then scrambled to his feet, went around to his wife and pecked her dutifully on the cheek. "I'll be back soon, darling."

He jogged across the yard to the same trail Kessa had just taken and vanished in the forest.

Chapter Thirty-Eight

As Gray drove up the driveway to the Avens' mansion, Kessa's jeep was backing out. He pulled right behind, blocking the jeep. Immediately, he shut off the engine and hopped out of the car, walking swiftly up to the jeep.

He stepped back as the door opened. "Kessa," he said, then gaped. It wasn't Kessa getting out, it was Mora Aven. In her hand was a gun, and it was aimed at him.

"Oh, Deputy," she purred. "You do get around, don't you? Well, at least we don't have to go looking for you and go to the trouble of setting a trap, here you are right in our laps. Put your hands up."

The pleasant smile disappeared into a nasty scowl. Waving the gun at him, a warning when he didn't do it right away. "Don't be a fool, I know how to use this. We live in the country remember. Get all sorts of varmints out here need exterminating. Now up with them."

Raising his hands, Gray put on a cool, relaxed demeanor to cover his confused surprise at seeing the matronly doctor's wife climb out of Kessa's truck with a pistol and amble amiably to him.

Seeing Mrs. Aven instead of Kessa was grossly startling, and frightening. It meant Kessa was incapable at some level of freely driving her car.

Struggling to keep his expression and voice friendly, he said, "Mrs. Aven, I would-"

"Save it, handsome. I know why you're here. You've come for the girl. Skip said you would, he said you had a thing for her. You've pretty much got things figured out haven't you?" Mora set a hand on her ample hip keeping the gun aimed at his heart.

"Pretty much," he replied honestly, lowering his hands.

"Oh no, son, up, keep 'em up. I hate to get blood on our lovely lacquered slate driveway, but," she shrugged, "if I must, I will. Up!" she ordered, waving the gun.

He raised his hands. "Can we talk about-"

"No," she said cold and final. "We are not going to talk. As soon as Skip gets back I'll have him take care of you. Now, take out your gun and set it very carefully on the ground, slowly, we don't want any accidents do we?"

Gray pulled the gun out of the back of his jeans, crouched and set it on the ground.

"Very nice. Now, take out your cell and set it down."

He plucked the phone out of his pocket and set it next to the gun.

Mora smiled. "That's a good boy, now the other phone. Those jeans are tight enough honey that I can see the outline of the other phone in your pocket." She waved the gun at him.

"By the way," she said as he bent over to set the other phone down. "I must say I do appreciate those tight jeans, dear. They don't just outline the phones and your wallet, you know." Her middle-aged face puckered in a coquettish wink. "I'll let you keep your wallet, for now."

His face a blank slate, Gray waited politely for her to give the next order. He could easily get the gun from her but he needed her to take him to where Kessa was.

"Okay, honey, move around the back of the house. We don't need any neighbors moseying by and getting nosey do we? Move it. Slowly, around the house."

Gray turned and trod towards the side of the house and walked around on the stone path that circled the house to the back.

When they arrived behind the house, Mora led him to the terrace. She told him to stop at the steps. "Oh dear, Skippy isn't back yet, I guess we should go up and have a seat and wait for him, he shouldn't be long. Go ahead, honey, up the steps with you."

Gray turned very slowly, said nonchalantly, "So, where is your husband, the good doctor?"

She snickered. "Oh wouldn't you like to know!"

Gray took a step towards the raised patio. "What harm is there in telling me, Mrs. Aven, what can I do about it anyway?" His face remained a guileless mask.

She thought about it, shrugged. "Okay, you're right, you're not going anywhere." Standing on the walk in short heeled pumps, dress a pendulum around her calves, she wrapped an arm around her plump waist, rested her arm on her stomach with the elbow of her other hand on her arm to hold the gun steady at him.

Arrogant in her security that Gray could not do anything about his predicament, or Kessa's, she said, "My darling husband, as we speak, has probably chased down that Kenton girl by now, and is, you know," she made a snapping motion with her hands indicating he was breaking her neck.

Gray's heart stopped. He had to breathe deeply to speak casually. "I see." He watched the lady's eyes shift slightly back to the forest bordering the yard. It was the second time she had done it. Even from where he stood he could see an opening into the woods.

"All right, enough stalling. Get your hunky body up those steps and sit dow-" Gray lashed his hand out and chopped the gun right out of Mora's hand. Before she could register the action, Gray kicked the fallen gun out of the way and wrapped his arm around her thick neck.

Forcing her head back with his arm under her chin, Gray said into her ear, "Make no mistake, Mrs. Aven, I will kill you in a heartbeat if you don't do exactly as I say. Understand?"

Hardly able to move her head in his stranglehold, she squawked, "But you're a policeman you can't-"

He tightened his half-Nelson. "Don't try to figure me out, Mrs. Aven, you're bound to be unhappily surprised." He pulled her head back so far she couldn't speak.

"Okay," he said, "up on the porch. Go." Bending quickly, he snatched the gun off the ground and stuck it in his belt, then keeping his arm around her neck he pushed her up the steps to the patio.

"Sit down." He gave her a small shove, she plopped on a chair. He surveyed the area then saw some electrical tape over on a shelf near the side of the house.

Retrieving the tape, he tied her hands and legs to the chair then found a towel and tied it over her mouth.

Without another word to her, he sprinted down the steps and across the lawn to the opening in the woods and disappeared inside.

On the porch, tears of frustration streamed down Mora's face, making her nose run. Her thought at the moment was *what if someone came by and saw her trussed up like this crying*, she'd look such the fool.

Chapter Thirty-Nine

Hitting the woods, Kessa ran blindly along the trail.

Slapped by twigs, tripping over rocks, she kept moving as fast as she could. She didn't dare look back.

The trees went by in a panicked jumbled blur. She knew she should get off the path as the doctor would be able to follow her effortlessly, but she was too frantic and scared to take her eyes off the trail.

Not hearing footsteps behind her, she slowed a fraction to glance around for an opening to leave the path, but the forest was a dense thicket that she would not be able to get through.

A thick gnarly branch gouged her arm then her foot caught a root and she was airborne a few feet before she landed on her hands and knees with a painful '*oomph.*'

Scrambling to her feet, she faced the way she had come from and held her rushing breath.

There was not a sound, no footsteps pounding the dirt, no birds, no wind, nothing. She felt almost transported back in time. It was the same feeling that day with her sisters.

Running in fear, then stopping, listening, and all was quiet.

She shivered like someone walked over her grave. The last time she'd hidden behind a tree, waiting, listening for whatever was coming, then she had been confident enough to go back to look for her sisters.

Gray shot Kessa a grin complimenting her on her trick of blinding Aven with the hot tea. "Good for you, babe." He said to the doctor, "We would have tied you in eventually. The problem was all the rosters they gave us, none included you."

"Yes, well, doctors like nurses and maids, no one notices us, don't think of us, like we're part of the scenery. They didn't think to add me to the jump school's roster."

"We have reams of videos from cameras around the area to scan. We would have eventually spotted you and looked into your history." Suddenly angry, Gray blasted, "You killed those people in cold blood, a boy for heaven's sake. You killed defenseless women, you are a-"

"It's your fault they're dead, Whitewolf." His nose in the air Aven accused.

"No, you killed them, Doctor. You're the only one at fault here." Gray's eyes so direct and hard at the doctor made Aven squirm.

Gray decided to give him more to squirm about. "The child, Hope, was found buried there, at Goldbrooke's house. You haven't heard that yet, have you, Doc?"

Kessa gasped. Aven's jaw slackened. "Oh? No, I hadn't heard." His forehead creased, skeptical. "You're bluffing..."

Gray glanced at Kessa then quickly away. "Behind but near the house." He watched Aven shift his eyes back and forth trying to determine if Gray was still trying to bluff him.

Gray shot home, "Under the stones, Doctor." A taunting brow rose. "You know the ones, they're only in the driveway, and over the," he flicked a look at Kessa and back to Aven, "grave."

He watched in satisfaction as the doctor blanched, suddenly unsure of his position. Gray didn't want to see Kessa's reaction.

"So," the deputy said, "there was only a handful of people coming around the desperately ill Mrs. Goldbrooke's house at that time. The priest, who was much older than and nearly as frail as Goldbrooke, and other elderly visitors, mostly her prayer group friends. And you."

He watched Aven's brows peak, thrown off guard with the information about the grave.

Thinking about it, Aven said in a shrewd drawl, "There's no proof it was me." Amusement relaxed his features as he wiped his sleeve across his damp forehead.

"There are no more witnesses. This one here," he tapped the gun against Kessa's head, "was the last loose string. Actually, Mrs. Aven and I were talking only today that we should dispose of you as well. If we'd known you were coming for the girl we would have waited."

"Really, doctor? You think I'm here for her, not that I came to arrest you for the murders?" Gray's lopsided smile looked sincere. He didn't want Aven knowing how important Kessa was to him.

The doctor thought, *that would mean others know about his deeds.* Agitation pushed the doctor's amusement aside, briefly. Then he shook his head. "No, you came for her." He smiled. "I had a feeling you might. One can see even now it's as plain as the longing lust on your faces when you look at each other."

His laugh was a thunderclap when he saw them wince ruefully at each other. "Now, let's get on with it, set the gun down."

Trying to distract the doctor, Gray said quickly, "The mark, you left your mark on her. Show him Kessa."

Both Aven and Kessa were confused.

Gray nodded at Kessa. "The mark on your arm."

Her eyes rounded as she understood. She held her arm up and showed Aven the mark on her upper arm.

"It's your ring," Gray said. "I recognized the design when I was just in the hospital. You never recognized it as a ring mark, Kessa, because you always saw it upside down."

Aven looked shaken, seeing a perfect imprint of his class ring imprinted in her skin. Then his thin lips curved in a smile.

"Doesn't matter, only you and she know that, if anyone else knew you wouldn't have come here alone. In a moment neither of you will be around to tell anyone."

discreet, she kept her job although only part time as not to look suspicious. The reason why I didn't take her out was because," the arm holding then gun lowered further. "Let me get this straight, wait," the thoughts traveled across his face.

He lifted his hand away from Kessa's neck to pinch between his eyes then looked towards the sky. "She was my wife's sister's first daughter's godmother. Until now Mora wouldn't let me do anything to her, I tell you-"

Gray flicked his eyes up then sharply down at Kessa, then in a flash he jumped up, drew his arm back, Kessa dropped to her knees, and Gray threw a rock like Babe Ruth straight at Aven's head hitting him square in the temple.

Aven's eyes popped wide shocked, then he crumpled to the ground.

Kessa ran to Gray and flung herself into his arms. He kept one eye on the doctor while wrapping his arms around Kessa. Pulling her head to his chest, Gray laid his cheek on the top of her head and stroked her back and her hair.

Her arms wrapped around his waist, Kessa willed herself to stop shaking. She crooked her head back to look up at him. "How did you learn to throw a rock like that?"

A shoulder moved up then down in a half shrug, he said, "I played baseball in school and when I was a military cop. We had long stretches of nothing to do so we played a lot of baseball."

Emotion hitting him like an avalanche now that she was safe, no longer able to hold himself back Gray cupped her chin, raised her head and hungrily covered her lips with his.

She responded with passion blazing like heat off the sun. The kiss strengthened, deepened, burned like a field on fire.

With arms like iron rods, Gray held her against him. One hand on her lower back, he pulled her even closer, the other around the back of her neck urgently tugging, pressing their mouths together.

Inflamed, he devoured her, groaning against her mouth, "Kessa," he kissed her neck, her face. He wanted to lose himself in her but didn't dare take his eyes off the doctor.

Her lips trembled with sobs of relief and desire.

He lifted his head, holding her chin with his fingers. "Don't cry baby, you're safe now. Besides, you're getting my sweater all wet." He smiled, letting out a shuddering breath.

Wiping her tears with his thumb, his voice husky, he whispered, "Your eyes look like sodden turquoise flowers." He bent his head and tenderly kissed both lids.

Kessa touched his face softly, then both hands clutching his hair, she brought his mouth back to hers, kissing him with unbearable need.

He bent and swooped her up in his arms, carried her over to a boulder and sat down with her on his lap. She laid her head on his shoulder.

His voice ragged, needing to catch his breath and slow things down before he went too far, he said, "Listen to me," then took a deep breath, steadier, his pulse slowed its racing.

"I'm serious about you and, and the danger," he attempted to sound austere, but his voice broke. "It's driving me crazy worrying about you. I've got to know you're safe."

She raised her head and wound her arms around his neck pulling him back down to her. Blistering flames surged between them, hot scorching sheets of passion.

After a few indulgent moments, Gray forced her away, his shaking hands holding her shoulders back.

Drinking in her heavy-lidded sultry envisage, he moaned, "Aw, Kessa, how can I have a serious conversation with you when those eyes are all dewy and glazed with passion. I can't stop-" he brought his mouth to hers briefly, then gently pulled her away from him.

His eyes dropped to her swollen pout. "You taste like honey," he said with a hungry smile looking back up at her. She twined her fingers in his hair tugging him to her, to consummate their kiss, but he held her still.

"I- I can't. I either have to stop right now or," he swallowed hard. Not looking at her, he said, "As I was saying, I let you do things your way, now you're going to do what I say."

She blinked at him.

His voice grew hard but still low, throaty, "You are staying with me until Matt comes back. No arguments. I swear to God, I won't touch you. But I can't be working and worrying about what idiot is going after you next. Maybe my mother's house, yeah, that would be better, out of temptation, you can stay there. You'll be safe there from thugs…and me."

Kessa slid off his lap. Her face set, she crossed her arms. "Gray, I'm not going anywhere with you. I just kissed you now, because…because…I had to. But, I'm not going to be with a man who's making love to me one minute and off with another woman the next."

She turned her head from him, staring off to the edge of the grass where it dropped a hundred feet or more.

Gray leaned his forearms on his knees and clasped his hands.

"I've told you, Kessa, we can't be together anyway. I'm not good enough for you, and I am not going to let myself…ruin you because you're so trusting, and innocent."

Kessa's head jerked towards him, her mouth open.

"But for the record," he stood up. "The redhead you saw at my house," the corner of his mouth pulled in at her scowl. "She was an informant of mine. She's the one who was telling me when the drugs were being smuggled into Cache's Bar."

"Even worse, Gray, taking advantage of a poor-"

"No, no." He crossed his arms, shook his head. "I never, we never, she was just an informant."

"Come on Gray, I saw her in your arms,"

"I was," he drew in a breath. "You don't understand. She was a prostitute. She was under Sheriff Lombardo's thumb. Now that he's been arrested she's free to do whatever she wants. She came to my house to thank me. *She* was hugging *me*. She was there to thank me and say goodbye.

"She's going back home, to Kentucky, to live with her parents. She wants to go to school, get her GED and then college. There was nothing, absolutely nothing between us other than cop and informant. And friends now, I hope."

Kessa's expression was decidedly skeptical.

"I'm telling you the truth, Kessa. I swear. Since I met you I haven't thought about or been with another woman. Believe me, if I could have gotten you out of my head I would have. But I couldn't. You can ask Donna, the informant, hell you can ask Rick.

"I swear, even though you and I can't have a relationship, I still, I just have no interest in anyone else. For the first time in a long time, I want a...a real relationship, like Rick said, someone at home waiting for, wanting to see me. I want you there. But that's not going to happen, you're too good-" his pupils enlarged in despair.

"Gray, you can't tell me what I can-"

"Look out!" he yelled.

Dr. Aven had leapt to his feet and was running head on at Gray.

Gray darted past Kessa catching the doctor around the middle, knocking him back. Both men fell to the ground, rolled and jumped to their feet.

"Come on, Doc, don't make me do this," Gray implored, his fists up and ready.

Aven rushed at him with a roar, Gray punched him in the stomach then slugged him in the jaw. Aven tottered backwards, his arms flapping, he was on the crest of the cliff.

Gray hit him again so hard the doctor's feet left the ground. His arms flailing like windmills, he staggered backwards then went over the cliff yowling.

Kessa ran over to Gray and threw her arms around him. They both cautiously peered over the edge.

Aven was sprawled on the ground at the foot of the cliffs.

"Do you think he's dead?" Kessa asked.

"I sure hope so," Gray muttered.

Kessa leaned back, looked up at Gray. "This seems to be becoming a habit."

"Uh huh. I know. Between your past and my job, like I said, too much danger. That's why you're coming to-"

Kessa stood on her tiptoes, her hands stroking up his chest and around his head, pulling him down to meet her lips.

He resisted. "Kessa, I'm not that strong, I can't just kiss you and move on."

She pulled harder, he lowered his head absorbing her lips, body, soul. It was like a tidal wave crashing over them, sweeping them away, breathless, intoxicating magic.

Dragging his head away again, Gray moaned, "I'm telling you girl, I can't-"

Kessa put her hands against his chest and shoved him away. "Now you listen here, Grayson Whitewolf, I've had enough of this 'I'm no good, you deserve better' crap," she mocked his words.

Slamming a hand on her hip, she pointed at him with the other. "Who the hell do you, and my brother too, who do you two think you are to decide for me, a grown up adult, what is best for me. I will choose what and who I want and you two can go screw yourselves." She crossed her arms angrily, face flushed, eyes flashing.

Trying to bury a happy grin, Gray asked somewhat meekly, "Are you choosing me?" When she didn't answer right away his face fell.

She shook her head with an eye-roll. "Gray, you are such an idiot. Of course I choose you. I don't go around kissing every other Tom, Dick and Jerk in the woods for Pete's sake. I want you. I've always wanted you."

Her voice softened, head tilted beguiling him to come to her.

And he did.

Chapter Forty

Gray and Kessa only yielded to a quick kiss knowing they needed to get back, call the police and an ambulance for the doctor in the far chance that he was still alive.

Which, as it turned out, he was.

As soon as they arrived at the station, Gray was called into his commander's office.

Commander Ross told him he was on desk duty until the whole mess was straightened out. He was to have someone take Kessa to a safe place and not see her until he was cleared to do so.

Gray wasn't even allowed to attend the arraignments of Jimmy Lombardo, Wayde Smith, Bruce Sutton, Taz Cache, and the other offenders.

Char's husband Jaspar was arraigned handcuffed to his hospital bed. The beat-down Gray had given him kept him in the hospital for a month.

Mrs. Aven was arraigned separately for her crimes, and when Doctor Aven was well enough, he was wheeled into the courtroom in a wheelchair.

When he is eventually found guilty by a jury of his peers, he would be spending the rest of his life in prison trapped in a cage in a wheelchair.

Char thought that was perfect justice, see how he liked being crippled, vulnerable and helpless.

As it turned out, Matthew returned the next morning. Gray's call had frightened him so much he hopped the first red-eye he could get on.

At least Gray didn't have to worry about Kessa being alone and vulnerable while he was under orders not to see her.

After a solemn, heart-wrenching ceremony, Hope was finally put to rest. At least they finally knew where she was.

Gray had called Kessa to tell her that although as much as he wished he could, he couldn't be by her side at the funeral.

She understood, but felt half of her was missing even though she was in the circle of her family. Kessa hadn't forgiven Sophie for compounding abandoning and rejecting her daughter by letting DeBarra loose on her, but she was cordial.

Tonight, everyone was having dinner at the Kentons' house at Geordie's insistence. He no longer kowtowed to his dictatorial wife. He said he'd already lost too many precious years of being without his exiled child. From now on, he determined, the family will be a united unit.

Clean for the first time since she was 11 years old, and feeling exhilarant freedom, Char divorced Jaspar as fast as she could and had invited her minister, Hunter, now beau, to dinner to meet the rest of the family. They sat at the dining room table cooing at each other like lovebirds. Char lost weight and Aria gained some healthy pounds.

Aria moved in with Rick a week after he'd taken her home from jail. A first time offender, she was sentenced to probation. Due to his lengthy criminal history, Peter was in the pen for the long haul.

Rick helped Aria get a job as a receptionist, and got her enrolled in Adult Ed. They sat next to each other with their heads together giggling and whispering.

Geordie sat at the head of the table beaming contentedly at everyone.

Sophia sat regally at the foot trying desperately to look pleased.

The dining room was close to the front of the house, Gray jumped up when he heard a car coming up the drive.

It had been months, and finally Gray's commander lifted the ban on his seeing Kessa. Matthew was supposed to be bringing her and they weren't there yet.

Gray couldn't believe he was so keyed-up he was sweating with nerves and anticipation. He and Kessa hadn't seen each other since the day at the Avens'. They talked every day on the phone and skyped, but he couldn't wait to lay eyes, and hands on her.

He excused himself from the table and hurried down the hall to the foyer. As he got there Matthew came in the door, alone.

Confused and frowning, Gray asked, "Where's your sister?"

Matthew gave him a big grin. "Hey, thanks for the warm greeting, bro, nice to see you too." He walked past Gray into the living room and laid his jacket over a chair with Gray hot at his heels.

"Matt, where the hell is she?" he demanded.

Matthew dropped in a chair. "You're lucky we talked things out and she wants you or I'd punch you in the nose right now, bro."

Impatiently, Gray stood in front of Matthew. "So take a swing, whatever. Where is she?" His hands on his hips concern crossed his face. "Matt, is she-"

"Yeah, yeah, she's fine, she's coming. I just had to get back at you a little after breaking your oath to me to keep your hands off of her. She had to do a 3-way conference call with her agent and publisher. She's out in my car finishing. She'll be here any minute."

He wiggled a leering brow at Gray. "She told me she wasn't coming home with me after dinner tonight."

Visibly relieved, Gray said, "Actually, technically, I haven't had my hands on her yet the way you mean."

"Oh? I can't imagine you having such restraint, what gives?" Matthew asked, knowing Gray would not lie to him, but having a hard time believing the self-described bad boy hadn't yet taken his sister to his bed.

Crossing his arms over his chest, Gray frowned again at his friend. "First of all, I did have restraint. If what I felt for her was only lust, hell, I'd have gone and taken care of it with an array of other women rather than disrespect you."

Discomfited, he stuck his hands in his pockets. Slightly ashamed about his typical rakish behavior, his gaze dropped to the floor.

Then he raised his eyes seriously honest and frank to Kessa's brother. It was important to him that Matt believed him.

"I found myself wanting to see her, talk to her, listen to her, tease her."

He sucked in a deep breath and said, "Just be with her. It hit me like a ton a bricks that I wasn't just watching out for her because of you, or because she was an innocent, vulnerable young woman in peril with no one to turn to. I…I realized I cared about her, really cared about Kessa Kent.

"I missed her when she wasn't near, I hated to leave her when she was. My heart froze every time she was in danger. I wanted more from her than I have ever had from another woman."

Setting both feet on the floor, Matt made to get up. "Gray, you don't-"

Gray held up a hand. "Hear me out. I'm not one to spill my guts, you know that, so you're only going to hear this once."

Matt stayed seated, said, "Okay."

Gray went on, "Matt, I'd lay down my life for her. I care about her as a person, not just for sex. However, I admit, my feelings for her are not *all* in my head, there were times I had to get away. I couldn't trust myself alone with her. I wanted…" his sheepish expression filled in the blanks.

"Anyway, I tell you, it was not easy. There were times it took every fiber of my being to walk away. Just remember, Matt, this is all with her compliance, she wants…me. I tried to back away, she told you that." He ran a fretful hand through his hair, tousling it then tried to neaten it with his fingers.

Chuckling, Matthew leaned back against the cushions and languidly crossed his legs. "I know bro, I'm just busting your chops. So, why haven't you two, you know," he asked before he remembered this was his younger sister they were talking about.

He waited for Gray's answer anyway, he was too curious to know how Gray the man he knew to have little restraint when it came to women, managed to keep his distance.

Gray stuffed his hands in his pockets. He was wearing dress slacks, the crease sharp thanks to Mrs. Butler, and a button-down long sleeved shirt. He'd gotten his hair cut right after being put on desk duty but already the black locks curled over his collar.

"I was assigned desk duty since the case closed. I was given a direct order to not see Kessa as she was a material witness in all of this chaos. They didn't mention not speaking to her, so we've been in contact every day, we both told you all this."

Matthew grinned. "I know. I just found it hard to believe you didn't go after her anyway. It's just, if it was me, I'd probably have snuck around and seen her anyway. And we both know you're more a dog than I am." He grinned to mellow out the barb.

A corner of his mouth pulled in, Gray replied, "Yeah, well, I am a man, but I'm also a cop. If I don't follow the law how can I expect others to?"

"Uh huh. I've known you to stretch, really stretch the law sometimes, bro."

Gray shrugged. "That's when it's benefitted others, when it was necessary for the good. This is personal. Besides, I don't want anything to happen to screw up what we have. I'm following the book on this one." He looked up at the ceiling.

Pulling his hands out of his pockets, he studied them. "I can't believe I'm sweating, I'm as nervous as a schoolboy." He grinned. "I can't wait to see her, bro, you have no idea."

Smirking, Matthew nodded. "Oh yeah, I have an idea. I've never seen you like this before. Cupid shot a big fat arrow right through your black heart, my man. No one deserves it more than you do." He snickered, "Ha, I can't believe it took my little sister to tame you."

"Matt, you-"

The front door opened, both men turned to look.

Epilogue

Kessa stepped into the doorway.

She was wearing a dress.

"What a dress," Gray muttered under his breath.

Shimmery silver and ivory, the skirt was snug enough to show her figure but loose enough to move sensuously around her slender legs. As she walked in, the halter top drew Gray's eyes like a magnet.

He strode over to her, whatever he was going to say to Matthew had gone right out of his head.

Matthew sat gleefully watching the greeting play out in front of him. His sister and his best friend, couldn't be better.

Gray closed the door and stopped so close to Kessa her light fragrance purled around his senses. They stood like shy teenagers. His smoldering pupils drank in the face he'd waited months to see in person.

He could see his reflection in her eyes, she looked at him like she was an addict and he was her hit. The heat pulsated instantly between them.

Gray lifted his hand and caressed her cheek. Smoothing back a wisp of hair, he gently settled his hand on her shoulder. They stood smiling at each other like giddy lovers. He stroked his hand down her arm, took her hand and started to say something,

Alice entered the room and announced, "Please, Mrs. Kenton is requesting your presence in the dining room. They're waiting on you. All of you." Her attention swept the three of them then she rotated and walked out of the room.

Matthew lazily rose to his feet and followed her.

Slowly, Gray skimmed his hands up Kessa's arms then slid them around her, pulling her to him, her softness melded to his powerful body.

He lowered his head, she raised hers, their kiss at first a satin caress, just to soak in, taste, momentarily enjoy the embrace, after their long separation, feel the warmth of their skin touching.

Kessa stroked the powerful chest, the strong arms that had picked her up and held her, fought for her, saved her. Her hands glided over his shoulders, fingertips tracing the face that took over her dreams, and around his neck to pull him more tightly to her as if being so close they could join together, become one.

His hands on her waist moved up her back and into her hair feeling the silkiness slide through his fingers. He kissed her eyes, her face, her throat. As he kissed her lips, this time she moaned his name, "*Gray.*"

Already feeling the flames of desire, her breathy whisper of his name ignited, striking him red hot. The rumble of intense sensation seethed into desire so strong it poured like burning lava from the tops of their heads, rolling over their shoulders down their bodies until they were both on fire.

Against her lips, Gray whispered, "God, I never want to let you go again, Kessa."

Smiling up at him, she murmured, "I don't want you to. Ever." Locking lips again, they were immersed in their own world, transported into a delirious tantrum of passion.

"Geez guys, get a room for crying out loud. You get this hot over a kiss you're gonna need an ice bucket when you really get together. I'm picturing a bunch of nieces and nephews, real soon," Matthew teased, breaking into their intimate coupling.

Gray growled against Kessa's neck, "Go away Matt…"

They could hear Matthew's heavy sigh from the entrance. "I wish I could, but, I have orders. I was told 'don't come back without them.' "

Gray kept Kessa folded in a tight embrace. His lips still on her neck, he said, "Fine. Then sit down and shut up." His mouth covered hers so torching torrid Matthew blushed.

"Come on, you know that ain't gonna happen." Matthew turned so the couple wasn't in his direct line of vision. "Seriously, next Dad or Mother herself will be in here. Give us all a break. You guys can do whatever you want after dinner is over. I'm hungry."

Gray dropped his head back and cursed at the ceiling. Wiping a sleeve across his hazed eyes, he smiled weakly at Kessa so tightly enclosed in his arms.

Her lips apart, she peered at him through heavy lids, he knew if he took her to his truck right now she would go home with him without question. He could feel her quivering against him, it almost undid him.

Gray garnered the strength to set her from him. At once he felt bereft and cold. He took her hand. "All right." That was all he could croak out.

"By the way," Matthew said, inciting trouble. "I thought you get all bent out of shape when my sister is wearing stuff like she has on now. You said she was courting trouble when dressed like that."

Gray tucked Kessa's hand under his arm and smiled. "What I said was, a woman shouldn't dress like that unless she's on a man's arm and under his protection." He patted her hand.

She grinned at him, whispered, "Chauvinist."

Gray smiled. "Now she's on my arm and under my protection. Always, from now on."

Matthew tucked the tips of his fingers in his back pockets watching the pair. "Uh huh. And who's going to protect her from you?"

Kessa laid her head against Gray's shoulder as they made their way down the hall. "Dear brother," Kessa's words trailed them. "I don't want to be protected from him."

Everyone cheered when they entered the dining room.

"About time, you guys," Rick cajoled from his seat. "You guys got all night, the rest of your lives, get a grip, we're starving!"

Aria piped in, "If you'd done it the day after you met like we did, your heads would stop spinning and you could get on with other things. Right Rick?" She gave her lover a devilish grin, especially delighted hearing her mother choke.

Matthew and Gray and Kessa joined the others at the table.

Sophie made sure that Gray and Kessa weren't seated right next to each other. Sophie couldn't believe her daughter had chosen a common policeman to dally with. Crazy good-looking, but a cop nonetheless.

Gray and Kessa had to make do with sidelong glances and quick glimpses looking around others to see each other.

The conversation rolled around Aria and Rick getting together, then Char and her minister's connecting. They teased Matthew about when he would be next.

Aria gestured to Gray and Kessa, "I'm predicting a winter wedding."

Gray and Kessa blushed, everyone chuckled.

Char said seriously, "It seems as if our Kessa returning to Resilir has been a good luck charm for all of us." She raised a glass of water to her sister in a toast. "Thank you, my sister, for saving us all."

Everyone toasted in agreement. Sophie did the action with the others but said not a word.

Devouring their way through a crown roast, stuffing, pearl onions with potatoes, bread, salad, Sophie was cutting a piece of meat. "So, Faith dear," she said, "have you heard from Dr. DeBarra since your date?" She hadn't been apprised of what had occurred, and whenever she asked about it she couldn't get any straight answers.

Kessa set her fork down furiously. She and Gray had made their solid interest in each other clear as crystal. How dare she bring that man up in front of Gray, it was so disrespectful. She could practically hear that vein banging at Gray's temple.

"Really, Mother, you-"

"I heard," Char swallowed a forkful of beef and stuffing, then leaned in and said salaciously, "I heard rumors that a husband caught the doctor doing his wife, and the husband gave him a terrible thrashing. Huh." She snorted. She'd never liked the guy herself, there was something smarmy about him.

"I saw him last week when I stopped by the hospital for a check-up." Char shook her head. "He's lost those movie star looks. He has scars now, and they don't enhance his appearance. They don't give him that edgy, sexy, dangerous pirate thing like Gray's do."

Kessa nearly spat out her mouthful of potatoes.

Matthew hooted at the end of the table. "Yeah, dangerous and edgy, Gray, she called that right. But pirate?" He scrunched up his nose. "That's a little too swashbuckling romantic for me."

"That's good, Matt, 'cause the last thing I want from you is romance, bro."

Everyone at the table roared with laughter.

Sophie asked Gray about his family, how many siblings he had, where did they live.

Gray told her about his parents and sisters, then waggled his eyebrows at Kessa and said to Sophie, "Next week Kessa is coming to my parent's house. They can't wait to meet her." There, he thought, that should shut the old bag up about DeBarra.

His mother, Shonna Whitewolf, had been gaga for weeks making plans to meet the girl that had stolen and won her son's heart.

Lexi had been his first real serious girlfriend after a series of casual dating. They had been physical but not in love.

Shonna had told him maybe this young Kessa woman could change him, change his attitude about women and his chauvinistic ideas. Gray had laughed at her.

After dinner, the group gathered in the living room to visit further.

Twenty minutes later and Gray finally had enough. He went up to Sophie and politely thanked her for lovely evening, chatted briefly with Geordie, kissed Aria and Char on the cheek, shook hands with the minister, bumped fists with Rick, slapped Matthew on the shoulder and went to Kessa and took her hand.

She was startled when he pulled her over to the door.

Opening the door, Gray said loudly, "Say goodnight to everyone, Kessa."

Her eyes widened at him. He was smiling, but he was also dead serious.

She turned to the room and said gaily, "Good night everyone."

Before anyone could respond, the couple went out and Gray pulled the door closed behind them. They walked arm in arm to Gray's truck. He helped her in, buckled her seat belt before she could do it.

"You did that just to touch me, you lech," Kessa teased him. When DeBarra had done it, she'd felt dirty and abused. However, Gray hadn't touched her inappropriately, just his shoulder on her arm, it only made her want more.

He kissed her lightly on the nose. "You're absolutely right. And I plan on doing a lot more." He closed her door, went around and got in the driver's side.

"Finally, babe," he stroked a finger down the side of her face. "We're alone. Just you and me."

Seeing something big in the 3-quartered back seat, Kessa twisted her body to see what it was. The entire truck smelled of raw leather. "Gray, why do you have a saddle in your truck?"

He grinned. "Damn you're nosy, girl." He stuck the key in the ignition but didn't turn the engine on. "It's for you. I felt a woman needs her own personal saddle."

Her brows jumped over popping eyes. She swung around to get a real good look at it. After a few moments of ooing and awing and touching the leather, turning back to him, she said quietly, "For me? Really?"

He nodded. "Yeah, it's time for you to start putting roots down, collecting your own things, not renting stuff." He patted her knee.

She sat dumbfounded. Took her a minute before she murmured, "Thank you," so quietly he almost couldn't hear her.

Gray knew it would take time for her to settle down and trust him not to abandon her, but it would come.

He never thought he'd get over the pain of betrayal; that no one and nothing would ever get through the wall he'd built around his heart, and all it took was a pair of turquoise eyes.

Gray laid his head on the back of the seat and gazed warmly at Kessa. His pupils large and glittering black, his mouth a set line, he said, "I love you, Kessa."

Her smile brilliant and happy, she replied, "I love you, Gray."

He leaned over, only touching his lips lightly to hers, then sat back and put his seatbelt on. "That's all you get for now, or we won't make it home."

Turning the car on, gazing tenderly at her again, he said, "To *our* home. As soon as I can, I'm putting a ring on that finger," he reached over and nudged the ring finger of her left hand. "I want to make you mine, and I want the world to know that you are loved and that we are claimed."

"I like the sound of that," she grinned. Her contented smile floated around him like a cherishing mist. "Kato can be our ring bearer."

Kessa faced ahead to look out the window as they drove off to their future.

The End

Dear Reader, thank you for choosing <u>Blood is Slicker than Water</u>!

I know you could have picked any number of books to read, but you chose this story and for that I am extremely grateful.

I hope you enjoyed this novel, and if you did, **please leave a review** where you acquired it, and look for other exciting titles in my name!

About the Author

Louise Furley loves writing romance with a huge helping of suspense. Sunny Florida is home where Louise is a graduate of St. Thomas University with a master's degree, and lives with Bob, her own hero.

Louise is the author of numerous published novels. When not researching or writing, she is dreaming of unique plots, and discovering fresh ventures she hasn't yet experienced in the world. Ride along with her as she travels new and thrilling journeys!